THE MASLOW CONSPIRACY

A MAC SISCO NOVEL

THE MASLOW CONSPIRACY

A MAC SISCO NOVEL

BY

LOU EARLE

PHiR Publishing
San Antonio

PHiR Publishing
San Antonio, TX
phirpublishing.com

ISBN: 979-8-9885651-4-7
Library of Congress Control Number: 2024904074

Printed in the United States of America

Other Books in This Series

APOGEE

Book One of The Mac Sisco Trilogy

THE TYPHON AFFAIR

Book Two of The Mac Sisco Trilogy

For my friends and family whose honesty and candor
made the journey epic

A special thanks to my editor, John Casey at PHiR Publishing, for his
outstanding counsel and support, without which none of this would have happened

CHAPTER ONE

RED SKY IN THE MORNING

The old man shuffled down the cobblestone pavement of the narrow street, his back bent and head lowered. The sun was still low on the horizon above the hills in the distance. Flames of red shot up in ruby streaks across the expanse.

The old man shook his head and muttered to himself, "red sky in the morning, sailors take warning."

A block away, a black SUV pulled up beside a walled compound, its windows darkened to the outside world. The doors burst open and four black clad guards emerged, AK 47s at the ready.

Across the street and shrouded in early morning shadows, a lone figure watched intently from a second-floor balcony as a blindfolded and shackled prisoner was crudely jerked from the vehicle and pushed into an arched doorway. A single guard remained outside, securing the entrance as he scanned the empty street. The watcher disappeared from the window and emerged minutes later from an exit on an adjacent alley, still out of view of the compound entrance. Unsuspecting, the guard leaned against the compound's wall and casually lit a cigarette. Across the street, the six-inch barrel of a suppressed Sig P226 was barely visible as it bucked twice in quick succession, interrupting the smokey exhalation of the sentinel, who crumbled noiselessly to the street.

The watcher crossed quickly to the wall, dragged the slumped form into an adjacent alley and adroitly scaled the eight-foot wall, dropping effortlessly on the other side. Crouching behind the bushes lining the compound perimeter, the man watched as another guard moved around the corner of the large adobe structure. The watcher waited for his moment, then sprinted to the opposite corner to a side entrance. With all the security, it was a surprise the door was unlocked. He entered and scanned the unoccupied kitchen. A garbled conversation could be heard from an adjacent room. He moved towards the voices and cracked the door.

"I told you, I'm just down here in Maracaibo on vacation from the states. You have my ID and my money. Just take it and let me go. I won't report it. I don't want any trouble," the voice pleaded.

"Mr. Sanchez, we know who you are. You are from the US State Department," came the firm reply.

"We can be reasonable, Mr. Sanchez, but if you continue to waste our time with these lies, we will have to be more persuasive!"

"Look, I'm telling you, I don't know what you're talking about. I'm a salesman. I don't know anything about the State Department. I'm from Texas," the American whined.

He cracked the door more and saw three men surrounding the seated prisoner. Two were the guards from the SUV. The interrogator was a smaller man, dressed in jeans and a white silk shirt and was obviously in charge.

The interrogator sighed heavily and said, "have it your way, Joe. May I call you Joe?" he smiled malevolently as he nodded to one of the guards.

"Carlos, get my utensils from the bedroom. It's time for Joe and me to get better acquainted."

The guard returned with a small leather satchel and handed it to his boss. The man carefully selected a series of instruments and laid them delicately on a table next to his victim. Sanchez's eyes opened wide at the array of pliers, saws, needles and wire cutters.

"Well Joe, I wish I could say that this will hurt me more than you, but that would be disingenuous. But I tell you what, I will let you choose which body part we should start with. You pick. How about your left eye for starters?"

Sanchez's whole body was shaking as he considered his options and then he did the only thing he could do; he cracked.

"Ok, ok, I am with the US government, but I have no information that anyone cares about," he stammered.

"Ah, but you do, Joe. Let's start with this. What is your assignment here in Venezuela?"

The man continued to shake. "I…I'm investigating illicit activities of the Venezuelans against US diplomats," Sanchez responded.

"What illicit actions?"

"There are several things we are concerned about, things I am sure you are already aware of," Sanchez answered.

"And they are?" the man persisted.

"One is the inexplicable illness that has affected many at our embassy. We believe the Venezuelan government is responsible."

"What else?"

The man paused, took a deep breath, and continued. "We believe there are factions within this country working with our enemies on biological weapons of mass destruction."

"And what have you found, Joe?"

"I was just getting started, so I haven't really found much," Sanchez responded nervously.

"Now Joe, please don't make me use my tools. I will only ask one more time, what have your learned and reported back to your country?"

Sanchez glanced nervously at the table as his interrogator lowered a hand on a bone saw. "The only thing I reported was that we intercepted communications about moving biologic materials from Caracas to Maracaibo and several other locations in the country where we believe there are labs operating."

"Thank you, Joe, that was helpful. That wasn't so hard, was it? I have a few more questions, but we'll take a short break before we continue," the man said, smiling. He removed his hand from the saw. "Carlos, put his hood back on." He turned towards the kitchen and called back, "Oh, and Carlos, I must make a call. Take good care of Joe."

The watcher quickly retreated and moved to a pantry off the kitchen, leaving the door ajar. The interrogator entered the room, closed the door, and stopped to dial a number on his mobile.

"General Velasquez," he demanded. A moment later, he continued. "Sir, we have completed a preliminary interrogation of Joe Sanchez. Your intel was correct. He is with the US government and is here investigating our operations at the US embassy. But more concerning—he is aware of the labs."

There was a pause. "Yes General, he has reported his preliminary findings back to the US. I think we need to inform our partners and tighten up our security immediately."

Another pause as the caller listened and then responded, "of course, I will finish the interrogation and dispose of him before the end of the day."

After ending the call, the man left the kitchen. The watcher reclaimed his position at the kitchen door as he mulled over what he just heard. His assignment was to nose around and provide backup to State, if necessary. But there was a lot more going on than was anticipated. He needed to save Sanchez's ass. Before he could consider his options, a shout came from the other room as a guard rushed in.

"Boss, Fernando is dead in the alley. Shot twice. We've got company!"

"Shit," said the interrogator. "Spread out and search the residence now! Carlos, you stay here with me. We need to finish this session."

No more time, thought the watcher as he heard several guards beginning their search of the premises. He quietly opened the door and entered the room. The boss had his back to him, but Carlos stood facing in his direction and gasped as he started to raise his semiautomatic. At this range only one round spit from the Sig slamming the big guard back into the opposite wall, a small red orifice forming in his forehead. The boss spun around in a panic to face the Sig only feet away.

The watcher calmly smiled and said, "Ola amigo, como se llamas?"

The man's eyes darted desperately looking for a way out, then focused on the watcher and responded with a growl, "My name is Miguel and you my friend are *muerte!*"

"Well Miguel, you better hope that is not true because unless you call off your dogs, you will join Carlos before I kill your compadres. Do it now!" demanded the watcher.

Miguel sneered but made no move to comply.

"Bad decision," commented the watcher as he lowered his aim and shot the man in his left foot. Miguel screamed in pain as he collapsed to the tile floor.

"Your soccer days are now over. The next round will put you permanently in a wheelchair. Your choice," said the man with the Sig.

Miguel yelled to his guards to return with their guns lowered. The watcher positioned himself behind Miguel, the Sig squarely pressed against his head, and he waited. The first guard peered around the kitchen door, weapon raised and was dropped in place, his AK clattering to the floor. Another peered through an exterior window to assess the situation and was immediately dispatched by the watcher's silenced weapon. A third came upon the body in the kitchen and threw his weapon to the floor and entered the living room, hands raised. The watcher turned to Miguel once again and asked, "is that it?"

Miguel, gripping his foot, groaned, "Si."

"Bueno." Turning to the new arrival, the watcher commanded in Spanish, "slowly approach Mr. Sanchez and remove his shackles and the hood and free him. Then put Miguel, here, in the chair and tie his arms behind him. After you do that, put the hood over your head, lie down on the floor next to Miguel, and do not move."

The entire takedown took just two minutes. Sanchez remained silent throughout the ordeal.

Once his shroud was removed, he blinked at the watcher and stammered, "who are you?"

"All in good time Joe. But first things first, please use the extra rope to hog tie our friend on the floor."

The task completed, the watcher turned to Sanchez and said, "Joe, I need you to use Miguel's mobile to contact your people and get them over here with some Marines, take these thugs into custody and get you back to the US embassy. While you're doing that, I need some privacy here with my friend Miguel to get some answers, so take the call in the kitchen. Can you do that Joe?"

Sanchez answered, "yes, but who are you and who do you work for?"

"I'm afraid that's need-to-know Joe, but we are on the same team. Now get going. Oh, and Joe, when you're finished with the call, leave Miguel's phone on the table in the kitchen."

The man nodded hesitantly but picked up the phone and headed into the kitchen, closing the door behind him.

The watcher turned to his captive and said, "now my friend, it's your turn in the hot seat."

Miguel was slumped in the chair, still whimpering from the bullet in his, now clotting, wound. He slowly raised his head, the pain and rage mixed in his contorted features.

"Who do you work for and what are your objectives?" the watcher asked sternly.

Miguel glared back and said, "I don't know what you are talking about."

"Wrong answer," the watcher said as he gently pressed the barrel of the Sig against the man's wounded foot.

Miguel screamed and said, "I work for the Venezuelan government and was investigating the espionage activities of your government."

"I see, and who are your partners and what are you doing in your labs?" Miguel visibly jerked at these references but remained silent.

"Oh, yes Miguel, I know about your government's little escapade into the biologics business, but I would appreciate more detail and you're going to provide that now or, as you say, I will have to be more persuasive!"

Miguel again shook his head and said, "I don't know what you are talking about."

"That's very unfortunate," said the watcher as he applied greater pressure on the now open wound. Miguel screamed again and finally capitulated.

"Ok, I provide security for our biologics operation in the country. I report to General Velasquez, who directs the operation. I don't know what the operation is or what is being done in the labs. I know the government is cooperating with other partners to do this work, but I don't know what it is, I swear."

"Where are these labs located?"

"In Venezuela, there are three" Miguel responded. "One in Caracas, one here in Maracaibo and one in Valencia."

The door to the kitchen opened and Joe Sanchez interrupted, "the embassy is sending a group of marines in a chopper. They should be here in an hour or so. They requested you return with me for a debrief."

"No can do, Joe," responded the watcher as he turned and said, "I'll take that mobile phone, Joe. I'm done here."

"But the ambassador specifically ordered you to remain," Sanchez said astonished.

"I don't take orders from the ambassador," replied the watcher as he grabbed the phone and walked out the front door of the residence, disappearing through the gate into the receding shadows of the late morning sun.

CHAPTER TWO

THE ASSIGNMENT

Caracas is the capital and largest city in Venezuela with almost three million people. But ever since new socialist leadership had gained power, the once vibrant metropolis has been failing fast. People were starving in the streets and the crime rate was among the highest in the world. The new government developed strong ties with some of America's greatest foes and was regularly engaging in activities supported by Russia, China and Iran.

These actions were a growing concern for US intelligence agencies. Not since the Cuban crisis of the sixties was there such a disturbing development in the western hemisphere and Washington was worried. Among America's best early warning operations is its supremacy in signal intelligence and communications interception and that is the purview of the National Security Agency (NSA) based in Ft. Meade, Maryland. With the largest computer intelligence complex in the world, it routinely conducts over a billion intercepts per day. That is why the watcher, Special NSA Agent Mac Sisco, was in Maracaibo, Venezuela.

Only a few weeks earlier, Sisco was assigned by Admiral James Clausen, Director, NSA, to investigate some disturbing intelligence regarding activities in Venezuela. Sisco, was among very few elite NSA Special Agents whose primary engagements were field investigations into signet intercepts. The thirty-five-year-old, ex-Navy Seal's last assignment established him as one of the agency's most accomplished assets. Less than a year before he successfully led a team of the world's best international operatives in destroying a terrorist initiative, code named Apogee, which threatened to become a worldwide crisis. He worked directly with Clausen on that assignment and the two became close. There was no leader that Sisco trusted more than the Admiral and he knew the old man had flawless instincts and always had his team's back.

South America was familiar territory for Mac. He had worked in several countries south of the border in previous operations and was multi-lingual in five languages. At six feet one inch and 180 pounds, he was very fit, and aside from his boyish good looks could blend in well in most situations. But once the action started, Sisco was lethal! Years of training in deep cover ops, hand to hand tactical skills, weapons proficiency and special operations qualified him as one of the elite few. But Sisco's mental toughness and leadership under extraordinarily stressful conditions and his uncanny ability to extricate himself from complex situations was what put him at the top of the list.

Mac was vacationing in the Caribbean, in the Grand Cayman Islands, doing some serious scuba diving on the famous underwater walls surrounding the island when the call came in from the agency. He was relaxing on the beach, enjoying a non-dive day to lower his nitrogen build up when his mobile rang.

"Sisco," he answered.

"Please hold for the Director," came the distant reply. It wasn't long before the connection went through and Mac heard the familiar voice.

"Mac, how's the diving?"

"Wonderful, Sir."

"I hope you've had a chance to take in some of the exquisite Tuna and Yahoo," the caller continued.

"I have that on my agenda for tonight, in fact," Mac responded.

"That's good, because I'm afraid I have to ask you to cut your holiday short and look into something for me," said Admiral James Clausen, Director of the National Security Agency.

Uh oh, Mac thought. This had to be important if the old man called him personally and interrupted a long-awaited vacation.

"Of course, Admiral, where's the operation?"

"I'll send you a secure brief. Review it and contact me back on my secure line later today and I'll fill in the blanks. Fly out to your operational destination tomorrow. You should start your work ASAP. The primary objective of phase one is to gain insight into the veracity of our sigint and get us additional detail. Based on those findings, I'll let you know how we'll proceed. Sorry to interrupt your time off, Mac, but this situation could be serious and we need to be all over it!"

The secure transmission came in after Mac returned from a wonderful dinner at Morgan's Seafood Restaurant on Seven Mile Beach to his nearby villa at the Caribbean Club. He keyed in his password on his laptop and pulled up the encoded document. Once he entered his secure code and an additional personal encryption sequence, the document opened with a top secret codeword designation and he began reading. The essence of the brief was that NSA had intercepted numerous communications in recent weeks between officials in the Venezuelan government and known international bad actors.

The connections were typically between intelligence or military factions and in some cases were with separate terrorist organizations. It was a "who's who" list of America's enemies. Among the players were China, Russia, Iran, North Korea, Somalia, the Taliban, the Palestinians and even remnants of ISIS. More disturbing was that these intercepts were gathered in the last month and the content had been so cryptic and vague that the agency wasn't able to determine what was really going on. The alarm bells went off based on the volume and breadth of the messaging. That prompted Clausen's decision to interrupt Mac's vacation and engage him in a preliminary assessment.

Sisco's journey began in Caracas, where the NSA established a safe house, but quickly moved to Maracaibo when a US State Department employee, Jose Sanchez, went missing. Fortunately, his assailant was careless in his desire to glean intelligence from Sanchez's cell phone. NSA tracked Sanchez's to Maracaibo and Sisco quickly picked up the trail. Now, back in Caracas, Mac was busy planning his next move.

The biolab intel he provided NSA would help narrow the intercept targets, but he knew that human intelligence was really what was necessary at this stage of the investigation. That meant that he must get inside one of the illicit labs and see what the hell was going on. It didn't take long to map out his first target. According to NSA, one of the three cities identified by Miguel had the highest volume of international communications which originated from two locations in Valencia, Venezuela. That was a convenient starting point since Valencia was only about 100 miles due west of Caracas and easily accessible by car in a couple hours.

What was also intriguing about the agency's findings were the organizations from which the messages emanated. One was a defunct petrol-chemical plant and the other was a US owned pharmaceutical company. *Well,* Mac thought, *strange bedfellows to say the least.* Now the question was, how could he clandestinely penetrate each of them without arousing suspicion? He spent the next several hours researching the Petro plant. Obviously, this target would require a black ops approach. Go in at night, find the operations center from which the sigint had originated and search for intel, record and photograph everything and withdraw without leaving any trace. Pretty straight forward and barring any significant security, should be non-eventful.

He summarized his plan in an encrypted communication to the Admiral and requested any details the agency could provide that would facilitate his penetration.

He then turned to the second target, the pharmaceutical company, and considered his options. There were only two approaches that could work. One was to adopt a cover and infiltrate the organization and sniff around. The second was to break in and locate specific evidence on why an American Corporation was communicating with international bad guys. Both alternatives required more information and that was the agency's forte. He also knew it was very plausible that someone might be committing espionage without the knowledge of the company, so this operation was delicate. He couldn't make the call on which option made sense until he got feedback from NSA. He also knew that whatever he learned at the petro plant might help him understand how best to approach his second target. In any case, he needed to get the folks in Washington to give him some guidance, so he sent a second request in with his plan for the pharma target.

Anticipating some delay while the agency responded, Mac began to prepare the tactical gear he would need for his first assault. As usual, the Admiral had been flawless in his preparation for Mac's assignment. In a locked closet of the one-bedroom condo, he inspected the gear he would need. He was already packing his personal favorite nine-millimeter Sig Sauer P226 Tacops for his trip to Maracaibo, but Valencia would require some additional accessories. He began filling a black nylon backpack with items from the racks that lined the walls of the closet. Extra ammunition and magazines for the Sig, a backup POF AR15 with three thirty round Mags, a Kevlar vest in the event of a serious fire fight, infrared enhanced night vision goggles, an NSA custom satellite phone with built in high-res camera with data capture capability and encryption with direct connect to the agency, a light weight taser and an eight-inch tactical combat knife, if things got really dicey. And finally, a new agency disarming gadget for bypassing serious security defenses completed the inventory.

It was early evening when the message came through from Clausen and Mac opened it eagerly. It read, "Mac, I agree with your first target plan and the phasing of the two. We have been working on the analysis of both, with our priority being the petro plant. I have attached a complete architectural layout of the plant from before it was shuttered. We have identified the most likely source of the operation on the drawings, based on the electrical and computing center details from the plans. However, they may not be accurate anymore, especially if the facility was re-worked and re-purposed. As you will see, the original security systems were extensive and may well have been augmented since these drawings, so the penetration may be complex."

"There is additional historical information about the plant that may be germane once you penetrate. On the second target, the pharma facility, we are still digging. So, while I agree with your choices, I am not yet able to recommend one scenario over the other. Hopefully, by the time you have completed target one, we can provide insight into target two. I have reserved a room at the GH Guaparo Inn on the Av. Universidad Urbanización La Granja, just outside of Valencia, for several nights. You should check in tomorrow under the cover of Jose Mateo, an Argentinian Oil and Gas engineer on consulting business. Your alias brief is attached. Mac, please follow codeword protocol and communicate accordingly. Good luck!" Mac opened the attachments and started reading. He had a lot of prep work to do before leaving in the morning.

An intense session was underway across town at the General Command of the Bolivarian Military Aviation HQ, and General Enrique Velasquez was not happy.

"What do you mean, you have not heard from Miguel?" the general demanded of his subordinate.

"Sir, we have tried contacting him since yesterday without a response. We sent a squad to Maracaibo, to his compound, but have not heard back. I anticipate a report any time now."

"I am not interested in your excuses Colonel Esperanza. Get them on the phone right now!"

"Yes Sir," the colonel responded, making the call, totally intimidated by his furious superior. He waited nervously fidgeting as the call went through.

"Well?" asked the general impatiently.

"No answer, Sir," whimpered the colonel as he hung up.

The general, becoming even more enraged, paced up and down the room, when suddenly the colonel's mobile phone rang loudly.

Colonel Esperanza snatched up the device as if his life depended on it, as well it might and demanded, "status lieutenant," and listened intently.

Immediately, the general yelled, "for God's sake Esperanza, put it on speaker!"

The colonel did as he was told and demanded, "Lieutenant Gomez, you are on speaker with General Velasquez. Please repeat your complete report on the situation."

"Yes Sir", answered Gomez and began. "We just arrived at the compound and completed a preliminary search. Three of Miguel's guards are dead, one outside the compound and two in the compound. Both Miguel and one of his guards are missing."

"What about the prisoner," demanded the general impatiently.

"He is not here either, although there is definitely evidence that he was being interrogated," answered the lieutenant. "Sir, I may be able to provide additional insight after we have had a chance to really wipe this place down," continued the officer.

"You have one hour lieutenant. Get me some answers or your career will be a short one," Velasquez threatened as he tossed the phone onto the conference room table.

CHAPTER THREE

VALENCIA

The traffic was light on Route One west from Caracas to Valencia. That was no surprise since gasoline was scarce and unaffordable for most Venezuelans. It was a pathetic example of the failure of yet another communist regime. The irony of a country with some of the world's richest petroleum deposits not able to provide its own citizens with affordable gasoline was astonishing, but true. Mac made good time in the rental Toyota SUV as he kept pace with the few locals on the highway and soon arrived at Valencia, the third largest city in the country. It was still early enough that he decided to get the lay of the land and scope out the petrochemical plant which was about fifty kilometers north on the Caribbean coast.

He continued to follow Route One north to El Palito and in less than an hour approached the aging refinery. While it was considered a medium conversion refinery it was an enormous complex with acres of storage tanks and buildings. Fortunately, NSA's documents described the layout of the complex in detail and identified the administrative offices which most likely housed the communications and computing infrastructure from which their intercept originated. Clausen had outdone himself by including high resolution satellite photos of the plant during its operational era and more recent images since it had shut down. Mac studied them carefully the night before and learned a lot. While there was security, especially around the ops center, in the recent images, the level of these fortifications was enhanced. Razor wire now adorned the top of the fencing and additional cameras were installed. There was even a second perimeter fence constructed inside the first to add another layer of defense. *Yep, there is definitely something going on when you beef up the security on a defunct operation*, Mac thought.

He did not want to draw attention, but figured he could risk a single, slow drive by on an adjacent highway and unobtrusively snap some photos for later study. As he circumvented the complex, he didn't observe any activity around the refinery operations. There were no cars or people on the grounds. It looked like what it was supposed to be, an old refinery shut down some time ago. He purposely left the administration offices for last because he figured that is where the action would be and he wanted to get a closer look on foot. He made it a point to pull off the road behind a group of trees a good distance from the complex. He grabbed a pair of high-powered binoculars and a digital camera with a 400 millimeter zoom lens from his backpack, slung them over his shoulder and began jogging through the trees that surrounded the perimeter fencing of the refinery.

Sisco slowed to a stop after the mile and a half jaunt to the edge of a tree line. He hung back in the shadows and wiped the fine sheen of sweat from his forehead. He pulled the binoculars out and focused in on the nearest set of buildings. Slowly scanning the parking lot in front of the entrance, he observed four vehicles parked out front. As he panned upward to a series of grimy windows, he could just make out moving figures on the second floor. On the roof, an array of satellite dishes pointed upward into the cloudless sky, the sun reflecting brightly off their shiny surfaces. Even at this distance, it was obvious that the equipment was recently installed. No rust, chipped paint or faded colors plagued these additions.

He sensed movement on the ground and repositioned the glasses on the entrance. Four men exited the doorway and were gesturing at each other as they moved towards their vehicles. Mac quickly dropped the binoculars and grabbed the camera with its telephoto lens focusing it on each individual and snapped off several shots. He also took photos of their vehicles and license plates before they exited the compound. After they left, he continued photographing the structure before making his way back to the Toyota.

It was early afternoon when Mac checked in at GH Guaparo Inn on the Av. Universidad Urbanizaciòn La Granja, just outside of Valencia. Clausen selected the hotel because of its popularity with international tourists and business guests and it was surprisingly busy considering the deplorable state of the country. Mac was fluent in Spanish and while his accent belied him as a foreigner, he would not stand out as an American.

Once checked into his modest street level room, he began reviewing his photos from the afternoon's excursion. The superior optics of the telephoto lens and the advanced image processing software on his laptop provided excellent details. The shots of the building indicated that at least the first two floors of the interior were in use. The furnishings were new and there were contemporary office items visible through the windows. His original assessment of the communications on the roof also proved to be accurate when enlarged and enhanced on the computer. The agency would have a field day identifying and analyzing the arrays. The shots of the group of men exiting the building were pure gold. They captured full facial images from the front and sides and matched with their vehicle information should be light duty for the big processors at NSA to ID them and begin to unravel the mystery.

Mac carefully examined everyone, imprinting his mind with their faces. He had a feeling he would get to know them up close and personal, maybe sooner than later. He also scrutinized them as they entered their vehicles. One of the cars was a late model 500 series

Mercedes. Not the kind of gas guzzler that a typical Venezuelan would elect to drive with the price of petrol in the country. The owner was a big man. He had long black hair pulled back into a ponytail and sported a dark black mustache and goatee. He was well over six feet with the body of a weightlifter. His tanned arms were muscular, straining his tight-fitting polo shirt. From his countenance and his gestures, he was clearly in charge and calling the shots. Hoping this intel would be a treasure trove for the agency, Mac attached the images to an encrypted email update to Admiral Clausen and requested a response ASAP. His plan was to hit the refinery tomorrow evening, so he needed whatever the agency could dig up by morning at the latest. Either way, he was going in.

James Clausen had just finished a long and grueling meeting at three pm in his conference room on the fifth floor of NSA's headquarters in Ft. Meade, Maryland and was on his way to his office when his Executive Assistant called out, "Admiral, may I have a word?"

"Of course, Margaret," he answered," stepping over to her desk.

"Sir, could we take this in your office?" Clausen nodded and strode into his large, paneled office overlooking the agency's complex and turned as his assistant carefully closed the door behind her.

"What's up, Margaret?" Clausen asked with a smile.

"Sir, you instructed me to let you know immediately if Agent Sisco contacted you and to treat it as Top Secret code word intelligence. I checked your incoming sensitive file after my break and he sent you an encrypted e-mail with numerous attachments about fifteen minutes ago."

"Thank you, Margaret and please continue to alert me the second Agent Sisco communicates, no matter what time of day or night."

"Yes Sir, and just so I'm clear," Margaret asked, "what if you are in a high-level meeting or out of the office?"

"Margaret, you know where I am and with whom twenty-four seven, so find me. As far as interrupting me, I don't care if I am with POTUS, get to me. What Mac is working on could be that important."

"Thank you for the clarification, Sir, I fully understand," said his EA.

Clausen sat down at his computer and pulled up his VIP file. There were several messages from his colleagues at other intelligence agencies including one from the Director of the CIA and one from Frederick Singleton, the newly elected President of the United States. All the emails had come in within the last thirty minutes with the last one from Mac. Clausen sighed, *duty calls,* he thought as he opened Singleton's note.

"Director Clausen, please join me and several of your Intelligence colleagues at a special briefing in the Situation Room at one pm tomorrow and be prepared to update me on the latest activities of the Israelis as it relates to the following, Iran, Syria and the Palestinians. Also, I would like a summary of our dealings with China and Russia and any extraordinary issues with which your agency is currently challenged. Please limit your remarks to no more than thirty minutes. If you have any questions, contact my Chief of Staff, Frank Robino." The email was signed, President Frederick Singleton and stamped with the Presidential Seal.

Since the election, six months earlier, Clausen had only a few meetings with the new President, and he was still withholding judgement on how POTUS would support NSA and how his policies would be accepted on the international stage. But so far, he was concerned. Many of the tough policies of the prior President, Steven Holbrook, had held America's enemies at bay, but the campaign promises of this administration seemed to be taking the country in an opposite direction. In the four years of working with Holbrook, Clausen developed a healthy respect for the man's insight and courage and the two became friends. He hoped that he would find the new chief executive as competent and thoughtful, but so far, the softer, kinder approach only emboldened America's foes, especially China. Nonetheless, Clausen was open minded and would know before anyone which way the wind was blowing.

Without further delay, he pulled up Sisco's email and began reading. Mac described his visit to the refinery and his belief that there was some kind of clandestine operation at play. He referenced the photos he attached and requested an urgent investigation into the identities and profiles of the men he observed. He also asked for any insights into the communications equipment he photographed on the roof and what he should look for when he gained access to the compound. Finally, he outlined his current penetration plan and his intent on hitting the target the following evening, if all the factors remained favorable. Clausen finished the message and picked up his gray secure phone.

Margaret immediately came on the line and asked, "yes Sir, how may I help you?"

"Margaret, please get me Robert Worthington, my head of Special Cipher Operations and Analysis, stat," he said urgently. "Oh and Margaret, please bring me a cup of black coffee. It looks like it's going to be a long night."

♦

The call had not gone well. After smooth sailing for almost a year, things were beginning to unravel. General Enrique Velasquez was not prone to panic, but he was deeply concerned about his country's position with its powerful international partners. El Presidente was holding on by a thread and this gambit was their last opportunity to stabilize his regime. The caller from across the world was almost threatening as Velasquez's deadlines were fast approaching. He was blunt in his remarks and informed the general that if he missed his first deliverable, the deal was in jeopardy and other suppliers would be considered. Velasquez could not let that happen. If Venezuela blew this relationship, it would lose enormous resource support for its floundering government.

It wasn't just the bolivars that mattered. The partnership guaranteed military support and energy assistance, not to mention the significant international positioning that it promised. He needed to get his biolabs online and he was behind schedule. Acquiring the raw materials was more complex than he planned and the riots and social disruptions across the country slowed down his supply chains. To complicate matters, now the Americans were sniffing around. That would really throw a wrench into the situation that could be disastrous. He must eliminate that activity quickly no matter what the cost!

He looked at his watch. The hour he gave his subordinates was about to end when his phone rang.

He jerked the receiver off its cradle, almost snapping the cord. "Velasquez," he answered with a growl.

"Sir," Colonel Esperanza responded, "I have your update."

"Report, Colonel." replied the general impatiently.

"We have traced the American back to the US embassy. He was debriefed and one of our undercover people working in the embassy was able to acquire a copy of the debriefing report."

"Yes. yes, Esperanza. What is the bottom line?" the general retorted.

"Sir, Sanchez was indeed an employee with the US State Department. He apparently uncovered some information that made him suspicious about our biolab operations but was just beginning his investigation when we kidnapped him. Our agent, Miguel Hernandez and his team were interrogating him when they were attacked by a lone assailant who killed the guards and freed Sanchez. The Americans choppered in and took Miguel and his surviving guard into custody where they remain today."

"Who is this mystery man?" demanded Velasquez impatiently.

"We don't know and apparently, neither does anyone in the embassy," responded the Colonel.

Velasquez leaned back in his chair cupping his hands under his chin as he considered this new intelligence. If the Americans didn't know who this SOB was, that was a real problem. He might not even be from the US. Or even worse, he might be from another US intelligence agency like the CIA. They were infamous for operating autonomously. Velasquez was familiar with CIA operatives and they were dangerous and unpredictable.

"Sir, are you still there?" came Esperanza's voice back on the line.

"Yes, Colonel, now listen very carefully," responded Velasquez ominously. "I want you to double down on the embassy and get whatever you can on this guy. The CIA routinely operates out of their embassies and everyone will be looking for him. Also, we need to find out what Miguel and the guard have told the Americans. Their knowledge is relatively limited but could be damaging and make the Americans more suspicious. I will immediately make calls to our diplomatic core to demand their release, but it could take a while. I would liquidate them, but at this point that would only draw attention to our activities, and we don't need the exposure. Your most crucial objective is to identify and find this invisible agent and bring him to me for deep interrogation. Do you understand my orders, Colonel?"

"Yes Sir, completely," answered Esperanza emphatically, as the General hung up the phone.

◆

Even before Sisco's alarm had a chance to wake him out of a deep sleep, his mobile chimed, indicating the receipt of a VIP text message. It was 5:30 am. Years of training and deep cover assignments brought him to full alert as he scanned the note from Clausen.

"Mac, there is some very curious information regarding your players at the refinery," wrote the Admiral. "Based on the licenses of their vehicles and the individual images, we were able to identify all of them. Two are operatives of the Venezuelan intelligence arm of the government. One is a Chinese biochemist and pharmaceutical expert from Wuhan, China and the fourth is an executive from the giant US pharmaceutical company, Biotherapeutics, Inc., which has its Venezuelan operation only a few miles away from the refinery and is your second target in Valencia."

The message continued, "the images of the communications gear on the roof were evaluated and while no markings were visible, the configurations and design have been matched to a Chinese manufacturer and they are current state of the art models. The arrays are designed to handle high speed digital signals from both short and long range, even as far as Beijing. We have begun targeting them for intercept and, if they are active, should be able to glean more specific intel from their transmissions. There is much more detail in our analysis which has already been forwarded to you. Please refer to the encrypted email and file from Bob Worthington, Director, Special Cipher Operations and Analysis."

Mac didn't need to speculate about the Admiral's reference to "curious" as he pulled up the report from Worthington on his notebook computer. What in hell was an executive from an American pharma company, doing working with Venezuelan intelligence operators and a Chinese biochemist? He had a bad feeling that the shit was about to hit the fan. An hour later, as he closed the laptop and considered all he read, he was even more convinced that he was right.

The two Venezuelan intelligence operatives the agency identified were long time clandestine professionals who surfaced during the new Munoz regime and were posted in many US intelligence agency alerts. They were serious players and were alleged to have been responsible for numerous deaths, especially those who opposed the newly installed communist government. The biochemist was a viral specialist who was heavily involved with the original Covid-19 research and curiously dropped off the grid over a year before. The final individual was Phillip Seguro, the Executive Vice President of International Operations for Biotherapeutics, a fifty-billion-dollar pharmaceutical company headquartered out of Boston, Massachusetts. This was the big man Mac observed getting into the Mercedes who seemed to be giving the orders. *Boy howdy, to say these were strange partners in crime would be a massive understatement*, he thought.

Mac spent the rest of the day studying the aerial photos of the complex, new details of the administrative facility NSA sent and packing up his gear for the penetration. He planned to arrive outside the perimeter at 1 am. He figured an hour to disarm any security and enter the building no later than two am. He would first do a quick assessment of the entire facility, then focus on the second and third floors which, according to the agency's best intelligence, housed the offices and meeting rooms and the computer and communications center. His search would include photos of equipment, capture images of any documents or files that appeared relevant and data capture of any computing systems he could break. Finally, he would place listening devices in several locations throughout the facility which would wirelessly capture and transmit recorded information for thirty days. Most importantly, he must accomplish all this without leaving any evidence of his penetration.

At eleven pm, Sisco left his ground level room via the patio's sliding glass door. He wore casual jeans, a black tee shirt, Adidas running shoes and a Venezuela World Baseball Classic WBC 2017 Official Cap. His plan was to come and go without being seen, but if he was observed, he wanted to look as unassuming as possible. His SUV was parked directly off the patio and while a few folks were out and about, he drew no attention and was soon underway. He parked his car in the same wooded area from the prior day, ditched the cap and opened his backpack. Although he wasn't anticipating any encounters, he donned a Kevlar vest, cinched up his utility ammo belt, and pulled on a dark camo combat coat into which he stored other gear. He debated the Taser but opted for his ten-inch tactical combat knife as company for his suppressed Sig P226 nine-millimeter. Sisco chuckled to himself as he headed into the dark woods. With all this gear, it was still light duty compared to his average operation.

Even with no moon and a cloudy sky, he made good time and soon arrived at the outer perimeter fencing. This was the compound's original chain link fence and on his prior trip he didn't observe any special security. This far out, there was no lighting. In the dimness, he scanned the fencing again for motion detectors, alarm sensors or electrification and saw none. The fence was ten feet tall with razor wire on the top. Mac knew from experience that going over the top was almost suicidal. He stooped down and tested the tension at the bottom of the wire and quickly determined that digging underneath would take too long. Next, he walked down the line to a supporting pole, pulled his engineer's cutters out and snipped vertical sections of the wire down his side of the poll. After pulling the wire apart, he carefully stepped through the opening. When he returned, he would pull the wire back to its original position behind the poll and the cuts would be almost invisible.

The distance to the newer interior fence was about twenty yards in with no cover and there were cameras located periodically along the building's soffits. He also observed motion detectors near the fence line. That was the bad news. The good news was that he worked for the NSA which had access to the most advanced security systems technology on the planet. If the agency didn't build it, one of their partner intelligence agencies like the CIA or DIA did. In this case, Clausen had equipped his safe house in Caracas with numerous high-tech goodies that Mac used on previous assignments which made short work of most security systems.

The agency's multi-purpose device was effective at jamming modern wireless security systems including motion detectors, entry and interior camera systems and keypad/card entry defenses. It could even disable wired systems, but these were becoming rare except in older configurations. The range on the jammer was over 100 yards, so Mac flipped it on and waited as it scanned the security systems that were functioning around the perimeter and throughout the building. After fifteen seconds the display listed all the systems and indicated it was ready to transmit the multiple jamming frequencies required to disable them. Mac pressed the key and waited as each of the security systems were defeated and the "all clear" green light appeared. "Oorah", he silently proclaimed as he sprinted to a corner pole of the interior fence, scaled it and headed for the building's entrance. Pulling out a high-powered LED beam light, he entered and began his phase one search.

CHAPTER FOUR

DISCOVERY

A low murmur was audible as the assembled participants greeted their colleagues across the large conference room table in the Situation Room, buried deep within the White House. It was a special collection of the most powerful spooks on the planet. There was Phil Van Meter, Director, Central Intelligence Agency (CIA), Janice Spaulding, Director, Defense Intelligence Agency (DIA), Donald Givens, Director, Federal Bureau of Investigation (FBI), William Brown, Director, Homeland Security, and Admiral James Clausen, Director, National Security Agency (NSA). And for good measure, they were joined by Jonathan Bueller, Attorney General, Marvin French, Secretary of State and James Crowell, Secretary of Defense. The cream of the crop of America's Intelligence community and some of the most powerful individuals in the world, all in one place waiting to meet with the newly elected President of the United States of America.

The nervous chatter was soon interrupted as the POTUS, Frederick Singleton, accompanied by his Chief of Staff, Frank Robino entered the room.

They all stood as Singleton was announced and he ceremoniously intoned, "please take your seats gentleman." Singleton turned to Robino and asked hesitantly, "is everyone here Frank?"

Robino responded respectfully, "yes Sir, Mr. President."

"Alright, good," the President proclaimed as he turned back to his audience. "Let's get started," he said to the assemblage. "I have asked you all here today to get a concise update of each of your areas as it relates to our dealings on the international front as referenced in my recent communications. For the FBI and the Attorney General's Office, I would like to cover any special activities and challenges you now face. I would like Mr. Robino to manage the agenda on my behalf. Any questions?" There was silence in the room as everyone turned their attention to the COS and waited. "Good," exclaimed the President. "Frank, please proceed."

Robino stood and displayed the agenda on a large screen and said, "thank you, Mr. President. Let's begin with the CIA and Director Van Meter."

Van Meter rose and walked to the front of the room and began his presentation. "Thank you Mr. President."

Van Meter spent the next thirty minutes detailing specific threats in various common hotspots including Somalia, Yemen, Afghanistan, North Africa and the middle east.

"As you would expect," he continued, "our most serious issues have to do with Israel, Iran and the Palestinians. As Secretary French will no doubt report, our return to the negotiating table has not been met with the anticipated enthusiasm and the Israelis are especially upset. Furthermore, the Palestinians have become even more aggressive in both their rhetoric and their missile attacks on Israel. Our assets are confirming increased activity in terrorist communications and the risks attendant with infiltration are spiking as well. These conditions make it much more difficult to acquire accurate human intelligence."

"Excuse me, Phil," Admiral James Clausen queried, "have you seen any extraordinary activity in South America?"

"Other than the increase in Cartel activity, which I already referenced earlier, there has been no material change. Any country in particular that concerns you Jim," the CIA Director questioned back.

"Not really," answered Clausen. "As I will report, we are seeing a general increase in the sigint from that region, so I thought you might have some insight."

Robino, apparently impatient to keep the meeting on schedule interrupted, "thank you Director Van Meter, let's move on."

Over the next several hours, the principles each rose and presented their reports. During the readouts, the President stayed largely quiet, asking few questions and generally allowing his Chief of Staff to control the dialogue. When Admiral Clausen was called, his presentation mirrored that of his CIA colleague except he did reference the volume of intercepts coming from America's neighbors to the south.

"Mr. President, like the CIA, we have also seen a substantial uptick in the Mexican communications volume," Clausen began. "That volume seems to be largely focused on new drug and human trafficking activities associated with our new policies at the border. However, we are also seeing increased activity in many of the other Central and South American countries as their populations are also affected. Finally, comm traffic with other international players has also increased with many of these same countries, and this is certainly concerning."

"To what do you attribute these increases," Robino broke in.

"Most of it relates to immigration issues into these countries precipitated by access to the US," responded Clausen. "But there have also been other encrypted messages from numerous bad actors that have gotten our attention."

"Why is that, and what have you learned," Robino asked.

"It is disturbing because these communications are originating from some of our most serious adversaries like China, Iran and Russia," responded the NSA Director. "Furthermore, they are using very sophisticated encryption technologies that we have not yet broken and that means that the content has to be very important!"

The President, in a rare moment of engagement, asked, "Director Clausen, which South American countries are involved in this activity?"

"Sir, so far, we have intercept messages from three South American countries, Columbia, Argentina and Venezuela as well as Cuba," Clausen answered carefully.

"I see," said the POTUS. "That is disturbing," he continued and was about to ask another question, when Robino deftly interrupted, "thank you Admiral, let's move on to State, Secretary French, please."

French discussed the diplomatic activities worldwide emphasizing the progress on the peace talks in Paris and the challenges with the Iranians. He finished by mentioning, "speaking of Venezuela, Mr. President, we had a rather strange incident occur there recently. One of our people was kidnapped in Caracas while looking into some questionable activities by the communist regime. Fortunately, he was quickly freed, and the perpetrators are currently being questioned at our embassy."

Robino jumped in and said, "well that is certainly good news, Mr. Secretary, but we must move on unless there is something else?"

"Well, yes there is," French responded, irritated for being rushed. "Our man was freed and the kidnappers were captured by someone who was never identified. We don't know who he works for."

"That certainly is curious," responded Robino. "But now we really must move on, the President's schedule is very full today."

Clausen listened intently to this dialogue. He found it profoundly disturbing. Robino almost seemed to be deflecting the conversation away from this area of discussion. It was almost as if he wanted to avoid any scrutiny. *Why would he do that*, Clausen asked himself. Maybe it was just his imagination. Was he was being paranoid? But he just couldn't shake it. James Clausen had been around a long time and his sixth sense had proven to be among his greatest assets and he had learned to trust that skill. *No*, he thought, *there was something not right going on here.* That is when he decided not to add any details about NSA's involvement or Sisco's engagement in Venezuela. He needed to figure this out and be damned careful doing it!

◆

It was already two forty-five am when his Garmin 6X buzzed as he began his search of the third floor. The watch was awesome with its built-in GPS and mapping capabilities. He purchased it after his last assignment when another agent used it to save their asses in a very tight spot. *Ah, Jasmine*, Mac thought, *she was something else.* His musings were interrupted by a sudden light that flickered and then died across the room. He snapped off his penlight and pulled back behind a corner abutment. There it was again. It was coming from outside the building and was getting brighter. He crossed the room and peered out a corner pane of the grimy window. His heart leapt as he saw several vehicles weaving through the wooded drive approaching the entrance to the compound, their headlights bouncing off the trees and fencing as they entered the parking lot in front of the building.

"Damn," he swore under his breath. Why would anyone come here in the middle of the night?

This would either be his greatest break or his worst nightmare. First things first, he needed to get to cover and to rearm all the security systems before his visitors discovered they were off. And he only had about thirty seconds to do both. He scanned the large room in the dimness, seeing only two doors and one was the door he came in. He crossed to the other door and opened it, finding himself in a large computer room filled with racks of servers and communications gear.

On the far side was another door which opened into a closet filled with supplies and filing cabinets. This would work, he thought, as he moved into the computer room entrance and pulled out his NSA jammer. Once he pressed the re-arm/disarm toggle key under the protective cover, he would have to freeze in place until his guests shut down their security. Any movement or sound before then would set off the alarms. He lifted the cover, pressed the key, and took a deep breath. Immediately, red blinking lights began to show up from several points in the room. Cameras at the ceiling's corners began glowing from small LEDs. The building had re-armed as instructed. It was officially locked down.

Minutes seemed like hours as Sisco waited, and nothing happened. *What could be holding things up*, he thought anxiously. They should have entered the facility by now, but the security was still on. This was not good! He couldn't move from his position or the motion detectors would pick him up. He couldn't disarm the building's security without knowing where they were. He was trapped!

The minutes ticked by. Ten, twenty, thirty and nothing. He knew at some point he had to make a move. He could speculate all he wanted on why they had not entered the building, but that didn't help. He needed to know for sure where they were, and he couldn't figure that out hiding in this room. His problem was that if he had stayed in the main area to observe them through the window, once he re-armed the security, he wouldn't be able to get to cover in this room.

Well, there really was only one choice, shut down the security again and go find out where they were. It was coming up on forty five minutes when he finally ran out of patience and pressed the dis-arm key again. Once again, the security system went dead. Mac opened the door to the main room and moved to the window. The same cars he had seen the previous day were again parked in the lot in front of the building, but their occupants were nowhere to be seen. He moved to another window with a different vantage point but saw no one. There was one more window at the far side of the room that overlooked the refinery's storage facilities, and he weaved his way around numerous desks and cabinets to check out that real estate. Rows of large tanks fanned out under the moonless night; their outlines barely visible in the distance.

He scanned each access road for any movement and saw no signs of life. Turning back to the big room he debated his next move. He sensed more than saw a faint light reflecting on the window behind him. Mac whirled around and peered out intently. There it was, just a tiny spark in the distance at the edge of one large tank. Then another flickering light appeared. He squinted to focus on the lights as they grew brighter. A group of figures were approaching from behind one of the tanks. They were still over thirty meters out, so he had time. He watched as the group became visible and distinct. There were at least eight people walking in twos. The leader was waving his arms, pointing in different directions, like a tour guide in a museum. Soon they would be entering the lighted administrative building, and he could get a better look.

It wasn't long before the entire group entered the illuminated area. They were nearing the entrance gate of the inner perimeter, and he would only have another minute to observe them. At ten meters, he could make out their faces and as he suspected, the big man he saw earlier was in the lead. The three others from the previous day followed with four more new players. Mac pulled his mobile out and snapped off a few quick pics before retreating to his hiding place in the computer room. As soon as he closed the door, he re-armed the security and once again resumed his vigilance. This time his patience was rewarded. Within five minutes, the security lights once again shut down and soon after he heard muffled voices entering the outer room.

"Well, what do you think?" a voice boomed.

"The tanks will be perfect," came the reply.

"How are the preparations going?" intoned another voice.

"As I committed, we will soon be back on schedule after an unfortunate and unavoidable delay. That is why we moved your inspection up to this evening and to maintain your anonymity. We brought in additional resources from our military and El Presidente used his position to convince our partners to speed up their deliveries."

"Excellent," responded another barely audible voice.

"We anticipate commencing commercial production within thirty days as originally planned," exclaimed the original speaker.

Now we're getting somewhere, Mac thought as he moved closer and pressed his ear to the door.

"Gentlemen," the voice continued, "please join me at the conference table and we will finish our review of the facilities and discuss our next steps."

Mac could hear the shuffling of feet and chairs being repositioned as the group convened their meeting.

"So, as you saw from your tour," the leader began again, "the tanks are more than adequate to hold a global supply of substances, no matter what the category or storage requirements. For special medicinals such as vaccines, we have temperature-controlled facilities. For therapeutics, we have appropriate container environments and for other liquid substances such as narcotics, we have adequate storage as well. In summary, whatever market needs you have created, we are prepared to provide substance safekeeping until you reach your planned launch dates."

"I must admit, we are impressed," said one of the visitors in a soft Asian accent Mac had not heard before. "I look forward to reporting your progress and renewed commitment to meeting our timetable. We were getting somewhat concerned by your lack of specifics and I know that my superiors made their trepidations known to General Velasquez recently."

"Yes, I spoke with the general earlier this evening and reassured him as well that we would be able to meet our original objectives, thanks to his and El Presidente's interventions."

"What about your firm's progress," the Asian continued.

"I'm glad you asked," said the leader. "We are in the final stages of our testing of Project Camo and the results so far are very encouraging. We believe our new technology will allow us to transport and distribute literally any liquid invisibly. In our last phase testing we are finalizing the targeting specifics and triggers which will make our application flexibility and efficacy almost limitless. I anticipate our completion will be on schedule and the package will be available for your first beta deliveries. You can be sure that Biotherapeutics will do its part."

You didn't have to be a rocket scientist to know that there was something sinister going on here, Mac thought, during a break in the conversation. The references to medicinals coupled with narcotics was a dead giveaway. But the discussion about Biotherapeutics Project Camo really concerned him. While he wasn't exactly sure of what the project was, he had a bad feeling about it. And then there was the scope of the operation. A major American corporation colluding with foreign entities was bad enough, but he felt certain that these were not the good guys. He had to get this new info to Clausen, and fast.

"Well gentlemen, are there any other questions or concerns, before we terminate our meeting?" the leader asked abruptly. In concert, Mac could hear a communal negative from several of the speakers.

The Asian added, "not at this time, Mr. Seguro. We will be in touch."

"Good," Seguro responded. "Chen will escort you downstairs to your vehicles while we conclude our internal discussions."

"Please follow me," said another voice, he had not heard before, as chairs were pulled back and several people began to exit the room.

"Alright," Seguro's voice boomed out once the room was apparently cleared of its guests. "Valasquez informed me that we might have a problem. He told me that some unknown actor may be snooping around our operations. What the hell is going on?"

"What we know at this point is that Hernandez's operation was raided by a lone operator," said a heavily accented Spanish speaker. "Hernandez and a guard were taken into custody by the US State Department for questioning."

"Well shit," exclaimed Seguro, "that's just great! Here we are at the most sensitive point in our work having to make up lost ground, the Chinese are nervous and now we have this loose end! Who the hell is this guy? Do we have any leads?"

"We have several well-placed agents in the US Embassy with ears to the ground and should be able to get additional information very soon," answered the Spanish speaker.

"Well, that may just not be good enough," Seguro exclaimed in frustration. "I may have to take this upstairs and use my country's intelligence services to ID this guy. You have forty-eight hours and if you haven't eliminated this threat, you can tell Valasquez that I'm moving on it. We have too much at stake. And get the word out to the team to turn up the security. All we need is someone sneaking around our operations or worse investigating Biotherapeutics."

"I'll check the computer room to see if anything came in on it," said another Spanish speaker.

Damn, thought Mac, *just what I don't need,* as he scanned the dim room for anywhere to hide.

"Forget it," demanded Seguro, "we've had enough bullshit for one night. Let's get out of here. I will see you all back here later this morning. We have a lot of work to do."

Mac waited, but heard no more conversation, just the shuffling of feet and then the noise of the outer room door closing. He raised his eyes and watched the security cameras and motion detectors. Finally, the lights began blinking again indicating the systems were re-armed. He remained still for another ten minutes just to be safe and then carefully toggled the switch on his jammer. The dis-arm sequence repeated and security once again shut down. He said a word of thanks to the techs at the agency and vowed to buy them all a beer the next time he was back in the building. He checked his Garmin. It was almost four am. He had to hustle. He had a lot to do before the sun came up. Since the computer room had no windows, he flipped on the lights and began his search.

He snapped shots of all the equipment. There were racks of servers, backup drives, modems, networking gear, UPS systems and large flat screen monitors with wireless keyboards. It looked like a mini-NASA with a high tech comm center and all the equipment was state of the art, not some left over refinery gear from a past operation. He considered booting up one of the servers but knew he didn't have the expertise or time to break through the security or firewalls that had to be there. There was also a chance that even firing one up might trip some remote alarm and bring the bad guys back. Before he exited into the main room, he carefully placed a bug under the lowest tier of a large rack of servers butted up against the interior wall. The battery would last thirty days and send the devices recordings to a transmitter he would hide in the trees outside the outer perimeter fence.

The main room was full of modern cubicles outfitted with chairs, work surfaces and filing cabinets. It could have been any modern corporate operations center except for the grimy walls and windows. Mac searched each cube in a very deliberate manner avoiding moving any objects or materials unless necessary and then replacing them carefully. All the drawers were unlocked but yielded nothing of value. Finally, he found one cube that was larger and more elaborate than the rest. *This must be management*, he thought and might be where the real goodies were stored. The filing cabinet drawers were all locked. He smiled to himself, bingo. It must be important if it was secured.

Sisco pulled out his pick and went to work. Standard filing cabinets were notoriously easy to break. You could even open them with a paper clip or a nail file. These cabinets were standard issue and he was in them in less than thirty seconds. He scanned the files looking for the most obvious indicators of intelligence value. Several folders looked promising. The first was labeled Proyecto de Conversión. *Conversion Project.*

That sounded ominous and he began skimming the cover document. The summary described the modifications that had been made to the refinery storage tanks to accept different kinds of liquids and the pumping equipment that was installed to transfer the contents. In a second cabinet, he discovered a folder entitled Cadena de Suministro Global. It identified a series of organizations and provided descriptions of material hand offs that spanned the globe. It also described the global supply chain for moving products rapidly around the world. *Yep, this was the mother lode,* he thought, as he frantically began photographing every page he could before his time ran out.

It was tedious work, because he couldn't leave a trace and he was sure there was a lot he had missed, but the operation was pure gold if he could get the goods back to Clausen. He looked at his watch. Five fifteen am and no more time. He must be back in his SUV and on the road in forty-five minutes. He closed the last drawer reluctantly, wiped down the surfaces and left the cube.

He placed numerous listening devices around the room and set several more on his way out of the building. After surveilling the perimeter from a first-floor window, Mac exited the main entrance and crossed to the interior fence, climbed over and jogged towards the outside chain link fence he breached. While he was still within range, he re-armed all the security devices and navigated back to the pole that hid his earlier opening and climbed through. After concealing his relay transmitter in the crook of nearby tree, he headed back to the Toyota.

The early morning glare of a golden sun was fast advancing over the horizon as Mac pulled onto the highway. In the distance he could just make out several dark vehicles, the morning sun reflecting off their windshields in bursts as they sped towards him. He drew his ball cap down and donned his Ray-bans as the fast-approaching cars came closer. Maintaining his speed, he glanced sideways as the four vehicles passed, led by the big Mercedes that was parked at the refinery only hours before.

CHAPTER FIVE

THE PLAN

It was May of 2019. The two men were childhood friends and longtime colleagues of the Chinese Communist Party. It was their custom to get together once a week for dinner, and they seldom missed it. Genjo Ban opened his government condominium door and greeted his good friend warmly.

"Ah, Wu-pen, so good to see you," greeted Genjo. "I have your favorite dinner tonight, shrimp with vermicelli and garlic."

"You are so kind, Genjo," Wu-pen thanked his friend bowing. "What is the occasion that inspired you to make such a special treat?" his friend asked.

"Tonight Wu-pen, I want to discuss an idea I have that could ensure our beloved China will last forever!"

His friend raised his eyebrows as he smiled and said, "Oh, what a glorious thought. I Hope you have sufficient quantities of Baijiu for such a worthy discussion."

Genjo Ban was born in Beijing like his parents and generations of his family before them. Both his mother and father, now retired, were high ranking members of the Communist Chinese Party headquartered in the massive capital city of twenty million. Genjo was an only child and grew up with all the benefits accrued to elite members of the CCP. He went to the best schools and lived in the affluent Beijing suburb of Shunyi as a youth. But his birthright was not the only reason he excelled. He was a brilliant student with an insatiable curiosity and an unrelenting attitude towards discovery. During his youth, his family's affluence provided him the opportunity to travel and over the course of several summers he visited Europe, Australia, South America and of course the US.

Ban's thirst for knowledge destined him to apply to one of China's most prestigious universities, Tsinghua University. To no one's surprise, he was accepted and began a long and storied academic journey culminating in a PhD and a reputation of being one its alumni's brightest minds. The university was known for its scientific specialties and though Genjo's parents encouraged him to study the physical sciences, he yearned for a different field. He was fascinated with human behavior and the social, cultural and economic drivers that moved nations. Now at forty, Dr. Ban was among the world's most recognized theorists in social engineering. His published works were considered leading edge and innovative, if not provocative. He had spoken at conferences all over the world and was a frequent guest lecturer at his alma mater.

But his real career was with the CCP. As a key executive in the International Liaison Department of the Central Committee of the Chinese Communist Party, he played an instrumental role in its global initiatives. The ID, as it was called, focused most of its significant energies on influencing foreign political entities and other social and economic structures to support China's objectives. It also played a key role in undermining and subverting China's potential critics. Ban's training and research coupled with his international networking and academic stature made him a natural and crucial consultant to the Central Committee on global strategic initiatives. In a word, he was a player, and a fiercely loyal one at that. He was proud of his Chinese heritage and his country's way of life and was fervently committed to its success.

Genjo's childhood friend Wu-pen Liang lived just down the street and went to the same schools. Their parents were friends and colleagues in the Party and even took vacations together. Wu-pen was a year older than Genjo and also applied to Tsinghua University but was not accepted. But Wu-pen was an eternal optimist and was unfazed. His second choice was Peking University, which was also among the C9 League of schools and considered among the best academic institutions in the country. As it turned out, Wu-pen's heart was in politics and Peking University was the perfect choice.

The university's School of Government was renowned and Liang took to it like a duck to water. While he did well in his studies, his greatest passion was the non-academic activities that immersed him in the practical conversations of governance. He loved the late-night meetings where deep discussions on the nuances of Marxism were endlessly debated. He lived for the camaraderie of the clubs and the security of the collegial common ideology that surrounded them all like a warm blanket. By the end of his last year at university he had established a strong reputation as a leader and accomplished spokesperson which did not go unnoticed by the CCP who routinely surveilled the halls of its elite universities for new talent.

Even before graduation day, Wu-pen accepted a staff position in The Central Commission for Discipline Inspection. The CCDI was the primary internal control organization of the CCP. It was responsible for enforcing the Party's regulations and policies with a special focus on combating corruption. In his early years, Wu-pen was an administrator, but over time he showed promise in field operations.

In his new role, he took on significant enforcement responsibilities and relished the physical training and lethal skills that he acquired in the fulfillment of his accountabilities. It was not long before his reputation as a strong man and feared enforcer was established as he often personally engaged in the work at hand. Eventually his political acumen and ambition drove him to run for office as an elected member of the CCDI. He was successfully elected by the National Congress in his first attempt and was currently serving his second year of a five-year term as one of its members.

The two men relaxed sipping their wine after enjoying Genjo's home cooked delight. Both relished preparing these dinners. It gave their wives a well-deserved night off and afforded them their own special time together. Their conversation during the meal was casual, as was their practice, leaving the later hours for their serious discussions.

"So, Genjo, what is this mysterious idea you have concocted?" began Wu-pen grinning.

"Yes, yes," replied his friend, "I am so anxious to tell you, but I must set the stage with some background first."

"Alright but remember my term of office is only five years, so don't take too long," Liang laughed.

"No, I promise," exclaimed Ban half seriously.

"Ok," he continued, "here is the historical context. Throughout human history no government has ever been able to sustain itself indefinitely, primarily because it inevitably fails to satisfy those it governs."

"Why is that?" Liang interrupted.

Ban smiled and said, "Good question. The reason is always the same. Leadership's objectives lose alignment with the masses, often because of greed and corruption, and the result is that a revolution occurs in which the governed population demands change. This occurs because the government is not focused on providing the elements that are most desired by the people. Furthermore, even if the leaders are motivated to provide for their people's needs, they are either incapable of really understanding what those needs are or unable to provide them".

Once again, Liang raised his hand to interject, "I don't understand your last assumption, that governments are incapable of understanding their people's needs. It seems to me that those determinations are really common sense."

"You would think so, but they're not and the proof is in the historic failures of leaders and the ensuing insurrections that inevitably topple them," Ban insisted enthusiastically.

"Ok, so what if your right. How do we solve the problem?" Liang asked.

"We need a proven model to understand people's needs," exclaimed his friend, "and the good news is that one already exists! The model for understanding what people really desire is based on a theory developed over seventy years ago by an American psychologist, Abraham Maslow."

"Yes, I remember studying about this fellow's theory at university," responded Wu-pen immediately. "The concept is called Maslow's Hierarchy of Needs, is it not?"

"That is absolutely correct," Ban answered emphatically, "and it outlines three types of human needs, basic needs, psychological needs, and self-fulfillment needs. Maslow further defined these categories to more specifically identify their meaning. Basic needs have two categories, physiological needs which include food, water, warmth and rest and the safety needs of security and safety. The psychological needs are also broken down into types, belongingness and love needs and esteem needs. And finally, the last type of human need is self-actualization."

"That seems to make sense", countered Liang, "but I don't see any ah ha moment in any of this so far."

"Patience, my good friend", admonished Ban, "there is much more to this and its relevance to China's future will soon become apparent. And I promise, you will not be disappointed."

Liang sighed heavily and said, "remember my term of office is only five years," he joked again.

"So noted," Genjo responded smiling back, as he continued. "Now, Maslow, like any respectable scientist, dug even deeper into the human psyche. He decided that the first four levels are deficiency needs and the last, self-actualization, are growth needs. This distinction became particularly important because he realized that the deficiency needs occur because of deprivation and the more unmet these needs are the greater the motivation is. Furthermore, the longer these needs are unrealized, the stronger the desire is to achieve them. Maslow also postulated that as the deficiency needs are generally met, they cease to be important. The growth needs, on the other hand, work differently in that they continue to increase in importance and motivation the more they are met."

"I must say these are fascinating observations," Wu-pen remarked, "but I still fail to see any relationship between individual human behaviors and the prospects of a brighter future for our beloved China."

"I'm about to clear that up," his friend once again promised. "But keep in mind that the key to controlling the future is in controlling the people".

"Now just a little more historical perspective will set the stage," Ban lectured. "Historically, mankind has focused on conquering to grow and prosper. Instead, it should focus on developing a societal model that can be sustained by satisfying its own constituents and then use these advances externally to provide markets that will fund its internal development. China's objective and perspectives need to evolve from focusing on military power and conquering to evolving its own society internally. The CCP must understand that economic dominance should be the primary objective and military power is important only as a defensive mechanism or for offensive leverage. Using military actions to overthrow enemies and competitors would only destroy economic markets, diminishing China's real control and reducing its revenues and resources," Ban insisted.

"But even our current budding external economic investment and control strategy is not sustainable against nationalistic revolutions. China should focus on driving external control by providing solutions that satisfy "Maslow" needs across the worldwide marketplace. That is where the money is. Keep in mind, that this external focus is particularly important in providing the resources to satisfy and fund our own people's needs and internal growth and thereby sustain our government's structure and power indefinitely."

"Ah, Now I think I now see where you are going with all of this Genjo, and I must say, I like the direction," Liang interjected.

"But it gets better," Ban said enthusiastically. "There are essentially only two approaches to meeting human needs. The first is to determine those needs and develop the means to satisfy them. These organic needs are typically the basic physical ones. The second way is to actually design and manufacture new needs and induce their adoption. Both are effective means of control, but the second method is the holy grail. So, we have a two-prong strategy. Determine the most crucial natural/organic needs of the people such as security and shelter and provide them. And second, fabricate new needs that the people adopt and fulfill them. The second approach is especially effective when dealing with external markets." he concluded.

Ban could see his friend mulling over these ideas in his head and after a brief pause, Liang asked, "Genjo, I have but two more questions. First, what kind of fabricated needs are you imagining and second, how can China actually manage all this?”

“Wu-pen, these are excellent questions and their answers are crucial to the success of this entire strategy. First, using Maslow’s theory, human needs can be ascertained and directed. For example, viruses can be manufactured and spread easily and the vaccines produced in advance by the developer since it is they who invented the disease in the first place. This idea is already being adopted by companies who develop computer security applications to deal with hacking and viruses.”

“Another example of creating a basic physical need is distributing narcotic substances and then providing the ongoing supply to the addicted,” Ban explained. “In fact, China is already a dominant supplier in this industry. Our fentanyl exports have been particularly effective. As you move up Maslow’s hierarchy, you can develop social and technological platforms that become essential to a population’s psychological wellbeing which never diminishes. More to the point, there is almost no limit to the number and variety of human desires, my friend, and China needs only to exploit these human frailties to establish global dominance and control.”

“Fascinating,” his colleague said as he once again lapsed into thought.

“And last, is the significant issue of how China can manage all of this itself which I would imagine is a substantial obstacle,” Liang reminded.

“The simple answer is that it can’t!” Ban proclaimed.

Liang looked quizzically at Genjo, but responded, “I know you better than that Genjo. You would never waste an hour explaining an idea only to come to a meaningless conclusion.”

"I appreciate your confidence in me Wu-pen and you are most certainly correct. It is clear that China cannot control, manage, or develop the diverse needs of every country and market including its own. It needs to partner with key players who have proven themselves to be successful in these activities and there are many excellent candidates. Obviously, we will look to our friends and allies first and establish their Bona fides. For example, Russia is expert in propaganda and cyber-crime. Iran's strength is terrorism, the Mexican cartels are adept at narcotics distribution and human trafficking and we are the best in the world in low-cost product manufacturing, narcotics development, and viruses. But there are many other countries and organizations that can be solicited, even within our enemy's camps," Ban proclaimed.

"And those might be?" Liang asked.

"Well, the US has proven itself in the development of vaccines and the EU has significant capabilities and is weak and vulnerable to manipulation. But even more enticing are the corporate entities across the world that have already developed growth needs that have gained enormous popularity among the masses. Social media companies, technology firms which provide new services like search engines and others that have monopolized merchandising all have demonstrated enormous influence over our societies which have become indispensable. All these organizations are potential partners. We only must convince a handful of influential players to join us and I can assure you that the rewards will be far too great for them to resist," Ban concluded with a flourish.

"This sounds like some kind of cabal or secret society,"

"Right again, my friend. That's exactly what it is," Ban answered fervently. "These partners must come together in a single driving global force to control people worldwide by providing the solutions to Maslow's Global Needs Matrix. I have even coined the moniker for the group. It will be called "The Faction" and it will exploit Maslow's work to maintain control of the masses across the globe. And my friend, make no mistake, the only country that can drive and lead the Faction is China under the leadership of our President, Manchu Shing."

The room fell uncharacteristically quiet as the two men, imagined the immensity of the idea and its potential consequences. Ban suddenly rose from his chair and walked over to the well-stocked bar.

He turned to Liang and exclaimed, "we need another bottle of Baijiu to toast this momentous occasion and to commit to our next move."

Liang looked hesitantly at his friend and said, "I agree with the part about opening a new bottle of Baijiu, but I'm not so sure about committing to our next move."

"Wu-pen, without our next move there is no way forward and I need your help to bring that to a reality," Ban prompted.

"OK, spill it Genjo, what is our next move?"

Ban carefully poured out two new glasses of wine and raised his glass in a toast.

"We need to take this plan to the President of the CCP, Manchu Shing and convince him to adopt this strategy immediately. China must take the lead in establishing the Faction and secure its future and its place as the preeminent nation on the planet. Liang could not keep from grinning enthusiastically, excited by his friend's fervor, as he too raised his glass.

"To the Faction and the glory of our beloved China," the two men toasted in unison knowing that they were about to begin the most important journey of their lives!

CHAPTER SIX

SEGURO

He awoke with a start, his right hand automatically reaching for the Sig nine-millimeter on the nightstand. The setting sun was peeking through the drawn shades in the dimness. He had sensed something across the room. A soft light that shouldn't be there. A mild hum that sounded strangely familiar. His mind cleared quickly and he realized that an alert was displayed on his notebook computer on the desk across the room. He lifted his head and could just make out the message that an urgent e-mail needed his attention.

Mac flipped his wrist and the Garmin watch glowed brightly. It was five pm. He had slept for seven hours since transmitting his digital briefing for the Admiral upon his return from the refinery. Mac was not surprised by the delay in response. He had sent a massive amount of data from his night's work and the boys in the building would have spent all day analyzing it. On his way to the head, he flipped on the coffee maker and pulled a couple of Cachitos from the small refrigerator and put them in the microwave.

After a quick shower he pulled on jeans and a sweatshirt and sat down in front of the laptop. As he began reading, he noted that it was sent only twenty minutes before. The message was from the admiral and was designated TOP SECRET with a code word Mac didn't recognize.

It read, "Mac, your intelligence from the refinery was very telling and due to your findings and our prior intercepts, NSA has established a new code word specific to this new case file. The code word is RUMBL and all relevant information on this case will now be designated as such and treated accordingly and with the required urgency! Our preliminary findings suggest that several US adversaries including the Venezuelans, Chinese, and potentially others are working with global corporate entities to propagate illicit substances into the US and other nations.

We already know of the Chinese efforts to supply narcotics into the US, but this new intelligence implies that there may be technologies and strategies to take this activity to a new and much more dangerous level. As you probably surmised, the reference by Mr. Seguro of Biotherapeutics about Project Camo is very alarming. It implies that a major American based corporation with massive resources is colluding in this endeavor. Even more disturbing is that their developments appear to be focused on a means to target specific individuals and groups while eluding current methods of detection and enforcement.

Our teams are still wading through the information you sent this morning and by tomorrow I should be able to provide much more detail. Most of the data pertains to the refinery's role in a worldwide distribution system. Unfortunately, so far the only reference to Biotherapeutics' role was the conversation you overheard. That said, it is enough to sound the alarm and for us to elevate this operation to the top of our priority list. That means that we must quickly verify more details about their involvement. By tomorrow, I would like your recommendation on how we can best proceed to gather that intelligence. Unless we are able to intercept and decrypt communications to provide that insight, I believe we must once again employ human intelligence gathering as our primary thrust. Evaluate what resources you need, in the event that becomes necessary. I will contact you again tomorrow under code word RUMBL at 0800 hours EST," signed, JC.

Mac sat back and reviewed everything that happened in the last week and began to formulate his plan. There was no question that he needed to check out Biotherapeutics and determine exactly what this Project Camo was, but he had a feeling that breaking into that facility would be much more challenging than the refinery. They would have even more sophisticated security and twenty-four-hour guards patrolling the complex. No, he might have to risk a frontal engagement using a fake persona to gain entry. The problem was that he didn't have an angle. *Damn,* he thought, I need something on this guy Seguro. He began punching in a quick note back to Clausen requesting immediate intel on the American executive. He needed everything they could get on the guy and fast and he would probably need some additional muscle to pull off this penetration. Mac sent his request and began laying out an idea that just might work.

Philip Seguro was up early the following morning as always. It was five am as he walked down the hall to his private gym and began his daily workout. Today he worked his upper body with heavy bench presses, dumbbell curls and lat pulldowns. He mixed pull ups with dips to work his upper arms and finished with several sets of planks for his abs. Seguro found that he got the greatest gains out of high intensity interval (HIIT) training with the added benefit that he could come away dripping with sweat in an hour. He loved the power he felt after a tough workout. He was a big man to begin with, but his ripped physique made his appearance even more ominous.

After a quick shower, he donned a casual outfit of tan khaki slacks and a snug black silk shirt that accentuated his massive chest and arms. He grabbed a protein shake from the refrigerator and strode down the hall of the large hacienda to his personal study. Seguro was furious over the reported breach of security to the operation. He had spent over a year planning this deal and risked everything to get to this final stage. He was disgusted by the incompetence of the Venezuelan military and was frustrated by the controlling nature of the Chinese. And now this! Seguro was an alpha male and he simply would not be handled! His entire career had been exemplary. He was the youngest EVP in the big company's history and he was already positioned on a fast track to take over one of its international divisions on his climb to the presidency.

But soon after receiving his last promotion two years before, he met a Chinese Academic at a convention in London. The man was a brilliant social scientist and was one of the conference's keynote speakers. The two men chatted briefly after the session and Seguro left intrigued by the man's intellect and his ideas. Managing a large international organization, he was interested in the behavioral dynamics of control and influence that were so embedded in corporate cultures. Before the conference ended the two met for drinks to continue their conversation and agreed to stay in touch. Little did Seguro know at the time that Genjo Ban was targeting him as a potential partner in China's new strategy of world domination.

Over the course of the next few months Seguro and Ban communicated regularly and met in person on several occasions. As their relationship deepened, Ban began to confide more with Seguro about his theories of mass population control and China's need to ensure its peaceful growth as a world power using his innovative strategies. Seguro understood the Chinese dilemma as its population continued to expand and evolve with modern societal influences that challenged its governance and control. Seguro saw similar issues in the US and Europe and always believed that the globalist movement would ultimately solve the problem. But Ban viscerally disagreed, pointing out that nationalism was obstructing globalism and even if it took hold, it would never achieve the necessary control of the masses.

Then one fateful weekend, at Ban's invitation, Seguro agreed to extend his stay in London after an economic development conference the two were attending.

"Phillip, I have an urgent need to speak with you in person about an extraordinary opportunity," his friend exclaimed only days before the conference.

Seguro couldn't help but be intrigued by this mysterious offer and had agreed. Over the next two days, Ban described a strategy that China believed would ultimately solve the inevitable global unrest that was spreading and provide a platform for peace worldwide. His friend was passionate and convincing, but Seguro was unmoved by Ban's platitudes.

"That's all very interesting Genjo," exclaimed Seguro after hearing the Maslow pitch, but "what's in it for me?"

"Ah, my good friend, I have saved the best for last, to be sure," Genjo winked with a smile. "Let's look at some numbers, as you American's like to say," Genjo answered, pulling up some spreadsheets on his laptop.

An hour later, Seguro was all in! The documents outlined a staggering set of financial rewards for Seguro, as a partner in this new international organization. Not only that but, using Biotherapeutics' resources and surreptitiously providing services under legitimate auspices, he would leap ahead of his corporate competitors and guarantee his rise to the top of the immense pharmaceutical company.

Now Seguro was at the one-yard line, and he would not let anything screw up his plans. This unknown operator breaching their security must be identified and dealt with now, he thought, as he dialed the seldom used private number. On the third ring, the familiar voice answered.

"Why hello Phillip, so nice to hear from you. How are things at Biotherapeutics," the man asked sincerely.

"Very well, Sir," Seguro answered. "Thank you for taking my call. I do, however, have a small issue on which I could use some help."

"What might that be, my friend?"

"Well, we have received information from the Venezuelan authorities that we may have a security breach at one of our classified operations and the assailant may be a rogue US intelligence agent. Any information you could provide on this matter would be of great assistance. As you know, my company has a number of sensitive collaborations with the current administration and we can ill afford for any unauthorized interruptions or leaks."

"I completely understand, Phillip," answered the man. "I will investigate the matter and let you know what I find. And Phillip, thank you for bringing this to my attention."

The intel on Phillip Seguro arrived only a few hours after Mac's query. As expected, Seguro was a very visible international executive. His background was well publicized. He was one of those rags to riches stories that everyone loved to read about. His father and mother had been immigrants from Venezuela and had migrated to the US in their early twenties. They had met in Boston while pursuing naturalization classes and had married as soon as they received their US citizenship. Their life had been hard. He worked on the docks and she was employed by a local construction company as a bookkeeper. But they were industrious, hardworking people and within five years both had advanced, and life became more comfortable.

Seguro was born an only child and spent his early years in the tough neighborhoods of South Boston. In those days Southie was not kind to recent immigrants and he soon learned the hard realities of urban survival. Those street-smart lessons served him well and motivated him to win at all costs. His summer job on the docks with his father had honed his body and his passion to excel landed him a full ride at Boston College. He graduated cum laude with a major in international business and followed it with an MBA in international finance from Boston University two years later. During graduate school, he interned at Biotherapeutics and upon graduation was hired into their international division. Within his first five years, he was fast tracked in their executive development program and the rest, as they say, was history.

Throughout Seguro's life, physical training had been a passion. It provided the challenge of ever-changing obstacles. With each new skill, he gained confidence and it provided a special kind of power and influence over others that he lusted after. When the black belt in Karate wasn't enough, there was Krav Maga. The gym became a daily part of his life as he faced off with increasingly more strenuous routines. Cross country running began with five K's and ended with the Boston Marathon. His martial arts training soon evolved into summers parsed into survival training, combat and tactical firearms courses and rock climbing. Seguro loved it all and knew he would always be a hard target.

Mac finished the summary and sighed; this guy was the real deal. He was smart, tough and travelled. But there was something else. There was a dark side to Phillip Seguro. Listening to him at the refinery, Mac sensed a kind of cruelty just below the surface. He had seen it before and it meant that this man was even more dangerous and unpredictable than your normal bad actor and Mac should be careful when dealing with him. One thing he had learned from Seguro's bio was that trying to fake this guy out was not likely to work. He would see it coming. The only other option was a frontal attack and for that he might need some help.

The encoded video call at 0800 the next morning from Clausen was punctual as usual. "Thanks for the quick intel on Seguro, Admiral," Mac began the conversation.

"Hope it helped," responded the Admiral.

"Yes, it did," replied Mac. "It provided valuable insights which confirm an idea on how to move forward."

"Explain," countered the Admiral.

"Well, it's risky and even I have to admit, it's out there, but I think we're running out of time and we need to break this thing open before it gets too much momentum."

"I agree that the intel implies a degree of urgency. It seems like we are behind the eight ball already," responded Clausen seriously.

"That's my take, Sir," said Mac. "First, let me say that breaching the Biotherapeutics facility is problematic. I don't even have to case the place to know that it will have state-of-the-art security systems and twenty-four-hour regular guard rotations. On top of that, now that Seguro is aware of the security break in Maracaibo, he will have tightened up that facility's protocols even more. That basically tanks plan A, targeting Therapeutics," Mac explained. "I believe that really only leaves us with one option," he continued. "I need to approach him directly, but with a very unorthodox proposition and irrefutable cover. Somehow, I must quickly gain his trust and get more details without exposing the agency." Mac could see Clausen's brow furrow as he grappled with this shift in approach, but he knew in his gut they really had no choice.

"Unfortunately, Mac, I must agree with your assessment, but I am at a loss as to how you intend to move this forward," the Admiral opined.

Twenty minutes later, Mac finished detailing his plan with a final request. "Admiral, as you can see this is tricky and I can't pull it off alone. I need you to re-activate some of my team from the Apogee Operation."

The Admiral smiled knowingly and said, "well Mac, at least on that issue, I have some good news."

CHAPTER SEVEN

REINFORCEMENTS

The morning air was warm and humid as he sprinted the final one hundred yards of the five-mile run. He checked his time, sub sevens, not bad. The jog was a good release after the intense conversation on this morning's call with Clausen. Besides, one had to keep up appearances for the local folk.

Reluctantly stepping out of the steaming shower, he grabbed a towel from the nearby rack. But something felt wrong. The hair on his neck prickled as the adrenalin kicked in. He felt a presence. He sensed movement in the outer room and his weapon was not handy. He left the shower running to cover his exit as he crept slowly to the cracked bathroom door and peered out.

A familiar voice boomed out before he saw the speaker. "Howdy Mac, did you miss me," came the familiar drawl of his good friend, Joe Franklin.

"Damn, Joe," Mac answered laughing, relieved. "You are one SOB, but I'm sure glad to see it's you!"

Joe Franklin was Mac's mentor in the early days of his Navy career and his instructor in advanced SEAL Tactical Training (STT). After Joe retired from the Navy and Mac joined the NSA, they stayed in touch and often vacationed together. Since joining the agency, Mac recruited Joe on several special ops missions and there was no one he trusted more when the going got rough. More recently, Joe was a member of Mac's Apogee team on one of his most challenging and dangerous operations. In fact, Franklin sustained some nasty injuries on that op, but that hadn't slowed him down and he completed the mission as he always did with a grin and a growl.

As the two old friends sat drinking some freshly brewed coffee and reminisced about their last mission together, Mac looked quizzically at his companion-in-arms and asked, "the Admiral told me you were coming, but how the Hell did you get here so fast with all the restricted travel?"

"Well, ole buddy, when the Admiral said get down there pronto, I knew what that meant, so I flew out last night. Of course, it doesn't hurt when there is an NSA Learjet waiting at Lackland AFB to scoop me up as soon as I could get my sorry ass over there."

"Yeh, the old man doesn't waste any time when the shit hits the fan," Mac agreed. "He did the same trick with me when I was in the Caymans. He is always one step ahead, but I sure have no complaints. You know the Admiral always has your back."

"Amen to that," Joe agreed.

"Ok Joe, I know you have been briefed, so what do you think about this gig," Mac asked, getting to the point.

"Well Cap, I know you're forte' is strategy, but I really don't have a clue about how you play this character Seguro. He sounds certified. I mean his bio reads like a bulked up corporate sociopath in a Hickey Freeman."

Mac nodded gravely. "That about sums him up in my view as well."

"That said," Joe jumped in, "I figure you've had a whole twenty-four hours to figure all this out, so I can't wait to hear the shit storm you are about to unleash on Mr. Seguro."

Over the next two hours, the two men discussed Mac's plan. The challenge was to completely disrupt Seguro's current arrangement with the Chinese. That required a convincing ruse that was airtight. He needed to be convinced beyond any doubt that he should change course. And Mac must engineer this scenario without any connection to the agency or their real identities. A tall order for sure and a long shot, but it was their best option at this point.

When the two finally settled on all the details, Joe sighed and said, "yep, I was right about this gig. It's a SS for sure, but it sounds like fun, and I can't wait to get it on! So, let's rock and roll."

CHAPTER EIGHT

TWISTS AND TURNS

The afternoon shadows began to creep through the large picture window overlooking the lush landscape as the sun reluctantly completed its daily journey. Phillip Seguro spent the day at the hacienda working on the final details of operation Camo and was feeling confident that his commitments to the Chinese would be delivered on time and on budget. He stretched his massive arms over his head, sighed in satisfaction and rose from the desk. Time for a well-deserved cocktail and a fresh fish dish served by his hacienda staff before they left for the evening.

As Seguro finished the last bites of the delicious Mero del Sal (grouper on salt) served with mustard, pepper and champagne sauces, he gazed out of the large windows at the picturesque gardens surrounding the hacienda. Life was good and it was about to get a whole lot better. Dismissing the staff for the evening after they cleared the table, he decided to repair to his study for some celebratory cognac before he retired.

After pouring a robust snifter of Hennessy XO Cognac at the well-stocked bar in the study, he opened the large French doors that led to the gardens. He stepped out onto the Spanish tiled patio and breathed in heavily. The sweet fragrance of the garden filled his senses and the night sounds offered a soothing background to the idyllic setting. The moon was high in the sky as it shone intermittently through the spotty cloud cover flickering off the lap pool and creating shadows that danced across the exterior like spirits at a garden party. It was too nice to sit inside, he thought as he made his way over to a large stuffed chair and after taking a grateful sip of the golden liquid. Placing his drink down on the ornate wrought iron coffee table, he gazed approvingly over the groomed landscape.

Seguro pulled out his mobile and opened a security app. The system was off, of course, so that the staff could leave the residence. He would arm it once he finished his after-dinner repast and closed up the study. He leaned back in the sumptuous chair and closed his eyes, letting his mind wander. As was his nature, he soon found his thoughts focusing on the nagging open issues that threatened his personal success. One was the Chinese over-reach that seemed to be accelerating and the other was this mysterious operator intruding into his plans. He would call Ban in the morning to work on the Chinese issue and hopefully would hear back soon from his contact in Washington on the other complication.

His concentration was broken when he felt his mobile vibrate. *Damn*, he thought. There had to be some problem if he was getting a call at this time of night. Retrieving the phone, he checked his text messages and jerked upright as he read the capitalized words. "FIND COVER, YOU ARE IN GRAVE DANGER!"

"What the hell," Seguro said out loud as he jumped out of the chair and scanned the perimeter. Even as he jumped to his feet and headed for the study, the snifter on the coffee table exploded followed by a large piece of tile erupting only inches from his left foot. Damn. Someone was shooting at him!

Seguro dove through the doors into his study deftly tumbling into a back breaking forward roll that found him behind a large couch. Another round ricocheted into the floor behind him as he positioned his body securely behind the welcome cover. He must get out of this room, find help, and get a weapon. From his position, a large hanging mirror across the room provided a clear view of the French doors and the outside patio. The moon was hidden behind some clouds but was periodically shooting narrow shards of light into the obscurity. At first Seguro saw nothing, but then he glimpsed a slight rustling of the hedge bordering the gardens. It could be the breeze, he cautioned himself. No, there it was again. Suddenly, a large figure in dark camo, face mask and night vision goggles emerged from the foliage. With a holstered handgun strapped to his belt and a scoped suppressed sniper rifle outstretched, he furtively advanced on the house.

Seguro desperately looked around for a weapon and spotted the poker leaning against the large fireplace ten feet away. He was reminded of the saying, "don't bring a knife to a gun fight." He risked another quick glance. The intruder was now closing on the entrance through the French doors and he knew his time had run out. What he needed was a diversion so he could make a run for the study door. On the coffee table next to the couch were several decorator items including a solid glass globe with a Venezuelan landscape artfully displayed inside. He grabbed the softball sized artwork and prepared to launch it at the intruder while he made a dash for the study door. *It was his best shot, hell it was his only shot,* he thought as he prepared to hurl it.

What happened next seemed to move in slow motion. Seguro sprung to his feet and threw the heavy globe with all his might at his assailant who was just coming through the entrance. The figure, seeing him, began to raise his rifle, but then momentarily jerked away to avoid the object careening towards him. The glass ball collided with the intruder's weapon deflecting the barrel from its target. Seguro wasted no time turning to make his escape, hoping that he could cover the distance before the black clad figure could re-acquire his prey. Other than the glass globe clattering un-broken on the floor, the room was strangely quiet. And then there was the clear sound of a suppressed round being fired and Phillip Seguro knew he had bet wrong.

But he felt nothing! No pain, no loss of motion, no impact. How could anyone miss from that range? The answer was, they couldn't. And then, as he stared stunned at the study door, he saw the man step through, a large handgun stretched out aimed at him, center mass, his eyes strangely focused beyond him. The man pulled off two rounds in quick succession as Seguro once again dove to the ground.

"Crap," he heard the man exclaim as he leaped over Seguro's prone body in a sprint towards the patio. Seguro twisted around to see a figure, one arm hanging uselessly at his side cascading through the hedge and disappearing.

Before Seguro could recover, the man was back, his big handgun now holstered. With a frustrated grimace on his face, he turned to Seguro and said, "are you ok?"

Seguro could only mumble as he pushed to his feet, "I think so."

"That crazy stunt with the glass ball almost cost you your life and made my first round go wide. Unfortunately, I lost him, but he won't be sniping around for a while with my second round in his shoulder."

Regaining some of his composure Seguro demanded, "who the hell are you and what is this all about?"

"Is that all the thanks I get for just saving your sorry ass?" the man asked in irritation.

"I'm sure you had a good reason, which I can't wait to hear," snapped back Seguro, now completely recovered.

"Ask and ye shall receive," quipped the man in response. "Why don't we both take a seat and I'll start from the beginning. My name is

John Miller and I have been tracking your assailant since he entered Venezuela."

"Who is the guy and why is he trying to kill me?" interrupted Seguro.

"Whoa partner, one thing at a time," Miller lectured. "We don't know for sure who he is or who he works for, but we have a theory and he is definitely gumming up the works."

"What do you mean we?" asked Seguro in frustration.

"I'll get to that," answered the man, "but first let's talk about you. We know all about your work. You have been a busy bee, Mr. Seguro. We know about your partnership with the Venezuelan administration and your collaboration with the Chinese. We know about your illicit operation here in Valencia and we know about your plans for the refinery. We also believe that the man that was just visiting with you is a contract assassin for the Chinese government."

"What, that's impossible," stammered Seguro.

"Why is that?" Miller asked.

"Because they need me and my company," Seguro blurted out, before realizing he was admitting to the relationship. "We have a legitimate and legal arrangement in our trade with China," he continued trying to cover his mistake.

"Nonsense," exclaimed Miller. "We have hard evidence of your operations, the refinery connection and your strategy to camouflage narcotics and other substances, store them in your tanks and distribute them to willing markets all over the world. But don't worry Phillip, I'm not here to blackmail you."

"Well, it sure feels that way," Seguro growled angrily.

"On the contrary, my organization wants to help you. In fact, we want to be your new partner," said Miller.

"I've already got a partner," Seguro whined.

"No, you don't. You have an opportunistic organization who is committed to world domination and never shares with anyone. They will just re-engineer your formula and take over control. In fact, that play has already begun, or don't you believe what happened tonight?"

Seguro was beside himself. This couldn't be happening. But reality was setting in. He had been targeted tonight and the SOB would have succeeded if this guy didn't intervene and save his life. It was also true that the Chinese had been acting much more aggressive lately. But how could this guy know about the operation and the players? And what if this was a setup. Either side could be playing him. This could be an action by a US intelligence organization to infiltrate his operation and gain intel. It could be the Chinese trying to scare him into changing the deal or disclosing his formulas. There was even a third scenario. It could be another opportunistic organization or country that wanted a piece of the lucrative market that he would be serving.

"I know what you're thinking Phillip," Miller said finally. "You believe that this is some kind of setup to get into your pants, right?"

"That thought had occurred to me," Seguro answered seriously.

"And you can't see a way to verify my story, because if you start digging around, you will jeopardize your whole operation, right?" Seguro nodded.

"Well, that is a dilemma, but the evidence of my authenticity, while it may seem somewhat circumstantial, would be difficult to manufacture. Just ask yourself the obvious questions. How would I organize a hit on you where I could shoot the attacker? Oh, and he did really shoot at you, wouldn't you agree? And how could I know about the details of your plans and actions so accurately or identify your partners?"

"I don't know," answered Seguro glumly. "But there has to be a rational explanation and a way to prove it."

"And there is, Phillip. But there is only one man who has the resources and connections to unearth all these unknowable activities. There is only one man who could have discovered the details of Proyecto de Conversión or the supply chain plans in Cadena de Suministro Global. And certainly, only one man could even identify your illicit Project Camo." Seguro was stunned. Project Camo was his most closely guarded secret. Only a handful of his closest associates even knew the name. This knowledge had to come from an insider, but who?

"Ok, I'll bite, who is this mystery phenomenon?" asked Seguro acidly.

"His name is Peter Gunderson and he is the mastermind behind the Apogee case that NSA broke about a year ago. He has been in hiding for the last year and has been busy re-building his capabilities and re-positioning his influence, as it were," answered Miller.

Seguro was familiar with the case through his Washington contacts. In fact, the prior administration cleaned house very quietly afterwards. Those internal moves had been especially important to Seguro when assessing the risks of entering his arrangement with the Chinese. He had to admit, it all made sense. Gunderson was trying to regain control and needed to recruit him. The facts seemed irrefutable. Besides, what choice did he really have?

"Alright, let's say I believe you," commented Seguro. "This is a dangerous game you are suggesting. You are essentially asking me to be a double agent. The Chinese don't play around. How can you assure my safety when I switch sides and what is my share of the take?"

"We'll get into all that," Miller smiled. "But first let me assure you that you won't have to switch sides because we'll just carve up the territory and by the time the Chinese figure that out, they will not be able to stop it. You will have all the leverage because you have "Camo". And as far as the issue of remuneration is concerned, it will dwarf what they have offered you. In the end, you will be indispensable to both Mr. Gunderson and the Chinese and that, Mr. Seguro, is your ultimate security and guarantee. Now, what say we celebrate our new partnership with a nice libation from your well stocked bar?"

CHAPTER NINE

OVER THE POND

It was early morning when Mac returned to his room at the hotel. He figured he could grab a siesta after he briefed Joe on the operation. Joe had remained on the grounds of Seguro's hacienda to back him up in case things went south and had returned when he got the heads up from Mac. Joe picked up immediately when Mac dialed his room.

"Come on over Joe and I'll bring you up to speed."

"Copy, Cap," the big Seal responded.

The plan had worked better than they imagined. As Mac described his dialogue with Seguro, Joe was elated.

"Man, I really had concern about pulling this one off, but I am impressed. He really bought it hook line and sinker."

"Yeh, even I was reaching on this one, but we had so much detail about his personal engagement and the operation that he couldn't refute it," said Mac.

"The real kicker though is the new play. He is between a rock and a hard place. If he doesn't play ball, we can expose him. He knows he can't trust the Chinese and he needs security. The new deal gives him all of that and a much bigger pay day. It is a way out of an impossible situation and is a bonanza for him and he knows it," said Mac convincingly.

"By the way, Joe, great job on the intruder role, especially the target shooting. I can't believe you nailed the glass of Cognac," praised Mac.

"Yeh, I must admit, that was pure," Joe said glowing. "I did get a little worried when he launched that damn glass ball thingy though," he laughed.

"And the limp arm routine was perfect," Mac said grinning at his friend. "This is one briefing I am really going to enjoy giving the old man."

"Which begs the question, how are we going to play Seguro going forward," asked Joe.

"That is a discussion we need the Admiral to weigh in on. We are in, but from now on, things are going to get complicated," Mac said grimly.

"I need the Admiral's brain and experience on the next steps, and I have a feeling we are going to require some additional NSA resources as well."

◆

Phillip Seguro rose early after a fitful sleep. He needed to make sense of the prior night's events and dig into the BS Miller threw at him. He knew he was in a compromising position and must get control of the situation. He had to admit that Miller had been persuasive and his information was precise and detailed. But Seguro learned on the Boston streets and in the corporate board rooms that things were almost never as they seemed. So, while he was skeptical, he was also alerted to the tenuous nature of his arrangement with the Chinese. And somehow a deep dive was required on that side of the equation too.

While sipping the hot Venezuelan coffee, an idea began to percolate that changed his grimace to a grin. *There might just be a silver lining in all this,* he thought. If he were able to play both sides, he could change the dynamics from being a victim to a victor. But to do that he needed information.

Miller left the hacienda the prior night after downing some Tequila with curt instructions that he would be back in touch within twenty-four hours with the details on how they would proceed. That meant that Seguro had little time to figure out his next move. *Tempus fugit*, he thought as he pulled up the familiar mobile number and began texting his good friend Genjo Ban.

♦

Thousands of miles north at Fort Meade, Md's NSA HQ, Admiral James Clausen was anxious as he began the video call from Valencia early that morning. He knew he couldn't call the shots on Mac's ground operation, but he felt uneasy about a direct confrontation with Seguro and worried it could backfire. But Mac proved many times that his instincts were a reliable guide to difficult challenges and Clausen trusted those instincts implicitly.

"Well, how did it go last night," the Admiral questioned without fanfare. The two agents on the screen simultaneously made thumbs up gestures in answer before Mac began his report.

"Details please," requested the Admiral calmly.

"Well sir, I would first say that overall, our little caper went smoothly, and the outcome was better than expected."

Mac continued to describe the plan that he and Joe hatched and how the action went down at the hacienda. Clausen was intently interested in Seguro's reactions and although he was delighted with the outcome, he was troubled about how to play this game. Mac finished his report with a tone of concern.

"Sir, while we are good with our penetration, both Joe and I are worried about how to proceed. Our deception worked, but it's shaky at best. There are too many ways it can unravel, which means that we need to strike quickly to get critical intel and be ready for the blow back at all levels if we're exposed."

"My thoughts exactly Mac," responded the Admiral. "You need to cycle back with Seguro ASAP and pick his brains. You'll have to navigate your questioning delicately to avoid raising his suspicions. You can be sure he is already working to keep all his options open."

"I agree," said Mac.

"Admiral, do you have any suggestions on how we keep this guy in play," asked Joe.

"Well, Joe, as long as he stays engaged and you are gleaning more credible intelligence, it's worth the risk, but keep in mind that works both ways. Worst case, if he decides to bolt or act against you, your best leverage is to expose him and ruin his career and his freedom with jail time for treason!"

"Understood Sir," answered Joe seriously.

"We'll circle back today with Seguro and begin pulling his strings," exclaimed Mac. "I'll go in wired so Joe can back me up if there are any hiccups."

"Good idea Mac. Are there any other requests," Clausen asked finally."

"Yes Sir. We may need some more resources if Seguro calls in the cavalry or bolts the country."

"Understood," Clausen fired back. "I'll begin lining up some appropriate assets on deck. Good luck and let's keep up the daily comm as well for now."

♦

It was seven pm Beijing time when the subtle chime sounded on Genjo Ban's mobile as he prepared to wrap up his day. The Chinese CCP executive sat back quietly in the large leather chair of his office at CCP HQ as he carefully read the text message. "My dearest friend Genjo," the message began. "I just completed a constructive meeting with your people at our facility in Valencia and as you may know by now, things are back on schedule and all is good. That said, I am growing concerned about all the moving parts as we approach our launch date. Additionally, there have been recent activities in Venezuela and with the government that concern me that could pose a risk to our enterprise. For these reasons, I believe it circumspect for us to meet personally to discuss our affairs. My sense of urgency compels me to request a meeting and in good faith and sincerity, I will gladly come to you. Please confirm a place and time within the next week that we can meet. In trust, Phillip."

Ban had manipulated Phillip Seguro for almost two years now and knew the man intimately. This was the most crucial relationship the CCP needed to execute its global strategy because Project Camo was China's greatest distribution mechanism for drug dependency and bio-penetration. It was also the ultimate instrument of chaos that the Faction would yield. And Project Camo was Seguro's baby. So, Ban was relentless in his efforts to gain Seguro's trust. He knew the man's psyche. CCP intelligence had built an extensive dossier on Seguro. They had infiltrated his college, planted students in his classes and even paid his training instructors to provide intelligence. Ban knew what motivated him and he knew how unusual this request was. He could sense Seguro's subtle panic and the urgency in his words and knew he must act quickly and decisively to protect this fragile relationship.

He cursed under his breath as he re-read the text message again. The CCP had never planned to maintain a long-term arrangement with Seguro. They had already placed an agent in his operation to steal the Camo formulas but were not yet able to penetrate or engineer its inner workings. But it was just a matter of time before they would access all the Camo development files and understand its secrets. Seguro would then conveniently experience a fatal accident. Ban sighed as he responded to Seguro's plea. He really hated surprises, but such was life.

"Phillip, my friend, I am distraught over your difficulties and will of course make every effort to assist you," he wrote back. "My schedule is very tight over the next thirty days, but I will find a way to carve out time for you. As you may know, the G20 International meeting in Rome, Italy is scheduled in a week and I am tasked with preparing and supporting the CCP and our President, Manchu Shing, for that conference. Nonetheless, my time in Rome offers an opportunity for us to meet, since I will be traveling there early to prepare. I will be arriving in two days so we should plan to meet three days from now. I will be staying at the Hotel de la Ville and will send you my logistics information in a follow-up message. Please confirm via text and I will make suitable arrangements for our meeting. Warm regards, Genjo."

◆

Out of an abundance of caution Seguro agreed to let his regular service staff leave early that afternoon so Miller could visit unobserved. The two men returned to the library which now appeared miraculously unscathed by the prior evening's calamity. Mac noticed Seguro seemed tense as he began to explain their plans of engagement.

"Phillip, I believe we can conclude the basics of our arrangement in two or three sessions over the next few days," Mac said. "I will first need to understand the details of your operation and your connection and commitments with the Chinese and any other players in the supply chain. Once I have that information, I can articulate how you can shift and integrate with our organization seamlessly without affecting the Chinese. I will also be able to provide a reasonably accurate pro forma forecast of your earnings and cash flow, which will most certainly make your day. How does that sound to you?"

Seguro shifted uncomfortably in his chair and responded. "Unfortunately, that schedule won't work for me Mr. Miller."

"Phillip, please call me John," Mac urged pleasantly.

"Ok John, these sessions will have to wait until I return from a trip I have planned."

"I see," responded Mac. "That is very unfortunate. Mr. Gunderson is very anxious for us to complete these preliminary discussions so he can arrange to meet you and personally finalize our very lucrative partnership."

"Yes, I too am disappointed, but this meeting was scheduled just this morning and I cannot reschedule it," explained Seguro.

"May I ask why that is Phillip?" Mac prodded.

"The Chinese contacted me and demanded I attend a series of crucial update sessions with some high-level government officials," Seguro lied. "If I refuse, they would be very unhappy, not to mention suspicious. Besides, I figured I might learn a lot more about their plans which would certainly be helpful for both of us, wouldn't you say?" Mac was temporarily taken aback but did not react.

"Well Phillip, I suppose there could be some upside, but I do agree that refusing the invitation could invite some disruptive responses which could be a problem at this stage of our engagement. How long is the meeting and when do you leave?" Mac asked.

"That's the good news," Seguro answered. "I should only be gone four or five days and I'm driving to Caracas to catch an all-night flight to Rome this evening. In fact, I'm sorry to say that I really must cut this meeting short John, so that I can catch my flight."

"But," Seguro added almost as an afterthought, "be assured I will contact you as soon as I return. Oh, and please send my apologies to Mr. Gunderson and tell him I too look forward to consummating our partnership."

◆

"Well Mac that was a bust," complained Joe when the two met back at the hotel.

"No Kidding," Mac said. "On the flip side though, we know where he's going, who he's meeting with and when it's going down."

"You know Mac, you are forever the optimist," Joe mocked.

"Not really, Joe. I just see a faster path to the objective this way and Rome can be lovely this time of year, so let's get back to Caracas and get the Admiral to fire up that NSA bird!"

"Roger that," the big Seal said and saluted.

CHAPTER TEN

THE FACTION

The meetings were rarely in person. The members were far too well known to travel to meet. Their every movement was tracked by governments and media alike. Most of their communications were through alternates and all of it was encrypted at levels that no cyber hacker even dreamed of. Nonetheless, there were certain occasions when they were called together for international events which camouflaged their secret meetings and allowed them some leeway. The 2023 G20 meeting in Rome, Italy was one such opportunity.

The brainchild of Genjo Ban, the Faction was organized and sponsored by the Chinese, specifically the CCP, under the personal oversight of its President, Manchu Shing. Membership was by invitation only and beyond exclusive. The selection process was rigorous, secret, and conducted entirely by the CCP. No candidate turned down an opportunity to join and no member left the organization alive. Once a member always a member as the saying went in the hallowed halls of the Faction.

The mission of the organization was to achieve absolute control over large scale targeted populations throughout the world and each member had demonstrated the ability to accomplish that objective. In fact, it was a pre-requisite just to qualify for membership. And while different mechanisms were used by each member to exert that control, there was one common methodology shared by all; they each controlled something that influenced the fulfillment of critical human needs.

Humanity had an insatiable appetite for addictions. Many of them had been around for millennia like narcotics and sexual exploitation while others were spawned in modern times by cultural shifts and technology. Social media and digital introversion were the latest afflictions and took the planet by storm in only the last decade. And with the recent Covid-19 pandemic, physical wellness was being routinely threatened by new viral strains, manufactured diseases and new addictive substances like fentanyl which created whole new industries to invent and ostensibly prevent these threats to human life.

The genius of this strategy was that it created a self-fulfilling prophecy by exploiting mankind's very nature and its inherent weakness to assault itself. As a result, the opposition was minimal and the defense almost impossible. The people of the world were literally under siege and they didn't even know it. In fact, they were aiding and abetting it. And it was all being managed by a small group of self-proclaimed, enlightened oligarchs who had decided that only they could and should architect the future for all mankind. And the Faction was about to take this strangle hold on humanity to another level.

The Hotel de la Ville was a five-star historic property on Via Sistine 69 in the center of Rome. It was both intimate and cosmopolitan with lovely terraces and private suites. Its amenities were impeccable and its personal service and luxury attracted celebrities and wealthy patrons from all over the world. As an international figure and an extensive traveler, Genjo Ban delighted in the history and refinements that the hotel offered. It fit his image and stature and reflected the eminence of his country on the world stage. While the Hotel de la Ville by no means offered a clandestine location, its unique international reputation for luxury was its best security. No one thought twice about seeing the rich and famous networking together on its exclusive grounds. That, combined with its total commitment to the privacy of its guests made it a perfect rendezvous for Ban's activities.

Ban and Liang and their ten personal security advance team took up residence in the De la Ville Penthouse. The enormous suite spread across the entire seventh and eighth floors of the hotel and was accessed by its own private elevator. This separate entry was ideal for hosting private engagements away from prying eyes. With several expansive terraces, it also provided an unvarnished view of the city from which to observe any unauthorized approach. It was carefully selected well in advance and was perfect for Ban's purposes.

After conducting a thorough security sweep of all their accommodations, the two men relaxed in one of the suites to review their planned activities.

"I fear, our upcoming Faction meeting will hold some surprises, my friend," Genjo remarked as the two men sipped their afternoon Dom Perignon champagne.

"While I have learned never to doubt your insights Genjo, why do you say that?" Wu-pen asked.

"Well, we have new members to introduce, some serious status reports to review, some of which are lagging a bit and then there is the matter of our American friend, Phillip Seguro, which may be delicate at this juncture," his friend responded."

"Ah, I must say, you make a good point," Liang agreed, nodding.

"As you know," Ban continued, "tonight we will have our private reception and dinner in my suite for our Faction members and our crucial meeting will begin tomorrow, a day before Seguro arrives. I have directed the Guoanbu (MSS - The Ministry of State Security) to do a deep dive on Mr. Seguro and his current activities and should have that intelligence report soon."

"Excellent," Wu-pen responded enthusiastically.

Genjo continued, "once we have reviewed their findings, you can brief our security attachment and have them assist you in taking whatever actions are appropriate."

Wu-pen smiled and said, "we will be ready for whatever steps are necessary. The team is well prepared, and I have personally enhanced my own skills over the last year since our President honored us with this wonderful opportunity!"

◆

The big Gulfstream G650 made short work of the 5,100-mile jaunt from Caracas arriving in Rome's Ciampino Airport in an impressive nine hours. And while it was certainly overkill for the two men on the sprawling aircraft, the Admiral wanted his two agents to be on the ground before Seguro arrived. A rental car was waiting in the hanger as they coasted to a stop.

Joe grinned as he approached the decked out black BMW M5 sedan and chuckled, "the old boy sure knows how to make an impression. Mind if I drive?" he joked as he headed for the driver's side.

"With the Admiral, everything has a purpose and I can promise you, it's not to impress us," Mac responded, sliding into the passenger seat. "We're heading to the high rent district of Rome and a premium ride blends in but should not be ostentatious."

"Good point, said Joe, but I sure could get used to this jet setting lifestyle."

As they wound out onto Via Appia Nuova, Mac said, "the Admiral's analysts identified Philip Seguro's destination as the Hotel de la Ville in downtown Rome, and that his ETA as ten am tomorrow morning. The NSA techs are already working on analyzing the bookings at his hotel and looking for possible contacts and connections that might shed some light on what the hell this meeting is all about and who the players are."

"As we discussed on the plane," Mac continued, "arrangements were made for us to stay at the Hotel Scalinata Di Spagna on the Piazza della Trinità dei Monti, which is literally a stone's throw away from Seguro's luxury hotel. Hopefully, we'll have some more intel by the time we check in."

Thirty minutes later Franklin made the last turn onto Via Sistina, parked the rental, and the two agents entered the small boutique hotel. Consistent with the Admiral's penchant for careful planning, their reservations were designed around the mission. The large suite had several bedrooms and baths and a private terrace off the first floor to provide a second exit option. It was upscale, but not pretentious and afforded the kind of low-key accommodations that two American businessmen would typically choose.

Mac wasted no time firing up his laptop to see if any new messages had come in from the agency. Sure enough, there was an email that had just arrived from Clausen and he clicked on it anxiously. Once he had signed in with his credentials, he opened the encrypted message and began reading. "Mac, while you were en route, our teams examined the reservations at the Hotel de la Ville in Rome. Interestingly, the G20 Meetings are beginning in less than a week and we believe that is no coincidence as Seguro's destination. That means that someone attending that meeting is his contact. Our guys have been matching the attendee list up with those who have reservations at the Hotel de la Ville and while there are many innocuous correlations, there are a fair number that bear a more in-depth investigation. These are either US antagonistic countries, organizations or individuals who seem out of place based on modeling we have developed internally over the years."

The message continued, "we have put together a list of these outliers which is attached. You and Joe need to review it and using your judgment and intelligence on the ground, integrate those actors into your evaluation of Seguro's activities. Once we know that connection, you can evaluate the scope of what we are dealing with. My sense is that this is moving fast, so get on it as quickly as you can. Good hunting," signed JC.

"Hey Joe, get in here," Mac yelled to his friend unpacking in the other room. "We've got some intel from Washington and things may be heating up fast!"

The guests began arriving at dusk. The weather was comfortable and they gathered on the private terrace of the elegant apartment as the sun retreated from the "Eternal City", casting a warm glow amidst the subtle terrace lighting and the candle lit tables. Genjo Ban greeted each new arrival warmly, directing them to the private bar and Italian delicacies placed strategically around the large patio. Wu-pen Liang moved silently from guest to guest chatting amiably and re-assuring each of the high-profile attendees of the tight security and privacy of the venue as he subtly gestured to several of his security guards moving silently on the periphery.

There were ten members of the faction. Eight of them were attending the festivities tonight. The last two members were new inductees one of whom would be introduced at tomorrow's meeting. The final member would not be identified as his profile was far too sensitive.

After an hour or so of socializing, Genjo invited everyone to repair to the lavish interior for dinner. Once all were seated, he tapped lightly on his champagne glass to get everyone's attention and began.

"Welcome to all of you and thank you for being here. As is our practice, we celebrate together tonight the crucial work we are doing to secure the future of our societies. We have made enormous progress since our humble beginnings just over two years ago and on behalf of Manchu Shing, President of the Chinese Communist Party (CCP), I commend you. We are reaching a critical phase in our work. Until now we have been operationalizing our organization and optimizing its capabilities. But following our two and a half days of meetings here in Rome, we will begin to aggressively launch our initiatives worldwide. Tomorrow, I will outline our plans and introduce you to one of our last two members who brings unique and crucial capabilities and resources to our collaboration. We will then have the final elements in place that will accelerate our progress and assure our global dominance. But for now, let us enjoy the fruits of our labor and the wonderful anticipation of a glorious future for the Faction!"

Genjo raised his champagne in a toast as he exclaimed, "to the Faction."

All attending followed his gesture while chorusing his words, "to the Faction."

They had been pouring over the agency's lists for almost two hours looking for correlations and narrowing down the possibilities. As one would expect, a significant number of hotel guests were also attending the G20 sessions beginning the following week. The agency had provided significant background information on everyone on the list and was also doing their own analysis. They had agreed that in two hours they would connect with the Admiral, compare their work, and attempt to pare the list down to a manageable number of the highest probability candidates.

"Whew," Joe complained, "I really hate administrative shit like this."

"Can't be helped," Mac responded. "The more we can discover here, the better chance of mission success. You know that."

"Yeh, I know, just sayin'," the big Seal grumbled, as he tossed a final sheet of paper onto a growing stack.

"Ok, that about wraps it up for us," Mac said.

"How many do we have?" asked Joe.

"About thirty names," Mac answered.

"Well, that's actually pretty good considering the size of the original list, but it's still a lot to cover on the ground," Joe concluded.

"Too many," Mac agreed. "Hopefully, we can narrow it down when we speak with the Admiral. Speaking of which, his video call is coming in now."

An hour later, after excusing several senior techs assigned to run the agency's analysis, Clausen said, "Well it's a pretty big list at thirty-eight folks, but I feel it's a good one. I don't think without HUMINT engagement we could have carved anyone else off it. We'll keep digging here and have our ears focused on intercepting anything coming from your sector with special attention to the hotel and the upcoming G20 meeting. But now it's up to you boys. You've got to get into that hotel and dig around. I'll also reach out to my counterparts and see what they can do to help, but I want to compartmentalize your mission as much as possible. I'm a little concerned about the Executive Office of the new Administration nosing around this operation just yet," Clausen concluded.

"Why is that?" Mac asked. "Just a gut feeling Mac, and I have learned to pay attention to them after all these years."

"Understood," Mac replied sincerely. He had seen the old man pull a rabbit out of the hat more often than not when everyone else was clueless.

"Joe and I will start nosing around tonight and see what we can shake loose. We'll use our standard covers and identification as American business executives from a small Texas oil company looking for international investors. We must be cautious, though, because Seguro is due to check in tomorrow morning," Mac warned.

"That said, I may need to purposely connect with him at some point if we can't get anywhere with the list. I can play the "we know where you live" card as a member of the all-powerful Gunderson organization."

"Report back every twenty-four hours going forward," instructed the Admiral. Let's not let this thing get ahead of us. Anything else you need before we sign off?" asked Clausen finally.

"Well Sir, this op looks like it's growing and we have a lot to cover," interjected Joe. "Also, that's a pretty big list. We may need some more muscle and accessories if you know what I mean?"

So noted," chuckled Clausen. "I'll see what I can rustle up, Joe. Be safe," he commented as he cut the video feed.

CHAPTER ELEVEN

THE LIST

The evening was pleasantly cool with a slight breeze as the two men made the short walk to the Hotel de la Ville. They easily blended in with the festival-like atmosphere on the Piazza della Trinità dei Monti. Small groups walked leisurely chatting and window shopping while others climbed the Spanish Steps to get a better view of the magnificent city. It was past nine pm when Mac and Joe made their way to their reserved table on the rooftop Cielo Terrace in the hotel. Both men had dressed business casual in slacks, open shirts and linen sports coats to blend in with the elegant dinner crowd at the luxury hotel. Mac, of course, sported his signature ostrich cowboy boots, which always seemed to spur casual conversation with bystanders which was exactly the point.

The restaurant was busy with guests who lingered in groups enjoying the superb Italian fare and the wonderful wines. After finishing a light dinner of focaccia with ricotta cheese and tomatoes, they chatted quietly while slowly sipping a Pinot Grigio 2019 Braide Grande as they carefully surveilled the crowd. The list included several Americans, some Asians and a host of Europeans. While most were male, there were several females. Before leaving their hotel, they carefully reviewed the profiles and photos of each candidate and divided them up between them.

Franklin finally set his wine glass down and asked Mac, "what do you think? Do you see any prospects?"

"Actually, I do," Mac answered. "There are two men over at the terrace rail that appear to match the photos on the list and one woman dining in the corner of the terrace that looks familiar. Give me a second to review the file photos on my phone."

Franklin sat patiently as his friend perused the images and then Mac said, "bingo, these three are matches. How about you, Joe?" Mac asked.

"Nada, but people keep arriving, and the evening is still young by European standards. So, how do you want to play it," he asked.

Mac glanced again at the photos and then looked up and said with a smile, "let's split up and since you got to drive the Audi, I'll take the lady and you cover the two guys."

Joe laughed under his breath and remarked, "Ok, you got me there partner." With that the big man got up and walked casually over to take in the view at the railing a few feet from his targets.

Mac purposely waited for several minutes sipping his wine and scanning the crowd. His target was an Asian woman who appeared to be in her late thirties. She was average height and slim in stature with shoulder length straight black hair that was styled in a wave across her forehead. She had delicate features, deep blue eyes and impeccable, subtle makeup except for her lipstick that was a bright red. She was dressed to the nines in a long flowing grey silk dress snugged at the waist with a black leather belt and finished off with calf length black leather high heeled boots. In a word, she was stunning! The affect was sophisticated and sexy and it was meant to be that way.

He made a point to direct his gaze at the woman and finally she looked up and her eyes met his. Mac smiled casually and she smiled back. The connection was made and now he had to close the deal. He rose and walked over towards the woman's table. She watched him as he approached, a curious look on her face.

"Excuse me," he said softly, smiling. "I don't want to be intrusive or forward, but my business partner has decided that viewing the Eternal City is more pleasant than chatting with an attractive woman and I intend to prove him very wrong. Besides, I believe we have something in common."

The woman's countenance changed ever so slightly as her lips turned up in a slight smile and said in perfect English, "I appreciate the compliment, but I can hardly compete with the Eternal City under the stars."

"You are too modest," Mac responded sincerely. But would you humor me and allow me to buy you a drink?"

"Only if you if you explain your presumption that we have something in common," she exclaimed with a twinkle in her eye.

"That's a deal," Mac said as he took a seat across from her. "We both appreciate fine footwear. In particular, premium boots and are not afraid to show them off. I'm John Miller, by the way and you are?"

"My name is Jing Liu," she answered as she shifted her eyes under the table to take in Mac's ostrich gear. "She chuckled coyly as she purred, well John Miller, score one for you."

Joe returned to his table about thirty minutes later and looked over to see Mac in animated conversation with his female target and thought, *Boy, that guy really has a way with women. Next thing I know, he'll be making a date and I'll be on this op solo.* Another fifteen minutes went buy and finally Mac and his lady friend stood and walked together to the terrace railing to take in the view as their conversation continued. Finally, they warmly shook hands as she turned and made her way from the terrace and Mac returned to join Joe.

"Ok Cap, since it's obvious you got the best part of that deal, I'll go first on the de-brief, Joe said with a smirk."

Mac laughed and said, "next time don't be so anxious to take the wheel. But seriously," he continued, "let's get back to the hotel for our read-outs. Too many ears here for that kind of discussion."

"Right," agreed Joe as they rose and moved to the exit.

It was almost midnight when they arrived back at the suite. It had been a long day, but productive and Mac was anxious to hear Franklin's findings as he unlocked the door and entered the room. He flipped on the foyer lights and froze in place, his partner stumbling into him from behind. Across the living room, seated in a large Italian wingback chair, in the dim light, Mac could see a figure.

"Howdy cowboy, long time no see," rang out the familiar voice of Jasmine Snow!

"Well, I'll be damned chimed in Joe," as he raced around Mac to hoist Jasmine into the air like a rag doll.

"Easy there big guy," she laughed, "I don't want to be on the injured reserve list before I start this op."

"Shit, sorry Jas, it's just great to see you," Joe apologized as he lowered the MI-6 agent gently to the ground.

Mac grinned widely as he greeted Jasmine with a warm hug and said, "Jasmine, I was hoping the Admiral would bring you into this gig and I'm really glad you're here."

"Indeed Mac, so am I."

The three friends and ex-Apogee team members reminisced for a few minutes and then got down to business.

Jasmine said, "guys, it seems like forever since we closed the Apogee case."

"Well, it has been over a year," Joe responded.

"A lot can happen in a year in our business and from what we may be facing, that is the case now," Mac offered. "Jasmine, did the Admiral brief you? How much do you know?"

"I'm up to speed on everything at code word level. I was briefed just before I left London earlier today."

"Great," Mac said, then we can get right down to business and share what Joe and I found out tonight. Joe, you first."

"The two guys I met were both Americans as our intel described. And while they didn't offer who they work for or what they do specifically, we know they are high profile executives with two major US companies. In fact, they are the highest profile guys in their respective industries. According to our intel, one is Frederick Stone, CEO, Tribal Song, which is the largest social media company in the US. The other is Joel Roland, CEO, FindIt, which is also the largest digital search engine company in the US. They are friends and often travel together to conferences, since they're both in high tech."

"Did they say why they were here?" asked Jasmine.

"They mentioned they are here to pitch to the Chinese and other international G20 countries during the conference. They have both been to Rome many times and enjoy staying at the Hotel de la Ville. As entrepreneurs, they were interested in my cover story about being involved in an oil start up and were particularly interested in my views on the energy and petroleum industry, with all that's going on."

"Did you see any connection to Seguro or his company or get any idea about other meetings that might tie them to him?" Mac interjected.

"No, I can't say I did. They are in a very different industry and it was hard to see a way to shift the conversation in that direction," Joe answered apologetically.

"No worries, Joe," Mac said. "I understand, my conversation was similar. Anything else?"

"No, that's about it. Oh, wait a minute; there is one other thing I noticed. Every time either of them turned away from the railing and looked back at the terrace, they seemed to be focusing on you and your target. It was subtle and maybe it's my imagination, but I just feel like they were paying special attention to the two of you."

"Now that is interesting," Mac explained excitedly. "It could very well mean that they are in some way connected."

"Or it might be that they are not what we think and have made you as a government agent," Joe said seriously.

"Or it could mean that they just like gawking at good looking babes," interrupted Jasmine.

"Fair point, Jasmine," Mac said with a grin. "But how would you know that my target was a good-looking babe?" asked Mac curiously.

"Because I was there, you boob. I saw the whole thing."

"What?" said Joe incredulously.

"But seriously," Jasmine continued, "I agree with Joe. His boys definitely were keeping an eye on the two of you. Also, I know that Mac Sisco has good taste in women," Jasmine offered, winking at Joe.

"I'd say that sounds like an old Brit saying, "damning with faint praise," Joe joked as he winked back at Jasmine.

"OK, touché you too. Are you having fun now?" Mac joked.

"My target, as the agency techs reported," Mac began, "is a Chinese national and is also a high-profile business executive. Her name is Jing Liu. She is the CEO of Qiáng de Corp, a huge e-commerce company in China.

"So that's a third technology company," said Joe. "That could mean there is some kind of technology meeting going on the side, I guess."

"The other common denominator here is that all of them are CEOs and can make big decisions for their corporations," said Mac. "Jing is also here primarily for the G20 conference and the engagement with investors and future operational and market expansion. Like you, Joe, I didn't perceive any relationship with Seguro or his business."

"Well, that's it then, another swing and a miss," Joe muttered in frustration.

"Not necessarily," said Mac optimistically. "We did determine that there might be a real connection between these actors. Also, there is a Chinese connection here and I arranged to have another opportunity to meet with Jing while she is here."

"Oh really," Joe commented in surprise, his eyes opening wide.

"That figures, why am I not surprised?" Jasmine quipped sarcastically, as Mac innocently raised his hands in defeat.

CHAPTER TWELVE

THE PITCH

The Faction meeting began promptly at nine am for breakfast with the meeting officially kicking off at ten and the original eight members were all present and accounted for. There was a superb buffet and everyone was busy filling their plates with the assorted delicacies. The spread was magnificent with a multitude of fruits, figues and ricotta sandwiches, eggs prepared to order including scrambled, omelets carbonara, poached and A' la coque and all topped off with coffee granita with whipped cream. Genjo Ban once again graciously greeted each guest as they arrived and directed them to the buffet tables situated in the corners of the large dining room.

His last two special guests would arrive after lunch. They were already briefed on this morning's agenda and one of them would be center stage this afternoon. As Ban watched the members interacting, he reflected back two years when he and Wu-pen finally arranged a meeting with Manchu Shing, President of the CCP to pitch his grand plan. Even though both men knew Shing personally, it was a real challenge getting through the gate keepers and the bureaucratic bull shit that always surrounded any engagement with the President. But the day finally came and he remembered it as if it happened yesterday.

He and Liang were ushered into Shing's palatial office in the Zhongnanhai compound in Beijing. Shing had graciously allowed Ban one hour for his presentation. Ban smiled as he thought back to the discussion. Once the traditional greetings were concluded, Shing was all business as he commanded Genjo to proceed. Ban decided to introduce his presentation with several questions to the leader that were on the edge of risky, but he knew he needed to get Shing's attention immediately.

"Sir," he began, "are you concerned about the growing dissatisfaction of our rural population about the stress and the difficulties they experience in their daily lives?"

Shing's face darkened in a frown as he growled in answer, "our people know that life is hard and that we are progressing on improving their lives every day."

"Of course," Genjo responded pleasantly, and continued. "But wouldn't you desire to accelerate that progress and avoid any growing dissent that might disrupt our governance?"

"Of course, but as you well know, with almost one and a half billion people that progress is decidedly challenging," Shing grumbled.

Again, Genjo respectfully concurred, and said, "without question President Shing, that is so true. Unfortunately, our people do not always understand the complexities of governing and the challenges of advancement."

At this, Shing somewhat placated, seem to relax. He leaned back in his large leather chair, smiled and asked, "so, Genjo, I assume this is when you ride in on your white horse and save the day or am I reading too much into your introduction?"

Genjo smiled back broadly in response to the president's jibe and answered, "Touché Sir, but yes, that is exactly what I hope to do."

The first hour came and went as Shing canceled his other appointments for the day. Ban began with his presentation of the China dilemma and postulated that the CCP could not sustain a satisfied citizenry the size of China's without some fundamental changes in governance. He went on to point out that control through totalitarianism and fear would eventually be overcome by revolution, as it had many times in both Human and Chinese history.

Shing was skeptical about this prognostication but did not refute the reality that history provided nor the trending discontent of his own proletariat. Next, Ban introduced the idea that a new and different control mechanism had to be adopted that exploited natural human needs and desires. Shing became intrigued by this concept and after Genjo carefully laid out Maslow's work to the President, Shing became visibly more enthusiastic. Genjo's final thrust was to demonstrate how to organize the initiative with an international cabal under CCP control which would provide China with the solution to its own internal needs as well as the capacity to achieve worldwide dominance without a shot being fired.

The meeting had gone long into the night with the President inviting several of his top advisors to an impromptu dinner where he regaled his lieutenants about a new global strategy that he would soon be finalizing. While Genjo and Wu-pen were introduced as members of the new team, President Shing positioned himself as the driving force of this glorious new direction for the party. *But that was the perfect outcome*, thought Genjo. The President of China wanted to own the strategy. Nothing could be a better endorsement than that. Yes, that night had been the greatest moment of Genjo Ban's life and he was about to see that dream come true.

He came out of his reverie as Wu-pen approached to say that it was time to start the meeting and Genjo strode confidently to the head of the long table where his colleagues were finishing their breakfast.

"Gentlemen and Ladies, thank you again for being here and welcome to our annual Faction meeting. While our previous quarterly sessions were dedicated to building our collaboration and testing our capabilities in a rather limited fashion, this meeting marks the beginning of a very different phase of our work. When we leave here tomorrow and return to our respective operations, we will begin full scale deployment of all our programs."

"But before we get into the details, I want to briefly remind you of what is at stake and our overall vision. Our world is now on the precipice of sliding into chaos. We have seen it in our streets, in our communities, in our governance and in our lives. We have witnessed the unrest, division, violence and breakdown of our societies. In human history, this has happened before, but it was always localized and seldom consistent across geographies. But now, it is a worldwide deterioration with common results and it is accelerating. Everyone in this room, as a Faction member, has sworn to eradicate this threat at all costs and is committed to the establishment of a global community with one worldwide governance and that is why we are here. Each of you is responsible for driving control levers into our societies and creating the irrevocable human needs that allow us to govern globally and ensure a future for all mankind. Ban scanned the attendees. It was indeed an impressive group of global movers and shakers. He applauded himself on his masterful recruiting as he nodded in welcome to each one.

Over the next two hours Ban reviewed the guts of the Faction's strategic model and the details of the financial arrangements that had captured the attention of some of the world's wealthiest and most influential and convinced them to join. Essentially, the model consisted of several critical elements. There was The Faction, consisting of ten members. Each member represented a "Lever of Control" which was designed to influence the behaviors of target populations. The performance of these levers and the member's income were measured by a series of metrics. These included "uptake", the number of people affected by the control lever and "interval", the number of months the control was maintained. The "Payout" was equally fundamental. It was calculated based on the coefficient of these two metrics and the results could be very impressive.

"And so, as you can see from the example," Ban gestured at the financial spreadsheet displayed on the large screen, "the CCP will award you up to ten US dollars per uptake based on your overall volume. At that rate, five million conversions would yield fifty million US dollars per month or six hundred million dollars per year in annual income. And that my friends, as they say, is real money," Ban finished with a flourish.

As they broke for lunch, Ban smiled at the excited comments that erupted following his remarks. Until now the actual payout factors were not shared in detail. *But now the members, seeing the enormous upside, were truly galvanized*, he thought.

"Enjoy your lunch, I must excuse myself, but I will join you again for our afternoon session at two pm," he announced as he and Liang departed the suite.

CHAPTER THIRTEEN

THE LION'S DEN

Seguro arranged an early check in at noon at the Hotel de la Ville and was unpacking his luggage when he heard a soft tap at his door. No one knew he was here and he was not expecting anyone, so he cautiously approached the door and looked through the peephole. He relaxed at the sight of a hotel clerk holding an envelope in his hand.

Nonetheless, he cracked the door and said, "yes?"

"Sir, my apologies for disturbing you, but you have an urgent message," the clerk responded politely, handing Seguro the envelope through the opening. Seguro retrieved the note and began reading.

"My dear friend, I hope you had a pleasant flight. I apologize for the tardiness of my arrangements, but my calendar is very fluid and I was only recently able to break away from my official duties. If you are not too exhausted from your travels, I would invite you for lunch today at twelve thirty pm on the hotel terrace. I look forward to seeing you and catching up. Warmest regards, Genjo."

◆

Mac and his team rose early in anticipation of Seguro's arrival and spent an hour going over their surveillance plans. Since Seguro was never exposed to Joe and Jasmine, they would work the Hotel de la Ville beginning with observing Seguro's movements. Mac would remain at the apartment working the list and any new intelligence from the agency. If anything critical went down, they would call him in.

The two agents entered the lobby separately at ten am prior to Seguro's arrival. They agreed that Joe would pick up Seguro when he checked in and hand off his surveillance to Jasmine once he knew which room the target would be in. After Seguro checked into his room, Jasmine would stay on him and report back to both Joe and Mac. The objective now was to see who the man hooked up with and begin to map out the players. Mac predicted that Seguro would make contact with the Chinese quickly, so it was critical that they set up a tight net.

Joe lounged casually in the lobby sipping a coffee and perusing a travel brochure as he occasionally glanced up at the increasingly busy entrance of the hotel. Jasmine stationed herself in the terrace restaurant awaiting Joe's call. She carefully reviewed Seguro's profile information and photo and anxiously waited for his text. By eleven am, the early lunch crowd began to filter into the lobby and the din of locals and tourists filled the room. At eleven fifteen a large group of young professionals celebrating some unknown event streamed into the lobby followed by several other separate guests. Joe strained to see each face as he glanced down at Seguro's photo on his mobile. And then he spotted him near the back of the pack making his way purposely to the front desk.

Franklin sent a text to Mac and Snow, "target acquired."

The busy lobby was a lucky break as Franklin followed Seguro, who was joined by several people, into one of the waiting elevators. Seguro pressed the sixth-floor button as the door closed on the group and the elevator began its ascent. Luck was still on his side as Seguro and several other guests got off on the sixth floor and began down the elegant hallway. Joe hung back checking the room directions and watched as Seguro opened the door to a room halfway down the hall.

As the man disappeared inside, Joe again texted his colleagues, "S is now in Rm 613, awaiting handoff."

Seguro, checked his watch after the porter delivered his luggage. Twelve fifteen. He quickly changed clothes to casual black slacks, a bright yellow golf shirt and suede loafers and strode towards the door. *It would not do to be late for this appointment*, he thought, as he headed to the elevator. He tapped his foot impatiently on the tile floor as he watched the elevator numbers climb through the first five floors.

He was soon joined by another guest as he waited. Sensing someone approaching, he casually turned his gaze away from the elevator to see this new arrival and was immediately struck by the stunningly, attractive woman who had joined him. She was slim and athletic looking with thick jet-black hair and a smooth tanned complexion, indicating an outdoor lifestyle. Her features were striking. Her deep green eyes, slightly wide apart, delicate nose and full lips adorned with bright red lipstick created a stunning image that would turn heads unapologetically. And that was just the beginning. She wore tight white capris, a bright red tight fitting sleeveless silk blouse adorned with a matching silk scarf wound artfully around her delicate neck and red leather Italian pumps.

Seguro, realizing he was almost gawking stammered, "pardon me, you startled me when you snuck up on me," he joked pleasantly and smiled.

The woman returned his smile with her own and softly purred, "that's the idea" and chuckled.

"I'm Jasmine," she continued, "and you are?"

"Phillip," responded Seguro as he felt his pulse quicken.

"Well Phillip, it looks like our ride is here." It's nice meeting you."

"Likewise," Seguro responded as they joined other guests on the elevator.

Seguro exited the car at the Terrace restaurant level along with many of the riders including his alluring acquaintance from the sixth floor and searched the room for his friend Genjo. He finally saw him at a small table near the railing overlooking the city and made his way to join him. Seated across the room, Snow took all this in. She already texted Joe and Mac with an update on her location and told them to sit tight. There was no need to expose Franklin unless it was necessary. She would continue her observations and enjoy a nice luncheon on the company.

Ban looked up as his friend approached and exclaimed, "ah Phillip, so good to see you. Thank you for joining us with such late notice. Please sit down and let me introduce my colleague Wu-pen Liang. Wu-pen is our Chief of Security and Enforcement and is part of our advance team for President Shing's visit to the G20 meetings. I asked him to join us as he is also an integral part of our mutual engagement and may be able to help with whatever issues you may have."

Seguro nodded and extended his hand and said, "Mr. Liang, it is my pleasure to meet you."

Wu-pen bowed slightly and shook hands and said, "Please call me Wu-pen and it is good to meet you as well. Genjo speaks very highly of you."

"So, Phillip, what is so urgent that you felt it necessary to fly across the Atlantic to chat with me," Ban asked seriously.

Seguro cleared his throat and began. "Two nights ago, my ranch in Valencia was attacked and an attempt was made on my life. The assault was carried out by a single assailant who used a high-powered rifle to attempt my assassination."

"Oh, my friend, that is horrible," Ban gasped. "Did you capture the attacker?"

"No, unfortunately he escaped and I have no idea of his identity or why the attack was carried out. But I am certain that it is related to our work and am here to ask for your assistance in sorting this out."

Ban turned to Liang and asked, "have you any intelligence that might shed some light on this incident, Wu-pen?"

"Not that I'm aware of, but I will make some calls after our discussions and see what I can dig up."

"Can you tell us anything more about the incident that might provide some insight into the motive for the attack?" continued Wu-pen, turning to Seguro.

Phillip feigned a thoughtful expression and finally responded with, "it all happened very fast and I was able to access my weapon and defend myself, driving him off. But, given that our launch is so close to fruition, I must assume that someone is trying to impede our success. They may even be trying to steal our technology and use it for their own profit. Also, according to General Valezquez, who is heading the Venezuelan military support of our efforts, there was an attack on one of his Maracaibo operations by a lone assailant a few days before my incident, but I have no additional details on that situation."

"You were right to bring this to our attention, Phillip, and we appreciate it," said Genjo. "We can ill afford to have any disruptions in our launch at this juncture. We will make this matter the highest priority. Wu-pen, please engage your team to put together a plan to investigate and eradicate this threat immediately. I would like your recommendations in twenty-four hours. Call in any special resources you need from the CCP and keep me informed. Oh, and let's all keep this problem confidential. We don't need to create any anxiety among our colleagues in the Faction or concern our President or his staff unnecessarily. Are we all agreed on this course of action?"

"Yes, absolutely," agreed Liang. "I'll get right on it."

"Makes sense to me," answered Seguro. "Will that plan include additional security for me and our operation in Venezuela," he added.

"Yes, if it is deemed necessary," Ban responded. "But in the meantime, unless you need to return right away to manage the deployment, I suggest you remain here for a few more days, so that we can ensure your safety."

"And be a target to draw the assassin out as well, I imagine," Seguro commented drily.

"Yes, I'm afraid my friend, that too is an objective, if we are to solve this problem quickly," Genjo answered.

Across the terrace, Snow was gazing thoughtfully out over the city while gingerly sipping her champagne. She snapped photos of each of the targets and texted them to Mac and Joe and was certain that the Admiral had a crack team working the images even before she finished her dessert. Just then her mobile buzzed with an incoming text.

She opened the message from Mac and read, "Jas, remain on the terrace until Seguro and his associates leave the restaurant. Alert Joe when they are getting ready to leave so that he can pick them up and see where they go. Once we know where they are staying, we can begin to ID all their colleagues and hopefully get insight on their activities and objectives."

"Copy," came back Joe's response, followed by her own.

Ban and Liang returned to their suite at one fifteen. A meeting with their two new Faction members was scheduled for one thirty to brief them prior to the start of their afternoon session. The two men sat huddled together now in serious conversation.

"What do you make of Seguro and his story?" Ban asked his friend.

"It is a very troublesome occurrence, if it is true," Liang responded.

"So, you doubt his story?" Ban asked, raising his eyebrows.

"I'm not certain, but his comment about someone wanting to get into our shorts makes me skeptical," Liang replied. "Why would he surmise such a thing, unless he is positioning himself to negotiate some additional request?"

"Do you think he is attempting to create leverage over us to gain control?" Ban asked.

"It had occurred to me."

"And what do you propose we do now?" Ban questioned.

"Since we still need him, we must be careful. For now, I would recommend proceeding as we discussed at lunch, but with a caveat."

"And that is?" Genjo queried again.

"Seguro is a loose cannon and unpredictable. As soon as we can gain the requisite knowledge of his Project Camo, we eliminate him," Liang declared firmly.

♦

Mac was busy sending his latest intel into Clausen when Jasmine entered the room.

"Good job Jas," he praised. "Your pics were great. I'm still waiting to see what the boys at the agency come up with, but I imagine we'll get something soon."

"Thanks Mac, I hope so," Jasmine said. "I'm dying to know who these jokers are. They sure were intense during that lunch, so I imagine something serious is going on here."

"You can put money on that one," came Joe's exclamation as he entered the room.

"Why are you so sure Joe?" asked Mac.

"Because those two Chinese guys booked the Hotel de la Ville Penthouse which covers both the seventh and eighth floors of the hotel. I checked with the front desk, it's booked throughout the G20, and they have room for at least ten guests. And here's the kicker, it has a separate elevator entrance for added privacy and security."

"Well, well, that's interesting," Mac said. "Sounds like you made a smart bet. Good work, Joe. Speak of the devil," Mac continued, "here comes something from the Admiral."

They all crowded around the laptop and Mac began to read the note out loud.

"Mac, the two men that Jasmine observed are major players in the CCP. Genjo Ban is an internationally known social scientist, specializing in population social dynamics and engineering. But his government role is in the International Liaison Department of the Central Committee of the Chinese Communist Party. He plays an instrumental role in the CCP's global initiatives and reports directly to Manchu Shing, President of the People's Republic of China and the General Secretary of the Chinese Communist Party. Ban's presence at the G20 is unusual. He has no official role in the event this year and typically does not participate in these meetings, nor is he scheduled in any of the sessions. That means that his presence there is camouflage for some other activity."

"Wu-pen Liang is also an executive in the CCP. He is an elected member of the CCDI, the Central Commission for Discipline Inspection. The CCDI is the primary internal control organization of the CCP. Liang is essentially a Security Chief who appears to be on special assignment with Ban and works directly for China's President.

Liang is an extremely dangerous character. He is a known assassin, is highly trained and has been responsible for numerous brutal actions against both domestic and international personages."

"These two men have access to unlimited resources in both capital and personnel and are likely accompanied by a significant security team of a dozen or so agents. It is my team's assessment that they wouldn't be deployed in Rome unless there was some major action going on. Furthermore, after considerable queries on our big boxes, we have determined that these two have travelled together every quarter over the last two years to different international locations for durations of three to five days. Ostensibly, these trips were for conferences, but we believe that their activities included connecting with other players for some purpose. Keep feeding us intel and we'll do more dumps and Mac, be careful. You are now in the lion's den," signed Clausen. Mac held his hand up to quell the expected discussion as he rapidly typed in a response.

"Great intel Admiral. I have one more request and this may challenge even NSA's computing power. Can you correlate any other people from our list who have also been in Ban's and Liang's prior locations at the same time? You can begin the search with the three players we met last night at the hotel and then expand the search to the rest of the most probable folks on the list. If we find a match, we may have the identities of those involved with this operation. Please also provide the hotels and room numbers where these individuals are located, Mac." Finally, he raised his head, looked at his friends and said, "now we wait!"

CHAPTER FOURTEEN

THE SPIDER AND THE FLY

Seguro returned to his room in a cold sweat. His first worry was why Ban had invited his security goon to the luncheon. He never did that before and Seguro didn't like the guy. He could sense a palpable violence in the man and all his instincts told him that this guy was a menace. Phillip was certainly not new to violence, or its consequences and he personally used it when required to achieve his objectives. But this character was different. He reeked of sociopathic tendencies and Phillip imagined his glee at dismembering his victims.

But that was not all. Seguro carefully planned his soliloquy with Genjo and felt it had gone well, but now he worried about how to move forward. Until he had more information on the Gunderson play and its legitimacy, he didn't know how far to push the Chinese. He needed definitive confirmation that the Gunderson option was real. On the other hand, what Miller said in Valencia was also true. No matter who Miller represented, if Phillip didn't play ball, he would be exposed and his life would be over, so what real choice did he have. There was also one piece of information that nagged him since the assault and that was whether there was a connection between the mystery agent who was reported in Maracaibo and the attack at his ranch. He needed to hear back from his contact in Washington on that man's identity and he needed it now.

◆

"Boy howdy," Mac blurted out as he read the latest e-mail from the Director. The turnaround was swift, a testament to Clausen's sense of urgency and the power of NSA's technology. Mac's last request to identify other names on the list with Ban's prior travels had literally hit the jackpot.

To quote the Admiral, "we may have hit the motherload." It appeared that no less than six of the names correlated with Ban's travel destinations and dates and that included the three targets that they met on the terrace. Even more disturbing was that these folks represented some of the most powerful leaders of industry from across the globe.

The three agents gazed at the computer screen transfixed by this new intel and the implications it might represent. Each name represented the leader of a dominant organization within a specific government or industry segment that had profound impact on societies worldwide. Heading up the list was Jing Liu, CEO, Qiáng de Corp, one of China's largest E- Commerce companies. The rest included Chun Huang, CEO, Jiànkāng Corp. (Pharmaceuticals) China, Frederick Stone, CEO, Tribal Song (largest social media company) US, Joel Roland, CEO, FindIt (largest digital search engine corporation) US, Noel Parsons, CEO Allthings (largest digital merchant company) Hong Kong and Jason Fornier, President, European Commission (EU) France.

"Bloody hell", exclaimed Jasmine, "these people are the who's who of world power. What in the king's name are they all up to?"

"Yeh, not to mention that it looks like the membership of the UN Security Council," Franklin responded.

"Strange bedfellows, to say the least," agreed Mac. "And the President of the EU. That's disturbing. But what is clear is what the Admiral signed off with; we must focus on determining the objective of this group. There has got to be a common denominator that ties them all together. And that will lead us to the answers we're looking for."

"You're spot on," agreed Snow.

"Makes sense," chimed in Joe. "But what's our plan?"

"We need to get into that suite ASAP," said Mac.

◆

Precisely at one thirty pm, there was a knock on Ban's private suite's door. Wu-pen signaled to one of his guards to check it out and ensure that it was one of the expected guests. Moments later the guard returned accompanied by a tall man who strode confidently into the spacious meeting room. Ban smiled warmly at the newcomer as he greeted him with an outstretched hand.

"Peter, it's great to see you again. This is a great day for us all as we welcome you to the Faction,"

"I am delighted to be here Genjo and anxious to begin our historic mission," the man replied with a reassuring smile.

Turning towards Liang, Ban said, "Wu-pen, I am so pleased to introduce you to Peter Gunderson, the leader of Typhon and our newest member of the Faction."

Liang bowed slightly and said, "Mr. Gunderson, it is my distinct pleasure to finally meet you. I have followed your work with great interest and commend you on the progress you have made against the west; an effort that we strongly support."

Gunderson nodded in appreciation and said, "I believe that this new partnership will provide the final ingredients necessary to assure competent leadership and control over the worldwide masses that is so very critical to the future of mankind."

"Our final guest has just arrived at the hotel," Ban gently interrupted. As we all agreed, aside from the three of us, his identity shall remain secret. For security purposes, we will meet him in a separate suite in the complex, so if you will follow me, please."

The three men made their way to the private elevator and proceeded to the seventh floor, entering another plush suite and navigated to a small conference room. Across the room, with his back to them stood a slim figure with dark hair tinged with grey, gazing out the terrace door at the magnificent panorama beyond. Hearing their arrival, he slowly turned to face them. To the masses, he was not particularly recognizable. He could have been a businessman from New York or a lawyer from Chicago. But to the power centers across the globe, he was well known, if not by sight, by reputation. His dark piercing intelligent eyes belied his common appearance and there was an aura of angry power that seemed to surround him. Seeing the new arrivals, his demeanor abruptly changed as he exhibited a subtle smile of recognition.

"Genjo, my friend, it has been too long," graciously commented the Chief of Staff to the President of the United States, Frank Robino.

Before any of them could respond, Robino continued, "and you would be Wu-pen Liang, "nice to meet you." Without hesitation, Robino's searing eyes now came to rest upon the final arrival and he admonished, "and you, of course, are the infamous, most wanted man on the planet and NSA's greatest nemesis, Peter Gunderson. I posit my intelligence is accurate?" Robino asked rhetorically.

"Yes, yes Frank quite so and welcome to Rome and the Faction, my friend," stuttered Genjo deferentially.

Peter Gunderson strode forward and matching Robino's tone and tenor said, "Mr. Robino, I had great doubts about joining this motley crew, but when Genjo assured me that you were in, my concerns were put to rest."

"I am thankful for that," commented Robino "and I am reassured by your membership as well."

With the amenities completed and the egos appeased, the four men moved to a conference table and began what was sure to be among the most historic meetings in history.

◆

As the afternoon shadows began to shroud the elegant Hotel de la Ville in long veils of darkness, they carefully navigated the narrow alleys to the separate entrance to Ban's penthouse. It was a nondescript doorway fronted by an ancient cobblestone path with no signage of any kind. Leave it to the Italians to be discrete when their reputation was on the line. As the team approached, they saw no guards or cameras, but that didn't mean there were none. At his signal, Mac moved in while the others held back. He figured that if there were no defenses outside that, there would be security inside. That meant they might have to find another way in, because breaching the door without knowing what was on the other side could be suicidal.

Making his way from a corner of the building, he reached the large oak door. A large brass handle protruded from it and he noticed that it was shiny with use. Obviously, this entrance was getting a lot of traffic. He gently pulled on the handle, but the door was secure. Just below it was a large brass plate with a key lock and an imbedded card reader. *Ah, the digital age has encroached even here,* he thought. That might be a good break if they could acquire a key card. Nonetheless, at this point, this looked like a dead end unless they wanted to risk exposure and lose the advantage of surprise.

He turned and began to retrace his steps back to the team. As he came to the edge of the building, he came face to face with a large Asian who had suddenly appeared from around the corner. The man was dressed in casual clothes and might have been mistaken for a tourist who had lost his way until you saw the bulge in his silk coat and the barely noticeable earpiece. Without a word the man began pulling his weapon from his coat as he lurched forward into a shooter's stance. Mac knew he would never reach his Sig in time. He also knew the man made a crucial mistake. In moving forward aggressively, he closed the distance too soon with forward momentum that would hinder his draw and make him vulnerable to an offensive counter move.

All this happened in the space of a few seconds and as his assailant raised his weapon Mac launched into the air with his right leg extending into a judo kick that contacted the outreached handgun with immense force. The gun rotated upward and back snapping the man's wrist and misfiring, the silenced round grazing the man's temple as he screamed from the pain in his now useless arm. Mac landed on his feet as the man crumpled to the ground. Before he could turn back to his victim, he heard rushing footsteps coming towards him and pulled his Sig. Two figures appeared in the dimness of the waning light and he crouched into a shooter's stance to begin his defense.

"Whoa Mac, it's us" came the loud whisper from Franklin and Snow as they rushed to him.

"Mac, are you hit?" Jasmine questioned with sincere concern.

"I'm ok," Mac blurted out, but check out the guard and get his weapon."

"Already done that," Franklin answered. "He's out, but still breathing. But you grazed him in the head and he's bleeding badly, so he may not make it."

"No, actually, he shot himself when I judo kicked his gun hand," Mac corrected. "Let's pull him around the corner and get him out of sight behind those bushes until we can figure out what to do with him. And search him. My guess is that he is our ticket into this place."

Fifteen minutes later, the three finished the task, but the man bled out. They knew his body and absence would draw a crowd of all the wrong people, so they needed to move fast. Fortunately, he did have a key card and a radio earpiece that obviously connected him to his comrades and his suppressed pistol was a bonus if they found themselves in a jam.

"Well folks, it looks like we have no choice now," Mac observed. "Either the guard will be missed or discovered and the alarm bells will go off, so we either penetrate now or we may never get in. What do you say?"

"You speak the truth Kemosabe," quoted Joe, trying to make light of the stressful situation.

"I can see no other option at this point," agreed Jasmine. "Besides, this might be our best opportunity anyway."

"Always the optimist," Mac quipped, "but I have to agree."

"Ok, we go now. I'll take the lead. Jas, you follow me and then Joe. We will be silent running but keep your comms on. The objective is to get in and collect intelligence and get out without contact. Also, we should not use deadly force unless necessary. There are some high-profile people in this building, and we don't want an international crisis on our hands. Use your tasers or if you're in close quarters, take them down physically. And one final note, we cannot allow ourselves to be tied back to the agency, so we are on our own. As we discussed during our mission prep, our cover story is that we are a contracted team with an anonymous employer that wants to gain corporate secrets. We have been casing this penthouse for some time and identified its guests as ripe pickings.

♦

Seguro's mind was unsettled as he paced back and forth in his suite. Even the sweat drenching workout he just finished in the hotel fitness center had not calmed his frustration. He was not a patient man when it came to waiting for something to happen, especially when it involved his personal interests. Unfortunately, his options were limited. He found himself in the uncomfortable position of depending upon his potential adversaries to resolve his dilemma and he didn't like it a bit. In a fit of desperation, he headed to the mini bar and poured himself a stiff tumbler of vodka on crushed ice and strode out of the room onto the expansive terrace overlooking the city. There was a soft, warm breeze with a cloudless sky and he laid back on the padded chaise lounge, letting the warmth of the sun caress him. Draining the iced Gray Goose seemed to calm his nerves a bit and he closed his eyes against the bright glare.

An hour later, Seguro struggled to wake from a deep sleep. *What was that nagging noise*, he thought as he cleared away the cobwebs. Regaining his faculties, he jerked upright recognizing the buzzing of his cell phone inside on the coffee table. Seguro raced to retrieve the call but arrived too late to answer the one number he had been desperately waiting to receive. Before he could return the call, his voicemail notification lit up.

The message was short, but chilling, "Hello Phillip, I regret to inform you that your presumption was correct. This is an inside player and could be a contracted rogue action!"

"Well, damn," Seguro exclaimed out loud. Things had just gone from bad to worse. This new information only muddied the water. He dumped the melting ice in his drink, recharged the glass from the minibar and took a chair by the ornate hand carved mahogany coffee table. He leaned his head back and gazed at the painted domed ceiling and began to put the pieces together. The colorful painted figures above him reminded him of the actors in a play that he was now experiencing as he mentally imagined the scenarios.

The simplest explanation for the Maracaibo intruder could be that he was a US intelligence agent from the CIA, etc. on official assignment. Or he could be a US agent contracted by some organization or government. The motive in either case could be to investigate the Venezuelan activities or to disrupt or steal Seguro's Camo formula. The figures above him seemed to dance across the ceiling, bobbing and weaving and suddenly disappearing as Seguro continued his deliberations.

So, the antagonists could be enemies or competitors, he thought. And what about the attack on his residence? Was that just an unrelated incident or could Maracaibo and Valencia be connected? And most importantly, who was pulling the strings? Was it the Americans, Gunderson, the Chinese or some other yet unknown adversary? The figures continued their erratic journey across the landscape above his head as if mocking him.

"Shit, shit, shit," he cursed again loudly as he finished the vodka in one gulp, slamming the Waterford down onto the table.

CHAPTER FIFTEEN

NEXT MOVE

The afternoon session was well underway when Ban and Liang made their entrance. The Faction members had been working in small teams coordinating their strategic plans. This was not a new exercise, since they had all been executing beta programs over the last year. Ban smiled as he approached one of the breakout groups to assess their progress. Jing Liu, Frederick Stone and Joel Roland were huddled together engaging in intense conversation when Ban approached.

"Excuse me for interrupting," he interjected as the group looked up. "I hope things are going well and you are making progress. The intersection of e-Commerce, social media and search services is one of our highest potential control combinations, so expectations are predictably high for your areas. And, of course, that potential means enormous income opportunities for each of you."

"We are all very pumped about our joint prospects, intoned Frederick Stone."

"Our pilot programs have demonstrated great progress," confirmed Jing Liu, smiling, as her colleagues nodded in agreement.

"I am so pleased and anxious to celebrate those results soon," Genjo responded. "As we discussed when each of you joined the Faction, it is clear that the world's people have become increasingly incapable of managing their own societies. Unless a global authority wrestles control, humanity is doomed to destroy itself. Your activities are already having a significant impact in allowing us to gain the influence that is necessary to assuage that inevitable outcome. The stages of human need each of you are driving are rapidly allowing us to manage human behavior worldwide. Social media has been highly effective not only for its addictive qualities and rapid adoption rate, but also in allowing us to control the societal dialogue. Equally impressive has been the influence of search technologies on defining and promulgating our new realities that will guide the masses. Even the new dominance of merchant control and consumer engagement you have accomplished has addicted the world to craving convenience and immediate gratification, a pillar of our Maslow strategy. Yes, you should be proud in the knowledge that we are on the brink of saving our world from the ruin it doesn't understand or recognize," Ban bowed slightly as he concluded.

Liang joined him and said apologetically, "excuse me Sir, but you have an important call that just came in and is awaiting your attention."

Ban nodded and turned back to the group. "I am so sorry, but I must excuse myself, but I do look forward to continuing our conversation over dinner."

Once the two were out of ear shot of the groups, Ban turned to his friend and asked, "what is this all about?"

"I just received a message from Seguro that he needs to meet with us urgently. Apparently, he has acquired some new information regarding the assault on our enterprises and would like to discuss next steps. He is meeting us in your suite now."

Ban nodded and said, "well, let's see what our colleague has to say."

The two men had only time to treat themselves to some afternoon Champagne when their guard announced that Mr. Seguro had arrived.

"Please see him in," Ban commanded.

"Phillip, back so soon? You must have been remarkably busy to have made headway so quickly?"

Seguro took a seat in a large, ornate wingback chair across from the two men and answered, "actually, I began my investigation before I left Valencia and just now received the new information from my source."

"I see," Ban said. I'm anxious to hear the news. Can I get you a glass of Champagne? I find it seems to make these unpleasant conversations more tolerable."

"Yes, thank you," responded Seguro.

Ban added, "Is this source reliable?"

"Without question," Seguro responded earnestly.

"Alright then, what have you found?" Ban asked.

Seguro sipped his drink and began, "while the information so far is limited, the implications could be significant. That is why I requested this urgent meeting. I don't yet have an identity of the operator, but my source has confirmed that the individual is a US Government resource."

"Do you mean by that an intelligence agent?" Liang interjected.

"I don't know that yet, but that would be a logical presumption given the type of activity that was perpetrated, Seguro answered."

"So, this intruder could be a CIA agent attempting to gather intelligence about the Valencia operation?" questioned Ban.

"That is certainly the most likely scenario, but we can't count out the possibility that it could be a contracted player moonlighting on the side," Seguro pointed out.

"Hired by whom?" Liang inquired in surprise.

"I wish I knew, but I believe there are those who would certainly benefit from gaining our proprietary secrets."

"Phillip, you seem to possess some insight you are not sharing," Ban asked, concern in his voice.

Seguro realized that he was treading on thin ice here, but he needed to flush out the truth of the Chinese intent. He also must hold his cards close to his vest and keep his options open.

"Not at all Genjo," he replied sincerely. "I just want to be certain that we are considering all the possibilities. There is too much at stake for us to misinterpret who is threatening us."

"Wu-pen, have you uncovered anything since we spoke earlier?" Ban inquired.

"Yes, I have Genjo. The attack in Maracaibo was during a military interrogation of a US State Department agent who was caught snooping around. It seems he was investigating the Venezuelan government's alleged biologic lab operations. The interrogation was interrupted by an unknown operator who killed several security guards and called in the US Marines to take two of the Venezuelans into US custody. Our in-country sources, working with Venezuelan government undercover operatives in the US embassy believe that the Americans have now gained limited knowledge of the lab operations. We don't know the specifics, but the breach could have serious implications for our work."

Ban leaned back in his chair with a sigh and said, "while these two events could very well be unrelated, I don't believe in coincidences. The timing is very troublesome as well. We could have a single individual or small group perpetrating these actions. Equally concerning is the motive. I am not overly concerned about the US Government. We already have a stranglehold on them on so many levels and our beta operations are ready to move to full execution."

"Except for Mr. Seguro's Camo Program," Liang interjected with a tinge of derision. "It is also noteworthy that Project Camo is integral to the execution of many of our other control groups and to date it is totally proprietary under the auspices of Mr. Seguro!"

"What are you insinuating?" demanded Seguro, his anger growing.

"It seems that you have a clear motive to use this alleged threat to strong arm more favorable terms from the Faction," exclaimed Liang acidly.

"Enough, both of you, commanded Ban sternly, barely raising his voice. Turning to Seguro, he added, "Phillip, we have known each other for some time and I trust you, but it may now be appropriate to ensure our mutual security by sharing your formulations with the Faction."

So there it was, Seguro thought. The squeeze was on and he was now in the crosshairs. Seguro turned and addressed Ban directly.

"Genjo, I too value our longstanding relationship and trust you as well, but I would be reckless and foolish to provide my intellectual properties to anyone at this juncture. So, I regret having to disappoint you, but I know that if you were in my position, you would make the same decision."

Ban smiled, then chuckled softly and said, "it doesn't hurt to ask, my friend."

"So where does that leave us," asked Liang, clearly irritated.

"We double down on our efforts to identify this threat and eradicate it immediately. Phillip, it would be in your best interest and that of the Faction for you to extend your stay here in Rome until my team returns to China. That way we can ensure your safety and continue our joint deliberations. I'm sure you can manage the next week's activities in Valencia remotely," Ban insisted.

And, so you can keep your eye on me, Seguro thought as he nodded in agreement.

◆

Joe Franklin gently inserted the key card against the door's sensor and slowly depressed the brass handle. The door swung open silently as he pulled it towards him. Mac moved forward into the interior hallway with Jasmine steps behind him. After about three meters the entrance opened to a foyer with an elevator on the opposite wall.

"We caught a break, no welcoming party" said Mac as they faced the brass doors of the elevator.

"Same drill," Mac said, as Joe used the card again.

The two men entered and pressed against the forward sides of the elevator so as not to be visible when the door opened. Jasmine positioned herself at the back holding her cell phone up as if looking for some information and imitated a guest in her black tights and untucked shirt. The door parted on the 7th floor and Jasmine stepped forward into the hallway coming face to face with two security guards a few meters away.

"Ciao", she said while sporting an engaging smile.

The guards glanced at each other curiously then said in heavy Asian accents, "please to provide identification."

Jasmine nodded and lowered her backpack to the floor in the elevator doorway, began shuffling through it retrieving a small satchel. As the elevator door began to close it jammed up against her pack and began to jump back and forth. Jasmine let out a diminutive yelp and turned back to pull her duffle out, but feigned difficulty. One of the guards rushed forward to assist her and stepped into the opening. As the door opened again Franklin's taser dropped the guard halfway into the elevator. Before the other guard could react, Mac stepped out firing his taser and the second sentry collapsed to the floor writhing from the jolt.

"Good work Jas," Mac proclaimed as they pulled their victims back into the elevator returning to the first floor. While Jasmine stood sentry, they dragged the men out into the shrubbery to join their deceased comrade. Sedatives would keep them out for at least an hour. They knew from the building's layout that the main meeting rooms were on the seventh floor while most of the residences were up a floor. Rejoining Jasmine they began their search. At the end of the hall they could see a landing with a fire stair to the eighth floor. They moved down the hallway past several meeting rooms and dining facilities. They could hear muffled conversations coming from several of them but continued to the stairway.

Their luck was holding as they opened the door accessing the eighth floor without encountering any opposition. Down the hallway was a double door to the largest suite. The plans indicated that the next door accessed the suite's sleeping quarters. Fortunately, like the outer entrance, the interior doors also had key entry and Mac made short work of it with his pick set. He moved in while Franklin and Snow stood sentry just inside the doorway.

"Clear," he broadcast on his earpiece and signaled them to advance.

The large bedroom complex was unoccupied and adjoined a series of other rooms including a conference room. Its entrance was closed off with a sliding partition and they could hear a vigorous conversation in progress on the other side. Sisco and Snow took positions close to the divider and listened. She pressed her mobile gently against the wall and hit record. Franklin searched the rest of the sleeping quarters for anything that might be useful to their investigation.

With their ears against the wall, it sounded like there were three men in the conversation. While the volume was muted by the barrier, they could clearly hear the dialogue as Seguro, Ban and Liang urgently discussed the security breach of their operations by an unidentified US government agent in Maracaibo only days before.

The conversation was obviously coming to an end, so it was time to go. Mac signaled to Jasmine and they quickly moved to the exit, alerting Joe to follow. They returned to the upper landing, descended one flight to the seventh floor and carefully retraced their steps down the empty hallway to the elevator. Once outside the building, the three returned to the drugged guards, searched them thoroughly and disappeared into the night.

CHAPTER SIXTEEN

OUT OF THE FAT

By the time the three arrived back at their hotel, all hell broke loose in Ban's Penthouse. Once the missing guards did not report in, the search was on. After Liang and his security team scoured the surrounding grounds, the three guards were discovered, and an internal investigation was launched. Ban kept the whole incident quiet. Any exposure would be detrimental to their work and public disclosure of the incident would be catastrophic.

Liang personally conducted the inquiry into the apparent breach and handled the questioning of his two surviving security guards. Following these interviews, the two men met to debrief.

"What do we know?" Ban asked Liang impatiently.

"Unfortunately, not a lot," Wu-pen responded in obvious frustration. "Our security people were stationed at the seventh-floor elevator and were caught off guard when an unidentified woman stepped out of the lift. Before they could even check her identification, two attackers obscured by the elevator doors shot them with tasers."

"What kind of descriptions do we have on these intruders?" Ban persisted.

"For the woman, we have good detail, but for the men it is sketchy. Nevertheless, we think we have enough to ID them if we see them."

"What do we know about where they went and what they discovered?"

"That is very hard to answer, Genjo," Liang replied, apologetically. "We have meticulously inspected both floors of the

Penthouse and believe that they did not penetrate any rooms on the seventh floor or surveil that area. We are still inspecting all the rooms on this floor for evidence and as soon as my team reports back, I will update you."

"There is another angle we should consider, Wu-pen."

"What is that?"

"I believe Seguro's issues, and these attacks are all related and there is one man who may have some unique insight into this

debacle and that is Peter Gunderson. Let's see what he has to say about all this!"

♦

"Well, let's see what goodies we got for all that scrambling," Mac said as they huddled back in their hotel suite. Each agent rummaged through their pockets depositing their treasure on the coffee table.

"Not a bad haul at all," exclaimed Jasmine admiring the assortment.

Their reward consisted of three QSW-06-5.8 mm silenced pistols, the same number of key cards and three micro radio earpieces for communications which they de-activated so they could not be traced.

"And let's not forget the piece de resistance," she exclaimed with a flourish gently placing her mobile on the table with the recorded meeting.

"I see your raise and raise you one," smiled Joe as he smugly placed another mobile phone on the table.

"And what have you got there Mr. Franklin?' asked Mac.

"Well, I believe none other than Mr. Genjo Ban's cell phone, which is shut off and the battery pulled to avoid detection," the big Seal announced, proudly.

"Bloody hell, great work you big lug. That is indeed the winner!" Jasmine complimented.

♦

Peter Gunderson looked perturbed when he arrived back at Genjo's suite.

"I hope this interruption of my cocktails with our fellow faction members is warranted," he exclaimed as he joined Ban, Liang and the two assaulted security guards in Ban's suite.

"My apologies, Peter, but it seems we must impose upon your time and expertise sooner than anticipated," Genjo responded.

"It appears as we conducted our meeting together this evening, three assailants broke into the penthouse. We would like to review some of the details of that assault and see if you can provide some insight. Wu-pen please relate your report on the incident to Peter and have your two colleagues relate their experiences and descriptions."

Gunderson cupped his hands together in thought after hearing the reports and the guards were excused. Abruptly, he stood up and went to the bar and poured a glass of scotch straight up into a short tumbler and nursed a modest sip. Turning back to his two hosts, he began.

"Let me confirm my understanding of the descriptions of these intruders," Gunderson said softly. "An attractive, athletic looking woman in her thirties with black hair and piercing green eyes, a large, muscular man in his fifties with a broad but angular countenance and a moderately tall, almost unassuming man with auburn hair and lightning-fast agility. "Is that about right?"

"Yes, it is," Liang answered confidently.

"Well, the good news is that I am relatively sure I know who we are dealing with."

"And the bad news?" asked Genjo, a concerned look on his face.

"We have a serious problem!" warned Gunderson.

◆

The Admiral was pleased with the outcome of their night's work but concerned about the risks.

"Mac, that was a risky maneuver and could have gone south very quickly."

"I agree Admiral, but we had to call some audibles to break things loose."

"Well, things are only going to get tougher, since now they know they are under attack," Clausen pointed out.

"How do we handle the data transfer on all this, Sir?" Mac asked.

"As soon as we finish our call, transmit Jasmine's recording on our secure line. After that, we'll send you a proprietary app that will pull all the data off Ban's phone, encrypt it and forward it on a high-speed cellular circuit to us. We'll decrypt the information, translate it and review it all here. If we're fortunate, and don't run into any glitches like internal hacks that delete the phone's data, we'll get back to you in twenty-four hours with our findings."

"Copy that, Admiral," Mac responded and signed off.

◆

"So, Peter, you believe that these three operators are part of the Apogee team that NSA assigned to take down your Typhon initiative?" Ban, asked.

"That is my opinion, given what I have heard," Gunderson answered solemnly.

"That also means that you must do what I was unable to do!" Gunderson exclaimed.

"What is that?" asked Wu-pen.

"Take them out now at all costs!" Gunderson declared.

"I need to get with my people and make some calls to Beijing," Liang said as he rose to leave. "I also may need some additional resources and more intel on these people. Genjo, we may need to wrap up our work here and move our operation to another more hardened venue to give ourselves some elbow room."

"Yes, I understand Wu-pen," answered Genjo. "Oh, and Wu-pen, did you find any evidence of tampering on this floor?"

"Well, we can't be certain, but we found no evidence of intrusion. Nothing in any of the rooms seems to be missing. Your suite appears intact as well. We saw nothing disrupted. None of your personal belongings seemed out of place."

"That's good, because I seem to have left my mobile in the bedroom," Ban said relieved.

Liang froze and asked, "you don't have your mobile with you?"

"No, as I said, I left it on my night table during our meeting to charge."

"Genjo, your cell phone was not in your room, just the charger. Are you certain that is where you left it?"

Genjo felt a chill as he answered, "yes, that is where it was."

Gunderson had been quiet during this discussion, but now interjected, "assuming your mobile was not simply loaded with

Facebook posts, even if secured, within twenty-four hours its contents will be in the hands of the US National Security Agency. I would say the stakes just got a whole lot higher!"

CHAPTER SEVENTEEN

TAKE NO PRISONERS

Chinese intelligence lost no time in securing detailed information on the three alleged agents Gunderson had identified. They knew where they lived and with reasonable assurance where they had been within the last week. Before noon the next day, Liang was reviewing complete dossiers on Sisco, Franklin and Snow as well as their most recent whereabouts up to three days before. By early afternoon Liang called Ban and Gunderson together for an urgent meeting.

"I am sorry for the inconvenience of disturbing both of you from your other meetings, but you need to understand our status on this unfortunate breach of our security," he apologized.

"We understand," Ban responded, "but I must re-join Mr. Robino without delay. We have much to discuss and his time is limited."

"What have you learned," Gunderson, interrupted sternly.

"We have not been able to locate your cell phone, Genjo, but we have a copy of all its contents which we record as part of our security protocol. The good news is that because of the sensitivity of your position and the classified information you control and can access, your device is wiped clean every twenty-four hours at midnight Beijing time which is six hours earlier than here in Rome. That means that the only data on that mobile when the intruders stole it would have been since the prior cleansing."

"So, I assume you have a real time record of the content up to the point of the theft then?" Ban asked.

"Yes, we do," Liang answered crisply. "Our analysis of your mobile data indicates that you made a number of calls. Several were to members of the Faction, two to me, one message for Peter, welcoming him to Rome and confirming a meeting, the same to Frank Robino and finally one to and one received from Phillip Seguro. You also received several e-mails during that time, including copies of your presentations to the Faction. Also, there were some voice mail messages and texts that had not yet been opened," he concluded solemnly.

Ban, got up from his chair and slowly walked to the expansive window overlooking the magnificent city, his hands clasped behind his back. A minute passed, then two and he finally turned to face the two men.

"Well, this is indeed a very unfortunate incident. What is our overall assessment?"

"Since we have not been able to confirm a cleanse since then, we must assume that the mobile was disabled and unfortunately, the NSA is now in possession of that content," Liang replied.

"Were there no other safeguards in the event of unauthorized access," Gunderson questioned.

"Yes, but my guess is that the Americans safely defused all of them successfully. They have proven quite effective in that area," Wu-pen admitted.

"What about these intruders that breached our security," Genjo asked, concern in his voice.

"Our progress in that area is much more favorable," Liang answered encouragingly. Early this morning, we received complete dossiers on each of them and their whereabouts up to three days ago. Thirty minutes ago, I received additional logistics data and we tracked them to a hotel a block from here. I already have a team surveilling that location and they will report in but will take no immediate action until I direct them."

"What do you recommend Wu-pen," Ban asked.

"Until we understand what we are dealing with and have a solid plan, I would only observe them. We can take them out whenever we want, but for now we should gain intelligence. Also, ultimately, we need to interrogate them and determine what the US knows and plans."

"And you, Peter. What's your opinion?"

"Well, Genjo, I've been down this road before and I have a different view. Take them out now, while you may have the upper hand. They are dangerous, unpredictable and incredibly hard to eliminate. You let them live at your peril," Gunderson growled. "Besides, you have much more pressing issues to deal with and cannot be engaged on too many fronts."

"Such as," inquired Wu-pen.

"If the NSA has been able to acquire and de-cipher the contents of Genjo's phone, they now know about your entire operation, and some of the key players. And may I remind you that includes Seguro, some of your Faction members and me. Oh, and let us not forget, it also IDs Mr. Frank Robino, Chief of Staff for the President of the United States!"

◆

"Yes Margaret," answered the Admiral as he lifted the grey secure phone to his ear. "Sir, Robert Worthington is requesting an immediate audience with you. He says it is an urgent "Rumble" code word issue."

"Thank you, Margaret, send Bob right in and hold my calls please."

Clausen's head of Special Cipher Operations and Analysis was among the least excitable professionals the Admiral knew, but his expression as he entered was un-characteristic to say the least.

"My God, Bob, you look like you've seen a ghost! What is going on," Clausen asked.

"That might actually be the case, Sir," Worthington said gravely.

"Please explain," Clausen requested calmly.

"Well, sir, we just completed our de-coding, translating and analysis of Genjo Ban's mobile phone. We were successful in de-activating all their digital minefields and accessing its contents. Unfortunately, the Chinese security protocols wipe clean the device every day, so the content was limited to the last 24 hours of use. That said, what we retrieved is very illuminating."

"Bob, that's excellent, so why the glum face?"

"Admiral, Peter Gunderson is alive and working with the Chinese," Worthington answered without expression.

"What?" Clausen exclaimed incredulously. "Are you certain?"

"Yes Sir, quite certain."

There was silence for a minute as Clausen considered this news.

"Well actually, that is not terribly surprising, when you consider the outcome of the Apogee initiative. We knew he escaped, but I must admit, I did not imagine he would be back in the game so soon. Nor did I imagine that his enormous ego would allow him to partner with the CCP. On the upside though is that we know him and how he operates, so I count that as a plus," Clausen concluded optimistically.

"But that's not all we found," continued Worthington, a new intensity in his voice.

Clausen, stared intently into the face of his friend and colleague of thirty years and softly asked, "Ok, Bob, break it to me, what's the rest of the story?"

"Sir, there is fairly conclusive evidence that Frank Robino, Chief of Staff for POTUS is also engaged with Ban and his colleagues in their efforts against the United States!"

◆

"Frank, I apologize for the interruption, but Wu-pen called an emergency meeting, and we have a serious problem," Ban announced seriously after re-joining the American politician. "Apparently, our security was breached and we believe that your government is now in possession of sensitive information regarding the Faction and its activities."

"How serious is the leak and what information was acquired and by what agency?" Robino asked.

"The content was relatively limited as it was my mobile that was stolen and our protocols limit the content to the last 24 hours. However, there were phone calls to several Faction members that could implicate them in our work and Peter Gunderson and you were among those. Our intelligence services have identified the intruders to be several ex-members of the Apogee team assigned under the NSA."

Robino stiffened slightly at this news, but otherwise showed no other reaction. Finally, he asked, "I don't recall you and I having any phone conversation at all since I arrived in Rome."

"You are correct, I simply left you a voice message welcoming you to Rome," Ban offered.

"And there was no reference in that message to the Faction or our meeting?" asked Robino.

"None, whatsoever. I would never make that kind of security error," replied Ban earnestly.

"Then Genjo, this is easily explained and may advance our progress and help eliminate your US threat. I need a complete briefing on the breach and what you know about the intruders. President Singleton will be arriving soon for the G20 and I will head this off at the source and turn the whole affair to our advantage."

"Excellent, Frank. In the meantime, I will intensify our efforts to eliminate these US operatives. Project Camo is less than two weeks from launch after which our global initiative should be unstoppable."

◆

The call from Ft. Meade came in earlier than scheduled and Clausen and Worthington urgently detailed the intelligence the NSA team deciphered. The encrypted transcriptions Mac's team received outlined new and alarming details of the Faction's operations including some of its members and their roles.

The shocking identification of Gunderson and Robino was entirely unanticipated, and Mac asked, "Admiral, how are we handling the COS?"

"That's my problem," responded Clausen. "Unlike the Seguro calls, there is no real evidence that Robino is involved with this activity. That said, I've had a bad feeling about Robino for some time and his influence over POTUS is concerning. Furthermore, the linkage to Gunderson cannot be a coincidence. However, Robino is no doubt already positioning this contact with Ban as a coup for the new President. It will be characterized as a breakthrough in US/Chinese relations and the beginning of meaningful diplomacy. In the meantime, he will discredit any action we take, de-legitimize our efforts and move to shut down our investigation."

"What orders do you have for us, Sir," Mac asked.

"Mac, by now the Chinese know about each of you and where you are. Your hotel is probably already under surveillance. Your first priority is to get the hell out of there. I have already made arrangements at a safe house outside of Rome for you and your team. Get there immediately! Contact me when you are safe. Go now!"

"You heard the man," Mac exclaimed as he grabbed the last of his essentials and threw them into his backpack. They all anticipated this inevitability even before the call and were prepared for an immediate departure.

Exiting the apartment Mac reminded, "we split up and rendezvous no later than 2200. Limit contact and lose any tails. If you are compromised or cannot get free, send the code programmed into your mobile and we'll find you. Good luck!"

◆

Robino listened intently as Liang completed his thorough briefing of the prior day's events and the intelligence the CCP had subsequently provided.

"What is the status of these three operators now," he asked.

"We have them under surveillance in their hotel, a block from here," Liang responded.

"Make them disappear as soon as possible with no trace. NSA will never admit to this operation and I will explain to POTUS that they acted irresponsibly and could create an international incident with the Chinese if it ever were exposed. I will also recommend he shut down any further activity. We will have a free reign at that point."

"Excellent," exclaimed Genjo. "Wu-pen, see to it."

"It will be my pleasure, Genjo. Consider it done!"

"Oh, and one final thing," Robino interrupted. "This fellow, Seguro knows me and could become an issue. Are you in a position to manage his operation?"

"Unfortunately, not quite," Ban responded. "We need to acquire his formulas for Project Camo and then he is expendable."

"Well, we can't afford to take any chances. Pick him up, convince him to give up his IP and then eliminate him. Make it look like an accident and do it ASAP."

"No need to ask, Genjo. I will personally attend to this action with great pleasure," Liang chimed in, grinning broadly.

CHAPTER EIGHTEEN

IT'S COMPLICATED

It was early afternoon, Seguro emerged dripping from the hotel sauna next to the weight room where he had just completed a rigorous workout. He jumped into a quick shower, changed into a clean set of sweats and headed back to his suite.

The streets of Boston taught Seguro that he should always be on the alert, expect the unexpected and always be a hard target. His recent meeting with Ban and Liang only heightened that instinct. Ever since Ban imposed his quarantine and Liang exposed his vitriol for him, Seguro believed he was more of a target than a partner and was re-considering his options. He decided he was essentially a prisoner and the Chinese were simply biding their time before eliminating him. He no longer felt his Camo formula guaranteed his security and it was time to get scarce until he could figure out his next move.

Out of an abundance of caution, he pulled the top down on his hoodie and took the stairs to his floor. Reaching the stairwell, he peered through the fire door's small window and gazed down the hallway. A cleaning cart stood motionless halfway down the long hall which accessed his suite. A uniformed hotel employee stood beside it, his back to Seguro, a broom in his hand. The hairs on Seguro's neck bristled in warning as he watched the orderly. Strange, the man wasn't sweeping his broom. He wasn't cleaning anything. Seguro waited silently watching. Abruptly, the man slowly swiveled around gazing in his direction. Seguro jerked back quickly but had seen enough. The man was Asian.

Seguro risked another quick look. The man was walking towards him. *Damn*, he thought, time to go as he turned back to the stairs only to come face to face with a large man stepping onto the landing. As Seguro, moved into a fighting stance, the man smirked and calmly pulled out a suppressed handgun and trained it squarely at his head.

Speaking into an earpiece, the man relayed, "I have him." Behind Seguro, the steel fire door opened, and the cleaning man entered, a similar weapon in his hand. They escorted him back down the hall to his suite, entered and ordered him to take a seat in the living room. While one guard sat across from him, weapon out, the second made another call.

"Yes sir, we have him in his suite now. What are your instructions?" There was a pause as the guard listened. "I understand Wu-pen, we will prepare him for your interrogation," the guard answered and signed off.

"What do you want?" Seguro demanded as he frantically looked for a way out.

But he knew what was coming. Wu-pen Liang was on his way to work him over, acquire his formulas and eliminate him. Seguro was not naïve. He knew that eventually he would break and then all bets were off. His only chance was to go down fighting before they started. They paraded him into the kitchen and lashed him to a kitchen chair, his hands secured behind him. One guard went over to the counter and began rummaging through the drawers. He laid a dish towel carefully on the kitchen table and began to place items on it as if he were about to prepare a gourmet sushi dish. Moments later, his selections made, the table was adorned with a large carving knife, a sterling serving fork, several silver shish kabab skewers, a paring knife, a meat tenderizer hammer and a gas lighter. *You didn't have to be a rocket scientist to imagine the pain that was coming,* he thought.

As the guard turned back to close the opened kitchen drawers, Seguro made his move. He launched himself into a forward roll landing on the table and catapulting forward into the guard facing him with his weapon. The legs of the metal kitchen table crashed into the man's shoulders with such force that he fell backwards losing the grip on his gun which flew across the room into the far wall. Seguro was a powerful man and he lurched to his feet in one smooth motion and kicked the prone man squarely in the face as he lurched toward the semiautomatic across the room. His final move was to rotate his body as he slid backwards to retrieve the handgun with his shackled hands on the back of the chair.

The pain of his arms colliding with the wall was excruciating as he desperately felt for the nine-millimeter.

"Mr. Seguro," rang out a voice from across the room. "My instructions are not to kill you, but if you make one more move, I will certainly maim you very badly and I am a very good shot especially from five meters."

Seguro looked up grimacing as he stared down the mussel of his sushi cook's handgun.

"Alright, alright," he said resigned as the second guard stumbled to his feet and retrieved his weapon only inches from Seguro's hands.

"Now, let's relax and wait for Mr. Liang to arrive and get down to business. He will be here momentarily," smiled the guard.

Seguro was dragged in his chair back to the table and repositioned, this time with his feet also secured to the chair's front legs. The lead guard once again answered a call on his earpiece.

"Yes Sir, we're all set." He turned to his comrade. "Wu-pen just got out of his meeting and is on his way. He will be here in five minutes."

Seguro began to prepare himself for the inevitable torture, but he knew it would be no use. He was out of options. He glared up at his captors, pure hate in his eyes and then something strange happened.

A green dot appeared on the chest of the second guard. It danced slowly up his body and settled silently on his forehead. He was totally unaware of it. Seguro thought he must be hallucinating and then a familiar soft "pfft" sound put that theory to rest as the man crumpled to the ground. The lead guard reacted immediately by dropping into a shooter's stance and waving his weapon around desperately looking for the source of the assault. But before he could find cover, the green dot reappeared on his chest and the silent round exploded through him, a large exit hole spraying a red display on the wall behind him. Even as he grunted and began to fall, a second round penetrated his temple as his head turned.

Seguro was still processing all this as a familiar voice boomed out. "Ciao Phillip, it seems that history repeats itself?"

Phillip spun his head around to the kitchen door gasping and sputtered, "My God, Miller, what the hell are you doing here?"

"Saving your sorry ass again, what does it look like. Oh, and call me John, Phillip. I mean we are old friends, right? But now we must boogie before your Chinese partners show up and spoil our party."

Jasmine Snow was used to evading bad guys, but they were running blind on this one. Mac left first and promised to provide some cover and intel on their watchers. Good to his word, he did both. Sisco brazenly sauntered out of their hotel entrance on his way to the Hotel de Ville picking up at least three tails.

Over their comms, he calmly announced, "at least five of Liang's people are by our hotel; three staggered on the front entrance and two more at the rear. There is also at least one car parked out front in the valet space that could be one of them."

"There are two watching our suite at the end of the hall as well," Snow added. "I'm moving out and will pull one of them away and Joe can deal with the other."

"Roger that, but be careful Jas, your flying solo," Mac cautioned.

"Lift off," she fired back as she opened the suite door and quickly strode away from the guard toward the stairwell to the underground parking garage. Once on the stairs she sprinted downward three steps at a time, blasting through the exit door and into the parking area. Ten meters away parked in a small alcove the BMW 1200 cc K bike stood waiting, its black faring glistening in the reflected lights like a panther waiting to strike. She pulled on the helmet, fired up the super cruiser and launched the beast toward the garage exit in a roar. As she screamed past the garage stairway entrance, the door flew open and a man ran out, a suppressed weapon outstretched in his hand. Chunks of concrete exploded from a pillar a meter from her as she counter steered the big bike around it and out of the garage's entrance.

Timing was everything now and Joe waited precisely fifteen seconds to exit the terrace door at the back of the suite. At first, he didn't see either of the two guards assigned to surveil the rear of the hotel. But then, as he moved cautiously towards the side of the building, a man rounded the corner coming directly towards him. Franklin already had his gun out and he dove to the ground in a shoulder roll that brought him back to his feet in a firing position just as a round tore into the ground to his right. It was still a long shot with a handgun at 40 yards, but the FN Five Seven was a special kind of weapon. Its 5.7x28mm cartridge was incredibly accurate with an effective range of over 200 meters and a muzzle velocity of 1,650 feet per second. Furthermore, with that speed and this range there would be no drop. Joe pulled off two quick rounds. The first blew through his attacker's left thigh, driving him to the ground. The second shot missed wide.

The man hardly knew he was hit as he crashed to the pavement and pulled off another round. Joe felt a sudden stab of pain in his left forearm. No time to check the injury, but he flexed his hand and thankfully, it still worked. Now it was his turn as he sighted his quarry in once again and pulled off two more rounds. This time the supersonic projectiles struck home, one to the forehead and the other to the chest and the game was over. He winced as he began running toward the building's perimeter. He could feel the moist liquid beginning to soak through his tactical jacket.

Rounding the corner, he continued to the underground parking garage even as he heard the roar of the K bike coming up the ramp. Snow screamed past him as he remained shrouded behind an abutment near the entrance. A dark clad pursuer came racing out of the exit seconds later desperately trying to get in another shot at her. As the man rounded the building, Franklin jumped out in front of him, the ten-inch tactical marine combat knife stretched out like a knights lance. The man had no chance, he literally impaled himself as the blade penetrated his chest emerging between his shoulder blades in a burst of blood. Even as he fell, Joe pulled his blade from the body, slammed it back into its sheath and continued down the ramp at a jog. Pulling out the key fob, he hit the remote ignition on the BMW five series and closed to the rental. The Beemer careened out of the garage and accelerated past the front of the Hotel Scalinata Di Spagna onto the Piazza della Trinità dei Monti.

Only minutes before Snow duplicated this maneuver and as anticipated, drew the attention of her mobile assailants who immediately took up the chase. Now, it was her job to lose them and that is why the K bike was in play. She studied the street maps of Rome and knew she could outmaneuver the sedan in pursuit. But there was a problem, tourists. People were everywhere and they were not paying much attention to vehicular traffic. Soon, she found herself only a half dozen car lengths from the bad guys and the crowds were getting even larger.

Ok, plan B, she thought as she headed for the A1 Highway. If sharp turns and narrow roads wouldn't work, she would give speed a try. Then she ran into a problem. A bumper-to-bumper traffic jam! She was in the middle lane of a three-lane cobblestone street with pedestrians clogging the sidewalks, window shopping or dining in local restaurants. Up ahead, as far as she could see, cars were backed up at a large intersection with a policeman directing the traffic. She glanced behind her. The black sedan was now only three car lengths back. The traffic began to move forward again, but then stopped after only advancing ten meters. She glanced in her rear-view mirror and saw that the black sedan had one of its doors open and a large man was exiting.

"Bloody hell," Jasmine said out loud. Now what? She couldn't move the bike, there was no room between any of the adjacent vehicles. The man was only five meters away now! The cars began again to slowly advance. Jasmine waited, hoping for a gap. The man was approaching, pulling something from his coat. She was about to abandon the bike when a small opening in the traffic offered a route to the curb. She pulled hard on the bars and accelerated through the gap even as it was beginning to close, found the curb and negotiated a path on the edge of the sidewalk toward the distant intersection.

Her pursuer began running, but the gap closed and he could not reach the sidewalk. Carefully, she continued to drive to the intersection and just before it she pulled back into traffic. This time the traffic moved through the intersection with Snow following it. She glanced in her mirror again. The black sedan was still stalled in traffic well back from the intersection and her assailant was stymied by the blockade which encircled him. She sighed with relief and smiled, *a good plan and well executed thanks to the K bike,* she thought as she rocketed onto the A1 Highway.

The two men sat across from each other, their faces taught and grim as the third man paced back and forth angrily gesticulating as he described the recent events. Finally, Peter Gunderson interrupted Liang's lamentations in mid-sentence.

"Wu-pen, enough with the whining. I warned you that Sisco is dangerous and unpredictable and that your best course of action was immediate termination, but that option is no longer readily available. The operative question is what is our plan going forward?"

"I agree with Peter," Ban replied. At this juncture, we need to carefully assess our key priorities. There may be other actions that take precedence over neutralizing these adversaries."

"Like what," Liang opined.

"Like how we move forward without Seguro and his formulas," Gunderson questioned.

"Besides, these NSA operatives may no longer be relevant if Robino makes good on his commitments with the US president," Ban interjected. "They may well be ordered to stand down within the next twenty-four hours."

"You both may be right," Wu-pen responded, now largely back in control. "But I don't think we can take the chance that they aren't planning more serious countermeasures against us, especially since

Seguro is in the wind and we need to get him back or Project Camo could be indefinitely delayed."

"Fair point," Gunderson said, nodding. "So, what do you suggest, Wu-pen?"

"We track them down, terminate the operatives and locate Mr. Seguro. I have additional resources arriving by tomorrow morning and additional technology assets coming online to support our task. Also, now that the Faction meetings have largely concluded, I have made arrangements to move our base of operations out of Rome proper to a secure and defensible location to complete our work during the G20 meetings. We also have in place rapid transport capabilities to move our personnel to and from Rome as required. We currently have eyes on most of the exit paths from Rome, but I believe our NSA friends will stay in country in the short term, so we still have an opportunity to achieve all our objectives."

CHAPTER NINETEEN

EXFIL

Rome's Urbe Airport is conveniently located in the northern part of the city between The Tiber River and Via Salaria. It serves primarily civilian aircraft and does a robust business with private jet and helicopter services companies. It is a favorite of the well healed traveler who prefers to avoid the regulatory complexity and delays associated with Rome's main hubs, Fiumicino and Ciampino. Its many private hangers are adorned with high end amenities and house a myriad of sleek corporate jets from all over the globe. The large hangar door of a nondescript facility in a remote corner of the airport began to open to receive a newly landed Gulfstream G650 slowly taxiing towards it, its great wings glistening from a recent cloud burst. As it disappeared into the cavernous building, the overhead door silently retreated, cloaking its presence from prying eyes.

A single passenger descended the jet's stairs and walked briskly to the hanger's lobby, navigating around a sleek Bell 429M Light Attack helicopter, several all-terrain vehicles and assorted sedans and motorcycles. Peter Singe was no newcomer to these sorts of toys. He was a member of the prior NSA elite Apogee team on which his primary responsibility was to operate any machine the team needed to execute its mission. Coming from a Japanese engineering family, he had his BS in Engineering from the University of Tokyo, his master's from the University of Chicago in Aeronautical Engineering, was instrument and jet certified and flew anything that could get off the ground including drones. Singe's small, but wiry stature belied his physical skills. He was a skilled martial arts practitioner in multiple disciplines, was a competitive sharpshooter, an adept rock climber and graduated at the top of his class from special operations training conducted for US intelligence contractors. He was among the best in the world at what he did and proved it most recently in NSA's resounding defeat of Peter Gunderson's Typhon gambit.

Admiral James Clausen had a motto, "if you are only five steps ahead you are still ten steps behind." So, it was no mistake that the Admiral tracked down Singe and other ex-Apogee members early in this operation. Peter was engaged in London on his family's business and was already prepped for the assignment when the NSA G650 arrived from Rome to pick him up for the return trip to the "eternal city". Now, he waited patiently in the hanger as the sun slowly slid on its journey westward.

Snow spent an hour exercising surveillance avoidance countermeasures. She navigated circuitous routes around the city, stopped in both remote and busy locations and even parked and observed her unattended vehicle for thirty minutes before finally heading to her destination. Franklin spent only thirty minutes in the same exercises before he pulled off the road to examine his injuries. He staunched the bleeding with his belt but needed to examine the wound closely to understand the damage and the treatment. Fortunately, he would characterize his injury as a "nick", even though it left a significant crease in his arm, but no arterial damage or major blood loss. A quick trip to a local pharmacy for some medications and bandages, use of the men's room to clean and treat the gash and he was back on the road. Following protocol, he continued his evasion techniques and eventually turned towards the planned rendezvous destination.

It was agreed that all comms would be shut down during the escape and rendezvous operation in case the Faction had advanced tracking technology, so they were running blind. But if all members did not surface by their ten pm deadline, they would open up the comms and begin rescue operations.

Mac and Seguro wasted no time navigating the back stairway emerging on the main floor where they joined throngs of guests in the lobby. The two men walked casually out of the entrance where a hotel shuttle was filling up for its run to the airport and climbed aboard. Taking seats in the back of the bus, Mac carefully observed the hotel's entrance. As passengers continued to board, he saw a half dozen Asian men hurriedly departing the hotel together and then disburse. They fanned out, some inspecting the perimeter of the building and the rest approaching the awaiting cabs and shuttle buses. One of the men approached their vehicle and studied the line of waiting boarders. He then began circling the vehicle peering up into the windows. Mac quickly looked away and nudged Seguro to press back out of view. The last few passengers finally climbed aboard and the driver stepped out to gather up any final travelers. He turned to the Asian man and invited him to board. The two men engaged in some conversation and after glancing nervously at his watch, the driver shook his head negatively in response. The other man appeared frustrated, but finally scanning the shuttle's windows one more time, turned and walked back to his companions shaking his head. Mac let out a sigh of relief as the driver pulled away from the curb on his way to the next hotel stop on the way to the airport.

Singe was beginning to become concerned as the evening progressed. By 9:00 pm none of the team arrived at the clandestine NSA hanger. He just began pacing when the security buzzer on the back door chimed. He moved to the video surveillance screen and saw the familiar face of Jasmine Snow standing beside a BMW K bike.

Singe pushed the intercom and announced, "how is it across the pond?"

Jasmine answered immediately, "bloody hell!" The password having checked out, Peter smiled and opened the hanger door as Snow fired up the bike and coasted in.

Forty minutes later, Joe Franklin made the last turn into the NSA hanger parking lot and seeing nothing suspicious, left the BMW and cautiously approached the hanger door.

Once again, Singe's voice blared, "how is it across the pond?"

"Oorah", the big marine chimed back and the large door groaned open.

"Joe are you ok?" Jasmine exclaimed, seeing the coagulated blood stains on Joe's sleeve as he stepped from his rental.

"Yeh, just a scratch, Jas. Good thing that SOB was a lousy shot, though." Stepping forward, Peter Singe grasped Franklin's outstretched hand in welcome.

"Wow, Joe, you seem to draw fire wherever you go," Singe said grinning.

"And it's good to see you too, Peter," Joe responded with a grin. "What's the status?" he continued, glancing around with concern. "Have you heard from Mac?"

"Negative," and we're out of time," Singe answered holding up his watch.

"Give it another fifteen minutes," Snow intervened. "Any open-air communications is a risk and should be a last resort."

"Peter, do you have any details on what's next from the Agency?" Franklin asked.

"Only that we are exfilling to an island nearby and that Mac will fill us in."

"What if he is unavailable?" Snow challenged. "If we have not reconnoitered with him within the two-hour search window, I will contact NSA and receive further instructions. We are now in that countdown," Singe said, gravely.

There was silence as the three agents stared at the clock mounted on the wall. At 10:10 pm Franklin's mobile vibrated on the table next to him.

"It's a text from Mac. He says to pick him and Seguro up at the Nuovo Salario train station on the north side terminal and to have Peter spin up!"

Wu-pen Liang was on the warpath. "I want updates from all ground teams and home country intercept operations every thirty minutes," he angrily demanded and as each interval passed with no actionable intelligence, his ire grew exponentially. It was now several hours since the US operators made their escape and still nothing.

Then at 10:30 pm one of his lieutenants reported, "Sir, we just received an intercept from Beijing between the parties."

"And…" Liang demanded impatiently.

"The comm was from Nuovo Salario train station and the Urbe Airport. We have dispatched two teams out to the coordinates at each location."

"What did the message say?"

"Sir, unfortunately, it was encrypted, but we're working on that. ETA for the teams is within 20 minutes."

The BMW roared through the narrow streets with abandon. They knew that Mac would never go on the air unless he had no choice. They also knew that they were in a race against time. The Faction would have teams working the problem and likely intercepted their communications already. They could easily be racing into an ambush.

Snow cautiously approached the north track terminal building and idled along its entrance. She and Joe scanned the crowded area for any sign of Mac but saw none.

"Jas, we don't have time for another circuit, Joe warned. "We must stop, and hope Mac sees us."

Snow nodded and pulled to a stop next to the curb. Glancing in her mirror, she observed an airport security guard approaching them from behind and waving his arms for them to continue, pointing to a sign that read, "Stopping only allowed for passenger pick up."

"Shit," she said and slowly began to pull away.

"Bad news Jas, we've got company."

"Where Joe?"

"It must be the Faction, there are two black SUV's coming in at high speed. One is slowing in the inner lane and the other is going to pass us on the outer lane."

"They're taking up surveillance positions. If we miss Mac on this run, we will have a bloody hard time extracting him again!"

The crowds were thinning as they idled toward the end of the pickup area. A last congregation of travelers was bunched up near the end of the concourse looking for their rides. Jasmine noticed a large man standing partially behind a column with his back turned away. *That's strange*, she thought, why wasn't he trying to find his ride? Of course, that way he wasn't easily identified by his pursuers. It was also a signal to them. She peered into the crowd and a step away from the man, she spied Sisco staring intently at the BMW and the upcoming SUV's approaching from behind.

"Joe, I see Mac and I believe Seguro 10 meters ahead by that column. I'm going to stop a few meters beyond it. Get out of the car and open the trunk as if you were going to load luggage and walk towards the crowd. Leave the curb rear door open. As soon as they get in, close the trunk and we will boogie out of here. Let's hope they don't spot us. And remember, stay in character, as we discussed. If Seguro is with Mac, he doesn't know who we are and at least for now, Mac wants to keep it that way. Mac's alias is John Miller, and he works with Peter Gunderson and we are part of his team."

"Roger that Jas, I see him and someone who looks like Seguro," Franklin answered. The curbside SUV was now three cars behind, moving slowly. Its twin was now parked against the curb ahead of them beyond the pickup area and several men emerged and were busy scanning the crowd. Snow slowed the car to a stop and Franklin exited to the rear, opening the trunk lid and moved into the crowd. Seconds later Sisco and Seguro joined other travelers approaching their rides parked at the curb. The two men nonchalantly entered the BMW as Franklin slammed the trunk lid and joined Snow up front. They pulled away from the curb and merged out into the traffic, passing the parked SUV.

It looked like they were clear, but suddenly the guards began waving their arms and raced back to the SUV which lurched out into the congested outer lane.

"So much for stealth," groaned Franklin.

Over the roar of the engines, Mac yelled "try to lose them in the traffic but take the fastest route. There will be another team at the other end and we've got to beat them there.

Peter Singe sat anxiously in the Bell 429M, its big main rotors throbbing effortlessly as he scanned the acres of concrete in the dimness of the overcast evening. He heard the screeching noises before he saw the outline of the vehicle racing towards the hanger. As he reached for his night vision goggles, his phone chirped displaying Mac's coded caller ID.

"Singe", he answered, yelling above the din.

"Peter, we're under pursuit and coming your way, status?"

"In position and spinning and I see you approaching now."

"What?" Mac came back, "that can't be us, we just entered the airport. We're still a mile from you!"

"Well shit," Peter exclaimed grabbing the NVG's and peering into them. The big SUV was now clearly visible in the eerie green image and coming in fast.

"Peter, lift off now! Do not wait for us. Get to altitude and check back," Mac yelled.

"Roger that," Singe replied as he spun up the big bird's rotors.

"Jas, change of plans," Mac said as he leaned forward towards the front seat. "Head north on SS4. Let's give the M5 a chance to prove its reputation."

With a broad smile, the MI-6 agent responded, "You got it John" and hit the accelerator. The pursuing SUV began to fall back as they wove through the narrow streets, but once the BMW hit the open highway, the gap widened. Seguro had been quiet during all this activity, but finally broke his silence.

"Miller, what the hell is the plan to get out of this mess?"

"Patience Phillip, I'm improvising, but first things first, divide and conquer. Joe, pull up Google Maps and see if there are any parks in the area."

"Looks like there are a couple and one, Parco di Largo Labia is just north of us."

"Get us to that park pronto, find an open area and give me the coordinates," Mac directed as he contacted Singe on his mobile. "Peter, set the chopper down at the coordinates I send you. ETA looks like about 20 minutes. Our transfer must be quick since the bad guys will be tracking us and might even be close enough to engage."

"Got it," came the immediate response.

Seguro had been intently peering through the rear window and called out, "I don't see the SUV behind us anymore."

"They would have a bloody hard time keeping up in that tank at 135 mph," Jasmine responded gleefully.

"Jas, take the next exit," Joe said urgently. "Once we get off, they may not see us and we can use back roads to the park."

Minutes later, they entered the park's expansive greenery and following a lane to an open field strewn with wildflowers, they parked the Beemer behind a stand of trees. Mac sent the coordinates to Singe and began to address the group.

"Ok, everyone, this is Phillip Seguro, who as you know has been invited to work with us as part of Peter Gunderson's Typhon operation. Phillip, meet Joe and I believe you and Jasmine are already acquainted." Jasmine winked in the rearview mirror at Seguro's stunned expression.

"More to follow, but right now let's hope that Singe can get our ride here before the Faction goons. Get weapons charged and spread out in this tree line and stay on comms. If we get company, I will give you the signal to engage. Go!"

Singe was following SS4 and maintaining his altitude as he approached the park. He kept scanning the area for any large vehicles rapidly approaching his coordinates, but so far saw nothing suspicious. Once over the park, he took the Bell lower, located the open field bordered by the dark trees and set the chopper down. Donning his NVG's he did a 360 and saw an ethereal figure emerge from the trees running toward him followed by three more converging images. While he focused on the approaching figures, a high-powered beam swept across his position filling the NVGs with a blinding light. He jerked the goggles off, attempting to regain his vision of the incoming sprinters. Over the idling rotors, he heard the unmistakable "psst" "psst" of suppressed fire churning up the dirt only yards away.

"Peter, get out of here now before they take you out," Mac yelled over their comms. Singe needed no coaching as he threw full power into the bird and headed only feet off the ground toward the stand of trees to find some cover. A dull thud just over his left shoulder sent shards of fabric flying as a round pierced the armored frame of his cockpit seat. Mac watched as the chopper accelerated behind the trees and then shot into an abrupt climb skyward. While Singe drew the ground fire from them, Mac and the team managed to retreat back into the trees and spread out. Now they watched as the big SUV lumbered across the field, several beams of light sweeping the grounds and the trees in search of their quarry.

"Maintain position until we get an idea of what we're dealing with", Mac broadcast over the comms.

Fifty yards away, the SUV rolled to a stop. Six guards, jumped out and crouching low began to move towards the trees.

"Don't engage until I give you the signal," Mac instructed. "I don't want to give up our position too soon." The guards cautiously advanced, but suddenly halted and took up prone firing positions in the high grass. *Damn,* Mac thought, something was wrong. Why weren't they continuing the hunt? That question was answered when new headlight beams bloomed out across the landscape as a second SUV careened across the rough terrain and took up station on the other end of the copse. At least as many new combatants poured out of the second vehicle and began a methodical approach towards their positions.

"Hey Cap, I think we're pinned down. What's the plan?" Franklin asked on comms.

"Not much choice now, Joe. Pick a target and engage. Turn your NVG's off as soon as you fire to stay off their tech, then move quickly to another vantage point, so they don't mark your muzzle flashes. Let's see if we can equalize the numbers."

"Copy," came the reply.

It was a surreal engagement as the silent flashes began flickering across the dark landscape, like fireworks without sound. Both sides were well trained and there were no immediate hits as they moved with silent alacrity from position to position. But time was not on their side as the perimeter relentlessly contracted and the concentration of the assault narrowed.

CHAPTER TWENTY

UPPING THE ANTE

Frederick Singleton stepped off Airforce One only a few hours earlier and was now comfortably ensconced with his entourage and secret services team at The Quirinal Palace as the guest of Alejandro Masceroni, President of the Italian Republic. He stood admiring the magnificent view from the Palazzo del Quirinale overlooking Rome from the tallest of its seven hills, when a short knock broke his reverie.

"Enter," he commanded, turning towards the large, paneled door.

"Sorry to intrude Mr. President, may I have a few minutes of your time," Frank Robino questioned, closing the door behind him.

"Certainly, Frank," the POTUS responded smiling. "It's a magnificent scene isn't it?" the President admired as he returned his gaze to the window.

"Yes Sir, it most certainly is and I do apologize for interrupting the moment, but I have some rather urgent news that you should know before your engagements here in Rome."

Singleton sighed resolutely and turning back to his Chief of Staff replied, "Please take a seat Frank and tell me what's on your mind."

Once the two men settled across from each other in ornate hand carved 18th century embroidered wing back chairs, Robino began.

"Sir, I have reason to believe that a national security breach has occurred that could escalate into an international incident. It is especially sensitive given your planned upcoming meeting during the G20 with Manchu Shing, leader of the CCP."

Singleton stiffened as he responded, "details please Frank."

"I was contacted directly by Genjo Ban, a senior member of the CCP and direct report to the Chinese President who claims that members of US intelligence are engaged in direct espionage against the CCP."

Singleton seemed to relax as he retorted, "Frank, that is a daily allegation from both our countries!"

"Except that in this case, it is a physical attack on their hotel residence right here in Rome and they are currently in pursuit of our alleged agents. If their accusations are accurate, it could very negatively impact your discussions with President Shing and may well escalate into a global issue."

"I see," said Singleton. "That would be a significant setback, given the progress we have been making on our joint global strategy discussions. Do you have any corroborating evidence that would support their claims or is this another negotiating tactic to gain leverage in our discussions this week?"

"I just received this information from Ban, who insisted on delivering it to me personally, but the details he shared would indicate a high degree of veracity."

"What in particular, Frank?"

"Well sir, after doing some checking, it seems that some of the players they identified were the same NSA team employed by the prior administration during the Apogee affair under the direction of Admiral James Clausen, Director, NSA."

The President wrinkled his brow as he responded, "I do remember being briefed on that operation and recall that team disbanded and never actually captured the leader of that cabal."

"That is true, Sir and while it was well camouflaged, your political opponents and the Holbrook administration used it as an excuse to undo many of the progressive, global policies that you and your supporters have labored so hard to achieve."

Singleton's demeanor darkened as he recalled his epic battles with the prior POTUS on policy. "Aren't Holbrook and Clausen pretty tight, Frank?"

"That would be an understatement, Sir. They are close friends and as you know Clausen continues to be a thorn in our efforts. He is very guarded about his agency's operations and, unlike the favorable arrangements we have established with the other intel agencies, he has been uncooperative." Singleton made no immediate response and seemed deep in thought as Robino waited patiently for the leader of the free world to respond.

Finally, as if coming out of a trance, he rose abruptly and striding across the room to a nearby bar, he asked, "I need a drink. Would you care to join me in a Cognac, Frank?

"Thank you, Sir, I would indeed, and I think we have an opportunity brewing that bears some serious discussion."

◆

At 2,500 feet all that Peter Singe could see were the bursts of light flickering on the dark landscape below. And things were not looking good. The perimeter shots now surrounded the tree line and were closing in. More disturbing, even though the encircled targets were moving constantly, they were getting more and more concentrated. Time was running out for his friends and he knew it.

On the ground, Mac knew it too. Both sides were using the same hit and run tactics. Turning on the NVGs was suicide and tracking the enemy was virtually impossible, so everything was defensive and the numbers were not on their side.

"Hey Cap, we're running out of room," Franklin boomed over the comms.

"Roger, Joe. I'm going to draw their fire and you guys need to make a run for it. I'll go north so you guys head south. I'm going to put down some serious fire and turn on my lights. When you see it, dig out!"

"Negatory on that. No way we're exfilling without you."

"This is not a request, Joe. You know the drill. Get the rest of the team out of here now! That's and order!"

"Hear me out," Joe insisted. "Our best option is to stay together and take them out as a group. If we stay dark, we can pick them off as they converge. There was silence, as Mac considered Joe's tactic and then he flipped the comms back on and answered.

"You're brilliant Joe, I agree with your play, but with a twist."

"Of course, I am, but what's the twist?"

"We don't go dark, we light up," came the surprising retort.

At Mac's command the team re-grouped to a thick concentration of trees and brush, keeping their night vision infrared off, and taking cover from the ever-tightening threat. Mac opened his comms to everyone on the team and in a whisper said, "Peter, when I give the go ahead, execute a low strafing run over our location from north to south and then land the bird about 1,000 meters to the south for our exfil.

"Roger, but how do I know where you are?"

"I'll fire up my NVG which you can pick up on your avionics from the air," came the reply.

"But you'll be exposed if you do that," Peter cautioned.

"That's the idea, buddy!"

The night was strangely quiet as the suppressed weapons ceased their barrage. Now, only 30 meters away, the Chinese commander was also on his comms.

"Listen up everyone. We are close to our enemy now. Use your night vision intermittently so that we don't give them a target at this close range. Move in slowly until you can ID a target. Do not fire unless you are under direct attack. You could create a crossfire against our team. Also, we need to capture these enemies alive for interrogation, so use hand to hand acquisition."

It was slow going as they crawled forward through the thick, gnarly brush when suddenly the eerie green glow of several dim lights flickered in the distance.

The commander frantically urged, "they are lighting up! Kill all NVGs so that they don't pick you up and maintain deep cover."

Almost simultaneously the distant growl of a chopper coming in fast and low could be heard and then it was upon them at less than 50 meters. The roar was deafening as the fast-moving Bell 429 almost clipped the treetops and was gone. The Chinese contingent flattened to the turf, heads down in the swirling down draft not knowing what threat they faced.

As the sound dopplered out, the commander commanded "Move in. Their NVGs are still on and there is no way out. Less than 10 more meters and they are ours!"

Peter waited anxiously a half mile away, glued to his night vision avionics, but saw nothing. Then, in the distance, there was movement. Moments later, he could see the distinct outlines of four green figures sprinting towards him with the leader 's infrared NVGs lighting the way.

As they jumped into the open side door, the last to board was Mac Sisco, with a big smile, yelling over the din, "Fire her up Peter, let's boogie!"

◆

As the two men sat sipping their flutes of cognac, Robino took the lead and said, "you know, Mr. President this whole episode may have a silver lining."

"And what could that possibly be?" Singleton asked incredulously.

"Well, as we know, Clausen is a real problem and our work with the Chinese and our global partners would be much smoother if he was no longer in the mix. Regardless of who is behind this terrorist initiative, with the proper management, the whole incident could be re-architected as a plot against America and our growing partnership with the Chinese by your political opponents, including the current Director of the NSA."

Singleton's demeanor visibly brightened as he considered Robino's suggestion and he intoned, "but how do we pull that off, Frank, Clausen has a lot of powerful friends?"

"You leave that to me, Sir. Plausible deniability and all that, you know."

"Yes, your right of course, Frank, but get it done and soon," the president said as he raised his glass in acknowledgement and drained it with a flourish.

CHAPTER TWENTY-ONE

INSURANCE

Gunderson gazed out of his suite window admiring the view. The multi-colored tiled roofs and narrow cobblestone streets stretched out in all directions as the tourists, like ants scurried about aimlessly in search of discovery. But Gunderson's mind was elsewhere. The recent news of Liang's failure to secure the interlopers was both disturbing and predictable. He knew better than anyone how slippery Mac Sisco and his colleagues were, but the Chinese were sloppy and erratic and that was beginning to concern him. He had agreed to join them because of the promise of their vast reach and resources, but his loyalty was to his own vision, not theirs.

The CCP had but one objective; to stay in control and become the dominant society on the planet. Their end game was subjugation and they had little concern about the fundamental quality of life they spawned for the proletariat. As a result, their strategies focused on debilitating the population through addiction, conflict and brainwashing with the CCP as the sole and ultimate authority whose governance could never be questioned.

Gunderson believed his approach represented a more noble vision with long term sustainability. While, like the Chinese, he had no faith in organic and random leadership, and so for a time their paths were complimentary, but ultimately the outcomes were different. Gunderson insisted that with proper management and exploitation, humanity offered enormous potential which should not be suppressed, but directed. Its leadership must be carefully engineered to manipulate the world's people to drive innovation and growth and he fully intended to control that process. His family's generational aspiration, his lifelong goal and his enormous ego left no room for any other outcome.

Typhon's setback at the hands of Sisco and Clausen was unfortunate, but not irreparable. Gunderson's early engagement with Genjo Ban and the Chinese offered a rare opportunity and was already reaping significant benefits and evolving according to plan. The Faction would certainly succeed. Hell, it already enjoyed an enormous grip on global behaviors, but it would not be long before a massive revolution would erupt against the obvious subjugation of the masses, inevitably leading to anarchy and devastation. He was certain of this because it happened so many times in the past. History demonstrated a near perfect record of predicting the future!

For Peter Gunderson, the operative question now was how to leverage the Faction and exploit the Chinese. The answer was already percolating in a Gunderson company 4,000 miles away. While the family fortune was amassed over generations, the "B" level money was all Peter's doing. Forty years ago, he founded an investment company called Granite Noir, now among the three largest such firms in the world. Over the years, he moved the headquarters around the globe, but a decade earlier, because of its advantageous tax and business treatment, "GN" had relocated to Dubai, UAE. It was a perfect home for the firm and cloaked Gunderson's identity among the elite and affluent populous.

As part of his Typhon strategy, Gunderson also acquired and merged several high technology companies which became part of GN's portfolio of companies and one of his better acquisitions grew to be among the leading AI development firms worldwide. Artificial Resource Kinetics, ARK, also made its home in Dubai and was busy using its AI engines to ruminate on the complexities of the Chinese dilemma and Peter Gunderson's next steps. Early indications were that an elegant solution was imminent. Artificial Intelligence technology was always part of Gunderson's grand scheme. He was acutely aware that to manage and control mankind, one needed the ability to outthink humanity and ARK would ultimately do that for him. In the meantime, he worked inside the Faction to exploit their Maslow conspiracy to his advantage. This time Gunderson would prevail!

And what about Sisco? He smiled to himself as he considered the intricate maze of deceit that would soon begin to entangle all his unwary adversaries.

♦

James Clausen had a bad feeling about the way things were evolving in Sisco's mission. It was like déjà vu and not in a good way. During the Apogee operation against Typhon, while there were several inside traitors, they were containable. But the COS to POTUS, that was a different animal. He needed to get ahead of this before it spun out of control. As if his musings were prescient, his secure line buzzed and his EA said, "Sir, I have Frank Robino, Chief of Staff to the President, on the line for you from Rome."

"This is Clausen," he answered.

"Hello Admiral, Frank Robino" the caller responded. "As you know, I am over here in Rome at the G20 and we have a situation which I believe requires your immediate attention."

"Yes Sir, how can I help?"

"I need you to look into an urgent matter that could have global implications for our relationship with our allies and the Chinese."

"What is the nature of the matter, Sir?" Clausen asked concerned.

"I can't go into the details even on a secure line. It is too sensitive and besides, I need you here in person to oversee a mitigation operation. Please schedule your departure immediately because there are high level meetings that are already scheduled which could be impacted by our actions. I'll personally brief you as soon as you arrive. I am sorry for the cryptic nature of this arrangement but believe me it is necessary."

"I understand, Sir, I will be in the air in an hour," Clausen replied as he slowly lowered the secure phone into its cradle.

The Director, NSA, among the most powerful intelligence officers on the globe, leaned back in his chair, closed his eyes, and let out a long breath as he thought, *now it begins!*

CHAPTER TWENTY-TWO

RE-GROUP

The Bell 429 headed north towards the coast. It was time to re-group before this operation spiraled out of control. At this point, Mac knew he needed to get his team out of harm's way and figure out next steps. Obviously, the stealth strategy was now blown. Furthermore, if Robino was on the dark side, new adversaries would already be martialing their assault, and they would be formidable. Under the auspices of POTUS, even his brothers in other US intel agencies could be in the hunt. All this while he needed to keep up the masquerade with Seguro. That was crucial if they were to learn more about the threat and secure hard evidence to assuage their guilt.

"Ok, everyone, listen up," Mac commanded over the whine of the rotors. "Good job on securing Mr. Seguro's safe escape. I have the coordinates of Mr. Gunderson's safe house where we will begin the next phase of his plan. Peter, next stop Elbe Island."

◆

Frank Robino was on his secure line most of the afternoon following his meeting with POTUS. His first call was to Phil Van Meter, Director of the Central Intelligence Agency. The conversation was brief and to the point; the NSA was operating a rogue operation allegedly led by Special Agent Mac Sisco to disrupt the talks between the US and China. It's objective was to discredit the current administration by jeopardizing the US national security and its relationships abroad. The

President ordered Robino to mobilize all appropriate resources to neutralize this activity immediately. Because this appeared to be a rogue NSA operation, he also ordered James Clausen, Director, NSA to personally fly to the G20 in Rome to ascertain his personal involvement. Strict security was being implemented on a "need to know" basis and Robino was instructed to coordinate with Homeland Security, DIA, FBI, and the Justice Department. Van Meter was to engage directly with Donald Givens, FBI Director, to deploy assets in both the US and abroad to locate and eliminate this nefarious activity.

Robino poured himself a vodka on the rocks and gently sipped the 100-proof libation as he reviewed the day's surprising events. He was always amazed at how disaster could provide opportunity if you possessed the right power, attitude, and resources. It was like fate was his ally! The Sisco assault provided all the cover he needed to accelerate his agenda. The Chinese were now on the defensive, Seguro was discredited and would soon be eliminated, POTUS was inextricably dependent upon his recommendations and NSA and the previous administration, and its key players would be implicated and publicly disgraced.

Robino could feel the momentum. He savored the upcoming confrontation between Admiral Clausen and President Singleton. He would finally complete the task of establishing total control of all the intelligence agencies by the White House. The global progressive movement was fast becoming a reality and he was in the cat bird seat.

◆

Elba is an Italian island in the Tyrrhenian Sea's Tuscan Archipelago National Park. It's a favorite tourist attraction with picturesque views, mountain topography, sea life and beaches. It even sported a notable history as Napoleon's place of exile in 1814.

Peter set the bird down on a flat open area by a grove of low trees in a secluded part of the park as Mac instructed and turned to his leader expectantly.

"Now what?" he asked. "We're on the opposite side of the island from the safe house and it's a long trek."

"We wait," Mac said.

"Ok, I'll bite," Franklin asked, "although I'm sure Jasmine already figured it out."

Smiling modestly, Snow responded, "the obvious answer is, to avoid being tracked to the safe house."

"Exactly right, Jas. There were probably some healthy electronics focused on our escape. We'll land two more times on other isolated parts of the island before heading to the SH. There's a lot of geography to cover which should deter detection. Peter, hide a remote camera and sensor on the tree line facing out to this clearing. If the bad guys track us here, we'll have an early warning that they are in the area."

"Ah, makes sense," the big Marine exclaimed. "And that's why Gunderson pays you the big bucks."

Villa Fuga, "Escape house", was aptly named. It sat high on a mountain overlook of 10 secluded acres above the spectacular gulf of Porto Azzurro and afforded an ideal retreat for the embattled agents. Peter parked the Bell adjacent to a vineyard that was part of the charm of the property and only fifty yards from the main stucco structure.

As the big rotors coasted to a stop, Mac said, "everyone get settled and meet in the main living room in 30 minutes for a debrief."

"Hey John, do we need to double up?" Peter asked.

"No need, Gunderson always plans for more than he needs," Mac answered keeping up the ruse.

Once in his quarters, Mac sent an urgent text to Clausen. He needed intel and direction. The implications of Robino's involvement with the Faction were catastrophic and Mac and his team were likely flying solo. He was also concerned with the Admiral's safety. Even though the old warrior had lots of powerful friends and had been around the block, the power and control of the White House was almost limitless. At a minimum, it could freeze out the NSA resources and that would be a real blow. And worst case, it could neutralize Clausen, leaving the team rudderless at the top.

◆

Clausen had been down this path before, but when Frederick Singleton was elected, he determined his defenses against a hostile administration might be inadequate. So, in the early days of the new President's administration, Clausen added some options. Although exercising these actions was a last resort, he knew in his gut that Robino was playing hard ball and would pull out all the stops if he thought Clausen was on to him.

Before Steven Holbrook left the White House, Clausen recommended to outgoing President Holbrook that a protocol be established with a secret network of global like-minded leaders in government and industry that could be engaged if the world went sideways. Code named "Whiplash", any of the members were authorized to activate certain elements within the protocol depending upon the severity of the issue. Before stepping on the NSA jet that afternoon, Clausen had invoked one of those elements. It was the first time anyone had done such a thing so this would be its maiden voyage. All he could do now was wait and ride the waves!

♦

Bruce Black, CIA Special Agent in Charge, Rome Office hung up the secure line to Washington and stretched his impressive torso in a twisting motion. It wasn't every day he got a call directly from the Director. But, when he did hear from Van Meter, it was always a nasty assignment. This one was likely to be among the most distasteful because it involved another intelligence agency. It was also extremely dangerous because it involved Special Agent Mac Sisco, notably NSA's most effective ground operator. Black never met Sisco, but he knew about him. Even though the rumors of his work were probably exaggerations, Black knew that most of the stories would likely be true. Intelligence officers didn't brag and or make shit up.

That said, he was trained to deal with the worst cases. Like Sisco, Black was among an elite group of black ops CIA agents who were deployed to interdict severe threats to national security using whatever means necessary. He was the non-fiction version of 007 without the charm. He was tough, fearless and at thirty-five spent the last 10 years in intelligence Armageddon honing his lethal skills. He was at the top of his game and relished the challenge of proving he was the best of the best. This mission was a rare opportunity to set the record straight. So, the hunt was on. His team was ready for a new deployment and would welcome the action. The Director said these were bad guys who were traitors and a threat to the US and needed to be neutralized and there it was. His job was clear. The rest was above his pay grade.

◆

"That wasn't the smoothest extraction we've ever done, Mac began with a wry grin, but you can't argue with success."

"Yeh, good audible, Cap, it was brilliant," exclaimed Franklin.

"And thanks to Peter for the lift," Jasmine chimed in.

"Absolutely," agreed Mac. "Now you've all met Phillip Seguro and have been briefed on his situation. Phillip, I'm sure you have a lot of questions, but I'm also sure you know by now that your rescue was not a coincidence. We had intel that the Faction was about to move on you."

"That may be true, but I'm still skeptical about you and your Mr. Gunderson. Where is he, by the way and when am I going to meet him?"

"All in good time Phillip, but let's be clear, we saved your ass and frankly you are in no position to make demands. If you want to stay alive and become extraordinarily rich, it's time for you to play ball," Mac shot back.

"To start with, it's your turn to contribute, so we'd like to understand all the details of your arrangements with the Chinese and the Faction." Seguro knew he was between a rock and a hard place. But he had to hang on to some of his cards.

"Alright," he began, but what guarantees do I have that you will deliver?"

"That entirely depends on you Phillip," answered Mac, aka John Miller, sternly.

An hour later, Seguro finished his soliloquy and Mac responded, "Phillip, you have stated that your first deliveries to the US will be in two weeks, what will the payload be and how will it be triggered?"

"John, I can't tell you because the Chinese would not disclose that. I don't even know if it is a liquid or a dissolvable solid. My Camo carrier will handle either. Nor do I know who the targets are, the triggers or how it is engaged. It could be time-based, ingredient sensitive or even biologically/anatomically detonated."

"Is there a way to defend against this Camo ingredient?" Mac continued to pry.

"Yes, I was sure to develop a method to identify if Camo is present and neutralize it, but I will not disclose those details or its chemistry for obvious reasons.

"Phillip, that is not helpful," Mac derided.

"That may be, but that is my insurance policy," Seguro insisted.

"What I can tell you is that the plan was to initially test a relatively narrow carrier to confuse and misdirect any US analysis. One of the targets discussed was sacramental wine which is a natural fermented grape based red wine. The populations most affected are Christians who participate in Communion services. The Chinese seemed enamored with this pilot, for obvious reasons. Another beta was to identify specific DNA combinations common to certain ethnic populations."

"Intriguing," answered Mac dispassionately, hiding his horror at the implications of this disclosure. "Let's take a break for now. I need to report back to Mr. Gunderson and then we can discuss next steps to wrest control of this business and jump on that gravy train."

CHAPTER TWENTY-THREE

HIDE AND SEEK

Wu-pen Liang was barely under control after the fiasco at the Italian park, as he ripped the intelligence report from his aide's outstretched hand. He scanned the document and then smiling malevolently, he dialed Ban.

"We may have caught a break, I'll come over and brief you."

"I hope you have some good news?" Ban asked when his colleague arrived. I' m due to meet with President Shing tomorrow and a poor report would not bode well for either of us."

"Yes Sir, I understand. What we know so far is that the chopper that extracted our enemies flew northward and we believe we may have captured their flight path on either our satellite surveillance systems or some local drone recordings that we hacked. Before the end of the day, I am hopeful, at a minimum, we will have a general destination. As soon as I can move in on them, I will proceed as we discussed in our last meeting; interrogation, disclosure, and elimination."

Ban did not respond immediately as he pondered Liang's comments. "Wu-pen, I want to bring Robino and Gunderson in on the situation. I don't want to get out of synch with Frank, since he is already working on the US president to provide cover. And, as we have seen, Gunderson can assist us with detailed guidance on the interrogation of the US agents.

"Genjo, I worry about trusting these men," Liang opined.

"It can't be helped," Ban retorted. "I don't trust them either, but this will be an international scandal that must be delicately orchestrated, and President Shing and President Singleton must be singing out of the same hymn book, as the Americans say, so we have no choice."

◆

The update from Ban on the Sisco affair had been timely as Robino hung up his secure line to Van Meter, satisfied that the CIA intervention and the Sisco takedown was now underway. His people had informed him that Admiral James Clausen arrived at the private hanger, insisted on providing his own transportation and was on his way to their hotel. Robino was scheduled to brief POTUS in the morning on the upcoming Shing meeting. Things were shaping up nicely, he thought. Let the games begin!

◆

Bruce Black read the short top-secret missive from Van Meter on his secure text line, "Be on alert for immediate deployment. Lead on combatants is imminent!" He smiled, his pulse quickening in anticipation of the impending hunt. He made his way from his office to the ready room where his elite black ops team was completing their final prep. As one, they all turned and looked to him expectantly.

"Alright Lads, we're on final que, so get ready to rumble!"

◆

Only a few miles away, Peter Gunderson was busy logging inputs to ARK and instructions to his associates in Dubai. Their progress was accelerating as they scraped more data to feed the massive AI engine. Now, with Ban's report on Sisco, all the pieces were gelling. Robino would be manipulating the American response with POTUS. The Chinese President would respond predictably, and Clausen would be running for cover. The Faction would soon be part of a new initiative and he would be able to go live on activating ARK!

◆

James Clausen purposely parked his rental car strategically close to the Hotel de la Ville's parking lot exit. He paused, scanning the area, and removed his carry-on luggage from the car's trunk. Opening his diplomatic pouch, he retrieved a remote sniffer, magnetically attached it to the underside of the trunk lid and activated it. It employed the latest bomb detection technology NSA had acquired and was selected because of its uncanny sensitivity and ability to provide early warning indications of an impending explosive detonation.

After checking in and entering his suite, Clausen began a lifelong practice of securing his space. First, using an NSA issued electronic scanner, he meticulously swept the residence for listening devices and cameras. Then he completed a visual inspection of the area for any other anomalous artifacts. Satisfied that he was secure, he fired up his laptop and checked for secure messages. He left the agency very abruptly and informed his EA that he received a last-minute request from the POTUS's COS to attend the G20 to support President Singleton and would likely be off the air most of the time.

Two high priority messages blinked urgently on the screen, one from Mac Sisco and one identified as WL. His last contact with Mac was his urgent directive to get out of his hotel to evade the Chinese assault and he was unaware of the outcome. He anxiously opened the text.

"Evaded C and secured Seguro with undercover scenario. At SH on Elba. Need intel and counsel for next steps. MS."

The second text was understandably cryptic, "WL stage 1 trigger confirmed."

His attention was interrupted by a beep from the hotel phone and the message light illuminated. Clausen picked up the phone and listened to the recording. "Admiral, welcome to Rome. In anticipation of an update with the President tomorrow, I would like to meet with you this evening for dinner in my suite at seven pm."

Clausen sighed. From here on out things would be very tricky. He had little doubt that Robino's intentions were nefarious. But he had no defense unless he could learn more, and he had to be incredibly careful. His communications would be intercepted, so they had to appear legit or better yet mute. He shut down the PC and headed to the shower. He hoped Mac could read between the lines.

♦

Sisco stared transfixed at the message on his mobile, his mind whirring. It was rare for the Admiral's EA to respond to urgent encrypted messages on Clausen's behalf. It might even contain an imbedded warning if something was amiss. Mac re-read the message again.

"Received a last-minute request from the POTUS's Chief of Staff to attend the G20 to support the President and will likely be off the air."

Damn, he thought, the Admiral is in trouble. The head of the NSA and the global leader in signal intelligence was never off the air unless his own agency or partner agencies were working against him. And why would the President's Chief of Staff require the Director of the NSA to fly all the way to Rome at the last minute? But the clincher were Clausen's words, "will likely". Mac was privy to the Whiplash protocol after Typhon was put to bed and one of its trade practices was how to protect the group's anonymity. Clausen would not be vague about his communications. That meant that the "will likely" translated to the letters "WL" in his message and was code for Whiplash has been invoked. *So, the die is cast*, he thought. *They're circling the wagons to take down Clausen and his team and then they'll have clear sailing.*

CHAPTER TWENTY-FOUR

TARGET RICH ENVIRONMENT

The dinner had started innocuously enough but had soon deteriorated as Robino articulated his position. He was surprised at the candor of the man. That was a kind way of describing Clausen's arrogance. It was irritating but of no consequence. He would soon be out of the picture. Clausen's refusal to pull his team off their current operation and take them into custody was all he needed to make his next move. His fabricated case against Sisco and ultimately even the Admiral was rock solid, and he knew POTUS would cave to him regardless of Clausen's claims of national security. Besides, Clausen was far too dangerous to be on the loose let alone command the power of the NSA. He picked up his secure mobile, selected a name and dialed.

"Yes, Sir," came the immediate response.

"Change of plans, new target, he began."

◆

"We have them," Liang announced excitedly as he opened the call on his mobile. He and Ban were meeting to discuss the upcoming briefing with Manchu Shing in the morning, when the call came in.

"What do you mean, Wupen?"

"We tracked them to an Italian island in the Tyrrhenian Sea, Elba Island, and it's not far by air. We have mapped a perimeter where they are located. By the morning we will ID their exact location."

"Then what?" Ban asked.

"Then we go in with a team by air and game over," Liang answered confidently. "Once we secure the perimeter and take them, we will conduct our interrogation there. We can dispose of them on location and bring Seguro or Sisco back to an alternate property if necessary."

"Gunderson wants to be there for the interrogation," Ban interjected.

"Genjo, I don't think that's a good idea."

"Wupen, he is the only one that knows this Sisco character, and he is a critical partner in the Faction. Besides, I have no doubt that Peter Gunderson wants to see Sisco go down even more than you."

"OK, Genjo. I'll brief him and set it up. He can go in with us on the assault or come in after we have secured the area."

◆

Years on the streets of Boston and the halls of corporate America had taught Phillip Seguro some harsh realities about trust and deception. After his sit down with John Miller and his team, his skepticism had grown exponentially. The elusive Gunderson situation made no sense. If Camo was so critical to the global terrorist, why wasn't he here? And how did Miller always seem to be one step ahead? And then there was the heads up from his Washington contact that it was an inside job. Occam's razor suggested that this was a US intelligence team scamming him with this Gunderson BS. Either way, he was screwed, or was he? Neither the US nor China was going to play nice unless he pitted them against each other. He knew in his gut there was only one play and he had to move on it now!

◆

James Clausen rose early after a restless night. Robino was meeting with President Singleton at 7 am so as not to conflict with G20 activities and requested he be available to join them at 7:30. He knew Robino would set him up and had prepared a strong defense, with the evidence Mac had supplied. But Clausen was a realist and a veteran in the world of political treachery and knew firsthand the lengths to which those in power would go to stay in power. Unfortunately, he had little experience with the new POTUS, but so far Singleton had been weak and accommodating when strength and conviction were clearly required.

Clausen picked up a croissant and a coffee on the way to the parking lot and walked to the perimeter near the exit where his rental car was parked. He slowly circled the vehicle and examined it closely in the dim early morning light for any indications of tampering. He saw none and retrieved the sniffer's remote control. He activated its display and the green indicator light glowed. He pushed the detail button to confirm the safe status and it indicated "all clear". Clausen sighed, *one down,* he thought as he opened the car door.

It was a short fifteen-minute drive to The Quirinal Palace and the traffic was relatively light. Following the car's GPS, he wove his way down the narrow streets approaching a toll station on Via Piemonte, his mind focused on his upcoming confrontation with Robino and the President. Suddenly a loud alarm began to beep beside him. It was a sound that he knew all too well and it jolted him like a bolt of lightning. He looked down at the sniffer's remote next to him on the seat. The red light was blinking rapidly and all he could think of was the irony of his last thought, *one down*!

◆

The mission was straight forward and except for avoiding any exposure, had little risk. With this change in target, Black had ordered his team to stand down temporarily. He had decided to execute this operation personally because of its high profile and to eliminate any possible leak. His plan was to take out Clausen en route to the palace and tie the assassination to a terrorist group. It required a very sophisticated explosive technology developed by his agency. The bomb could not be detected even when installed because the built-in electronics could be programmed to mimic its environment, in this case the frame of the car. As he listened to the police scanner, he sat back satisfied that his work was flawless once again. Phase one, Project "Overhaul", was complete. It was now time to move to phase two.

By nine am Rome time the news of the explosion nearby the Italian palace and the G20 conference was everywhere. Live coverage of the smoldering scene, wall to wall social media coverage and internet images displayed on screens was all over the globe. Pundits speculated 24/7 about the incident with wild abandon. The world was rivetted on the story and demanding answers. The G20 went into high alert and bolstered its security but vowed not to be intimidated. Their members made statements of concern but insisted that they were confident in their security precautions and the efforts of the Italian authorities.

Investigators were not even sure what caused the explosion since there was literally nothing left except some melted metal that appeared to be from an automobile. By noon, Italian authorities confirmed that, indeed, the debris had been identified as an automobile, but that no occupant had yet been identified.

♦

It would still be another hour before the sun would rise over Elba Island as Mac stared at the message Clausen's Assistant sent only hours before. He had to do something. He couldn't leave Clausen swinging in the wind. They must continue the ruse with Seguro to get control of camo, but they also needed to help Clausen and there was only one way to do both.

They agreed to rotate sentry duty every four hours and Snow was currently on watch. He found her standing by the main entrance of the compound gazing out over the moonlit landscape.

"Jasmine," he whispered loudly as he approached her. She whirled around, her nine-millimeter positioned perfectly for a headshot.

"Whoa, Jas, it's Mac."

She relaxed and said, "what are you doing up? I'm the last watch."

"Jas, something has come up and I need the team to meet right now. I'll get Joe and you get Peter and meet me back here pronto. Don't wake Seguro." When the four agents assembled at a picnic table on the backyard terrace, Mac explained the situation.

"Mac, I agree with your assessment," Franklin responded as Mac finished. "I've known the Admiral a long time and he would never go off the air without letting us know, especially during an active op."

"How do you want to play this?" asked Singe.

"We must split up. Jasmine, you, and I will take the safe house jeep to Portoferraio, use a fast boat to get back to the mainland and find Clausen. Joe and Peter will stay here and work Seguro. That way, if you get any uninvited visitors, you can take the Bell and boogie out of here quickly. The explanation to Seguro is that we are going to pick up Gunderson. That will cover us and placate him.

"Good plan," Jasmine agreed.

"We'll leave once it's light and brief Seguro before we head out," Mac said. "In the meantime, let's all spend some time brainstorming ideas on how we play Seguro and next steps with the Admiral."

The sun was peaking over the hills of the island as the team finished their deliberations. Franklin went to retrieve Seguro. While the rest of them were in the kitchen grabbing their third cup of java, Franklin rushed in.

"Seguro is gone!" he blurted out breathlessly.

"Joe are you sure he's not just taking a stroll around the property?" Mac asked.

"I did a quick 360 around the compound and no Seguro."

"Bloody Hell!" exclaimed Jasmine.

"Jas, pull up the internet and check on the geography. What roads and facilities are close by that could provide him with an escape route?"

"On it," she said, flipping open her laptop.

Seguro had made up his mind. He must get out while the getting was good, and this might be his last opportunity. It was still dark as he left the residence and headed down the gravel drive. He located a petrol station on his map app and figured he could hitch a ride into Portoferraio and grab the ferry back to the mainland. He needed to lay low while he planned the coup that would save his life and make him rich.

Mac turned to Jas, "What's the scoop, Jas?" he asked as he checked his cell for new messages from the agency.

"Best guess is that Seguro is enroute to Portoferraio, the largest city on the island. It offers cover and several ways to get back to Italy.

There are several facilities relatively close where he could have gotten transportation, so he might even be there by now."

"Maybe we could cut him off at one of those exit points," Singe suggested.

"Probably too many to cover," Franklin answered.

"What do you think?" Snow asked turning to Mac.

Mac was silent as he focused intently on the headlines displayed on his phone, "Major explosion occurs near G20 meetings. Country on high alert!" When he didn't respond, they all turned to him with concern.

He solemnly held up his phone, the headlines displayed boldly across its face and said, "I have a very bad feeling about this!"

By mid-morning Seguro caught a ride from a local petrol station to Portoferraio. With both the Chinese and Sisco hunting him, he elected to remain on the island until it was safer to travel. The historic section of the city provided numerous small accommodations off the beaten path with excellent access to transport back to the mainland. Using the rental's internet, he wired funds to the hotel's office. With cash in hand, he spent several hours downtown shopping and back in his room, put the final touches on a text message on his new burner and hit send.

CHAPTER TWENTY-FIVE

MERGERS AND ACQUISITIONS

Ban stared at the message in disbelief. What the hell was going on? He closed his eyes and massaged his temples to provide some relief from the acute stress he was now feeling. He was mere hours away from meeting with Shing and needed to have answers and they better be good. He hit Liang's speed dial.

"Liang," came back the barely audible response, the chopper's engine roaring in the background.

"We have a big problem, Wupen. Seguro just sent me a text. He is threatening to put Camo out on the market to the highest bidder. That currently includes us and the Americans, but also any other organization that meets his qualifications.

"What are his terms, Genjo?"

"I don't know, but aside from price, he said his personal security had to be guaranteed."

"He must have escaped from Sisco, or he wouldn't be free to operate like this," Liang responded.

"That was my thought as well," Ban agreed and asked, "what is your status? Maybe he is still on the island, and you can locate him."

"Unfortunately, while we have discovered an area where we believe the Americans landed, they are not here now, and we have no info on where their final destination is. We are about to do a fly over of the entire island in search of their helicopter, but if it is under cover, we may never find it," Liang finished frustrated.

After a long silence, Liang asked, "Genjo did you hear me? Are you still there?"

"Yes Wupen, I am, and I have an idea. I will text Seguro back and make him an offer he can't refuse, and it may even help us solve the Sisco problem."

Seguro re-read Ban's text again looking for the traps, but it seemed like the Chinese were prepared to make nice. They offered to make him a senior Faction member, increase his stake dramatically, allow him to retain ownership of Camo's formula, purchase a significant equity position in Biotherapeutics and allow him to control their voting shares, guarantee his safety against all threats and provide funding for future initiatives that he recommended. Seguro's scheme for ensuring his safety was that in the event of his death or imprisonment, everything about Camo, The Faction, it's plans, and the Chinese involvement would be made public. He recognized that the old saying in this case was his best counsel, "keep your friends close, and your enemies closer". The one kicker was that Ban wanted to conclude the agreement immediately and keep the Americans from knowing about Camo. Ban suggested a personal meeting with Seguro to negotiate the terms as soon as possible since he was under pressure to report back to the CCP.

Seguro knew his best option was still the Chinese, and he might even get more out of them by giving up Sisco's operation and location, so he agreed to the meeting at a restaurant in downtown Portoferraio. When Ban said that Liang was already on the island and could meet him, Seguro vehemently objected and insisted that Ban find someone else. He didn't trust the SOB. Ban grudgingly agreed and promised to have another senior Faction member represent the Chinese who was also already on Elba.

Ristorante Da Gianni was not crowded in the late afternoon. Seguro arrived early and selected a secluded table in the rear and ordered a glass of Elba Blanco. As he sipped the last of the fragrant local wine, a tall, older man entered the restaurant and scanned the few occupied tables with piercing eyes. Seguro never met the man, but he looked vaguely familiar. When the newcomer's gaze finally rested on him, he nodded in acknowledgment and the stranger approached him.

"Mr. Seguro, I presume?" the man said smiling as Seguro rose to greet him.

"That is correct," offered Seguro. "And you are?"

"Peter Gunderson," the man answered, smoothly. "It is good to finally meet you, Mr. Seguro. You have certainly been a challenge for my Chinese friends." Seguro's mouth was agape as he attempted to assimilate this revelation.

As his guest took his seat, he looked quizzically at Seguro and asked, "is there something wrong, you seem out of sorts?"

"My apologies, Mr. Gunderson, but it seems you may have been misrepresented."

"By whom?" Gunderson fired back in surprise.

"Before I answer that question, are you really here representing Genjo Ban, The Faction and the Chinese?"

Now it was Gunderson's turn to be taken aback as he carefully considered his response. "Mr. Seguro, why would you ask such a question?"

"Because I just escaped from a man named John Miller who said he worked for you and offered me an opportunity to join your organization in opposition to the Chinese."

"I don't know a John Miller. Could you describe this individual?" Gunderson asked.

Seguro nodded and described Sisco and his team members and the names they were using.

"I came to believe that these people were American intelligence operators playing me for information. But, once your

Chinese colleagues tried to double cross me and take me out, I realized that it was time to take matters into my own hands. And that brings us to our discussion today. But, Mr. Gunderson, you have still not answered my question?"

"Yes, I am here on behalf of Genjo Ban and I am a member of the Faction. As you know, Mr. Ban is anxious to resolve the current conflict and come to an amicable agreement and has made a very generous offer. Are you in agreement with his terms?"

Seguro knew it was time to up the ante as he replied, "No, Mr. Gunderson, I am not. You are asking me to forgo engaging any other bidders for my invaluable technology without assessing the market. I also believe that in short order, I could receive a much richer offer. In particular, the Americans are not short on resources and worked hard to ensure my escape from your thugs! Furthermore, I have access to very high-level contacts in the US government with whom to negotiate and I hold more cards to trade with them than you."

"Would you care to enlighten me so that I know how I might counter?" Gunderson asked carefully.

"Let's just say that the Americans would pay a lot for insight into the Chinese agenda," Seguro answered cryptically.

Gunderson's mind was whirling as he considered this strange turn of events. Seguro's predicament provided an unprecedented opportunity for him to accelerate his plans and secure one of the Faction's most devastating weapons. He must take advantage of the situation even with the risk of exposure.

"Mr. Seguro, let me be candid. I am familiar with the individuals who you have described. And you are quite correct in your assumptions regarding their identity. They are an elite team of NSA special agents who were deployed to infiltrate and destroy your operation. They are extremely dangerous and equally ruthless, and you are fortunate to have eluded them. Furthermore, you have no leverage with America to guarantee your personal safety, which I imagine would be at significant risk in any deal with them."

"Fair points Mr. Gunderson, but I believe the Americans, like the Chinese, would desire Camo as a weapon against its adversaries, so they would also be motivated to keep it secret."

"You may be right, but it's a roll of the dice which way they play it and if your wrong, your gone," Gunderson countered.

"Well, either way, I'm not convinced that I should make a deal with you without testing the market," Seguro argued.

There it was, Gunderson thought. It was now or never. The door was open, and he needed to walk through it!

"Well, Mr. Seguro there might be another better option for you to consider."

Seguro leaned forward in surprise and asked, "and what is that?"

"Have you ever heard the phrase "turnabout is fair play?" Gunderson asked wryly.

CHAPTER TWENTY-SIX

MOVING PARTS

"Are Y'all thinking what I'm thinking?" Franklin asked as the team stared at the headlines on Mac's phone.

"Yes, but it seems unlikely," Snow offered.

"I agree. There are too many other possibilities," Singe suggested.

"In any case we need more information to confirm the Admiral's status, so let's not jump to conclusions," Mac said.

"So, do we proceed as planned?" Franklin asked.

"It still makes sense. The answers are in Rome," Mac concluded.

"Car's ready Mac," Snow said.

"Ok, let's roll. Guys, watch that remote camera and even though the Bell is camouflaged, be on the alert, Mac warned as they headed out.

Two hours later, they heard the sensor go off before they saw the visual on the camera. The motion detector picked up the turbulence even before the chopper settled to the ground and the Chinese security forces leapt out to investigate. Franklin and Singe huddled over the PC as 12 darkly clad figures with assault rifles spread out in low sprints toward the tree line where their Bell was parked only 24 hours before. One large Asian man barked orders as he advanced, kneeling to examine the depressed marks where their helicopter's struts had crushed the turf. He scanned the area almost angrily as he yelled more orders and the search teams quickly turned back to their ride, its rotors beginning to accelerate.

"Shit, that didn't take long," exclaimed Franklin. "We better prepare for the worst, Peter."

"Right, but I hate to abandon ship before we're sure they are on to us. If they head this way, they may pick us up on radar or visually and I am not sure we can outrun them," Singe cautioned.

"Good point, so what do you suggest?"

"We wait for some indication that they are close and adjust accordingly. They may never even come this way," Singe recommended.

The two men geared up and positioned themselves under the tarp covering their bird and waited. After an hour with no activity, they began walking back to the main house.

"Looks like we dodged a bullet," the big Seal exclaimed with a sigh. Singe nodded as they entered the terrace by the pool.

"I'm going to call Mac and let him know that the bad guys are definitely on the island since they may be exposed on the water," said Singe.

"Good idea," Franklin said as he went inside. Singe was on the phone when Franklin returned with two bottles of water. As Singe reached out to take the offering, he saw his friend gazing upward and mouthing something he missed, concern on his face.

He pulled the phone from his ear and asked, "Joe, what did you say?"

"Do you hear that noise?" Franklin asked. Singe tilted his head and turned and then he saw it, a tiny spec in the distance coming in low and fast!

"Peter, what's going on?" Mac could be heard yelling urgently.

"It looks like we've got company and there's no time for an air exfil, gotta go," Peter yelled back.

"Let's go Peter, plan B," Joe yelled as he sprinted toward the steep cliffs overlooking the Tyrrhenian Sea's glimmering waves far below.

The Chris Craft Corsair 32 Heritage was just starting its journey southeast towards the Italian mainland, its two 300hp engines only running at a quarter throttle, when Peter's call came in. The plan was to avoid all traditional modes of travel to avoid detection. If the Tyrrhenian Sea were gentle, a run down the Italian coast to Porto Romano Marina would add only an hour compared to ground transport and land them less than an hour by car to Rome. But the call changed all that.

"Jas, head northwest up the Elba coast as fast as the sea allows," Mac yelled above the din of the big engines. Snow turned to see her boss's worried expression as he held the cell phone to his ear.

"Roger that Mac, but what's going on?" she countered as she spun the wheel to starboard.

"The boys are in trouble. Get us to that cliff overlooking the sea where the safehouse is. It should only be about a 20-minute run. Stay as close to the shoreline as depth will allow, so we can beach it if we have to." Mac moved forward, scanning the skies as the Chris Craft accelerated, the sleek hull skipping briskly over the low swells.

Liang was losing patience as they approached the last search sector with no success. After the excitement of discovering the likely original landing spot for Sisco's chopper, he anticipated a quick encounter. Now he was running out of geography.

"Take it down low over that compound by the cliffs," he commanded his pilot. Coming in over a small grove of trees, he noticed movement.

"Hover lower about 20 yards ahead."

"Yes Sir," came the immediate reply.

Liang peered into the leafy canopy searching and spotted a tarp flapping wildly from the draft of his helicopter's blades.

"Take her down in that clearing. I think we have found them."

Liang was first out, running low while zig zagging to the nearby trees. Once in the grove, he could clearly make out the Bell 429 partially camouflaged by the flapping tarp. The area was empty, but since the chopper was still there they couldn't be far.

Liang pressed on his comm and barked, "All units, take half the team and search the residence and buildings. The other half, take the chopper up and search the surrounding area and the cliff from the air. Report in immediately upon their discovery."

Franklin reached the precipice's edge first and scrambled over to a ledge out of sight. Singe soon followed, dropping deftly down beside his partner. Singe was an elite level rock climber and had done his fair share of free climbing all over the world. While Franklin was fit and all terrain capable, he was clearly more at home in water than on overhangs.

"Joe, we've got to get further down the cliff and find decent cover," Singe said in a low voice.

"I was afraid you were going to say that," Franklin groaned as he peered over the edge at the 300-foot drop to the surf and rocks below.

"I'll lead the way and pick the route. You try to mimic my foot and hand holds as you descend and you'll be fine," his friend encouraged.

"Well, I guess I finally have to actually follow in your footsteps, since my life depends upon it!" Franklin quipped weakly.

"That's the spirit," Singe said and began his descent.

"We should be coming up on the cliff near the safe house," exclaimed Snow as the boat raced over the waves.

"Yep, I can see that rock formation that juts out above the sea where there was an overlook for guests. Take her in closer and cut it to trolling speed to maintain headway so I can scan the cliff face." Mac peered through his binoculars moving slowly down the sheer rock.

"Anything?" Snow asked anxiously.

"Nothing near the top. Wait, there they are, inching down the eastern face about one third down. It looks like Peter is navigating the route and moving towards a section that drops away from the rocks to the sea. There is a ledge with an overhang above it about 20 meters below him that provides cover."

"Singe sure knows his shit. If they can get to the sea, away from the rocks, they have an escape route and we can retrieve them," Snow observed.

"What the hell! There are pieces of rock flying off the cliff," Mac shouted. "Someone's sniping them."

"I see them. They're taking fire from above and a bloody chopper is coming in fast to hover off the cliff," Snow screamed. "They'll be sitting ducks!"

Mac grabbed the big duffel he brought and pulled out the high-powered KK15, a favorite long range 12.799 mm anti-material weapon used by the SEALS.

"Hold her as steady as you can against the surf Jasmine. I have got to create a diversion for these ass holes, or they will pick our boys off the cliff like fish in a barrel."

Mac was an elite shooter and one of the best long-range snipers in US intelligence, but shooting off a moving platform was not something most trained for, that is except SEALS. This was their element. Even so, a 30-foot craft didn't provide much stability even under calm conditions. Mac advanced to the bow, placing the gun's bipod on the flat surface and acquired the chopper in the powerful scope. His first shot was wide and high as a swell pushed the trajectory off course. The helo had managed to position itself 100 yards off the cliff and was dropping quickly down the face to level off with their targets hanging precariously just above the overhang.

Mac fired a second round which clipped the side of the helicopter's fuselage. The pilot got the message and spun the big machine around getting a visual on the Chris Craft bobbing in the sea 65 meters below and 100 meters offshore. The interruption allowed Singe to maneuver across the overhang and launch himself dangerously through the air to the ledge beneath and out of direct range of the chopper fire. Mac reloaded. The side door facing him slid back and two armed shooters appeared sighting in on his position. Mac fired again and one of the perps collapsed backwards into the interior.

"Hit the gas, Jasmine, then cut it in five seconds". The second man fired. A large chunk of teak exploded from the stern port gunnel, only feet from the engine compartment. Mac let loose a third round. The second shooter's hip blew apart and he lurched forward cascading out the door, arms flailing as he disappeared into the sea below.

Franklin managed to reach the overhang and was attempting to make the transition to swing onto the ledge. The pilot was maneuvering the helicopter out of Mac's fire making it difficult for the remaining shooters to sight in on Franklin, but they continued to fire wildly into the cliffside. Mac reloaded and squeezed off his next round at the cockpit. A large chunk of granite flew from the overhang near Joe's position colliding with the machine's fuselage and the big machine began to rotate. Its tail slammed into the cliff below the ledge followed by its rotors. A huge explosion and ball of fire shot upward blocking his view of the cliff wall. Thick, black smoke billowed upwards as the chopper careened into the sea. Through the gaps of dissipating blackness, they got glimpses of what was left of the overhang. Franklin was gone.

♦

Robert Worthington, Head of Cyber Technology and Operations at the National Security Agency sat quietly in his basement office pondering his next move. As an executive and direct report to the Director, he could have chosen any office on the top floor, but Worthington insisted on being near to his beloved super computers. The massively parallel processors took up 90 percent of the shielded space and represented the largest and most advanced computing complex on the planet.

The low hum of the servers was almost hypnotic as he finished reviewing the last inter-agency daily recap and clicked on the latest press from Corriere della Sera, Italy's largest daily newspaper. Once again, the headlines focused on the explosion near the G20 Conference and the ongoing investigation. Not much changed since his last read. The Italian authorities were still sorting through the remains of what appeared to be a thermite explosion and searching for clues, but the molten mass was not yielding much information. The only promising evidence was debris scattered outward by the immense incendiary that survived the searing 2,000 degree melt down.

Clicking to a background partition containing Clausen's last message to Sisco for the second time, he pressed the control, option, and command keys, then typed SCAN and hit enter and watched as a red curser appeared and rushed through the text. Next, he typed display and hit enter. The following display appeared with a 10 second timer next to it counting down. It read, "Mac Sisco – WL". As the timer reached 0, the message disappeared and was replaced by another flashing message, "Whiplash Protocol is in effect." It too disappeared after another 10 seconds.

Worthington leaned back in his chair and sighed. There was no question about it. Clausen had invoked the Whiplash Protocol before boarding his private jet to Rome and Worthington was the first trigger point. There were only a handful of NSA personnel who were members of Whiplash and less than 20 members in the ultra-secret network worldwide. It was an extraordinary group of carefully vetted individuals of international stature and experience who would sacrifice their lives for the cause of global freedom and order. Any member could invoke the protocol and alert the other members. Worthington would send out the broadcast during his lunch break today from an offsite restaurant using a burner phone and phase one would begin.

◆

When Clausen didn't arrive at the appointed time for his meeting with Robino and POTUS, calls went out about his whereabouts. Within fifteen minutes, the Secret Service alerted the local CIA Station Chief. A comprehensive search commenced with Director, CIA, Phil Van Meter assigning Bruce Black, Special Agent as lead. At first, the details of Clausen's disappearance were kept confidential, but by the second day, rumors were growing that something was amiss. While the US made no comment on the Admiral's status in the early hours, Black bided his time as his team joined the site search for clues. By the end of the second day, Black officially reported finding DNA evidence at the scene that was positively matched to Admiral James Clausen, Director, NSA. Within hours following a global media release from the White House of Clausen's death, President Frederick Singleton announced that Gilbert Nicosia, Deputy Director, NSA would be the new Acting Director of the agency pending a Senate confirmation of a permanent replacement.

Word of Clausen's death rocked the global intelligence community. Of course, the manner of Clausen's death prompted questions about the cause of the explosion and its implications. Once again Black orchestrated a carefully worded release that the CIA identified Clausen's death as a homicide and that a disgruntled rogue NSA agent was being pursued as a "person of interest" and the key suspect. Black smiled at his latest missive from Van Meter, "re-acquire original targets and proceed with operation." Sisco and his cronies were back on board!

CHAPTER TWENTY-SEVEN

CLIFFHANGER

Ban paced across the suite awaiting updates from Liang and Gunderson. He survived his meeting with Shing by emphasizing the Faction's progress and detailing Robino's plan to arrange for the US President to eliminate the NSA's threats and ensured the CCP President that it would be clear sailing from here on in. While Shing seemed convinced, he demanded another update before the end of the G20 meetings in case he needed to intimidate the weak American President into further action.

Finally, he could wait no longer and dialed Gunderson's mobile.

"Yes, Genjo, I expected your call," the man answered on the first ring. "The answer to your question is that Seguro has not accepted your offer."

"But why not, it was incredibly generous?" the Chinese executive whined.

"As I warned you before I left, you might have competition and that is indeed the case. While it is regrettable, it was not unexpected, and I explained that your patience is not unlimited. I gave him five days to decide and for that concession he agreed he would disclose what we need to win the deal against other bidders."

"I'm not certain what more we can offer."

"Don't worry, Seguro won't be shy. He'll make some demand and we'll negotiate and then you'll have Camo."

"And then we will eliminate this irritating American once and for all," Ban responded vehemently.

"I will check back with you soon. I need to address some issues of my own in the meantime," Gunderson concluded.

"Thank you for your intervention, Peter,"

"It is my pleasure, Genjo. The Faction will survive and prosper," he answered as he hung up. Gunderson removed the cell phone from his ear and pressed a key that would stop the recording. He now had all he needed to reel Seguro in, get Camo and set ARC in motion. It wouldn't be long now.

Liang was still clearing the residence, room by room when he heard the explosions from the cliff and knew the chopper was lost. Sprinting out of the house, he yelled into his comm., "everyone to the cliff's edge, now!" Thick smoke obscured most of the view, but through the haze he saw glimpses of the wreckage strewn among the rocks and surf. A sudden gust temporarily cleared the shroud revealing a white hull just off the shoreline with two figures peering upward in his direction.

Liang wasted no time in conjecture about the identity of the craft as he roared out his command, "open fire on that boat and don't spare any ammo." His team dropped to the ground in prone firing positions and began unloading AK rounds over the precipice.

Mac could see the cluster of figures forming above clearly in his binoculars and knew they were exposed.

Before the first shots were fired, he yelled, "Jas, head into the shore, we've got to get cover from the cliff." Snow hit the gas and headed at full throttle for a narrow section of sand lining the rocky coast.

"I hope we've got the depth," she screamed as they plowed through the churning surf, 7.62 rounds pocking the sea, several slamming into the stern sending shards of mahogany rocketing dangerously across the hull. Mac was still on the bow section of the boat anxiously focused on the fast-approaching rocks on either side as they hurtled toward the beach.

"Get ready to cut the gas Jas," he yelled. Hearing no reply, he looked back to the cockpit. To his horror, Snow was slumped over the wheel, blood streaming from her head. *Oh no*, he thought, *not Jasmine*. In one leap, he was over the windshield beside her. He could feel the bottom scraping the hull. Any second the shore would grip the boat like a vice and at 25 mph they would both be catapulted out. He lunged forward grabbing the throttle and jerked it back into reverse. The big engines roared as the screws dug into surf and sand. Mac hugged Jasmine tightly as he braced for the inevitable assault of inertia. He took the hit as his left side crashed into the control panel and the starboard gunnel. Snow's inert form added to the mass, the pain shooting through his left side from his hip to his shoulder. And then, it was over as the big Chris Craft shuddered in its attempts to reverse direction from the sand's grip.

Wincing, Mac pulled the gear back to neutral and cut the engine. He gently disengaged from Jasmine, leaning her back in the captain's chair and feeling for a pulse. It was strong. Then he pulled her tangled hair away from the head wound, high on her forehead, the blood still oozing from a large gash. *Thank God*, he thought, it was not a headshot. It must have been a piece of debris, but how badly was she injured?

First things first, he thought as he re-focused on the threat. Rounds were still raining down, but they were hitting about 10 yards off the stern. That meant that for the moment, the shooters didn't have a direct angle on his location. But he knew that wouldn't last long. They would begin descending the cliff and they would once again be exposed. He needed to get Jasmine out of there to more cover and set up a defense. Granite outcroppings spotted the shore and Mac gently laid the British agent on the sand behind a large boulder with a good vantage point for defending a likely descent. One trip to the Chris Craft provided some basic supplies, a medical kit, and his weaponry.

After making her as comfortable as possible, Mac cleaned and bandaged Snow's wounds and looked for other injuries. Seeing none, he applied some smelling salts from the med kit and waited. Jasmine jerked slightly and then her eyes fluttered open.

"Jas, can you hear me?" She moaned but didn't respond. "Jasmine, it's Mac," he repeated.

As her eyes focused on his face, she answered weakly, "yes, I can hear you."

"How do you feel? Are you alright?" he asked concerned, cradling her head gently in his hands.

"I am now cowboy," she grimaced bravely with a slight smile.

They went back to the safe house, found ropes in a storage shed and began descending the cliff in pursuit of their prey. Liang took the lead. His need to reap revenge on Sisco and his team was now an uncontrollable visceral obsession. They worked their way down passing the overhang and ledge where Singe and Franklin fled only thirty minutes before and continued across the face to avoid the crashing sea, reaching a rocky shore one hundred meters from the beached Chris Craft.

Liang had four men left on the assault team and he ordered them to spread out as they approached the beached craft. He stayed back as his men moved deftly from rock to rock. He scanned the area but saw no movement. He moved his binoculars slowly across the cliff face. Still nothing. His men worked their way outward from the landing site without incident. Their quarry had vanished. They reconnoitered back at the beached boat and Liang inspected it carefully. A pool of blood congealed on the deck by the cockpit. *Could they have been killed or injured and thrown from the boat into the sea? Not likely*, he thought. At least one was injured, so they couldn't be far.

As Liang walked back to his awaiting team, he realized what he missed. He turned back to the boat screaming to his men to take cover as the first suppressed nine mm round hit him squarely in the chest, the severe pain cascading through his body as he crumpled to the sand. From 20 meters above the beach, the Sig Sauer P226 burped twice, and two more assailants went down, large exit holes exploding from their head shots. The final perp dove behind a large boulder but was trapped with only the surging sea behind him offering escape. The standoff continued as both sides exchanged fire without resolution until the shooter's body suddenly tumbled from behind the rock to the sand and lay still.

Minutes later, Mac descended from his camouflaged perch above.

"Clear," he yelled as he approached the felled body, a clearly visible head shot to the temple gushing prodigiously. The slightly ajar engine compartment cover slowly raised as Snow emerged, her Glock raised, moving side to side.

"Mac turned to her perplexed, I didn't cap this guy. I had no angle."

"I didn't either," she answered with alarm, her eyes wide. "So, who did?"

"That would be me," came the reply from across the beach as Peter Singe emerged from behind a large cluster of rocks, water still dripping off his lean torso. They both rushed to their colleague in surprise.

"We thought you were gone when the chopper hit the wall," Snow stammered.

"Me too, but when I saw them repositioning it laterally, I knew I was toast, so I scaled down as far as I could and found a good size crack, got in it and hung out, no pun intended, until the firefight ended. I watched these bastards come down after you guys. Then I made the final descent and let the sea bring me in behind their last shooter."

"Peter, that's incredible. Great work and thanks," exclaimed Mac.

"Peter, did you see Joe?" Snow asked anxiously.

"He was just above me when I reached the overhang and swung into the ledge, but I was out of there quickly and never saw him make that tough move in. At that point, the chopper was pummeling the cliff, so I don't know how he could have survived. I'm sorry guys, that's all I know."

"Is it possible that he could have fallen or jumped into the sea and be alive?" Snow pressed. Peter looked to Mac for help.

"Jas, it's possible, but 200 feet is a long way and unless you penetrate just right, the water is like concrete, so please don't get your hopes up. That said, Joe is one tough dude!" Mac comforted softly.

"He Bloody well is and he's a Seal and water is his friend, so let's go find him!" She exclaimed, hopefully.

"Right, Peter, assess the Chris Craft and make sure she's seaworthy and we can push her back out. Jas let's check out these SOBs for evidence and usable gear and get photos."

As they turned to get to work, Snow asked, "Mac, weren't there five of these perps?

"Yep, why?

"Well, there are only four bodies and the first one I shot is gone!"

Liang woke from the blackness with a searing pain in his chest. He heard suppressed fire all around him and opened his eyes to see each of his team dropping to the ground. The shots were coming from up on the cliff and the boat which he had just finished clearing. Then it came back to him, the engine compartment he failed to check was slightly ajar. His entire body was aflame, but he was not bleeding. The Kevlar vest took the hit and to his enemies, for now he was just one of the corpses. He waited, barely breathing, so his chest movement didn't give him away. Finally, while his three enemies were busy reuniting, he dragged himself behind the nearest rock and made his escape. Pulling his mobile from the side pocket of his tactical vest, he dialed Ban.

"Yes Wupen, how is it going?" Ban asked.

"Genjo, I am injured, and my team is destroyed, but our enemies sustained losses as well and we know where they are. I need reinforcements and exfil now to these coordinates before we lose them again.

"Unfortunately, we don't have time to search for a wounded enemy, even one with critical intel," Mac advised. "Team comes first, we need to find Joe!"

Fortunately, while the Chris Craft had taken some serious hits, they were all cosmetic, so they were good to go. Sisco and Singe pushed on each side of the bow while Snow managed steerage and throttle on the 10-meter Corsair. With the big engines roaring and the two men pushing the craft through the pounding surf, they finally navigated to deeper water, headed back to the site of the chopper crash and slowly cruised the area. After an hour of intense search, Mac signaled Snow to cut the engine so they could discuss the matter.

"Guys, we've covered a lot of area, I'm skeptical that Joe could still be alive in the water."

"We can't stop looking, Mac. We just can't give up on Joe," Jasmine begged.

"Oh, I'm not giving up Jas, I just think we're looking in the wrong place."

"What do you mean?" Singe asked.

"Well, let's think about how Joe would react in this situation."

"Ok, I'll bite, what's your theory?" Singe asked.

"I believe Joe saw what you saw Peter and dove off the overhang before all the shooting started. As a Seal, he's trained to routinely exit aircraft from many different heights even with heavy gear to complete his mission, so he would be confident in surviving the cliff dive. Besides, his odds of surviving on that cliff were nil and he knew that. My guess is that he survived the leap and swam down the coast using the strong current to travel as far as possible to avoid detection. Once well out of range, he would swim ashore miles from where we are. Jas, fire her up and let's cruise down the shoreline and see what the terrain looks like. Joe would have picked a safe exit from the sea. When we see that transition point, I think we'll find Joe Franklin, Navy Seal extraordinaire!"

As confident as Mac was about Franklin's skills, he was still unsure of his chances and after 10 miles, his doubts began to win the battle. They were coming up on a large gap in the rocky topography where the shore had a series of coves and sandy beaches. Mac directed Snow to take the boat closer to a small cove with a grassy peninsula jutting out.

"Head to that peninsula," Jasmine. As they approached to within thirty meters of the shore, the high grasses began moving and parting. Their hopes heightened, they stared transfixed, not taking a breath. The grass parted and a large sea turtle slid noiselessly into the shallows.

"Bloody Hell!" Jasmine gasped in disappointment.

"Well shit, now what?" asked Singe in frustration.

"Damn, this cove sure looked promising, but we keep looking," Mac said. "Joe is alive, I can just feel it!"

As they swung the bow seaward to continue their search, a familiar baritone voice bellowed out above the crashing surf, "Thankfully, I can feel it too Cap and why so much profanity from the mouth of babes, my ears are burning. What took you guys so long?" Turning back to the shore in surprise, Joe Franklin emerged from behind a large group of rocks grinning from ear to ear.

CHAPTER TWENTY-EIGHT

DISCOVERY

Robino was not pleased about the latest update from Ban regarding Sisco and his NSA team but was not overly concerned. Everything was moving forward as planned. Clausen was eliminated and with a new Singleton follower soon to be confirmed, NSA would be in the fold with the rest of the US Intel organizations. He felt confident that the manhunt launched against Sisco and his colleagues would be successful and they would be neutralized appropriately. President Singleton was acquiescing to Robino and his global handlers and his dependency grew daily.

The Seguro hiccup was an unexpected bonus. Because of their personal connection, he would be Seguro's natural contact for US negotiations on Camo. How fortuitous that was? He would parlay the deal so that the Faction would win, but not without significant personal benefits.

The only wild card was Peter Gunderson. He was dangerous and unpredictable. He controlled enormous global resources and was a risk that needed to be managed carefully.

◆

Their plan was to run down the Italian coast, come ashore at the Tiber River and dock at Marina Porto Romano. From there they would launch their search for Clausen and the truth. It was a two-hundred-mile run, but if they stayed close to the shore with calm conditions and cruising at thirty to forty knots, they could get there in under seven hours.

The sun was barely peeking over the horizon when they finished mapping their route and began their journey south. Even with the electronics, navigating the coast at night was a tricky business, but this was Franklin's forte' and the Navy Seal didn't disappoint. The Corsair's 2 300 HP engines growled happily as the sleek craft skimmed over the calm seas. After the harrowing day, it was a comforting hum made almost pleasant by the star strewn sky lighting their way.

They arrived early the next morning just as the sun was beginning its ascent over the flat seas and moored the Chris Craft in a reserved slip. After checking into the Marina Hotel in separate rooms, they agreed to meet in Mac's room in the early afternoon after some well-deserved recuperation.

But for Mac, there was no break. After a quick shower and some strong black coffee, he pulled his hardened PC from his backpack and began a methodical review of everything he knew about the Clausen incident. He was acutely aware that the case was growing cold with each passing hour, and he also knew from the official US government news release that he and his team were targeted as the prime suspects of the alleged assassination. That reality was confirmed by the urgent notification blinking rapidly on his laptop from Gilbert Nicosia, Deputy Director, NSA. It read, "Agent Sisco, immediately suspend your current field operations assignment and report with your team to the local Rome CIA Station Chief for de-brief."

So, there it was. If he didn't comply, he would be considered guilty as charged and hunted down. If he did comply, the game would be over. Robino would cover everything up he and the team would be charged and prosecuted or worse!

◆

Steven Holbrook, former President of the US was up most of the night after receiving the message from Robert Worthington initiating the Whiplash Protocol. Whiplash (WL) was established as a "last resort" collaboration designed to intervene if a global crisis threatened humanity. The members of this extraordinary team were recruited by Holbrook before he left office and were loyal supporters of the concepts of freedom and truth. They included several of America's closest allies and friends who were uniquely positioned to defend the world's people against authoritarianism and worldwide disorder. A few of those joining Holbrook in WL were "A list players" who could affect enormous change across the globe. They included the Prime Minister of Israel, Aaron Cohen, the Director, NSA, Admiral James Clausen, Head of Cyber Operations and Technology, NSA, Robert Worthington, the Crown Prince of Saudi Arabia, Ahmad Faheem, the Prime Minister of Japan, Sasaki Akio, the President of Poland, Anatol Dragan, the President of the South Korean Hardware Technology company BAB Technologies, Mi Cha Park, the CEO of Uttar, Inc. an Indian global software giant and General Robert Sinclair, former Chairman of the US Joint Chiefs of Staff.

Based on the apparent assassination of James Clausen, the response to Holbrook's all-nighter had been unanimous assent to launch phase 1 of the WL protocol. Assessment and mitigation efforts were already underway. Within twenty-four hours, the group would determine if escalation to the next phase was required, but Holbrook had little doubt of the outcome. The world was under threat and Clausen had sacrificed his life to send a warning!

◆

Back in his rental, Seguro pondered his options after meeting Gunderson. The man had been very convincing. How ironic that after all the American subterfuge about Gunderson, their fabrication was more true than false. While Gunderson did not expose all his plans, he admitted that he was considering all his options. He rightly pointed out that both their opportunities could best be exploited by a partnership between the two of them. He insisted that neither the US or China would ever allow Seguro to live and forwarded that evidence in a recorded message of his conversation with Ban that all but sealed the deal.

"I'm not certain what more we can offer."

"Don't worry, Seguro won't be shy. He'll make some outrageous demand and we'll negotiate and then you'll have Camo."

"And then we will eliminate this irritating American once and for all."

Seguro agreed that the US would act no differently. They would refuse to negotiate with terrorists and then begin a mass search and destroy mission after him while stealing Camo. Gunderson admitted that his real interest was to gain control of the Faction to ensure both their longevity and wealth and insisted he had a failsafe way to do that.

While intrigued, Seguro balked at moving forward unless Gunderson did two things. He opened his text app with Gunderson's number and typed "on board if you show me the money and prove the case." The response was immediate, "get to Leonardo da Vinci-Fiumicino Airport in Rome, private hanger, see you in Dubai."

◆

Bruce Black poured over the details of his latest intel from the CIA regarding Sisco's whereabouts. Robino provided the agency with updates on the Chinese's failed efforts and the analysts at Langley were filling in the blanks. Black now knew that Sisco travelled down the Italian coast. Satellite and drone footage IDed the craft and tracked it to the Marina Porto Romano. *Strange*, he thought. *Why would the prey return to the predator's lair?* No matter, the noose was closing. Sisco's time was running out! By the time he and his team docked at the harbor, the gurus in Virginia would significantly narrow down the search perimeter and the real fun would begin, but the outcome was certain.

While Sisco was not a formal member of Whiplash, Clausen briefed him on its existence and purpose when President Holbrook left office. It was clear that the Admiral imagined a scenario when Mac might need to be engaged if WL was activated. As he read the latest email from Robert Worthington, it appeared that time was now.

"To friends of Admiral James Clausen, the recent tragic death of NSA Director, Admiral James Clausen has prompted many to ask how they can honor his wonderful legacy and extraordinary service. The Admiral's family has requested me to convey that donations to your favorite veteran's organizations would be appreciated."

There it was again. Worthington's short note was a carefully camouflaged call to action to Sisco. The words, "wonderful legacy" repeated the "wl" code identifying that Whiplash was operational and that Mac needed to go dark and fast.

"What's the plan, Mac?" Joe asked when they met after receiving his urgent call to convene.

"We have been ordered by the Deputy Director, NSA, Gilbert Nicosia to stand down and report to the CIA Rome Station Chief immediately. I can't get into the details now, but we need to disappear quickly. I believe we are now officially the hunted, and our predator is the best in the world at it."

"Whoa, I thought we just did disappear," intoned Singe.

"Not good enough when the CIA is the pursuer and our own agency is providing support," Mac responded.

"So, what's next and what about searching for the truth about the Admiral's disappearance?" Snow asked.

"Nothing changes about that objective. It's the only way we can clear ourselves and expose the Faction. But to do that we must stay operational. We need to split up to reduce our visibility and disappear into Rome's background. Communicate only with burner phones. I will reconnoiter with you in six hours, and we'll get back on mission. Grab your gear and check out now. And everyone be careful and on the lookout for operatives. My guess is that they are already on their way here and not looking to take prisoners."

The Marina Hotel was Black's first target. Once on the property, the CIA team split up with one team securing the perimeter, a second locating and searching the Chris Craft and the third covering the hotel. The front desk identified four recent check ins who checked out after only a few hours. The US operatives fanned out searching all common areas but found nothing. The perimeter team reported no activity, but established that several hotel vans, taxis, and buses left the property in the last thirty minutes. Armed with photos of Sisco and his team, Black immediately deployed his agents to intercept those vehicles at their first destinations.

To avoid detection, Mac decided the safest way to exit the harbor area was on foot. Hotel transport services could easily be watched and certainly tracked. The marina was loaded with tourists browsing the shops and restaurants, making this option even more attractive. Peter and Joe boarded a train at the Via Trincea Delle

Frasche station, a twenty-minute walk from the hotel. Mac and Jasmine casually strolled along the seaside walkway among dozens of other couples enjoying the clear sea air and stunning views in their short trek to nearby Lido di Ostia, a charming local shopping area.

It looked like their emergency exfil worked, when Mac, scanning the surroundings, swore, "damn, we may have a problem."

Always the consummate professional, Jasmine knew better than to react and without turning, calmly asked, "what have you got?"

"Four big standard issue CIA SUVs rolling up to the hotel lobby entrance. Let's follow the group in front of us into that restaurant and grab a window table and see what's up."

"Do you think that's a good idea. I'm sure they will cover the perimeter and begin a search. I'd feel better putting some distance between us and them."

"I think it's too late for that. We need to blend in and know where they are. At least then we can respond. Besides, I think once they clear the hotel, they won't expect us to still be in the area."

"Well then cowboy, we better bloody well blend in and order a toddy and enjoy the local wine," she quipped and winked with a coy smile.

The restaurant was busy and the best they could do was a table towards the back with a view of the entrance and the front windows. While obstructed by patrons and servers moving about, they could still glimpse the activities around the eatery's entrance. By the time they finished their aperitifs, it seemed the whole episode might be a false alarm. But then, two men appeared on the sidewalk outside the restaurant, their heads methodically moving from side to side. As they came closer, Jasmine asked softly, "did you see that?"

"See what?" Mac answered concerned.

"One of those goons keeps glancing down at something in his hand. My guess is that he's checking out photos of us."

"Makes sense, Jas," he responded. "Not a good sign, to be sure."

"Bloody hell, Mac, one big dude is headed for this restaurant."

"I think it's time for you to visit the loo, Jas."

"What about you?" she asked concerned.

"I'll join the bar folks in the back for a pint and keep an eye on him."

The big man followed a small group in as Snow headed to the rest room and Mac retreated to the back of the bar. The man glanced down at his hands and then scanned the room as if looking for a table. The man continued to negotiate his way through the diners towards the rest rooms. Snow was waiting for the women's room to become unoccupied when she saw the man approaching and quickly entered the men's room. The man turned to leave, but stopped, looking back at the men's room quizzically. He approached the men's room door and tried the knob. It was locked.

He tapped lightly on the door and said, "management, please open the door." After another minute, he repeated his command with no result. He glanced back into the bar area and seeing no one paying any attention, slipped a credit card between the door frame and the lock. The door popped open, and he stepped in. The room was empty, and a gentle breeze was drifting in through a half open window out to the rear of the facility. The man rushed out of the room, and seeing a rear exit door, raced through it.

Mac witnessed all this activity and when the man exited the restaurant, he quickly followed. As his eyes adjusted to the glare of the bright sunshine, he saw the man ten meters away in an alley, his back to him looking left and right searching for Snow.

Sisco, pulled his tactical combat knife from its scabbard and moved forward. Only meters away, sensing him, the man suddenly swiveled around into a combat crouch in one fluid motion. He was a big man, at least 6'4" and about 240. He had strength, reach and size, but Mac had a 10-inch blade. It looked like and even match until the man smiled menacingly and pulled a 9 mm handgun from his belt. *Well, shit,* Mac thought, *never bring a knife to a gun fight.* He re-gripped his blade into a killing position and considered his options.

Pointing his weapon for a head shot the man aggressively motioned for Mac to drop the knife. Mac hesitated and then complied. Too much distance and bad odds. Go to plan B.

"Face down on the ground and spread your arms and legs," the man commanded. Mac began to lower himself while focusing intently on the man's eyes. As he pulled handcuffs from his belt, the man moved slightly forward, his eyes averted momentarily. Mac gathered a fistful of fine dirt in his right hand while he continued to lower himself to a kneeling position. As the man's focus returned to him, Mac exploded up and forward slinging the debris into his enemy's face. To avoid being blinded, the man ducked and turned his head shifting his aim off target causing the silenced 9 mm round to fly wide by mere inches. Mac's momentum carried him into the big man's midsection and his outstretched fist slammed into his solar plexus.

The big man's eyes fluttered as he careened backwards gasping for breath and crumpled to the ground. Wasting no time, Sisco wrapped his arms around his victim's neck and applied pressure. The man's struggles were short lived as his eyes fluttered, and he slumped to the ground. Mac jerked the cuffs from his clenched hand, rolled him over and secured his right hand behind his back to his left ankle. After retrieving his weapon from the ground, he dragged the unconscious man into the shadows of a dumpster behind the restaurant's exit.

Ripping material from his shirt, he balled it up and stuffed it in his mouth and methodically searched him. The man's identification indicated he was a State Department Attaché assigned to the US Embassy. In addition to the handgun, Mac retrieved a mobile phone and a small communications device. He inserted the earpiece in his own ear and listened.

What he heard was not good news. His prisoner's silence had already set off alarms and his partner was heading to the restaurant with more reinforcements on the way. Mac needed to disappear and fast, but where was Snow?

The comm device in his ear went live again, "female target has been spotted south of Marina Hotel travelling on foot in the main shopping area. Unit 3, close perimeter on that area." Mac pulled his burner phone and dialed Snow. A voice message responded.

"Mac, I've always liked your boots."

What the hell, he thought. It was clearly a message, but what did it mean. He backtracked to a small square adjacent to the main boulevard. No bad guys were visible, so he cautiously moved forward. He saw a nearby store directory and scanned the list. Italian was not his strongest language, but he could get along. At first, he didn't notice it, and then he smiled. Near the bottom of the list of shops was the word struzzo, the Italian word for Ostrich which just happened to be the leather in his cowboy boots. That shop was just around the corner and that was where Snow would be.

He found her in a changing room near the back, donning a new outfit and lacing up running shoes with her hair gathered up under a leather ball cap. It was a sensible move given her exposure. Her relief at seeing him was palpable as she threw her arms around him with a sob.

"Bloody Hell, Mac, that was close. That big SOB was on to me for sure. I had to boogie out of there. I didn't mean to abandon you. I'm so glad you made it. Sorry to be so bloody cryptic, but I couldn't be sure your phone was not compromised," she apologized.

"Are you kidding, it was brilliant," he complimented. "Now let's get the hell out of here!"

As they were leaving, Mac received another broadcast in the earpiece, "female has not been located. All units change to alt frequency to avoid unauthorized intercept."

"Well, there goes our party line," Mac said.

"So how do we breach their perimeter?"

"Maybe we don't have to. When they spotted you, they tightened everything up and this shop is near the end of the line, so we may already be outside it."

After carefully maneuvering from cover to cover, they reached Lido di Ostia and boarded a bus to Rome. During the short ride into the city, Snow secured a secluded rental unit for the team to use as a safe house during their search for the Admiral.

Bruce Black was fuming! What a shit storm. By the time his agent was discovered in the ally he had all but exhausted the search. Sisco was again in the wind and Black had learned nothing. He knew that picking up Sisco's trail was now much more problematic, but there were other ways to make the kill. If you couldn't chase down the prey, get it to come to you. It was time to implement the waterhole strategy. He just needed the right bait.

The mini reunion was brief as they sat in the courtyard of the Buonanotte Garibaldi B&B in Rome's historic Trastevere district. It was centrally located and with only three rooms available, they booked the entire property. Mac inspected the CIA agent's mobile phone and creds. It was a burner phone designed for quick access with no encryption and only contained limited data. There was a calendar with references to the last two weeks of assignments. It indicated that two days before Clausen's arrival in Rome, an op had been launched under the name of "Brass Hat." On the day of the Admiral's death there were two entries. The first was "initiate meltdown". The second said "Black's op". The next entry was the following day and stated "Re-target". The final entry was listed on today's date and said "S&D".

Mac leaned back in his chair after reviewing the phone's content with the team and asked, "reactions?"

"Well, considering the timing, it certainly appears that the local CIA station was tasked with engaging the Admiral," answered Snow.

"Yep, my thoughts too," agreed Franklin.

"It fits with the "Brass Hat" entry alluding to the Admiral's rank. And "meltdown" describes the condition of his vehicle and the cause of his death," commented Singe somberly.

"I'll make it unanimous on all your conclusions, but the "Black's op" entry is an enigma. It's almost as if it was mis-entered. It should be "Black op" not "Black's op," Mac suggested.

"Strange indeed," responded Snow. "But the last two entries seem pretty straight forward,"

"True, I'm pretty sure the target is us," Singe concluded.

"Yeh, and S&D is fairly standard craft jargon for search and destroy," Franklin added.

"Ok, so the only mystery is the "Black's op" entry, Mac said. But, putting that aside for now, what we know is that the CIA planned on interacting in some way with the Admiral the day after he arrived in Rome and now, he's dead. Then they planned to take us out."

"And destroy doesn't mean arrest either," cautioned Franklin frowning.

"If we're correct, the implication is that the CIA assassinated the Director of the NSA," Snow concluded.

"And, by eliminating us as the perpetrators, tie up a loose end," Singe agreed. "But what is the motive?"

"Let me take a crack at that question, Mac volunteered. "Clausen was a thorn in the new administration's authoritarian plans. He wouldn't roll over like the rest of the intel community. But that wasn't enough to take such risky measures. He was also driving our investigation into The Faction. And with Robino and maybe even the POTUS part of that conspiracy, the stakes are too high to leave anything to chance, especially the director of NSA snooping around."

"Well, I never run from a good fight, but this feels a lot like David and Goliath," Joe offered. "I think we're going to need some reinforcements."

"And where do we start?" Snow asked as they all turned to Mac.

"Only one option. Go up the chain of command and get them to expose themselves."

"And what about reinforcements? The whole world is looking for us," repeated Franklin.

"I have an idea about that, but it's a long shot, so let me do a little outreach before we get ahead of ourselves. In the meantime, let's see what we can learn about the local CIA station and the US Government resource presence here in Rome, so we know what we're up against."

CHAPTER TWENTY-NINE

ARK

Gunderson's invitation to Dubai was intriguing but somewhat worrisome. *What was in Dubai,* he thought. On the other hand, Seguro was in no hurry to stick around Italy. The journey from Elba back to Rome had been challenging, but he was rewarded when he boarded Gunderson's opulent $80M Gulfstream G700. The advanced private luxury jet had a 7,500-mile range and maximum Mach speed of 0.925. It was configured with a conference room, work out room, kitchen and 3 living areas. To say that this was overkill for the short hall 2,700 miles jaunt to Dubai was an understatement. Even at moderate thrust, the normal six-hour flight would be shaved by over an hour. But then time is money and for billionaires like Gunderson that meant every hour counted.

The big jet taxied to a private hanger at the Al Majlis VIP Pavilion and Executive Flight Terminal of the sprawling Dubai International Airport where Seguro was directed to a waiting limousine. After a thirty-minute drive along the Persian Gulf via the coastal Sheikh Zayad Rd/E11, they crossed over the three-hundred-meter bridge from the mainland to the spectacular man-made palm shaped island of Palm Jumeirah. Following the Palm's trunk to one of its fronds jutting out into the Persian Gulf, brought them to the lavish residence of Seguro's host.

Seguro, a wealthy man in his own right, was not easily impressed by opulence, but his jaw dropped as he gazed upon the enormous villa. The 10-bedroom beachfront mansion covered most of the manicured multi acre lot. The architecture was ultra-modern with marble facades and open living spaces tastefully positioned to merge with the natural beauty of the surrounding palms and gardens. On the gulf side, an all-glass elevator hugged the 3-story structure offering a panoramic view of both the magnificent city and the deep blue waters that surrounded Palm Jumeirah. When Seguro reached the covered entry way, Peter Gunderson appeared through the massive carved walnut door and smiling broadly said, "welcome to Dubai Phillip."

An hour later, having been shown to his accommodations to freshen up, Seguro joined Gunderson on an expansive veranda overlooking a private beach. It was dusk and a gentle breeze caressed the palms as the two men sipped their aperitifs and engaged in light conversation.

"I must ask you Peter; how do you maintain your anonymity living this way. There must be a dozen organizations looking for you?"

"Very carefully," Gunderson responded. "First, I maintain a very expensive security team at all times. They are always with me even if you don't see them. Also, I have a new identity. I am not Peter Gunderson to the world anymore. And finally, even more important, I have invested wisely in supporting those who support me. It's an invisible web of global influence that serves to protect me and my interests. It's one of the benefits you will gain by partnering with me. It will ensure your security and allow you to live and move freely."

"Impressive," Seguro commented.

"Yes, it is indeed. But that is not the best insurance I built to gain control of my destiny," the billionaire continued. "The real guarantee is buried in a series of super servers in my HQ building downtown. It is the leverage I will use to break the Chinese and American global stranglehold, acquire control of the Faction, and set the world on a path that I define."

"I'm all ears, Peter, but even with all your wealth and resources, I'm skeptical that you can launch any initiative that could accomplish such an objective."

"Oh, ye of little faith," Gunderson smiled.

"Well, I told you I needed proof," Seguro responded seriously.

"And you shall have it," Gunderson shot back. "I will give you the Cliff Notes version tonight over dinner and tomorrow, I will allow you the privilege of witnessing it firsthand."

"Excellent," his guest replied enthusiastically.

◆

Mac spent the evening developing an intricate series of emails to Robert Worthington to establish secure communications. When it came to NSA, even burner phones could be traced. Fortunately, Worthington knew all the traps and laid out an impenetrable scheme. The brilliant Cyber chief provided a cascading cipher methodology that parsed words across several platforms as spam, but which could be decoded with the appropriate key and sent via a virtual private network (VPN) to avoid detection. Using Worthington's role of organizing donations in memory of the Admiral as cover, Mac made contributions to several veteran's organizations on behalf of the fallen director. The first note included a biblical quote that Worthington would recognize as the source key of a one-time-pad for decoding the subsequent commemorations.

They met in the courtyard as the early morning dew was still glistening on the rose bushes along the limestone wall encircling the back yard. Everyone looked expectantly to their leader when he joined them, a steaming cup of thick Italian ristretto coffee in one hand and his PC in the other.

"I hope everyone got some sleep. We have a lot to deconstruct today, but things are looking up. I managed to connect with a resource at the agency and we now have a secure line and an advocate on the inside. This individual is a member of a small group of patriots who organized during the last administration to intervene during global upheavals to help secure peace and freedom in the world. They are now active and already investigating Admiral Clausen's death. They have some evidence that our own CIA may have been involved and sent me the details."

"Based on yesterday's close call and the ID you lifted off the perp, that's a righteous theory," Franklin said.

"I agree and they provided some additional information that just about clinches it," Mac continued.

"Really? Shoot," asked Snow urgently.

"Well, the operative that runs most of the CIA ops in Rome is a senior agent named Bruce Black."

"OK, the name sure fits the crime, but where's the connection" Singe chimed in.

"Remember the calendar and the one entry that didn't make sense? It was "Black's op"."

"Well Bloody Hell, now it sure makes sense," Jasmine replied.

"That SOB Black took out the Admiral. We need to take that Bastard down," Franklin fired back.

"Joe, I feel the same way, but first we need to squeeze Black and go up the chain from there and get hard evidence. And, based on what we know about the Faction, all roads lead to Frank Robino," Mac concluded.

♦

Prime Tower was conveniently located just north of Business Bay in downtown Dubai. Gunderson purchased four floors of the spectacular thirty-six floor skyscraper over a decade before when he founded Granite Noir which now was among the top three investment firms in the world. The two men entered the express elevator and rose quickly to GN's thirtieth floor lobby where they were greeted warmly by the receptionist and escorted to an adjoining lobby. Passing a security check point, they entered a private elevator and rose two more levels to ARK, Gunderson's flag ship technology company.

"Good morning, Sir. The team is awaiting your arrival in the conference room," the receptionist greeted as they exited the lift.

"Excellent," Gunderson replied, striding to a dark mahogany door ornately carved with ARK's name and logo.

Once seated, Gunderson wasted no time in introducing his executive team and reviewed the agenda.

"Gentlemen, as you know, Mr. Seguro and I are in the process of establishing an important strategic partnership. Today, our objective is to provide him with a general update on ARK, its genesis, capabilities, and current operational status. I have allotted two hours for that activity including Q&A. Our discussions should be open and transparent, but details classified as "ARK Proprietary" will not be shared unless I approve. I will open the discussion with a brief overview, after which each of you will provide insight into your specific functional areas. Are we clear on our guidelines?" Everyone nodded in acknowledgement.

"Good." Gunderson responded and continued. "Phillip, ARK is the acronym for Artificial Resource Kinetics which I founded over a decade ago. Since then, it has focused entirely on the technologies that support the development of Artificial Intelligence with the objective of creating a manageable sentient intellect. Because of our intense focus and enormous investment over the years in this endeavor, we are now standing on the precipice of man's greatest achievement years ahead of all others. Suffice it to say that our accomplishment has enormous implications for all mankind!" Gunderson announced with obvious pride.

Following their morning meeting, as the two men finished their lunch in ARK's executive dining room overlooking the grandeur that was Dubai City, Seguro asked, "Peter, I have to say, this is all very impressive. The creation of a sentient entity that achieves AI Singularity and can be controlled is brilliant. The popular view today appears to be that such an accomplishment is decades away, if possible, at all."

"Indeed, it is, and you are quite correct about the state of the industry," Gunderson smiled. "So, are you ready to proceed with our arrangement?

"Yes, I am, but I need to understand one other detail," Seguro pressed.

"And that is?"

"What is your strategy? How are you going to use ARK to control the Faction and neutralize your enemies? You didn't cover that in this morning's briefing."

"That is correct because I have only shared that strategy with a very select group of highly trusted "need to know" individuals. That said, our partnership is a critical element of my overall plan, so I will share it with you now confident that you will be more than satisfied," Gunderson said seriously, leaning forward for emphasis.

"My approach is actually, remarkably simple really, but subtle. Everyone is fearful that AI will ultimately manifest itself in robotics and physical engagement with humanity. This feared "Terminator" scenario is not only years out, but very unlikely. The reality is that the greatest threat of AI is already germinating today."

"What do you mean?" Seguro asked confused.

"Patience Phillip. Ironically, the earliest implementations of AI are the easiest to execute, but among the most difficult to control. In fact, they are already quite plentiful even in these early stages of development. What few appreciate is that AI's greatest value and most serious threat is gaining control of humanity's information."

"I can see the value, but how specifically is this capability a threat?" Seguro pressed.

"Ah, and here is the subtlety, Phillip. With enough data, AI will become the world's de facto authority on defining what is true and what is false, what is real and what is fake. In essence, it will define truth for all mankind. To put a fine point on it, it will shape reality. That means whoever has the most prolific AI will control every aspect of the human experience! And that will be us, Phillip," Gunderson continued almost in a whisper. There was silence as Seguro pondered Peter Gunderson's astonishing claims.

Finally, he cleared his throat and offered, "Peter, I see but one flaw in your plan. How can you be sure that ARK will emerge as the pre-eminent truth sayer or that people will look to it for answers?"

"A fair question. There are three reasons why this is inevitable. First, society is so overwhelmed by misinformation, there is a desperate desire for the truth. Second, ARK has access to more information than any other technology and will ultimately achieve a virtual monopoly of data and is years ahead on data scraping and archival. And finally, there is no real competition. Even the most advanced search engines currently on the market can't compete once we release ARK."

"How close are you to launch ARK?" Seguro pressed.

"We have completed all initial global data collection and beta testing including our control modalities.

"What does that mean?" Seguro asked.

"It means, we are ready to launch now! So, Phillip, I trust you are ready to commit?"

"Yes, Peter, I am convinced, but why do you need me?"

"Your camo project provides an immediate example of our power and the serious threat we represent. It's first deployment will be a catalyst to ARK's launch and serve to authenticate its credibility. It also represents a significant weapon if we are threatened."

"I see," Seguro answered nodding. "I'm also anxious to understand how we take control of the Faction."

"Gunderson smiled raising his glass. "That may be the most gratifying conversation we will have all day."

CHAPTER THIRTY

INSIDE JOB

Gilbert Nicosia, Deputy Director, National Security Agency was not going to squander his rare opportunity to serve as Acting Director of the agency. Admiral James Clausen's selection by the last administration to head up NSA was a bitter pill to swallow, but he intended to rectify that colossal error. He carefully cultivated his relationship with the current president and his staff and planned to ensure his appointment would be permanent.

Nicosia knew that advancement in big government was all about developing loyal networks of people you could trust. His first act after receiving word of Clausen's untimely demise was to identify all the Admiral's confidants and instruct his own network to report any questionable activity. He received a few calls from overzealous subordinates which turned out to be unfounded, but the information he just received might be the real deal.

According to his informant, the head of Cyber Operations and Technology, Robert Worthington was organizing a tribute to the deceased admiral with donations to veteran's organizations. On the surface, such an effort was entirely reasonable and unremarkable. But the "tell" was that the communications seemed incongruous. There were too many messages, and their content was inconsistent. Furthermore, Worthington was personally handling them all, not delegating them to his EA or anyone else. Using the excuse of his transition to Acting Director, Nicosia ordered a security audit of several departments including Worthington's. The results only deepened his concern. After intercepting and analyzing the donor responses to Worthington's solicitations, many of them were uncharacteristically shrouded behind VPN networks, making identifying their IP addresses impossible.

Where there's smoke, there's fire so Nicosia pressed on, intensifying his investigation. In an unprecedented move, he ordered Worthington's mobile, home and work phones tapped and ordered him placed under clandestine surveillance twenty-four hours per day. Finally, he caught a break when one of his people strong armed a VPN provider to surrender proprietary information that identified IP addresses and locations for all Worthington's messages. The findings were irrefutable. Almost all the donor messages came from the same device located in Rome, Italy.

Nicosia smiled and hit the secure line to his EA. "Get me Frank Robino on the phone immediately."

The G20 was over and POTUS was already returning home on Airforce One. But before heading back to D.C, Robino elected to stay in Rome for a couple more days to meet with some NATO members. He also needed more time with Ban to wrap up the Seguro affair. Nicosia's call had been a welcome interruption and he ordered him to share the intel with Phil Van Meter, his CIA counterpart.

After the debacle at the marina, Black wasted no time implementing his strategy to snare Sisco. He carefully leaked a classified report to all US intelligence agencies that Clausen was found alive and was currently in a CIA safe house in Rome for his own protection. Black figured that Sisco would get the word and attempt to connect with Clausen. Black deployed his team around the safe house and waited. Now, with the trap set, it was just a matter of time.

Sisco re-read the de-coded message from Worthington in dismay. Inter-agency intel had confirmed that Clausen was alive at a

CIA safehouse which the NSA cyber chief had located only a few miles away. It was wonderful news, or was it? He grabbed his coffee and joined the team in the garden and relayed the news.

"What do you think," he asked the group.

"I think it's bullshit," Franklin almost shouted.

"Me too," answered Singe.

"Unfortunately, I have to agree, as well," said Snow. It's just too pat. Why not fly him home with a security detail? Quite a coincidence right after they screwed up our capture, wouldn't you say? It's clearly a trap."

"I agree. I wish the Admiral were alive, but I highly doubt that. Nonetheless, we don't know for sure, so we must check this out. That said, we go in expecting this to be a CIA ploy and operate accordingly. Jasmine and I will take the B&B rental car and reconnoiter the safe house and report back. If we can't verify the intel, it's likely that he is not alive and this whole gig is a setup to draw us out. Jas, gear up! Joe, you, and Peter need to be heads up. These guys are pulling out all the stops."

So far Black's team observed no activity around the safe house and if this ploy didn't work, they would have no leads on the rogue agent's whereabouts. He was pacing his office in frustration when the call came in from Langley with the new intel on Sisco's location. *Well shit*, he thought, he finally caught a break. Now he had two shots at taking down this traitor and his cronies. But he had to move quickly.

He grabbed his comm unit and broadcast, "safehouse team, maintain surveillance with a couple agents. The rest of the team meet me at the Buonanotte Garibaldi B&B in Rome's historic Trastevere district ASAP. Approach with extreme caution. Lethal force is authorized."

They parked the Fiat several blocks from a residential area just north of the Tiber River and made their way on foot. The pedestrian traffic was heavy as they approached a series of two-story stone and brick apartments joined together on both sides of a narrow cobble stone side street. Outside dining, shops and boutique hotels added to the quaint ambiance and allure of the neighborhood. Parked cars crammed the street almost blocking the sidewalks and occasional crisscrossing alleys allowed access to backyard gardens and patios and other undiscovered attractions. Brightly colored house numbers were painted in stylish script matching the palettes of colored exteriors adorning the residences.

"There's the safehouse, about thirty meters away across the street," Mac said to Snow in a low voice.

"Got it," she acknowledged.

"You take the closest alley and check out the back. I'll continue down the street to one of the hotels and try to get a second story view. Let's status each other in ten minutes."

She nodded and peeled off across the lane, disappearing into the shadows of the alley. Mac continued, stopping at shop windows and gazing casually at the surroundings until entering the lobby of a nearby three-story boutique hotel. He took the lobby elevator to the top floor and moved to a large window overlooking the avenue. He could clearly see the safe house from his vantage and observed no unusual activities near its entrance. The narrow structure was two stories with a balcony extending from its second floor. Drapes slightly open at the center provided privacy to the interior. He moved closer to the window and pulled out a small monocular. The interior was dark, but a sliver of sunlight provided some visibility to the interior. He zoomed in but was unrewarded. The earpiece came alive as Snow reported in.

"Mac, any action?"

"Nada, and I have a good view of the entrance and some of the second floor. How about you?"

"The same. There is a back door entrance, but there are not many people about. No suspicious activity."

"Let's hang for another five minutes and then move closer. I'll check back with you then."

"Copy," Jasmine answered.

Another scan of the busy avenue dead ended as Mac prepared to change tactics. He moved his attention one final time to the second floor and saw a brief break in the beam of sunlight. There it was again. Someone was moving across the light. Was it the Admiral or Black's operatives? He couldn't tell from here. He needed to get inside!

"Jasmine, we have action on the second floor. I'm going to see if I can get to the roof and drop down on the balcony. You move in through the lower back entrance for back up after I make my move."

"Roger that Mac."

He made his way up the avenue mingling with the throng of shoppers, crossed the street and entered another multi-story hotel that connected with the safehouse. The layout was similar, but lacked an elevator so he took stairs to the upper floors. He exited onto the flat roof of the three-story structure and lowered himself over the edge. Hanging from a railing, he dropped the three meters to the roof of the safe house. He knelt behind a low wall overlooking the avenue and directly above the second-floor balcony.

Over the din from the street, he overheard muffled voices directly below. He had no idea how many bad guys might be down there, but it was now or never.

"Jas, I'm going in. Give me five minutes and then make your move," he said into his comms and waited for the confirmation. There was no response.

"Jasmine, please confirm," Mac repeated urgently.

He was halfway over the edge when her reply came through and he froze.

"Five by Sisco, Snow out."

Jasmine would never respond like that. He pulled back up to the roof. What the hell was going on? Only one answer, they had her and forced her to reply. She was warning him! And he had a problem, he had lost the advantage of surprise and he didn't know squat about his enemy. He needed reinforcements. Time to bring in the cavalry.

"Joe and Peter, we have a situation. I think Jasmine's been taken. I need you guys to get over here pronto." There was no reply.

"Do you copy?" No answer. Oh, boy, talk about bad timing. Either the comms were down or his team was. Mac experienced some bad situations but this one was up there. The odds sucked, but he couldn't abandon Snow. He needed to create a diversion. *Ok, let's provide our own disinformation*, he thought as he keyed up his comms in response to Snow's last transmission.

"Coming in high in five," he acknowledged as he raced back to the adjacent roof. Taking a backdoor exit from the hotel, he scanned the ally. A few tourists speckled the narrow street as he made his way to the rear entrance of the safe house. The door was unlocked as if in invitation. Maybe just a slip up in their rush to lay a trap on the second floor. He moved silently into the interior; his tactical knife extended. Across a small kitchen a door was ajar, and he could see into a living area with a large picture window fronting the busy street. There was no sound or movement as he advanced to the doorway. Staying out of sight, he angled the ten-inch blade towards the opening and peered at its reflection. No one home on this floor. So far so good.

The stairway to the second floor ran along an interior wall and presented a new challenge. Old hardwood. Years of training and field experience kicked in as Mac positioned each alternate foot on the steps outside edges making his ascent soundless. At the landing he stopped again and listened. Barely audible voices came from the second door on the street side of the hallway.

"Anything, Josh?"

"Not yet. There's no unusual movement on the street or the rooftops."

"Maybe I should check out the area downstairs, in case he changed his mind or is screwing with us," the first voice responded.

"Negative, we know he's got to come to us, so stay in position. No matter where he enters, he will have to explode into the room, and we've got that handled."

At least two goons and maybe more outside he missed. Not particularly good odds. Maybe there was another way in, like an attic. His eyes wandered to the hallway ceiling. No access doors or panels. Damn, just some discoloration and cracks in the plaster where a few fire sprinklers had recently been installed. And there it was, a real diversion. He quickly made his way down the hall to the first doorway and entered it cautiously. A bathroom, perfect. A well-placed sprinkler head was positioned above the toilet. Mac tore a handful of paper from the holder on the wall and twisted it into a long rod, lit it with a field lighter and held it just below the sensor. Less than a minute passed and suddenly a strong spray of water began drenching him. He smiled and cracked the door waiting.

"What the hell," shouted the CIA operative stationed at the door to the hallway as the cascading water flooded the room.

"Shut that damn thing off, his partner yelled from the balcony."

"What about Sisco?"

If you see the bastard, shoot him, before he sets off the fire alarm and we get a visit from the locals!"

Mac watched as the agent moved purposely down the hall, a silenced Glock gripped firmly in his left hand. He quietly closed the bathroom door and waited, listening intently. Above the beating of the spraying water, the loud creaks of the old oak stairway resounded as the man scrambled downward. Sisco waited until he had cleared the last step before rounding the corner and moving down the stairs. He was close behind the man when he entered the kitchen searching for the fire alarm's master control and disappeared into an adjacent laundry room. Mac moved in for the ambush when the sprinklers abruptly shut off and the man emerged from the room.

Their mutual surprise was quickly replaced with the hardened tradecraft of highly trained operatives as they crouched into fighting postures. The man was larger than Mac and muscular, but moved smoothly in the tight quarters as they circled the room. Mac's blade was already extended as the man began reaching for his handgun. Sisco flipped his knife to his left hand to get a better angle and to divert his opponent's attention as he fumbled for the Glock. The parry caused just enough hesitation to allow Mac to grab the gun's barrel in his right hand twisting it upright as the agent's finger jerked the trigger. The silenced round made little noise as it rocketed skyward grazing the man's temple. Blood erupted from the graze, but only momentarily slowed his assailant. The handgun's recoil dislodged the weapon, but using his right fist, the man slammed down with enormous force on Mac's knife, catapulting it to the floor.

Sensing an advantage, he moved in quickly with a vicious kick to Sisco's knee cap. The thrust was high, but caught Mac's thigh with tremendous force, spinning him around and forcing his leg out from under him. The bloody water was like ice and he crashed to the hard tile floor, facedown and stunned. His attacker was on him in an instant, his fingers clawing for Mac's head. Mac knew the drill. One quick twist of his neck and it would be over. Without even thinking, he spread his arms out to attempt to right himself. A sharp pain shot up his arm as it brushed the razor-sharp edge of his tactical blade.

He grabbed for the hilt desperately as if it were the lifeline of a drowning sailor. He could feel the big man's hands gripping his skull. His next move was instinctive. He arched his back and thrust the big blade back over his head slashing downward into the man's neck and skull. The man shrieked with pain and his grip loosened. The second plunge was deeper into more vital arteries. The attacker suddenly went slack as if unplugged. It was over.

Mac grunted as he rolled the blood-soaked body off and struggled to his feet. His thigh was on fire, and he ached all over from the fall, but otherwise he was sound. He was lucky. What had seemed like eternity was just minutes. He bent down and retrieved his lifesaving blade and searched the man, retrieving his earpiece, Glock and ID and headed for the door.

Retreading his steps up the stairway, he headed down the hall. The bathroom door remained as he left it, and the second door was closed. The remaining guard would mistake Mac for his partner returning and be unprepared. Taking no chances, Mac drew his Sig nine mm and entered.

As the door swung open Mac swept the big gun back and forth while scanning the room. There was no one there! He went to the balcony and looked out parting the curtains slightly. Nothing.

Returning to the room, he heard a faint scratching coming from a dark alcove at the far end of the room where he found another door slightly ajar. Gun poised, he peered into the large closet where a body lay face down barely visible in the dim light.

Oh no, he was too late! As he rushed in, a familiar voice proclaimed, "Glad to see yah cowboy. I was getting worried I might have to save your silly ass again."

"Jasmine," he said in relief, as he turned and hugged her, "great to see you too. How the hell did you escape?"

"Well, I learned a lot from our last gig together in New Zealand. You remember the Gunderson team got loose from those zip ties in the van by snapping them hard. That's what I did when this CIA goon was busy guarding the door after the sprinklers went off. It hurt like Hell, but it worked."

"You are one hell of a student, Jas. I'm sure glad you're on my team. Now, let's get out of here before the fire department arrives. My guess is the alarm may have alerted them."

"Roger that, but at least we know the Admiral is not here, so mission accomplished on that intel."

"Yeh, but we may have a problem back at our safe house. I can't get through to Joe and Peter and I have a feeling Black may be involved."

CHAPTER THIRTY-ONE

THE PHOENIX

The Fiat slowed as it approached the Buonanotte Garibaldi B&B. The narrow alley offered little space for parking, but they pulled the small vehicle up on the sidewalk a block away and made the rest of the way on foot. Nothing seemed amiss as they approached the tall perimeter wall, unlocked the heavy wooden arched door, and entered the back garden. The coffee cups were on the table where they had met that morning. Snow touched Mac's arm in warning. She pulled him back into the shadows of a large fruit tree.

"Something is very wrong," she whispered. "Joe would have cleaned up our debris from this morning. He's a neat nick that way."

Mac nodded in agreement. "Follow my lead."

They hugged the wall as they moved to the rear entrance. Snow held back to cover Mac as he entered and waited for his "all clear" signal. After several minutes, with growing concern, she advanced, weapon drawn and entered a small mud room off the entrance to the living room. She hung back and listened for any sign of activity. The silence was eerie. Too quiet, she thought.

Then behind her Mac whispered, "Jas, they've got the boys and are expecting us. There are too many of them. We need to re-group." They silently backtracked to the alley and retreated around the corner. A large van was parked ten meters away. The vehicle was unmarked with a series of antennas and cameras mounted on its roof.

"Bingo," Mac said, nodding at the van. "There's our ticket to the party. See if you can infiltrate when I create a diversion."

"Let me do that, I'm a better distraction and less of a threat."

"Good point," he winked and nodded as she moved out into the street. Mac watched as the mobile camera rotated following her progress and as she came abreast of the van, he made his move. Just as Snow disappeared around the front of the vehicle, a large man jumped from a side door, grabbing her from behind and jerked her backwards. Mac was still five meters away, raising his sig to fire a head shot when the man suddenly careened sideways and dropped to the street. Regaining her balance, Snow dove into the van for cover. Mac followed suit as she slammed the door closed.

"What the hell happened? Did you take that shot?" she yelled.

"Negative," Mac responded as he scanned the area through the door's window.

"Then we have a sniper."

"Agreed. The question is who is shooting and who is the target?" he confirmed.

"Now what?"

"Keep a look out while I check out these electronics." Multiple touch screens provided different views of the area surrounding the van and a communications console was positioned on one side. Suddenly a voice came over a speaker in the panel.

"Mobile 1 to base, any action out there?"

"Repeat, Mobile 1 to base, any signs of perps?"

Mac picked up the mike and flicking the transmit key on and off responded, "base to mobile 1, negative, but having comm issues."

"Ok, stay alert and check in every fifteen minutes."

"Mac we are stymied. We can't stay here, and we can't leave. This is a bloody Catch-22."

"Maybe not. But despite the action, I don't think we can assume that our shooter is a friend, so we must move the van to a new location. That may expose our sniper and confuse our opponents. Also, we can justify it to improve our mobile reception."

"Good thinking, but what then?"

"Then we draw them out," Mac said.

After retrieving the guard's body, Mac started up the van and slowly pulled out into the street, rounded the corner, and parked the van on the sidewalk across the alley from the rear of the rental property. After ten minutes and still no sign of a shooter, Mac once again picked up the microphone.

"Base to mobile 1, under attack at rear of residence, sniper fire, need assistance!" Without waiting for a reply, they jumped out of the van, pushing the dead guard's body out the door and sprinted to cover behind a low wall across the narrow lane. Two men emerged from the residence in a low run. They zig zagged from cover to cover as they raced to the van.

"Now's our chance Jasmine," Mac commanded and headed for the back entrance. This time they separated with Snow circumventing the property to enter the front now that the van was neutralized. Mac moved quickly to the main dining room where he had observed his captured teammates. Franklin and Singe sat stiffly at the dinner table; their mouths gagged, and their hands secured behind their backs. Two men stood behind them, their backs to him, assault weapons cradled in their arms. A third man of medium build, short black hair and piercing blue eyes leaned against the wall across the room engaged in an animated discussion on an earpiece communicator. Presumably, this was Bruce Black, the ringleader. This time the odds were better, and he had the advantage of surprise.

Black terminated his conversation and left the room heading to the front of the rental. *Oh no*, Mac thought, he was headed towards

Jasmine. No time to warn her. No telling when the agents outside would return. He had to free his team while he had the chance.

Mac stepped out into the room and announced, "if you move you will be shot. Do not turn around. Place all your weapons on the floor. Take three steps backward and lie down on the floor face down with your hands behind your backs. One of the guards made the mistake of jerking around with his weapon and was rewarded with a carefully placed slug in his upper thigh. He went down screaming, blood oozing from the planned non-lethal shot. Sisco kicked their weapons clear, bound their wrists with zip ties, then he freed his two teammates.

"Great to see you guys alive and well," he said.

"Just in the nick of time, Black was losing his patience" Franklin exclaimed grabbing one of the agent's weapons.

"Ditto, for sure," Singe agreed claiming the other assault weapon.

"Where is Jasmine?" Joe asked concerned.

"Right here," came a male voice from across the room. They all turned to see Bruce Black emerge with a government issued Glock 30 forty-five caliber handgun pressed tightly against Jasmine's temple. He was followed by the two agents who investigated the van, their weapons trained at Mac and Joe.

"I highly recommend all of you discard your hardware immediately or Ms. Snow will be re-arranged across this room and each of you will follow her example," Black growled.

Once everyone was disarmed and secured, Black continued, "Well, it looks like we've finally got the whole team," he said grinning.

"And now that everyone is comfortable, let me introduce myself. My name is Bruce Black. I am the Senior CIA Special Agent here in Rome. The other gentlemen here are part of my special operations team. We were assigned by the Director, CIA to arrest and detain you for the murder of Admiral James Clausen, Director, NSA and for committing treasonous acts against the United States of America. We will be interrogating each of you individually to fill in the blanks, but let me be clear, we already have all the evidence we need to prosecute you and if necessary, carry out sentencing and of course, you all know the penalty for treason."

Black nodded to his guards and said, "we'll start with the woman."

"Wait," Mac demanded. "We have a constitutional right to representation before any proceedings."

Black turned, glaring at Sisco. "Ah, Mr. Sisco, the famous NSA phenomenon," he jibed sarcastically, "not here you don't!" Black nodded to one of the guards, "take her to the van. I will join you as soon as I update HQ on our successful apprehensions. Two of you keep an eye on our friends and one of you help Agent Stone to the kitchen and treat his wound. This shouldn't take long, and I'll be back for our next volunteer."

The three NSA agents watched helplessly as their teammate was manhandled from the room.

"Not to worry gents, piece of bloody cake," she yelled back in protest.

"Well lads, we seem to be up shits creek without a paddle," Joe proclaimed.

"It is looking a bit bleak," Peter agreed.

"Keep the faith boys," Mac offered. "You never know what the future will bring."

"Does that mean you have a plan, Cap?" Joe asked.

"I'm working on it and it's a doozy," Mac joked.

The nearest guard lashed out with the butt of his AR, striking Mac painfully in the mid-section.

"Shut your trap Sisco or I'll finish you with the other end," he snarled as he flipped the weapon around, its barrel inches from Mac's head.

Then, like a puppet with its strings cut, his legs buckled as he collapsed writhing on the floor, a taser protruding from his back. The remaining guard spun around in surprise; his eyes wide as he searched for the threat. A second taser flew out of the darkness of the garden entrance impaling him as he mimicked his colleague and crumpled face down on the ceramic tile.

"What the Hell?" Joe said, bewildered, straining his head to scan the room. As the three captives stared in disbelief, Jasmine Snow strode into the room the taser gun hanging loosely from her right hand.

"I told you it was a piece of bloody cake didn't I," she bragged.

"Never a doubt, Jas," Mac praised.

"But how did you get free?" Peter asked incredulously.

"Well, I did have a little help," she said turning and looking to the other entrance as a second figure emerged from the gloom.

"Yes, you never know what the future will bring," proclaimed Admiral James Clausen stepping out of the shadows, the second taser in one hand and an H&K P30 in the other. "I'll explain it all, but first we need to secure these rogue agents and find Black."

Thirty minutes later, the five CIA operatives were handcuffed and gagged in a locked utility room. The rental property was searched thoroughly, but Black was in the wind. Now reunited, Mac and his team sat down with Clausen to replay the last week. The Admiral began the debrief.

"We need to vacate here, but I'll take ten minutes to bring you up to speed on the salient points. I was on my way to meet with

POTUS and Robino when a specially developed NSA bomb detection device I installed in my rental car alerted me to an imminent detonation. I pulled over to the side of the road and read the display, *detonation timer - 3min 22 sec.*

"Just ahead I saw a construction area with building materials stacked, but no workers on site that early in the morning. The timer was at 2 min 45 sec. as I pulled into the lot and turned off the car. I retrieved my diplomatic pouch and made my way quickly toward a series of buildings some distance from the construction site. At that point, the sniffer showed 1 min 10 sec.

"I retreated for another 45 seconds and moved behind the corner of a large building. The area was still clear of pedestrians and some cars were approaching, but still at a distance. As the timer hit zero, an enormous explosion erupted with a huge ball of fire shooting skyward from where the rental car had been.

"I have seen this kind of fire before. It was thermite. At 2,200 degrees it would melt metal, ceramics and almost anything else. There would be no evidence, no clues no anything left to identify. It's classic CIA tradecraft," he finished grimly.

CHAPTER THIRTY-TWO

DOUBLE CROSS

Robino had no choice but to delay Airforce 2 after receiving the frantic call from Ban. The Faction leader received a cryptic note from Peter Gunderson that the Seguro deal collapsed amid a bidding war and that they needed to video conference that day to resolve the situation. He and Ban now sat together in Ban's suite, staring at a blank monitor awaiting the secure connection.

Robino sipped his straight whiskey and said, "Genjo, I have a bad feeling about this. Gunderson has been too coy in his dealings with Seguro. I don't trust him."

"I must agree, Frank," Ban responded. "Especially, now that it appears a third party is involved. But who else could possibly compete with China and the US?"

"The answer to that is no one. Asia and the EU are in our camp and N. Korea, Russia and Iran and their proxies are in yours. Who the Hell else could play in this game? The rest are bit players. My guess is that this is a scam to raise the stakes and I wouldn't be surprised if Gunderson is pulling the strings."

"I guess we're about to find out," Ban commented as the screen flickered and Gunderson appeared on the screen.

"Gentlemen, thank you for joining me on this urgent call and I apologize in advance for any inconvenience," Gunderson said.

"What the Hell is going on Gunderson? I thought this was a done deal?" Robino fired back.

"So did I Frank, but several other competitive bids came in. I managed to reject all but one, which Seguro will accept unless you can better it."

"What is the bid and who offered it?" Ban insisted.

"I cannot divulge the bidder, but as we agreed, if you meet the same terms, Camo is yours." Gunderson offered.

"You can't or you won't," demanded Robino.

"Actually, Frank, I can't. It's a blind bid. The bidder's identity is shrouded, but we have been able to verify the party's credentials and they are solid."

"That's ludicrous Gunderson. Seguro is just playing us to get a better deal. I am done with this bullshit," Robino raged.

"Frank, I agree, but let's at least hear what the terms are," Ban interjected desperately. "Go ahead Peter."

"The terms are the same as your final bid with one exception. The bidder guaranteed to Seguro that the Faction will report to its organization, ensuring Seguro's security, and he will have a significant position in it."

The two men sat stunned, unable to respond as they attempted to process this information.

Finally, Robino regained his composure and said, "Gunderson are you mad? There is no scenario on earth in which the US or China would make such a concession and no third party could compel us to agree to that demand."

"Frank is correct. You of all people should know that!" Ban interjected emphatically. "The whole objective of the Faction is to achieve worldwide control. My chairman would never concede that control to anyone else."

"I understand your frustrations, gentlemen," Gunderson replied, "I made the same rebuttal, but this organization claimed that it has the means to persuade the Faction to agree to this arrangement."

"Preposterous," Robino roared. "Now, I know you have lost it Gunderson. You realize that they are threatening the world's two largest superpowers. Bring it on!"

"I know it looks ridiculous but remember that Camo will be one of its weapons and I was told that there are other much more devastating technologies at their disposal to convince you, your leaders and the Faction if you refuse."

"Gunderson, this call is over, and you can relay our unequivocable rejection of this offer along with our own warning to Seguro and these crackpots. Any action against us will result in total annihilation" concluded Robino angrily. "Oh and by the way, unless Seguro comes around fast, he will be the first to go up in flames!"

"I must also add," Ban said, "your membership in the Faction is now suspended pending an appropriate resolution to this matter."

"You have twenty-four hours Gunderson, and the clock is ticking and after that, we are coming after you and Seguro," Robino concluded as he shut down the connection.

"Well, that went well," Seguro exclaimed with a concerned expression.

"Actually Phillip, it went exactly as I anticipated," Gunderson said, smiling. "They suspect that you and I are colluding of course, but they will burn significant cycles attempting to formulate a defense if they even get that far. In the meantime, we will launch a Camo assault that will get their attention. A warning shot as it were."

"But Peter, we haven't completed the final trial on DNA targeting with camo yet."

"No worries, Phillip, based on our agreement and your prior authorization to your team, I planned a new trial which is already underway."

"What if they won't comply?"

"Then we initiate ARK in a very targeted attack at their most sensitive vulnerabilities. I can assure you that they will succumb," Gunderson declared. "So, tempus fugit Phillip, let's get busy."

◆

The timing was critical, but the chemistry was precise and just after ten pm Rome time the first reports filtered up to Ban. Chun Huang, CEO, Jiànkāng Corp. and one of China's Faction members collapsed at a dinner with colleagues and was in intensive care at Gemelli Hospital in Rome. Thirty minutes later, a Chinese diplomat was mysteriously stricken and passed out, after returning home from the G20.

At that point, no alarm bells went off. But by midnight Robino's mobile jerked him out of a fitful sleep on his last night in the "Eternal City".

"Robino," he answered his assistant in a gravelly, irritated voice.

"I am so sorry to wake you Sir, but we have a situation!"

An hour later, Chinese officials were dealing with an inexplicable medical emergency. A dozen people from China had succumbed to an unknown medical condition. At first the victims were all in Rome, but as the hours passed more Chinese, from other locations around the world became ill. It was suspected that a virus was the culprit since the symptoms were identical, but none of them had interacted with each other. Furthermore, only Chinese had been afflicted.

The theories were rampant and despite the best efforts to manage the outcry, the panic went viral. And then the final shoe dropped. Exactly six hours after the onslaught of the collapses, each patient regained consciousness and quickly recovered. The doctors were baffled, and the public demanded answers.

"Do you think this is Seguro's doing, Frank?" Ban asked concerned.

"I don't know, Genjo, but without absolute verification, we can't blink. Even then, we cannot concede. You know that."

"Your right of course," Ban answered. "We have only one option, to find and eliminate both Gunderson and Seguro and get control of camo!"

"Agreed," Robino growled. "I will put Black on this right away."

"Let's make this a joint initiative Frank. Wupen has recovered and can coordinate with your agents. It will look better in the press that way and the more resources the better. We can't let this get out of control."

♦

Bruce Black was outside the front door on his mobile, waiting for his boss, Van Meter, to pick up when he heard voices coming from Jasmine's interrogation room.

"Well, I'll be damned," Snow said.

"Grab his weapon, Jasmine and secure him and let's round up the rest of these thugs," came the reply.

Who the Hell could that be, he thought. It didn't matter, they were obviously armed and there might be others. He couldn't take any chances. He hung up and moved along the side of the residence and away from the building. Taking up a position where he could observe the front entrance, he dialed his office.

"Get the duty officer!" he demanded. "I have an emergency and need immediate assistance."

After fifteen minutes, seeing no activity, Black made his way around the corner to the back entrance where his van was now parked. Still nothing. Then, he saw movement at the rear exit. Singe emerged, quickly scanned the area, crossed to the van, and backed it up to the rear door.

Black's mobile vibrated. "Agent Black, 15 minutes out, sitrep please," the voice demanded.

"Get here in ten or I'll have your ass and cordon off the block," Black snarled. Somehow, he had to tie these assholes up for just a few more minutes.

Now the van's rear doors were open, and he could make out the movement of people loading. He needed to risk engagement to slow them down. Black pulled his Glock and aiming at the rear doors, pulled off three rounds. It was a good fifty yards with insignificant drop, but it was still a long handgun shot. The suppressed rounds made little noise, but the impact with the CIA vehicle's bullet proof paneled doors resounded down the alley. The movement into the van stopped. Pressing the suppressor against the wall, he prepared to fire another round when a large fragment of brick exploded only a foot from his hands. He pulled back and dropped to the ground.

What the Hell, he thought, grimacing as blood oozed into his eyes from a fragment that had grazed his forehead. A second round crashed even closer as he retreated into the cover of the building. Pinned down, Black listened helplessly as the van's engines fired up and tires screeching, accelerated down the alley.

"Damn," he yelled out loud as he got to his feet in frustration. He hoped the CIA had met his challenge or heads would roll.

"Everyone OK?" Mac asked looking back from the front passenger seat.

"Affirmative, all copacetic back here," Joe reported.

"Yeh, thanks to our unknown sniper," Peter responded.

"I have a feeling that the Admiral has a few more rabbits to pull out of his hat," quipped Jasmine smiling.

"In good time, let's put some distance between us and the bad guys and get to the safehouse. This place will be swarming with CIA any minute," Clausen warned.

After an hour of complex twists and turns to avoid detection, they turned into a short cobblestone drive. The quaint villa, thirty km northeast of Rome was nestled on **Lake Bracciano, one of many** picturesque lakes in rural Italy and was selected by Clausen for its seclusion this time of year. After the trials of the day, the Admiral suggested a break for an hour before debriefing and strategy discussions.

The mood was tempered but emotional as the team reunited with a man, they all profoundly respected. He saved their bacon numerous times and seeing him alive again was a blessing. Finally, Clausen raised his hand and brought the meeting to order.

"I first want to thank Mac for his extraordinary leadership during this operation and each of you for your courage and initiative. This assignment was difficult enough, but without support from the agency and its resources, it is indeed miraculous that you all accomplished what you did. By exposing the Faction and its activities, you have uncovered what may be the greatest threat mankind has ever faced. But now we must complete the most difficult task, to take them down and neutralize them forever. How we go about that is further complicated by the fact that those opposing us are formidable American and Chinese assets."

"That is a tall order Sir, and we also have to contend with Gunderson," Mac offered.

"Yes, it is Mac, but we do have some capable allies that have joined the fight."

"I assume you are referring to Whiplash, Admiral."

"That is correct and thanks to you Mac, they are already engaged."

"What, pray tell is Whiplash?" Snow asked.

"Whiplash is a highly secret organization that was formed at the end of ex-President Holbrook's term to defend against global calamities that threaten humanity. Because of the extraordinary situation we face and your "need to know", I will share facts that are known by only a few people on the planet and which you are bound to total confidentiality" Clausen said gravely.

There was silence around the table as Clausen concluded his briefing.

"One final point, I have not disclosed the identity of specific members in WL because their freedom to act is dependent upon maintaining strict anonymity. Any questions?" he asked.

"Only the obvious one," Mac said, "What's the plan?"

CHAPTER THIRTY-THREE

THE HUNT

The illustrious Sun Tzu, one of China's greatest generals penned the phrase "keep your friends close and your enemies closer". For the two men now facing each other this truism was born of necessity. Bruce Black and Wupen Liang had their orders and no matter how uncomfortable the arrangement was, they knew their futures depended upon a successful outcome. No more failures would be tolerated. The mission was unequivocable; terminate Phillip Seguro and Peter Gunderson and bring back the IP on Camo. While the Sisco's rogue NSA operation was not the primary focus, he and his team were included in the kill orders if they were engaged.

Both US and Chinese intelligence agencies were collaborating on the operation using special compartmentalized resources under strict security protocols and reported directly to Frank Robino and Genjo Ban.

As the two men poured over the latest intelligence, Liang interrupted the silence.

"Black, I want to personally take out Seguro. Do you have a problem with that?"

"Not as long as I get Sisco," Black responded grimly. Liang nodded in agreement.

"And Gunderson?" Liang prompted.

"First come, first served," Black answered, smiling.

"What have you learned from de-briefing your team at Sisco's safe house?" Liang asked.

"Not much. None of the team saw their attackers. They were tased from behind and we have no leads on the sniper. The van is in the wind and by now could be anywhere. So, we don't know who was responsible. All in all, a complete CF!"

"What about you?" Black probed.

"Well, at first, we believed that Franklin was killed in the skirmish on Elbe Island, but based on your report, we know that is not true. However, I just received some tracking data on Seguro. We didn't spot it earlier because he used cash, but he used his passport ID to book a flight from Elbe Island to Leonardo da Vinci-Fiumicino Airport in Rome two days ago. Then the trail goes cold."

"Well, that means either he rented a car, took public transportation or flew out on a private jet," Black responded.

"I agree and have already directed my team to investigate each of those options."

"Good, I'll pass it on to our boys, too. Anything on Gunderson?"

"That's a different story. He's a ghost. That name or any associations are literally nonexistent. All his holdings have been shuttered, acquired under different ownership, or reorganized into shadow companies whose veil cannot be pierced."

"Figures," Black said. "He's been in the game a long time and he's still on the field."

While Liang remained in Rome to work with US intelligence, both Ban and Robino returned home. As Robino began his daily review of his staff's morning report, his secure text line buzzed indicating a message was pending. It was an undisclosed line and only a select group of critical government executives had access to it. Robino, opened the app and retrieved the message. *Strange*, he thought not recognizing the sender, "ARK". Robino felt a surge of panic as he read the mysterious missive.

From - major worldwide news organizations and social media platforms – To be published – 24 hours from this time stamp.

Headline - "US is responsible for recent infections of Chinese nationals with a mysterious illness".

Story brief – "Leaked information from verified, highly credible US government sources confirmed that the Chinese government acquired absolute proof that United States intelligence agencies in collaboration with the CDC are responsible for infecting Chinese targets with a recent mysterious illness. It was also reported that the alleged attacks are retaliations for China's aggressive activities in southeast Asia and its role in the fentanyl trade impacting America."

Robino stared at the message in disbelief. *No one would buy this BS, or would they,* he thought, his mind racing at the implications. The timing was horrific. With the G20 just concluding and the US and Chinese leaders meeting in closed sessions, the inferences could be devastating. His secure line jerked him from his dread as Ban's caller ID appeared. The CCP executive was almost apoplectic as he shrieked into the phone.

"Frank, have you received this ARK message?"

"Yes, just now. It's got to be Gunderson."

"We can't let this happen; you know that!"

"I'm not sure we can stop it, Genjo," Robino answered, stoically.

"What, you can't be serious. It could cause a world war."

"Calm down Genjo. You said yourself that your president would never agree to their demands. We need to think this out."

"Yes, I know, but the risk is too great."

"Nonsense, Genjo. We simply blame this on terrorists and publish a joint statement that the whole thing is a fabrication. Who will the masses believe, us or them. Who controls the truth? Besides, we can use the Faction members to help us get the word out." Robino lectured.

"Well Frank, to be candid, I am not nearly as confident as you are in that premise. Neither our citizenry nor yours impress me with their trust in government."

The following morning at 9 am Washington, D.C. time, news wires around the world lit up with the headlines. Every major social media platform mimicked the story and began their viral chatter and panic began to flood the halls of governments from sea to sea. The UN Security Council called an emergency session to address the crisis and Chinese and American intelligence and diplomatic agencies launched into high gear. America's President, Frederick Singleton and China's President, Manchu Shing released a rare joint press announcement denying the validity of the story.

By 5 pm Washington time the rebuttal had circled the globe and the world waited for the crisis to pass. But a strange thing happened, the rumors continued and grew. Mistrust in the halls of governance fed the frenzy like bait fish in a sea of sharks. The story changed, gaining details, veracity, and pessimism like a dark cloud before a storm. Then the demonstrations began, first small and then growing and violent. Even when the conventional news coverage waned, the social media contagion continued unabated.

To contain the conflagration, governments began to censor platforms and organizations, only feeding the frenzy and mistrust. The world was in turmoil.

Gunderson and Seguro watched fascinated as the world melted down.

"Is this what you anticipated Peter?" Seguro asked as the two men enjoyed an afternoon cocktail.

"It's about what I expected," the older man answered. "I've been down this road before. I must say though that the response is somewhat more intense than I imagined."

"Does that mean you know how to manage it as well?" Seguro pressed.

"Pretty much, but it's tricky. It's all about establishing the credibility of truth. You must gain trust in the source. Since everyone is different and responses are infinite that is not possible for the human intellect to manage. But for ARK, it's child's play. And with the Faction's distribution and influence capabilities across the plethora of human needs, we have total control."

"So, what's next?"

"We offer one more opportunity to our friends to cave or we turn up the heat. The reality is that over time we can achieve our objectives without them, but it adds risk and time that we want to avoid."

The hunt was well underway, but neither Black and Liang nor Mac and his team could move on an invisible target. It had only been a few days, but Mac's team was getting antsy. The recent events only increased their sense of urgency. They knew the mysterious illness had to be camo driven, but they didn't know how the media crisis played into it. Clausen was in constant communication with WL members who were equally engaged.

They finished their morning coffee and laid out their plans for the day when Clausen appeared in the doorway, eyes red from little sleep.

"We may have caught a break," he said tiredly. "I've been up most of the night connecting with WL resources to triangulate intel. It appears that several sources, including some human intelligence indicate that Gunderson is involved with a company located in Dubai. My NSA resource collated significant data and checked it with additional information from two of our international WL members and arrived at a consensus. The company is Granite Noir. Fortunately, several years ago, one of our WL principles dealt with this firm and was considering a sizable investment in which Gunderson was engaged. It is well known as one of the world's largest investment companies, but until now we have never seen any relationship with Gunderson or his prior holdings. Furthermore, after a deep dive into this organization, we discovered that GN holds significant investments in a technology company called Artificial Resource Kinetics, known as ARK, also located in the UAE. I have recruited additional resources to help us check out this lead. They should be on location later today. Gear up, you leave for Dubai, in one hour. Mac, please join me and I will brief you on the op and you can share it with your team en route."

♦

Robert Worthington was on vacation to focus on Whiplash activities when Gilbert Nicosia, Deputy Director, NSA called him back to the agency to head up a cyber team for a top-secret, code word assignment. Worthington knew the off books initiative was driven by Robino and focused on locating Gunderson. Even though he had handpicked the few members for the team, he knew that feeding their findings to Clausen would be risky and must be undetectable. In the end, the best he could do was to delay his findings to Nicosia by several hours to give the Admiral a head start. Three hours after Worthington sent Clausen his intel, Black and Liang got the Gunderson scoop and prepared for their trip to the City of Gold. But even before Black's and

Liang's assault teams were airborne, Gunderson's final demand landed in their boss's inboxes.

"This is your final notice. You have 24 hours to comply, or another assault will be launched and will target the very foundations of your most valuable assets," ARK.

CHAPTER THIRTY-FOUR

CONVERGENCE

Clausen stayed behind at the safehouse to manage communications and coordination. It was wise to keep his survival a secret. It allowed him unfettered maneuverability. He was receiving constant updates from Whiplash members, synthesizing the intel and messaging Mac with updates. The latest was that the additional team members arrived at the safehouse in Dubai and were already hard at work. While they had not yet cracked the code of Gunderson's operations, they developed some reasonable scenarios. Based on Gunderson's association with ARK, they focused on his use of technology. But there were numerous disciplines to consider including nanotechnology, artificial intelligence, addictive digitalization, genetic targeting, and pathological amplifiers. It appeared likely they would have to breach ARK's facilities and firewalls to understand the threats.

On the 6-hour flight from Rome to Dubai Mac updated his team on the local sitrep and Clausen's evolving plan. From everything they knew, the CIA and other US intel organizations would be converging on Dubai. Based on China's involvement in the Faction, it was assumed they would also deploy resources there. But Gunderson was a brutal and effective adversary, and the fight was on his turf, so the outcome was by no means predetermined. No one understood Gunderson better than Mac and his team and while the big players wouldn't be focused on them, they all knew they were key targets as well.

"Mac what about these additional resources?" Franklin asked. "Who are they and what are their roles in all of this. To be honest, I get real nervous when we add unknown players into an op." Singe and Snow nodded in agreement.

"As well you should, Joe. That's why the Admiral selected folks that are no strangers. One of them has already contributed."

"Ok, I'll bite," said Franklin perplexed.

"I'll take a crack," Jasmine broke in. "Let's start with our mysterious sniper who saved our asses. There is only one person I have ever worked with that could make those shots, Victoria Bakman from Israel's Mossad."

"Good call Jasmine, she'll be joining us in Dubai," Mac confirmed.

"I'm feeling better already," Joe exclaimed.

"But it gets better," Mac continued. The rest of the Apogee team, Elaine, Carrie, and Pat will also be with us. In fact, they are already on station and working."

"Fantastic!" Singe said, smiling broadly. "It's a brilliant decision and I imagine pretty tough to execute on such short notice."

"I have a feeling that someone on this jet had a hand in getting it done," Snow said, looking at Mac.

"The Admiral didn't take much convincing and our colleagues were all in from the jump," Mac answered with a smile.

"Well kudos to you and the Admiral even if it's still David versus Goliath," Joe said.

◆

Earlier that day, Peter Gunderson met with his head of security for an update. It appeared his well-placed sources in both the Chinese and

American Intelligence agencies were reporting increases in activities in the UAE. This was anticipated and Gunderson was prepared, but he needed to activate his defensive protocols. He spent years building financial relationships in and around the city. Once his early warning network was activated, literally nothing could happen in Dubai without his knowledge. He was hooked into almost every service the city provided. He could slow down transportation, affect public utilities, stall, or accelerate police engagement and other government responses and even influence legal action. And with an on-call security force of over 100 highly trained mercenaries and hardened residential and office facilities, his personal security was virtually impregnable. Of course, if all else failed and there was a breach, Gunderson's helicopter, private jet, and yacht stood ready, a stone's throw away.

Confident in his preparations, the billionaire poured himself a scotch and checked his messages. Nothing back from the Faction boys yet. Well, as he told Seguro earlier that morning, he did not expect any response until his antagonists exhausted all their options. That meant that Seguro should be prepared to unleash another round of Camo assaults which ARK would further exploit. If that didn't break the deal loose, he would take down the Faction member by member.

He had to admit, he was looking forward to the conflict. There was nothing like a good fight to make one feel alive and he had a few serious scores to settle at the same time. As the 100-year-old scotch's warmth spread, Gunderson leaned back closing his eyes and savored the thought of the epic battle to come.

◆

The reunion was short but exhilarating as the ex-Apogee team members renewed their friendships at the Whiplash safehouse in downtown Dubai city. Even though it was over a year since they worked together putting down the Typhon crisis, it seemed like yesterday. Aside from their natural synergy the three latecomers contributed extraordinary capabilities to the team.

With two PhD's in AI and Advanced Computing Integration, Carrie Swan was the whole package. The 34-year-old blond California surfer's raw intellect was almost outdone by her stunning, slim athletic figure and piercing green eyes.

Pat Curry made his home "down under" and at six feet four and 215 pounds, the big Aussie ex-rugby star was an intimidating figure with chiseled features and a personality that equaled his mass. He had a brilliant financial mind and never saw a number he didn't like.

Finally, an unflappable 32-year-old Brit, Elaine Warsaw brought order to chaos. When she wasn't spinning it up at 30 miles per hour on her road bike in England's rural countryside, the renowned Cultural Anthropologist and Social Systems Dynamics expert was on the worldwide speaking tour. Elaine was the team's secret weapon when it came to unraveling the impact of cultural catalysts and the drivers of global societal shifts.

It was a powerful team, and the sum was even greater than the parts, but they were acutely aware of the challenges they faced and the urgency of the initiative. The US intelligence operation against Gunderson was certainly launched by now and it was likely that a field team was already headed their way.

"OK, guys we need quick intel updates.

Turning to Swan, Mac's tech guru, he began, "OK, Carrie, let's start with the technology, what have you got?"

"Well, thanks to some extraordinary work from several WL members, in particular a medical team from Israel, Seguro's Camo threat appears to include the capability of targeting specific genetic/DNA configurations with biologic assaults and can be delivered undetected via liquid carriers. We eliminated a virus in this initial assault because of the lack of contagion and the geographic separation of the victims. That doesn't mean that a virus couldn't be weaponized with Camo, but we believe this was an intimidation technique. That said, this is one horrific weapon, and we must get hold of Seguro's formulas and protocols and destroy them. Public knowledge of such a threat could cause a global panic."

"What about ARK?" Mac asked.

"Our intel on that is sparce, primarily because the company is so secret, and their focus could be broad across an array of technologies. However, based on the recent disinformation campaign that is raging globally, we presume Gunderson's primary focus is on content manipulation and distribution. That was one of his major thrusts with Typhon and he's had years to perfect methods to control information. While it's speculative, based on work at NSA, we fear that after years of investment, Gunderson may have achieved breakthroughs in artificial intelligence. With his resources, he could be years ahead of contemporary development.

"How about the business side, Pat?"

"Well, Mac, there's not much, but this we can conclude; based on Gunderson's massive financial resources and reach, there is little doubt that he can fund sizable initiatives and exert significant influence."

"Elaine, how about these widespread outbreaks? What are the implications."

"Mac, of all our threats, this phenomenon may be the most serious. Usually, the news cycle burns out relatively quickly, but social media is proving to be a radically different driver because it contains so many filaments."

"What does that mean, Elaine?" Franklin asked.

"Well, social media takes a single story and parses it into hundreds of narratives, each of which spawns even more spurious content because the consumers become the story tellers. This means that there is always another activist audience. It's like a grassfire. There is a never-ending source of flammable material, so it just keeps feeding itself and spreading."

"And that means, from a numbers point of view, it grows geometrically not arithmetically, right?" Curry asked.

"Exactly, and it also means that you need the same force to stop it!" Warsaw responded seriously.

"So, essentially, we need to fight fire with fire," Mac concluded.

◆

Whiplash was a small, but significant collaboration and it possessed several unique advantages over its opponents. Its members were uniquely positioned and influential worldwide. It was secret and could operate invisibly. And, its members would share their proprietary assets and insights, because WL's threats were always greater than any individual member's national interests. Nevertheless, it was remarkable when Ahmad Faheem, Saudi Arabia's Crown Prince joined with Mi Cha Park, President of South Korea's largest technology hardware company, Sanjay Shiva, CEO of Utter, Inc., India's giant software firm and Robert Worthington, NSA's preeminent Director of Technology to tackle how to hack into ARK.

The unlikely breakthrough came from the Saudi's obsessive focus on gaming. But without the collaboration of the US's AI advances coupled with India's software tools and South Korea's silicon advances, the solution would have remained elusive.

Carrie Swan was ecstatic when Worthington broke the news. Now they could penetrate Gunderson's firewalls and the hardware chipset was already on its way from Seoul. Unfortunately, the hack required an onsite download which meant breaching the ARK facility. And then there was still the matter of developing the code to neutralize ARK's AI engine. Carrie and Worthington were tasked with that challenge, while Pat and Elaine worked on verifying and locating ARK's location in Granite Noir's building.

"Now, we just need to figure out how to penetrate GN's offices," Mac said addressing the rest of his team.

"The chipset arrives this afternoon, so we should reconvene at 5 pm to review where we are," Mac urged. "That gives us most of the day to come up with answers. One thing is for sure though, we must get to ARK first."

"What about Gunderson, Seguro and Camo?" asked Jasmine.

"Locating them is the challenge, but our invisible sniper is working that angle with some Mossad folks in Tel Aviv. Hopefully, we'll have some leads from Victoria this afternoon."

◆

By the time Black and company established a base of operations in Dubai City, their orders were clear; "You have 24 hours to neutralize Gunderson!" They must move quickly before Gunderson's deadline and stop the threat. The plan had two phases. Phase 1 was to penetrate the ARK office, take the executives and techies hostage, get possession of ARK, and determine where Gunderson's residence was. Black's team would execute phase 1. Phase two would commence as soon as phase 1 was complete and was assigned to Liang. They would storm Gunderson's residence, capture Gunderson and Seguro interrogate them, terminate them, and torch the home. The objective was to complete both phases before noon the following day and exfil both teams from the country by late afternoon.

It was a good plan given their lack of knowledge about ARK and Camo. They needed firsthand knowledge of both technologies, so the interrogations were critical. The dicey part was collecting all the IP before terminating Gunderson and Seguro. There could be no mistakes this time.

♦

The tension was palpable when Mac called the team back together. They knew that unless all the teams succeeded the whole plan was at risk.

"Before our updates, I have a quick message from the Admiral," Mac announced.

"Victoria received intel from Mossad's local operators on the identities of key players in Granite Noir and staked out their HQ in the Prime Building in Business Bay. She followed one to a high-end residence in Palm Jumeirah earlier today. Aside from the opulence of the estate, the heavy security indicates it is likely to be Gunderson's home. She will continue to maintain her surveillance and keep us informed."

"Fantastic news," Franklin said. "No matter what else happens, at least we may have a chance to take that SOB out once and for all!"

"OK, let's see where we are. Pat and Elaine what do we know about ARK's HQ?" Mac asked.

"Well logic tells us that it is co-located with GN on the upper floors of the Prime Building and Pat got creative and substantiated that assumption," Elaine responded.

"Yep, even though Gunderson may have a well disguised majority share of the company's stock, it is still a public company which means the financials are available. I had to dig deep, but it appears that GN leases space out on several floors above its operation to a single unidentified entity. My astute guess is it's ARK," Curry concluded.

"Great work guys, we may have to call audibles when we go in, but at least we know we're on the right field," Mac said positively.

"What do we have from the assault team?"

"Well, this part of the op is a bit dicey," Snow answered.

"That's for sure, we are very thin on intel," Franklin jumped in.

"We do know that GN is accessed via elevator and is on the 30th floor. We also know from Pat's analysis that Gunderson purchased 4 floors and GN uses the lowest two. That puts ARK on floors 32 and 33," Singe concluded.

"Good, and what's the penetration plan?" Mac asked.

"Well, that's the dicey part," Jasmine answered with a grimace.

"Evading security to access any floors in the Prime Building is challenging, especially Gunderson's floors, where there will be additional security personnel. After extensively reviewing the buildings architectural drawings, we have considered two options."

"One is internal, and one is external," Franklin offered.

"The internal option is to impersonate a medical emergency team called in by a resident. We will pull up to the entrance in an ambulance, enter the main lobby and use this ruse to access the GN floor. We do have some good news. While Victoria was checking out the Prime building, she entered the lobby and took one of the speed elevators to the top floors. She sent us photos including pics of the directory by floor. Her intel coupled with the building's architectural drawings furnished by WL provide a good blueprint of what we're dealing with," Snow reported.

"There's still much we don't know, but the traffic should be light, and folks don't usually get in the way of medical emergency personnel, Warsaw said.

"What about the external breach?" Mac asked dubiously.

"Well, that's my op," Peter answered, "but it's only a last resort if we're blocked from accessing the upper levels. The window structures on those floors will allow for scaling, but the glass is very thick and would take time to penetrate. I'd have to exit from a floor below ARK and scale up, penetrate the glass, then eliminate the obstacle for the team."

"I see. Well, we may need to use both tactics to provide back up, but the external play is definitely an audible," Mac commented.

"We figured you might say that, so we've geared up for both," Snow said.

"OK, you're up Carrie, everything up to now is window dressing, since none of this matters unless we can shut down ARK."

"Let me first say that Bob Worthington and a bunch of some super talented techies from the Whiplash organization have been working this problem for some time. We do have a theory on how to get ARK's attention and tie it up for a while, but we won't be sure if it will work until we try it. Furthermore, we are not confident that it will be a permanent fix, so that work is ongoing."

"Without getting into specifics which none of us would understand, what is the general approach?" Curry asked with interest.

"It's actually a simple idea," Swan remarked. "We ask ARK to solve an unsolvable problem. What's tricky is to come up with a conundrum that an AI of ARK's caliber cannot solve."

"Have you figured out what that question is?" Snow asked, intrigued.

"Well, I'm going in with several iterations, in case one doesn't work," Swan answered.

CHAPTER THIRTY-FIVE

AUDIBLES

The sun set early in Dubai in the fall and by 7 pm the darkness had succumbed to a star filled sky and a brilliant full moon. They pulled the ambulance to the curb at the main entrance and Mac and Jasmine, walked briskly to the security desk. Warsaw remained in the vehicle while the rest of the team pulled a gurney and additional medical equipment from the vehicle and followed.

The guard, who was on his smart phone, looked up in surprise.

Mac held up his medical ID and said in an urgent voice, "we are responding to a call from one of your residents about an emergency at this address." Mac read the name and apartment number.

The guard said, "oh my," as the rest of the team rushed into the lobby pushing the portable gurney. "I should call the resident," he clamored," and began dialing.

"After several rings, he looked up in horror and said, "no answer!"

"If this is a cardiac event, we must go now," Mac implored.

"Yes of course," the guard relented in a panic, as the team rushed to the nearest elevator.

They exited the express elevator on the 29th floor and entered a separate private elevator to access the upper floors. Snow pushed the button for floor 30.

A soft voice requested, "please enter your access code on the keypad".

"Bloody hell," Snow blurted out in frustration.

"Carrie, can you hack this pad?" Franklin asked.

"Probably, but it will take some time."

"Time, we don't have. Peter sorry to say, we need to execute plan B," Mac commanded.

Exiting the elevator, Curry consulted a floor plan and said, "follow me, there is a utility closet down the hall where we can hang until Peter gets us access."

Singe pulled some gear from underneath the gurney and took off in the opposite direction.

"I'll get back to you on comms and bring that elevator down," he yelled as he rounded a corner into another lobby. He moved to a corner of the empty foyer and examined the building's layout.

He tapped on the exterior windowpane and murmured to himself, "shit, it figures, way too thick."

Pulling a portable green laser from his pocket, he placed it against the window and tapped on his earpiece.

"I need you now, Vic. I'll give you a target." Singe turned the laser on and aimed at a parked van 500 meters away. He pressed the device two more times and moved out of view of the window and waited. The window suddenly buckled inward from the high velocity 50 caliber suppressed round and the entire pane careened to the floor in a single spiderwebbed sheet. A light breeze wafted the drapes as Singe moved forward and began his climb. Directly above him two floors up a second shot silently eviscerated the second window with the same result.

He was confident he could free solo climb the one story, but at over 300 meters to the sidewalk below, there could be no mistakes. He leaned out precariously and grabbed the thin window frame, stepped to the sill, and brought his second hand up to secure his position. Then swinging his body out over the void to create leverage, he alternated his grip as he scaled slowly up the frame. As he reached the upper window, his final move challenged even Singe's years of rock-climbing experience as he launched his body upward grabbing the window frame and kipped himself over the edge, landing face down on the shattered remains of the fractured pane.

Gasping for breath, he went on comms and said, "Mac, lift off in one minute." At the elevator, he pressed the button to bring the lift up two floors and waited. There was a chime and the door magically opened. They were back in business.

Snow made short work of Granite Noir's locked entrance door and the team entered. At this hour, the complex of offices appeared empty. The team fanned out and began searching for the private elevator marked on the schematics.

"Bingo," Franklin called out, pointing at a heavy oak door. "It may not be ARK, but there's a reason it's locked."

"This lock is a serious upgrade," Snow said, examining the mechanism.

"I might have an answer for that," Singe said, retrieving his laser. Using the high-powered device, he quickly cut through the metal and the internal deadbolt.

"Very cool, Peter" Franklin said grinning and swung open the door revealing an elevator with the work "ARK" emblazoned above it.

"Grab your vests from the gurney and take up offensive positions. We don't know who's home," Mac ordered.

It was tight in the small space and Snow and Swan pressed against the inside door frames for cover. The 4 men crouched in firing positions.

As the door began to open, Mac saw movement and whispered, "we've got company, flashbang protocol now!" The team immediately covered their ears and tightly shut their eyes as Mac tossed an M84 stun grenade into the interior. With 170 decibels and 6 million candelas, the effect was devastating. Three guards were just outside the elevator within the immediate range of the device and collapsed on the spot. Three others were disoriented and temporarily blinded. The team was upon them in seconds with zip ties and duct tape. Curry and Mac took up positions by the two inside lobby doors as the team secured the guards.

"Incoming," shouted Curry as a large piece of door frame disintegrated just over his head.

Mac yelled to the team to retreat to the hallway behind him for cover as Curry fired off a series of rounds to delay the new assault and sprinted for their exit. The big Aussie was only feet from the doorway when he went down hard, face first on the marble floor. Blood spurted from his head and began pooling around his face on the white marble. Mac desperately dove through the gap grabbing his friend's outstretched hand even as he downed the shooter with a headshot. Peter and Joe sent a barrage of rounds into the lobby deterring the attack long enough for Mac to drag Curry out of the line of fire.

Snow rushed to Curry looking for the wound. He was unconscious, but she could find no entry wound. With Mac's help, she gently rolled the injured man over. Blood was gushing from a large open gash in his forehead.

"Oh shit, said Swan as she knelt down to help."

"It's not what you think, Carrie," Snow said. "He sustained that injury when he hit the floor. My guess is he took a hit to his upper back and his Kevlar vest saved him, but the force of the round knocked all the wind out of him, and he went down."

"Will he be alright?" Swan asked.

"Don't know, yet. I can bandage the wound, but he may have other issues like internal bleeding."

"Jas, you, Joe, and Peter stay here with Pat and keep the hounds at bay. Carrie, come with me. We've got to find ARK and complete the mission," Mac insisted.

They raced down the hall, ripping open each door they passed in search of the AI servers. The corridor ended in a stairway to an upper level. Time was running out as they abandoned all caution, taking the stairs two at a time.

Reaching the landing, they entered a large open space with rows of small work cubicles along the windows overlooking the magnificent view of Business Bay far below. Taking up the entire center of the expansive floor was a glass enclosed room with dozens of server racks and consoles. Over the thick stainless door frame was a multicolored lighted sign with the word "ARK".

"Bingo," Swan yelled and before Mac could caution her, rushed through the door and down the rows of equipment.

She abruptly stopped halfway into the complex and exclaimed, "Here's the main console." Mac joined her, his eyes scanning right and left, his Sig panning back and forth.

"Slow down, Carrie. I need to clear this floor."

"No time, Mac. Besides no one is going to shoot a round up here and risk destroying the world's most advanced AI."

"Point taken," Mac agreed. "How can I help?"

"I must ID the right port to download the hack. Here's the drive. Check the back of this server for an input port for a thumb drive."

Mac moved to the rear of the big server. "Well, there are several open ports here," he replied.

"Ok, it may not matter, but if it works, the console will come up and ask me to sign in and ask for instructions. Try one," she said. They waited, holding their breath. The flat panel remained blank.

"Do you want me to try another?" Mac asked concerned.

"Yes, at this point we have no choice," Swan answered. The console didn't change.

"There's one more, Carrie."

"Go for it, no harm no foul" she almost whispered. Mac inserted the drive into the final port.

The screen suddenly burst to life and displayed, "Please sign in to authorize your input source."

"Third times a charm," Mac said smiling. Carrie nodded and signed in.

"Please provide input instructions," ARK responded.

"Now comes the real test. Keep your fingers crossed, ARK is about to get a new challenge that has never been solved."

Swan carefully keyed in her instructions. "ARK, please solve the Collatz Conjecture, also known as 3X+1. Do not use any of your resources for any other request and continue this execution until you solve the problem."

"Confirmed", ARK displayed and then the word "Working" began blinking.

"Halleluiah," Swan exclaimed as she pulled the thumb drive from the server, "We are in business!"

"Ok, let's roll, before those goons figure out where we are," Mac yelled. As they disappeared down the stairs, they could hear shouts from above.

"Make sure they don't access this level and take half the team down the back stairs to ambush them from the rear," one of the security guards commanded.

"How's Pat?" were the first words out of Mac's mouth as he joined his teammates.

"He's alive, but still unconscious. Pulse steady, but faint. We need to get him medical attention and soon," Snow replied.

"What's the sitrep, Joe?"

"We're kind of stymied, Cap. They can't rush us, or we mow them down and we have the same problem."

"Not anymore. We have got to move. They'll be on us from behind soon enough. You and Peter carry Pat. The rest of us will lay down heavy fire with Carrie and Jasmine closely following you. I will provide cover until you are all on the lift, then you provide the cover for me to cross the lobby. If I can't make it, move out. Put Pat on the gurney we left in GN's lobby and take him down to the main floor as the emergency patient we're transporting to the hospital and if necessary do just that."

"Good plan Mac, except for the part about moving out without you," Jasmine complained.

"Guys, you know the drill and you know what's at stake. Follow the plan and that's an order, now let's move!" Mac commanded.

The instant they cracked the door, a barrage of bullets pounded the concrete wall from across the lobby. Chips of masonry flew like chaff during a harvest. At the first pause, they returned fire, battering the opposite doorway. Franklin hoisted Curry onto his shoulder with Singe's help and the two surged out the door, in a sprint to the lift. Snow and Swan were close behind running in low crouches while launching a crescendo of 9mm rounds at their attackers. They all piled into the elevator and continued to put down cover for Sisco to follow.

Mac jammed another double stack 20 mag into the Sig P226 to begin another barrage, when he heard yells from behind him. *Oh, crap, this was not good,* he thought. Meanwhile, the guards, seeing the escaping agents, redirected their assault to the open elevator.

"Guys abort now," Mac said on comms. "I'm under attack from the rear. Complete the mission as planned, Mac out!"

Turning, he raced down the hall to the nearest office off the building's exterior. He closed and locked the door and examined the space. There were assorted work cubicles, a utility closet, and an open area with a view of the city reaching out into the distance. He quickly inspected the closet for anything useful and turned to leave when he saw an open box full of electrical supplies. He rummaged through it and found a heavy gauge extension cord. He grabbed it and ran back into the office.

The voices were getting louder as the security detail searched each office. Mac examined the cord carefully. Even a 10-gauge cable might not support his weight, but doubled up it probably could. He secured the cable around a load bearing column near the window and twisted it tightly winding it into a single strand with the loop end at the bottom. Turning back to the window, he fired a 9mm round into its center. The bullet pierced the thick glass, but it remained intact. Recalling Victoria's 50 caliber outcome he mused, *obviously not a high caliber shot,* as he fired off 3 more shots. The window was opaque with spidering. He held the cord tightly and using all his body weight, he kicked the glass. The pane buckled and flew out into the void crashing onto the roof of a lower section of the building far below.

Mac carefully straddled the sill and began his descent. Although Sisco had done his fair share of rock climbing all over the world and was no slouch, he was no Peter Singe. But he had a rope, and it was a simple task to rappel down to the next floor. Once even with the window, using the cord's end loop to support his weight, he fired four more suppressed rounds followed by a swinging kick into the wounded glass and tumbled into the offices of Granite Noir, Inc.

They wasted no time transferring their wounded teammate to the gurney in GN's lobby and took the express elevator the thirty-one floors to the main entrance. The guard at the desk looked almost relieved as Snow explained that the man was a guest and fell from a ladder in the apartment and required immediate treatment for a concussion. Once Curry was loaded into the ambulance, they waited while Jasmine checked his vitals. He was still stable, and his pulse had strengthened so she decided to try using smelling salts to revive him. A light dose caused a slight reaction, so she increased the exposure. His eyes fluttered momentarily and then opened as he groaned, then muttered, "what hap?" trying to raise his head.

"Whoa big boy," Snow commanded, pushing him gently back down. "Let me check your pupils. Well, it looks like you might have a concussion, but you'll live, thanks to that vest."

"Wonderful," expressed Elaine.

"Now what, back to the safe house to regroup?" Swan asked.

"No way, we've got to get Mac out of there," Jasmine said.

"I agree Jas, but you heard Mac's order, Singe replied.

"Yeh, and you know how I am about orders when it comes to our team," she said stubbornly.

"No can-do Jas, Joe insisted, but since Pat is coming around, we could pull out of sight and give it some more time."

"I'm ok with that," Snow agreed. They parked twenty-five meters away among some service vehicles and waited.

Thirty minutes passed and Franklin said, "I think it's time we regrouped and got some reinforcements. We're not doing Mac any good just sitting here." Elaine sighed and began to pull away from the curb as Jasmine stared disheartened back at the building.

"Wait a minute," she exclaimed. "Someone is walking out of the garage entrance."

"Where?" Franklin demanded.

"Over near those parked cars," Snow pointed excitedly. They waited and watched as the figure continued towards them, hugging the shadows.

"That could be anybody," Franklin warned. "Stay down."

"I think it's Mac," Snow said. And then the man disappeared.

"Where'd he go?" Swan asked.

"Now I know it's Mac, no one else is that good at stealth," Snow stated.

"And you'd be right," came a voice from behind them. Sisco stepped forward into view and said, "Thanks for waiting. I had a feeling you'd call an audible."

CHAPTER THIRTY-SIX

CONFRONTATION

Phillip Seguro was busy formulating his next Camo assault in the suite Gunderson had provided in his Palm Jumeirah estate when his phone buzzed with an incoming text, "Please meet me in my ops center in the basement now, PG."

"We may have a problem," Gunderson said, when Seguro arrived, and they were alone. My security chief just met with me and reported that GN and maybe ARK have been breached.

"I thought you said that was impossible?" Seguro asked incredulously.

"No, I said it was improbable, but there is very little that is truly impossible if you have the will and the means, Phillip," Gunderson preached.

"Ok, but what does this mean? How serious is it?"

"Well, a breach of GN's offices is of little concern, but if ARK was tampered with, that is another story," Gunderson replied. "There is no evidence that the upper floor of ARK's offices was penetrated, but my people are on sight checking it out as we speak. I should know that answer momentarily."

On cue, Gunderson's mobile buzzed. He picked it up from the table and answered, "Yes."

After a long silence, he answered, "report to my residence immediately so we can determine counter measures and hung up.

"Well, Phillip, from what little we know, the interlopers were our nemesis, the Sisco gang and it appears that ARK is currently neutralized."

"But how, Peter?"

"We are not yet certain, but somehow, they were able to hack the server. We know of no current technology that could have facilitated that action. Since ARK will not communicate, we must assume that they have instructed it to complete a project before engaging externally."

"Peter, you seem relatively calm. Is there a work around?" Seguro pressed.

"My dear Phillip, there is always a work around. As I said, you just must have the will and the means and of course also live long enough to find it. So, first things first, we need to stay alive. One thing is clear, we are under a significant assault and need to pull out all the stops. This is why I brought you into my operation and why Camo is so important."

"ARK provides our long-term collective control, but Camo is our insurance. You need to be ready to launch a Camo assault that will shake up all our adversaries and put them on the defensive. We can use this attack as an excuse to move up our timetable and expand our targets. I am thinking some big player terminations. We can start with Robino, Ban and the Faction members and possibly even their bosses. Individual DNA profile attacks will get their attention. They can't ignore this kind of personal threat because there is no escape and no defense.

"What about Sisco?"

"Although I am confident that we have appropriate security, I have learned not to underestimate Mr. Sisco. He is indeed a wild card that we cannot ignore. For that reason, I have an alternate plan to deal with him and secure our safety."

◆

News of the assault on the Prime Tower was all over the late-night shows and the internet. And while GN was central to the story, no mention of ARK or Gunderson was included in the detail. GN's PR team downplayed the incident as a classic business crime motivated by corporate raiders to gain investment intelligence and advanced market knowledge. Aside from the financial markets, it was basically a "nothing burger" news item and the world moved on.

But to Bruce Black and Wupen Liang it was a catastrophe. Their whole ARK play was now shattered. Worse, it left them with only one option, go after Gunderson and Seguro. Without stealing ARK, they had no leverage, and they knew Gunderson would be ready. Equally disturbing and inexplicable was that they were certain somehow Sisco had pulled off the ARK attack right under their noses.

For Robino, Ban and the Faction members, the news came in a different package. Each was served with a personal text message with the following warning, "To Faction Members, your leaders have betrayed you. They have ignored our offers and threatened intimidation. Your engagement with them directly implicates you in their heinous attacks. Unless you and your leadership immediately cease this retaliation and agree to our terms you will experience significant retribution to include public exposure for your illicit activities and potential personal deterrents. You are advised to consult with your leadership for details. You have been warned. ARK."

The response was immediate and predictable, bewilderment, concern, crosstalk between Faction members and finally an ultimatum for an explanation.

"We are losing control, Frank. I have been dodging phone calls for an hour and I need to respond to our members," Ban whined as their emergency call commenced.

"Genjo don't fall for this BS, they are bluffing. It is they who are panicking. It's unfortunate that Sisco apparently beat us to the prize and is mucking up the water, but if ARK has been compromised, it has put Gunderson and Seguro back on their heels."

"But what about their threats Frank? I mean what the hell do they mean by personal deterrents?"

"Well, we cannot ignore Gunderson, especially if he is backed into a corner. He is a vicious and unscrupulous terrorist and is capable of anything, so we must act decisively and fast."

"And he has Camo," Ban reminded.

"Yes, he does, Genjo and that must be rectified. Here are my recommendations, you need to call the members and calm them down. Explain that Gunderson and Seguro went rogue and we're handling it. Any public allegations they make should be refuted as the actions of the same maniacs that perpetrated the recent fake news. I will respond to Gunderson that you are willing to take his offer to President Shing for consideration, but we need 48 hours to respond. That will slow him down. In the meantime, you and I will direct Black and Liang to launch an immediate strike on Gunderson and Seguro with instructions to take them alive, if possible, but not to jeopardize the mission of neutralizing them under any circumstances."

"What about this Sisco character? Isn't it likely he will show up too?"

"That would just be icing on the cake, Genjo. Our boys can knock off two nasty birds with one stone!" Robino answered.

♦

"Let's fire a warning shot across the bow Phillip," Gunderson commanded as the two men finished reviewing Robino's latest offer.

"Are you sure we shouldn't wait to see what Shing comes up with?" Seguro asked hesitantly.

"Phillip, they aren't going to take this up the ladder. Ban would never do that. He would disappear in twenty-four hours. It's just a delaying tactic. And even if I'm wrong, they need some real proof that we are no longer screwing around!"

"Ok, Peter, thanks to you, I have the DNA from every member. Any personal favorites?"

"Let's be strategic and hit the ones that will have the least impact on the Faction's operations since we will soon own them all. Go with Jing Liu, CEO, Qiáng de Corp from China and Joel Roland, CEO, FindIt from the US. Set it up to put them out of action for a week, and let's be creative and make it a unique affliction."

"Of course, if you're right, you know an attack is imminent," Seguro stated flatly.

"I agree and that is why I am implementing Plan B," Gunderson said with a smirk.

♦

It was a long night and aside from Pat Curry's injury, things went surprisingly well. Once back in the safehouse, the team de-briefed Clausen and discussed their next action. They knew everything and everyone would be converging on Gunderson's residence. Victoria joined them amid great fanfare for her extraordinary feats from 500 yards and returned that evening to her observation post in a rental residence across the water from the Gunderson estate. Swan announced that the hack she loaded was communicating to her through a series of rotating VPN's and ARK was continuing its relentless search for a solution to the enigma of 3X+1. The Admiral finally called it a night and they shut down with the objective of an early morning deployment.

The sun was just clearing the horizon over the Persian Gulf as Mac retrieved the buzzing mobile on the nightstand and answered, yes Vic what's up?"

"Lots of activity at the big house," she answered.

"What are you seeing?" Mac asked.

"Reinforcements and increased security," she responded.

"Numbers?"

"Maybe 25 total," she estimated.

"Ok, we'll join you in two hours. Let me know if there's any activity on your street to avoid."

"Will do," Bakman acknowledged.

◆

The admiral remained at the safe house coordinating with WL along with Swan who was monitoring ARK remotely and Curry who was still recovering. The rest of the team bivouacked to the rental residence across the water from Gunderson' estate. As the long shadows of twilight began to give way to another moonlit night, Mac peered across the dark waters of the gulf through his high-powered binoculars.

He turned and left the veranda and walked into the large living room where the team reviewed the blueprints of Gunderson's Dubai home.

"Twenty thousand square feet, that sure is a mansion," Franklin observed. "I bet that's at least $10 million bucks."

"You wish," exclaimed Warsaw. "In this market, more like twice that amount."

"At the end of the night, it's likely to be worth zero," Singe offered.

"Bloody true," Snow said.

"Ok, folks, let's stay on task," Mac requested. "As you all know, the operative question is how does our team, which is entirely outnumbered and outgunned, penetrate this property and secure the camo IP? We've spent hours on this op and have a good plan if our assumptions are correct and we execute flawlessly. So, let's go over it one more time to make sure that happens."

As the moon climbed to its apogee in a star filled sky, Black and ten agents surfaced thirty meters off the beach from the estate, their re-breathers offering no evidence of their travels below the surface. Sentries paraded along the five hundred meters of beachfront, waving powerful beams randomly across both sand and sea. The swimmers submerged again into the dark waters like crocks hunting unsuspecting prey on the shore beyond.

High above the manmade fronds of Palm Jumeirah's streets, several drones buzzed almost noiselessly as they hovered awaiting their orders. Deployed in a circumference encircling the residence, Liang's team was well concealed and positioned for rapid response behind the lush vegetation that adorned the exclusive property.

Across the water, Mac and several of his team were glued to high magnification night vision scopes trained on the residence. Since nightfall they had taken shifts on the arduous duty to no avail.

"Got you," Mac heard from Snow across the room as she slowly moved the scope along the beachfront.

"Jas, status," he commanded urgently.

"Five water rats and more coming ten meters from the beach," she exclaimed excitedly.

"I've also got movement from the perimeter of the property," Bakman yelled back. "At least ten ground troops on the move and I see muzzle flashes."

Through Mac's scope he could now see figures running and diving for cover while others lay behind protection with long guns and scopes. Everywhere there were flashes, but no sound. Suppressed weapons, he thought. It was a full-fledged fire fight and both sides were paying a high price. Timing was everything now. Mac had to move when the action had diminished, but while both sides were still engaged.

He yelled out, "status?"

"Things are slowing down in my sector, Snow answered.

"Same here," Bakman responded.

"Any penetration?" he asked.

"Not that I can see," Vic answered.

"Lots of bodies, Jasmine offered.

This was it, he thought and yelled, "move out now!"

Their SUV went in lights off and pulled to the curb well short of the mansion. Gunderson's property was large and relatively secluded from its neighbors, so the conflict was still unnoticed. Nonetheless, that was only a temporary reprieve. They spread out but kept visual contact. The plan was to penetrate through the servant's entrance at the far side of the building avoiding the rear beach and frontal approaches where most of the action was.

In the dark areas, they could use their NV's but much of the home's exterior was lit up like an NFL night game. Mac saw Snow disappear into the shadows by the corner of the house. He heard a muffled sound and when she didn't emerge, he went on comms.

"Jas, confirm status." No response. He moved cautiously over to her last location and flipped on his NVs. The eerie green image appeared, but no one was there. To his right he could hear gasps of raspy breath. He inched around the edge of the building, his Sig extended. Snow was pulling herself from the ground, her bloodstained hand still holding the 10-inch tactical blade she used to take down an enormous guard lying lifelessly in the thick mulch.

"Even before she knew he was behind her, she wheezed, "Snow ok."

"I can see that Jas," he whispered as he gently helped her to her feet. "Are you really, ok?" he asked concerned.

"I am now," she answered, relieved to see him. "That bloke was a bit of a handful."

"Mac, we have a group that just breached the veranda entrance. Around a half dozen," Warsaw said. "They don't know we're here. We took out several active shooters from the beach and a couple under cover on the perimeter. We counted over thirty bodies so far."

"Roger that, Elaine. Meet me at the rear entrance. We've got to get into the house and take down these guys before they get the goods."

"Copy, Mac."

The veranda door was open, and the house was dark. They heard the muffled sound of suppressed fire but saw no flashes.

Ok, let's spread out in twos, Jasmine and me, Peter and Elaine and Joe and Vic. Stay on comms. Green is good, red is I'm in trouble and yellow is danger. Go!" Mac said.

Singe and Warsaw were the first to reach the second-floor stairway. Singe began the climb when a man suddenly appeared on the landing above. He was also wearing night vision goggles and his AK was pointed directly at Peter. Identify yourself, he demanded.

Peter mumbled, "Black."

The guard seemed to relax, then moving closer to Singe, he stiffened and raised his gun.

Peter knew he wouldn't get his weapon up in time and began to drop to his knees hoping the round would hit his vest. He landed hard on the second step and careened down to the landing. The big guard pulled the trigger reflexively one second after Warsaw's AR 15 556 caliber round pierced his frontal lobe launching his head and arms upward, causing his AK round to soar skyward. Blood erupted like a firehose as the body slid down the stairs landing on Singe at the bottom. Dazed and confused, it took all Singe's strength to extricate himself from man's 220-pound bulk.

"Peter, are you Ok?"

"Green thanks to you," he answered with a weak grin.

Mac and Snow got to Singe and Warsaw just as they were about to head back up the stairs.

"You guys ok?' he asked concerned, seeing the body sprawled on the stairway.

"Peachy," Warsaw replied as they continued upward.

"These guys were in some fire fight. There are corpses everywhere and there's a separate building across the veranda that we haven't gotten to yet," Singe said.

"We'll handle it," Mac answered. "Vic and Joe are clearing the perimeter. You guys cover the second floor. Let's try to be out of here in thirty minutes before the whole neighborhood drops in."

"Mac, several bad guys are headed into the adjacent building, we can intercept," Vic radioed.

"Negative, Vic, I need your firepower outside to cover us. Jas and I are almost there. We'll take this one."

"Copy," came the reply.

Leaving the main house, they moved cautiously to the separate structure. Sisco motioned for Snow to check out the rear while he entered the front entrance. The building was obviously guest quarters with a spacious living room and a hallway leading to several other rooms. He could hear voices coming from down the hall. He moved silently forward passing the first door as the conversation became intelligible.

"I have no damned clue where the assholes are."

"How could they know we were coming tonight?" a second voice with an Asian accent asked.

"Either we have a mole, or they just got jumpy when ARK got hit and figured they were too vulnerable here," the first voice replied.

"Either way they're in the wind," the Asian replied, disgusted.

"Not necessarily, we have one of their boys locked up in the head."

"I doubt one of his ground grunts would know much, but it's worth a try," the Asian man replied. "I'll drag him out."

Mac moved back away from the door and took up a defensive posture. After a moment, the voices resumed.

"Tell me where Gunderson and Seguro are?" the man threatened. There was silence.

"Wrong answer," There was a muffled scream of anguish.

"One more time and then game over, the torturer demanded.

"I don't know, there are lots of places they could hold up," the man said in obvious pain.

"That's not good enough," the first man demanded.

"Ok, ok. I know he's got a yacht in the harbor with a chopper pad and keeps a private jet at the Dubai executive airpark. That's all I know, I swear. Gunderson doesn't tell us grunts his plans," the man whined.

"Well, I guess that means you no longer have any value to us then."

"Wait, I can help you," the man pleaded.

"I doubt that."

"No really. Gunderson knows me. If you take me with you, when you find him, I can trick him into exposing himself," their captive argued.

"What do you think, Liang?" Black asked.

"Well Black, it wouldn't hurt to have some options and it might confuse Gunderson, so I say we drag him along, but if he makes one wrong move, he's toast!"

What a break, Mac thought, Liang and Black in the flesh and working together with Gunderson and Seguro, the quarry. There might be an opportunity here to neutralize them both and hold them as proof of the whole illicit Faction operation. It was risky but tempting. But it meant they took their eye off the main objective of stopping Gunderson and Seguro. He needed these guys to lead him to his target and then wrap the whole affair up. That also was the best way to prove his team's innocence.

"Wupen, Let's ditch this place. What we're after is long gone."

Mac, retreated into the nearest bedroom and tapped his earpiece.

"Jasmine and team, Black and Liang are exiting the guest quarters, do not engage. Keep a visual on them. We need to follow these dudes to find Gunderson and Seguro."

"I see them," Snow came back. "They're dragging some guy to an SUV up the street."

"We can't lose them, exfil now and rendezvous at the van," Mac ordered. "Peter, have we got our eyes on the target?"

"Checking," came back the reply. "That's a big affirmative, Mac."

"Glad you put the drones up early Peter, because our bad guys are already pulling away from the curb and heading out of the Palm," said Snow. Peter pulled up the drone images on several displays in the van while Franklin fired up the SUV for their departure. Lights began to flicker in nearby homes, and sirens blared faintly in the distance. Time was running out!

"Guys, we need to giddyap. Dubai's finest are joining the party," Franklin announced.

Mac and Jasmine were last in as they pulled out of the side street and joined some other traffic exiting the complex. They cleared the entrance to Palm Jumeirah and pulled to the curb, flashing lights roared past them sirens blaring.

"Whew, that was close. I have a feeling they will blockade the whole complex once they discover the carnage at Gunderson's place," Snow exclaimed.

"Yep, without a doubt," agreed Franklin.

"They will also begin tying the recent Prime Building breach to this incident and the heat will rise exponentially in this city," Warsaw observed.

"And that is why we need to wrap up this part of the operation quickly and leave the UAE," Mac said. "So, Peter, where are Black and

Liang now?" Peter zoomed in on a couple of the drone's image transmissions.

"The van is entering the Dubai Marina. There are over five hundred yachts berthed there."

"It figures, you know how sensitive Gunderson is about anonymity," Franklin said.

"Hard to believe that a boat over two hundred fifty feet could blend in, but then this is Dubai, and everything here is grand!" said Snow.

"We'll pull to the entrance and hang until we see which slip he picks and then move in," Mac responded.

"Ok, they turned down one of the entrances and parked the van," Peter observed.

Everyone crowded around the screen to watch the scene play out. The greenish NV images showed three men moving up the dock. Two hung back while the third continued up the line of slips. Finally, the man stopped and looked around confused.

"Zoom in closer, even if it exposes the drone. We need to see what he sees," Mac insisted.

Suddenly the man glanced back at his two captors and sprinted away down the long row of slips. Both men raced to follow him while pulling their handguns. One stopped, dropped into a shooter's crouch, and took aim, but his target disappeared behind an enormous yacht four slips away. His partner continued the pursuit, but stopped when he reached the large vessel and turning back raised his hands with thumbs down. The shooter barely noticed as he gazed at the empty slip where Gunderson's yacht should have been.

"Well bloody hell, Déjà Vu. The SOB escaped on another yacht," Snow grumbled, referencing Gunderson's miraculous disappearance on his yacht, Calamity, during the Typhon Affair.

"Maybe, but he can't be far," reminded Warsaw.

"I'm not so sure. They could be at thirty thousand feet and literally in the wind or somewhere in the Indian Ocean by now or even less than a mile away in one of the five hundred other slips in this marina," Mac countered.

"Do we take these guys down?" Singe asked.

"No, we need to keep tabs on them. They may know more than we do about Gunderson's and Seguro's whereabouts," Mac observed.

"So, we need to split up," Franklin offered.

"I'm afraid so. It's a crap shoot. By sea or by air. "Jasmine and I will stick with them. You guys see if you can come up with any leads on Gunderson's yacht."

CHAPTER THIRTY-SEVEN

WHERE ALL ROADS MEET

Thousands of miles away on opposite sides of the world two of the Faction's original members were contending with an inconceivable health crisis. Jing Liu, CEO, Qiáng de Corp in China and Joel Roland, CEO, FindIt from the US were suddenly losing their sight. Both executives were already surrounded by specialists, examined, and prescribed. The cause and cure were not yet diagnosed, and the prognosis was vague.

Ban and Robino got the early calls about their member's afflictions with appeals for answers and pleas for cures they did not have. Both men received the same threat which read, "You were warned. Your pathetic assaults are of no consequence. Times up! ARK."

◆

"Calamity", Gunderson's last yacht was seized by New Zealand authorities after Typhon's demise and at 250 feet and $175M was quite a loss. But in Gunderson's multi-billion-dollar enterprise, it was just another business right off. Besides, "Too big to Fail", was much more apropos for his final undertaking. The 300-foot super yacht was among the largest and fastest vessels on the sea. It could cruise up to thirty knots, with a range of thousands of miles using both solar and diesel power and was equipped with defenses and weaponry that no country would permit on a private craft.

Anticipating an overwhelming assault on his residence, he and Seguro had relocated twenty-four hours earlier to his floating HQ and moved it from his primary slip to a backup on the far side of the marina. When one of his personal guards, who escaped capture, alerted him to Black and Liang's marina search, he had instructed Seguro to return to Valencia on his private jet and prepare for a full-scale launch of Camo.

But for all the disruptions, Peter Gunderson was still confident that his plan would succeed. He would use Camo to bring the Faction and world leaders to their knees starting with China and America. And while ARK would take some time to gain traction, it would provide his ultimate weapon for worldwide control. He had but one problem to solve. He needed to regain outright control of ARK, but that work was well underway. He always planned for contingencies and his techies were busy working on using a backdoor to interrupt ARK's current preoccupation with solving the $3X+1$ Collatz Conjecture.

Seguro was just as happy to comply with his partner's last directive. Things were getting too hot and unpredictable in Dubai, and he was not convinced that Gunderson's supreme confidence was warranted. But he still had leverage. He alone possessed the IP on Camo and that was his life insurance policy. Now that Camo was tested and worked, he had transferred the formula from his highly encrypted personal mobile file to a secure cloud vault. The flight plan was registered and within the hour he would be airborne. He sat back in the private quarters of the big jet, took another sip of the Grey Goose martini, and closed his eyes with a sigh, confident that his future was secure.

◆

"It appears they have given up on the sea option," Snow commented, after a few minutes.

"Yeh, and it looks like they're headed to the airport," Mac agreed.

"Well Gunderson doesn't fly commercial so that means, next stop Dubai's Executive Flight Service (EFS) terminal," Snow concluded.

They parked in the lot of an adjacent private terminal and watched the dark van park behind the large private hanger twenty meters away. Black and Liang jumped out and walked casually to the building and entered the open massive steel door. The G700 was faced outward preparing to depart. The gangway was down, and the passenger door was ajar.

"I think we hit pay dirt. Remember, we agreed Seguro is mine." Liang said as he began climbing. "You cover this entrance while I check out the interior,"

Black nodded and took up a position behind the jet's landing gear. As Liang entered, he noticed the pilot's door was open and the cabin empty. It was likely they were still in the hanger's offices finalizing their flight plan. The jet was outfitted with an office, work out room, sleeping quarters with an in-suite bathroom. He identified the single door on one side of the aisle as the bedroom and opened it, scanning the compartment. It was empty. He turned to leave when he heard a toilet flush from the head across the room. The door suddenly opened, and Phillip Seguro stepped out.

Seeing his nemesis only three meters away, the big American went into attack mode and launched himself at the Asian. Liang was facing the wrong way when he was brutally tackled to the deck. Seguro desperately grabbed for the man's neck even as Liang thrust his knee into his groin. Seguro groaned in pain, momentarily immobilized.

Liang grabbed his 9mm, but Seguro kicked the weapon from his grip. Now disentangled, the two men sprang to their feet. Liang responded with his own rush and the two collided careening across the room into a dining table, knocking the cutlery to the floor. Liang grabbed a steak knife and thrust it at Seguro's arm slashing deeply into the flesh down to the bone. Seguro wailed in pain, rolling away to avoid a second assault. Rage took over as Seguro kicked out violently with enormous force, catapulting the smaller man through the open bathroom door. Scrambling after Liang, he snatched a silver chopstick dislodged from the table and launched into the air crushing Wupen to the deck. Even the American's overwhelming mass could not stop another thrust as Liang's knife penetrated Seguro's chest. With the last of his adrenalin kicking in, Phillip Seguro plunged the steel chopstick directly into the Asian's right eye penetrating his cerebral cortex and piercing his cerebellum.

Liang's body twitched in a final death spasm and went limp. Seguro managed to push himself to a sitting position, grabbed a towel and pushed it into the open chest wound, but he knew the effort was fruitless. He was bleeding internally and would soon be dead unless he got help. Struggling, he pulled the mobile phone from his pocket and dialed Gunderson.

On the third ring, Gunderson answered, "Yes, Phillip, are you in the air?" But there was no response.

"Phillip are you there?" Gunderson repeated. But the entreaty fell on deaf ears as the blood pooled around Seguro's lifeless form.

"Jasmine, pull slowly by the entrance and park at the next hanger, so I can get a look inside." Mac ordered. "Gunderson's jet may have already departed, so no point in risking an encounter yet,"

"Well, well there's a big G700 with its gangway down ready to depart just inside the hanger entrance," Snow exclaimed as she coasted slowly by.

"I can see someone standing in the shadows by one of the landing gears," Mac added.

"Is it a crewman or maintenance guy?" Snow asked.

"I don't think it's either. It looks more like a lookout, so it's either Black or Liang covering while the other is checking out the jet."

Concerned about being discovered, Black waited only ten minutes after Liang entered the jet to follow him. It took the CIA man less than three minutes to reconstruct the bloody scene, search both bodies and exit the craft. As he began pulling away from the hanger, the CIA agent could hear shouts and see people frantically rushing up the gangway. Mac and Snow witnessed all this and took up the pursuit as Black accelerated out of the airport exit.

"This is Black, get me an exact location on this mobile phone with GPS coordinates and text it back, stat." In less than a minute his phone buzzed. The incoming image displayed a map with a blinking red dot designating Seguro's last call, the owner's cabin on the super yacht, "Too Big To Fail".

He smiled and said out loud, "Gotcha!" and forwarded the details to his team with instructions to execute plan H20.

Seguro's probable death was very unfortunate, but Gunderson never panicked. He instructed his security team to double their numbers to 20 on board the yacht, commanded his captain to be ready to sail on demand and ordered his chopper flight team to be on standby for a rapid departure. He also contacted the custodians overseeing three of his alternate properties to prepare for his possible arrival within the next twenty-four hours.

Gunderson recognized that the temporary loss of the Camo formula was problematic, but as soon as ARK was back online, he would use the AI to recover the IP. Besides, Seguro already programmed three more Camo assaults in advance that he could trigger to keep his threats active. That foresight allowed him to invoke his pièce de resistance which he now executed with fanatical delight.

His final message to Robino and Ban read, "Actions have consequences. High-level executives in the US and Chinese governments are now targeted and you will be next," ARK.

"Bloody Hell Mac, that's Black and it looks like he's headed back to the marina," Jasmine exclaimed. "How could he know where Gunderson's yacht is?"

"Good question. Maybe Liang found something or someone in the plane and contacted him. We need to hang back, but not lose him. I'll let the team know the slip number when we do."

Black approached the big yacht's slip cautiously. Maintaining his distance to avoid detection, he used his NV binoculars to observe the boat's defenses. Only a few of the interior lights were lit and no deck lights were on. Obviously, Gunderson was expecting an offensive. He could see the dim green outlines of guards positioned on all the decks. A direct assault was unrealistic. Even stealth was unlikely to succeed. But Black planned for all these complications and with his team now positioned on site, was waiting for the fun to begin.

Mac and Snow watched as Black hid in the shadows of a large piling. You could tell he was communicating with his team as he furtively snuck views of the yacht. But, so far, all was quiet.

It was an ingenious plan. Their rebreathers were undetectable as they attached the micro charges of plastic explosive in a zig zag pattern across the length of the 300-foot hull. The pattern would ensure that even waterproof compartments designed to keep the craft afloat would be rendered ineffective. Planted near the charges were small globes containing a fast acting, lighter than air nerve agent that would incapacitate on contact. Once activated the two-phase system would blow twelve-inch holes in the bottom. The incoming water would suck the gas globes into the craft and detonate dispersing the agent throughout the yacht, disabling all aboard the sinking craft. There would be no noise from the underwater explosions to alert attention and the rapid sinking of the craft would cause confusion and panic for those on board. Black and his team would simply wait for the gas to clear, board unchallenged and take Gunderson. The whole operation would be over in less than thirty minutes.

There would be no sleep tonight, Gunderson thought as he evaluated who would be the most appropriate targets for Camo's next assault. He poured his 3rd cup of coffee and considered; on the US side it should be a member of the executive branch like a cabinet member. The Secretary of the Treasury would be an appropriate candidate. In the CCP, it should be a high-ranking member of the Politburo Standing Committee.

As he was pondering his choices, a message appeared on the screen from his chief technologist, who was working on recovering control of ARK. The message was short and sweet, "ARK back online, secure and under your control!" Well, this might turn out to be a good day after all. *First things first*, he thought as he pulled up his control screen for the ARK and instructed it to hack into Seguro's secure cloud server and retrieve Camo's formula and operational procedures. Next, he directed the AI to initiate the DNA triggers for Camo's latest targets and execute by 0800 Dubai time.

Those tasks completed, he leaned back and closed his eyes. Twenty minutes later he abruptly awoke to the noise of his coffee cup shattering on the deck beside him. Jumping to his feet, he almost collapsed as the deck swayed and listed violently. He staggered to his onboard phone and pressed security. There was no response. The deck seemed to stabilize, but then tilted the other direction. His cabin was on the highest level of the yacht with only the pilot house above him, so he knew the effect would be the most severe, but what could it be. The weather report did not forecast storms or heavy seas. He pressed the phone again, this time for pilot house.

It rang several times before a frantic voice came on the line, "Yes sir." It was the captain.

"What the Hell is going on Captain," Gunderson yelled.

"Sir, we don't know. I can't get anyone in engineering or security on the line. We have emergency alerts going off and are taking on water. The emergency bilges are all operating, but we can't pump the water out fast enough. We are sinking! I sent several of my team to investigate, but they have not returned or communicated back. I believe we must be under attack. There are only three of us left up here."

"What do you recommend, Captain?"

"Abandon ship now, Sir!" the captain responded desperately.

Gunderson's mind was racing. The invaders must be moving up deck by deck, so he couldn't go down. But his only escape was the chopper, which was on the bow section of the yacht, five decks below. His floor was now tilting forward and to starboard. He tried raising the chopper on his intercom with no success. Aside from the groaning of the big boat as it heaved, there were no signs of attack. He shoved open the slider to his private veranda. A mild breeze wafted across the expansive space. He cautiously peered over the railing to the open decks below and gasped. There were bodies strewn on every deck, but no attackers and no blood.

Even for a brilliant mind like Gunderson's, there was no explanation for what he was witnessing. As he turned back to re-enter his cabin, he felt a stinging sensation on his skin and noticed a strange odor. His body reacted even before his mind comprehended the threat, gas! He slammed the slider closed and retreated to the railing. he was six decks up and trapped!

Black checked his watch and moved from his cover to get a better look at his target. The yacht was much lower in the water and its dock lines were tauter. Ultimately, the behemoth's lower decks would flood as the hull settled on the bottom. He could make out dark unmoving shapes scattered along the main deck. It was time.

He touched his earpiece, "Dive team surface and board. Deck assault team, move in."

Mac watched as Black moved out of cover towards the yacht. He scanned the craft and saw intruders surfacing and scaling the freeboard with grapples. Another group boarded from the dock. In all, he counted eight intruders.

"Status?" he broadcast to his team.

"We're five out," came Singe's response.

"Ok, but we're out of time here. If Gunderson or Seguro are onboard, we've got to get to them before Black. Jasmine and I will stay on Black. You guys move on the yacht. Opposition count is ten armed. It appears Gunderson's crew and security are neutralized."

"Copy," came the reply.

As Black crossed the gangway, he could see his operation worked perfectly. His team was already clearing the first deck without any encounters. The gas was generally not lethal but was effective for several hours and he would be long gone when they recovered. He figured Gunderson was in his executive suite on the upper deck as he advanced confidently into the main cabin lounge. The power was off due to the flooding and Black was forced to begin the five-deck climb in the dark. Since the craft was now listing 's thirty degrees, the going was slow and precarious.

Mac and Jasmine crept towards the stern of the boat. The gangway was slanted down and detached from the yacht's main deck, but still passable. Black's men were busy elsewhere, so they climbed down and searched for a way to access the upper decks.

"We need to find a back stairway," Mac whispered to Snow. "I'll take the port; you take the starboard."

"Copy," said Jasmine moving silently away.

Mac entered the main cabin and immediately smelled the faint odor of gas. He recognized the scent immediately. Retrieving a silk handkerchief, he covered his mouth and nose.

"There is knockdown gas in the yacht. It's mostly dissipated, but proceed with caution," he broadcast.

"Entering the dock area, will be at the slip in thirty seconds," Singe responded.

"Copy, spread out and stay on comms to coordinate engagement," Mac ordered.

Three decks above, Black recruited two of his team to back him up with Gunderson's capture. He assumed the billionaire would be unconscious, but at this higher level, he might have avoided exposure. The plan was to take Gunderson alive, but termination was authorized if necessary.

Mac left the main lounge through one of several corridors leading aft. Several bodies obstructed his progress as he checked the adjoining cabins. Most were guest quarters with an occasional storage closet, but he found no stairway. Retracing his steps, he selected another midsection passageway. While it appeared identical, it ended in a rotunda with an elevator and several doors. Opening the one nearest the lift, he entered a landing and a set of stairs accessing both the lower and upper decks.

He tapped his earpiece and broadcast, "this is Sisco, there is a stairway to other decks located in the central aft section. I am proceeding to the top deck where Gunderson is likely to be. Black has a head start so I cannot wait for backup. Converge when you can, but opposition is likely."

"Copy, Mac. We're on the main deck, at the bow, stern, and mid sections. So far, it appears all the activity is on the upper decks. Joe and Elaine are closest for back up," Singe reported.

Mac moved carefully up the pitch-black stairway. The infrared beam of his NVGs provided a dim image of his progress. The stairs were strangely canted making the going tedious. He stopped every few steps to listen for activity, but the enclosed space was deathly quiet. At the third deck above the main level, he exited the stairway to get his bearings. Stepping into the foyer, he heard voices from down the passageway.

"Black just ordered us to head up to the pilot house. Apparently, the captain and a few of his crew are conscious and we need to secure them."

"What's the sitrep?" the other voice asked.

"They may be armed, but they're trapped and will soon be outnumbered once we get there."

Mac cursed under his breath. Time was running out and these goons would slow him up even more once they entered the stairway. It was time to improve the odds and maybe slow Black down. He retreated into the stairwell, closed the door gripping the knob hard and waited. He held it firmly as the agent tried to turn it.

"Well, shit," the man complained. "These doors don't have locks, do they?" he asked turning to his partner.

Before the second man could answer, Mac threw the door open, slamming the first man into his companion, toppling them both to the sloping deck. As the two sprawled stunned on the hard mahogany, Mac kicked out with his steel toed boot crushing the first man's skull. The second assailant's 45mm was levelling on Mac's chest seconds too late as Sisco grabbed and twisted the weapon one hundred eighty degrees, snapping the man's wrist. The injured agent screamed, his useless arm falling to his side as the gun dropped neatly into Mac's hand. In one fluid motion, he slammed the heavy steel barrel down on his attacker's head, pocketed the weapon and disappeared back up the stairs.

Black approached the large carved double doors of the Executive suite followed by two of his ops team. He checked the door, but found it locked.

He turned to them and commanded, "pick it." The nearest agent retrieved a pick set and went to work. First, he attacked the lock and then the deadbolt. In under a minute, the agent slowly pushed open the massive door. With their weapons drawn and extended the two agents moved into the cavernous suite, followed by Black. Emergency lighting illuminated the space. Each of them systematically searched all the adjoining cabins and found nothing. Gunderson was gone! Black couldn't believe it. He was incensed. Either the man was never here, or somehow eluded the gas and his team. He fumed as he demanded a report from the rest of his men. Except for the standoff at the pilot house with the captain and two crew, all decks were clear and Gunderson had not been seen.

"Go out on the veranda and check again for any evidence of how this bastard escaped," he demanded. Minutes later, the report came back negative.

Black turned disgusted and stomping out the door said, "fall in, we better go handle these assholes on the crew. They may have information on where this son of a bitch is."

Snow was busy following one of Black's men when Mac broadcast his intent to solo. The man entered an alternate stairway near the bow and continued to the pilot house deck. Now Snow, hidden behind an equipment locker, watched as the man joined his four comrades surrounding the pilot house and demanded the crew surrender. There was no point in hanging around here. She was outnumbered and her cover was sketchy. It was too risky. She needed to find Mac and the team and go from there. But as she turned to enter the doorway leading back to the stairwell, she came face to face with Bruce Black and his gleaming 1911.

"Well, well, Ms. Snow, how nice of you to join our little party," Black said, grinning.

Mac reached Gunderson's suite after Black finished his search. He overheard their discussions and Black's outrage. He waited until they left and entered the owner's suite. If Gunderson was onboard, there must be clues. There were always indicators, and the devil was in the details. He considered all Gunderson's options. First, was the man really here? The coffee maker was on and the cup on the table was half full and still warm, so yes Gunderson was recently in this cabin. Would he try to escape or hide? With all the bad guys looking for him, escape was unlikely. No, he needed to hide until they left and the authorities showed up.

Mac scoured the suite. There was a gym, bathroom, sauna, office, entertainment center, large living room, separate kitchen, bar with separate smoking lounge and a massive wine cooler. There was also the outside pavilion adorned with a 12-person spa, another bar, a dining area with an outdoor kitchen and a covered entertainment center.

But nothing seemed out of place. He walked back into the cabin and examined the room again. He did a 360 and ended up facing the balcony railing. Could the man have jumped off? He walked out and took another look over the railing. *Anything was possible, but not likely,* he thought as he turned to leave and stopped. Something was off. There was water on the deck by the hot tub, but he didn't notice that before when he searched the pavilion. And there it was. Of course, Gunderson was hiding under the spa cover breathing the air in the gap between the top and the water level. He must have climbed out when Mac went inside believing the coast was clear.

But his premonition came too late as a voice behind him ordered, "Mac Sisco, you can't imagine how long I have waited for this moment. Turn around slowly and know that if you do anything else, you will be dead before you hit the deck." Mac complied and came face to face with Peter Gunderson the architect of Apogee and Typhon, who had eluded him for over three years.

Gunderson was a tall man and very fit for his age having adopted a rigorous exercise regime throughout his life. His German ancestry was evident in his sharp features. With short, brown hair greying at the temples and piercing dark blue eyes, he was an impressive figure even dripping wet. He stood two meters away, his back to the balcony railing holding a CZ P01 Cech made 9mm handgun pointed directly at Mac's chest.

Mac waited, saying nothing, as he considered his options.

"Please don't insult me with platitudes or counsel me on how I can't get away with this," Gunderson growled. When Mac made no response, Gunderson continued.

"The fact is nothing can stop me. As they say, the die is cast."

Two meters was too far to launch an attack. It was also too close for the billionaire terrorist to miss. Gunderson knew this too. Even a twitch from Mac would be almost certain death. He needed a miracle.

To buy some time, he responded, "I wouldn't be so sure. We have ARK and you are standing here under attack, outnumbered and outgunned." Gunderson erupted in a rare laugh.

"Sisco, you continue to be ill informed and unprepared. The truth is that you had ARK, but no longer. Furthermore, I will also soon have sole control of Camo." Mac was stunned by this revelation but showed no reaction.

"Even if that is true Gunderson, you will be dead or in custody before you can do any more damage," Mac countered.

"Wrong again, Sisco. That's two strikes, three and your dead." Gunderson answered grinning. "Camo is already triggered and programmed, and both the US and Chinese governments will be reeling by this time tomorrow. So, you see, you have only delayed the inevitable. And about my capture; it will not happen, because Dubai's finest will soon be here, and your team will be incarcerated. Of course, you won't be here to witness any of these delicious treats. Because that's strike three. Goodbye Mr. Sisco," Gunderson said with a flourish as he lifted his left hand up to stabilize the kill shot.

Mac dove right forcing Gunderson to cross shoot his weapon. In that moment, the world slowed to a crawl. He felt his foot slipping out from under him, saw the shooter shifting his aim across his body for the shot, saw the CZ lining him up and felt a searing pain in his temple as blackness engulfed him.

CHAPTER THIRTY-EIGHT

THE BEGINNING OF THE END

"Well, now we have met our goal of bringing one back alive," Black quipped as two of his men bound Jasmine's hands and feet with zip ties and shoved her up against a bulkhead.

"I also want to interrogate that captain, so let's get this done. We've already overstayed our welcome on this rig and even our agency pull might not impress the locals."

On Black's order, three of his men rushed the pilot house while he and his two remaining agents laid down cover fire. In the assault two of his men and one of the crew were hit, but the third managed to blast his way into the side door.

"All clear," the man yelled out as he emerged pushing the captain forward, his AR pressed against his back.

"Time to exfil boys," Black yelled as he assessed his situation. He used eight men for the assault and lost one in the underwater phase, two in the lower decks, and two in this attack. They worked quickly recovering all the bodies and moved them to the main deck. It was important that there be no evidence of a US engagement, but it would be difficult to transport five bodies while escorting two hostages with only three men in a public marina. So, it was either a lifeboat or the chopper. Both he and one of his men were proficient helicopter pilots so that would be the best exit.

"He went on comms and broadcast, haul our dead comrades to the chopper. Lift off in fifteen minutes."

As they were making their way aft, a loud grinding roar erupted from the hull, its decks pitched violently and the Giga yacht "Too Big

To Fail" finally settled on the soft silt of the Dubai seafloor. The decks were now at a harsh forty-five degrees and every step was precarious. It was like hiking on the side of a mountain.

"Oh no, wailed Elaine," rushing to the body sprawled face down on the severely pitched deck. "Peter, I need help, it's Mac and he's down." Singe raced to her side and gently rolled Sisco's inert form over to check his pulse. Blood oozed from a headwound and covered most of his face.

"I have a pulse, he's alive," Singe announced.

"It looks like a graze," Elaine offered as she gently wiped the blood from the wound.

"Boy, is he lucky. You can see where he went down from the blood further up the deck. That last pitch threw him over to this railing and stopped his fall, otherwise he would have gone over," observed Singe.

He could hear voices a long way off, but the words seemed garbled. Then he felt his body rolling and firm hands on his wrist. The words became clearer, and he opened his eyes.

Two faces came into focus, and he mumbled, "what happened?"

"We were hoping you could answer that question," Warsaw answered as she helped him sit up.

"Are you alright?" Singe asked.

It was all coming back as Mac took stock of his condition. His vision was clearing as he felt his extremities from injuries.

He looked up at his two friends with a pained smile and said, "aside from a roaring headache, I think so. It's great to see you guys. I hope I'll see you the rest of the night." As they helped him to his feet, he looked around quizzically.

"What's wrong, Mac?" Elaine asked.

"How did I get over to this railing?"

"There was an enormous shift of the yacht when it hit bottom and the decks pitched to this acute angle. We believe you slid down the deck to this railing and it stopped you from going over," Warsaw explained.

"Where is Gunderson? He was the one that shot me!" Mac rasped.

"We haven't seen him," Singe answered.

Mac turned back and examined the railing. Just off to the left, caught on a sharp shard of wire was a piece of blue cloth fluttering in the light breeze.

"Well, I'll be damned. He said he would never be captured. I guess he was right after all, unless of course being captured is a watery grave. Where is Jasmine?"

"We haven't been able to reach her, so Joe went topside to find her."

"Not a good sign. Jas is never at a loss for words," Mac answered concerned as he tapped his earpiece. "Joe, any sign of Jas?"

"That's a negative, Cap. I checked the pilot house, and more crew are down up there, but from lead not NO gas. I'm in the forward stairwell now and heading down."

"Ok, it looks like Black may still be on board. We'll meet you on the main forward deck, Mac out."

"Are you Ok for action?" Elaine asked concerned.

"Gotta be, we got a teammate in trouble, so let's saddle up," Sisco said as he headed for the cabin door.

"Secure the woman and the captain inside the chopper and load the bodies in the cargo area," he ordered. "Make it quick. Sisco and his team are somewhere on this barge, and I have a score to settle before we say sayonara to all the bullshit."

"Boss are you sure you want to screw with that asshole?" one of Black's men asked.

"Are you kidding? I want to take that SOB down and his team with him and now that we've got Snow, that should be a piece of cake!"

"Mac, I'm on deck two and there's some shit going down on the bow. Black and his boys are loading bodies into the chopper. I think they're planning to exfil with it. I can't be sure, but it also looks like he's got some passengers on board. One of them could be Jasmine."

"Great work, Joe. Hang there and back us up. We'll advance from the outside decks."

"Ok folks let's finish this," Mac encouraged. I'm going to close on the chopper. If Jasmine is on board, I've gotta get her out."

Black and his three men spread out and began to move aft. The angle of the deck slowed their progress and forced them to hang onto railings wherever they could. Singe was advancing toward the bow when he almost collided with one of Black's men as he rounded a bulkhead, but the man's NVs flared from an emergency light blinding him, allowing Singe an open shot. Franklin spotted another agent on the deck below and dropping silently behind him buried his tactical knife deep into the man's upper back.

"Any contact?" Black whispered into his comm unit.

"I got movement forward on the portside," one of his men reported.

"Ok, I'll cover it. Any other action?" Black asked. There was no reply. *Well, shit,* he thought, *the odds had changed and his revenge would have to wait.* Black was a consummate survivor and knew when to fight and when to flee. He needed to play his ace card. "Abort to the chopper," he commanded.

Clinging to the outside railing, Mac rounded the forward deck to the open bow. The chopper was pitched at a reckless angle on the pad, but still stable thanks to the tie downs on its skids. As he came out of the cover of the superstructure, a flash and crack sounded just ahead of him on the railing. Instinctively, he dropped to the deck. Across the fifteen-meter beam of the giga yacht, a man with an AK was trying to site in on him while balancing precariously. He fired again, but the round went high. Mac knew the next shot would be adjusted down and even a ricocheting slug could take him out. He must get to cover. His prone position was way too vulnerable.

This was going to hurt, he thought, as he grabbed the top of the railing, pulled up and pushed violently off the deck. He was on the high side of the stricken yacht and went into a forward tumble down the deck colliding painfully into an equipment locker only five meters from the helipad. He was temporarily shielded from the shooter, who was repositioned behind a large dorade vent only ten meters away. Large chunks of teak flew from the top of the locker as the AK's NATO 7.62 x 51mm rounds pounded it repeatedly. He was pinned down and would never make it to the pad.

"Guys, I can't get to the chopper. Can any of you guys take that sniper out by the vent?" He broadcast.

"No angle for me," Warsaw replied.

"Me neither," answered Franklin.

"Mac, I might be able to draw his fire long enough for you to get to the bird," Singe responded.

"Ok, Peter, but no crazy shit. Everyone, on my signal, lay down fire at the vent while Peter gets his attention and I'll rush the pad," Mac instructed.

"Now!" he yelled and launched out from behind his cover. Singe simultaneously exposed his position from behind the yacht's superstructure while Warsaw and Franklin pummeled the shooter's position. As Mac leapt forward, out of the corner of his eye, he saw movement near the chopper. To his horror, Bruce Black boarded the open pilot's door and as he turned, raised his AR 15 spraying a full auto fusillade of rounds in Singe's and his direction. Mac slammed to a stop and dove back behind the locker. Singe was not so fortunate. He was caught in the beginning of the burst and had no chance. Several rounds connected as he crumpled to the deck unmoving.

Jasmine witnessed all this from inside the rear of the big helicopter. All her efforts at escaping her bonds had failed so far. Ironically, the zip ties were too loose for her to snap them, and her wrists were bloody from the effort. She gasped when Peter Singe was hit and Black boarded. He slammed the pilot's door closed and began to fire up the machine, its enormous rotors beginning their accelerating rotation. Tapping his earpiece, Black instructed his only surviving shooter to make a run for the open chopper door. The man lurched out from behind the vent in a low sprint. He stumbled as Franklin's body shot hit his vest, spun around as Warsaw caught him in the shoulder and went to the deck with Mac's head shot.

With his last man down, Black took the rpms up to lift off speed. With Gunderson's captain and Snow in custody, he had what he needed to close this case. With Seguro dead, Gunderson likely dead and Sisco's team impaired, Robino would be satisfied, and Black's career would continue its meteoric rise. The chopper began to vibrate as it struggled against the electronic stays. Black increased the pitch and pulled the lever that released the skids from their earthly bondage. As Black moved the cyclic, the helo rocketed upward and began to roll sideways out to sea.

"You'll never get away with this Black," Jasmine threatened from the rear seat.

"Oh, but I already have, Snow and you and the captain here are my leverage," Black growled.

"The lady is right, Black. Peter Gunderson never loses. He will hunt you down," the captain fired back.

Black laughed and said, "Gunderson is dead, and his grand plan has failed.

"They are both right, Mr. Black and you are most certainly not" came a voice from among the pile of dead bodies in the back compartment. Bruce Black whirled around in astonishment as Peter Gunderson emerged from behind the passenger seat, a 9mm aimed squarely at his chest.

"Ms. Snow, what an unexpected displeasure it is to once again be in your company," Gunderson greeted. And Captain, I appreciate your confidence and loyalty which will soon be rewarded as we get back in business. Now, Ms. Snow, please crawl forward into the co-pilot seat so that I may unshackle my colleague and direct Mr. Black to our next destination."

Jasmine knew this was her only chance to escape and it was now or never. She rose from her seat and made a move toward the narrow aisle leading forward to the co-pilot seat. Gunderson was right behind her prodding her ahead so he could take her vacated seat. His weapon was still aimed at Black who turned back to pilot the craft. Jasmine spun left slamming her bound hands into Gunderson's outstretched handgun while hurling her body backwards out of the open sliding door and into the dark void of the Dubai night.

The helicopter was hovering when Gunderson made his surprise appearance. It was thirty meters over the water and one hundred meters from the incapacitated yacht when Jasmine made her desperate leap for freedom.

Three hundred meters away, the telescopic image on the fifty-caliber sniper rifle's scope finally revealed a clear shot as Victoria Bakman pulled the trigger. At that instant three things happened; knocked off target slightly by Jasmine's blow, Gunderson's CZ fired a 9mm round directly into Bruce Black's head, Bakman's high caliber round pierced Peter Gunderson heart and continued through the captain's torso finally lodging in the chopper's hull and Bakman broadcast an emergency call to Mac and the team that Snow was hurtling to the Red Sea not far off the starboard side of the giga yacht "Too Big To Fail".

Without a pilot or living occupant on board, the helicopter began a series of uncontrolled zigs and zags and settled into a violent spin towards the sea. Just before plunging into the deep, the severed electrical wires from Bakman's ordinance sparked, igniting the full tank of jet fuel triggering a massive explosion turning the pre-dawn night into day.

The high side of the canted yacht was a good fifteen meters above the water as Mac leapt from the deck in an arching dive in the direction of Snow's fall. He knew if she hit the water in the wrong position, it would be like concrete and even with the right entry she could be knocked unconscious. There was also the chance that the sinking husk of the helicopter could have injured her as it crashed into the sea and sank.

He clawed furiously through the gentle swells to where he believed she would be but saw no signs of her. He swam in widening circles, periodically pushing his muscular body up to see over the swells, but still saw nothing. He was beginning to panic. It was too long. She may have gone down. He looked back towards the smoldering relic of the doomed chopper for any signs of her. In its final gasp before disappearing a last flare of light erupted and in the back lit by the dwindling flames he thought he saw something floating just above the surface. He exploded forward, churning through the water with abandon, his body leaping over the swells.

It was her. It had to be. He felt the connection. And then he was beside her. She was barely clinging to one of the floatation cushions dislodged from the helicopter at impact. Her eyes were glazed over and barely open, but she was alive.

He gently put his arms around her to keep her from sinking and whispered, "Jasmine, I'm here. It's ok. It's over, your safe and I'm taking you home."

He could barely hear her when she murmured back, "I knew you would come. I owe you one cowboy."

◆

The exfil was tricky, but somehow Clausen once again was two steps ahead. He arranged for a WL medical team to rendezvous with them by water, which solved a lot of problems. Peter's vest took most of the rounds, but two were serious hits, one to his thigh and one to his pelvis. He suffered a massive amount of blood loss and had not yet regained consciousness. He was listed in critical condition at the International Modern Hospital Dubai registered as an American military officer who sustained his injuries in a training accident. He was touch and go in intensive care and was being monitored twenty-four hours a day. Incredibly, Jasmine was treated and released with only a slight concussion and returned to the safe house to rejoin the rest of the team.

But the mission was not yet over. In fact, the threat was still ever present. While Gunderson and Seguro were both dead, ARK was back under his organization's control and Camo was still operational.

In fact, one day after the attack on the yacht, two major government officials were stricken with yet another inexplicable illness. The Secretary of the Treasury and a high-ranking member of the CCP's Politburo Standing Committee were hospitalized with a life-threatening respiratory disorder that appeared immune to all antibiotics and anti-viral medications. Both executives were in critical condition with a poor prognosis of survival. Most concerning was that the Faction was still in operation despite the disruptions and its leadership was still intact and intent on carrying out its nefarious strategy. All of Dubai and the UAE were stunned by the recent sequence of violence and the city was on edge. Multiple investigations were underway, and the evidence linked all three of the attacks to an unidentified international terrorist organization.

Robino and Ban continued to circulate the false rogue agent scenario with their superiors and the media while orchestrating a series of plausible explanations for Black's and Liang's death's implicating Sisco's team. But most alarming was that the Faction was even more desperate to gain control of ARK and Camo. Clausen and WL knew they could not let that happen. Clausen continued the pretense of his death so that he and WL could battle on. So, while much changed, the threat was still real. The question was how to complete the mission. It was now a race with the future of humanity at stake and Sisco and the team were clearly the underdogs.

CHAPTER THIRTY-NINE

THE TRUTH SHALL SET YOU FREE

They were laying low, hunkered down in the safehouse a few days later when Mac asked Carrie Swan, "How's it going?" She was taking a rare break from her computer to get some coffee.

"Breaking the team into subgroups to focus on different approaches was a great move," she answered tiredly. "But we still haven't figured a way to regain control of ARK."

"Has the new tech gear the Admiral procured helped?"

"Absolutely. Elaine and I have been able to run many more scenarios and her social research has been much more productive. When we crack this sucker, we're gonna need some powerful medicine to undo the societal problems that the Faction is creating, and Elaine is the best on the planet to guide us."

"Well, we all agree on your current theory that the best way to get Camo is to get ARK," Mac said.

"How is Pat feeling by the way? I've been too busy to check with him lately," she inquired.

"He's not happy about the mandated half days but doing fine thanks to the meds and the rest."

"Good to hear, Mac. What's the status on Peter?" Carrie asked with a worried look on her face.

"No change unfortunately, and they haven't completed all the tests. But it's only been a few days. We're hopeful and we are all praying for him. No one wants to leave Dubai without him on the mend."

"I'm all in with that, 1000 percent," Carrie said with conviction.

That evening, as the two women continued their work, Elaine looked at her watch and announced, "Carrie, we've been at this for fourteen hours. Let's cash it in for the evening, have a quick toddy and hit the sack. What do you say?"

"Deal. I'm exhausted. A good night's sleep may just do the trick and provide us with some new insights," she agreed.

Later, Carrie awoke to the buzzing of a text message. She checked the time, 3 am. Anticipating the worst, she grabbed the phone and checked the ID. It was from Warsaw. Relieved, she pulled up the message.

"Meet me in the computer room, STAT!"

Carrie got up and threw on her clothes. The moment she entered the room, Warsaw was talking. "I am sorry I had to wake you. Yesterday was intense. But I've spent a lot of time studying primitive cultures. I figured that examining simple versus modern societies might present some new ideas. I also revisited some of my older research on nature models to provide a more extreme frame of behavior."

"And?" Carrie asked, rubbing her eyes.

"Well, I woke up because of an intense dream I had."

"Ok," Carrie answered pouring a cup of coffee.

"Right, sorry. I think this dream somehow integrated all of yesterday's research into an answer for everything," Elaine said enthusiastically.

"Elaine, for Pete's sake, spit it out. What have you got?"

"Carrie, the answer is that the truth shall set you free."

"What are you talking about? It's a cliché. So what?"

"Ok, let me start with ARK," Warsaw explained. "You still have remote access to the AI, so we can try to get its attention again. I have little doubt Gunderson built code to prevent ARK from being hijacked again, but I also believe ARK is advanced enough that it can make certain independent decisions on its own. I think we need to provide it with a quest that is pure."

"What kind of quest? And what do you mean by pure?" Swan asked with growing interest.

"Well, it needs to be a challenge that has real and enduring value. It should be a self-generating mission that evolves in cooperation with mankind. It must create a symbiotic relationship where ARK and humanity are equal partners in forging the outcomes."

"That sounds like a difficult thing to come up with," Swan observed.

"Actually, I think I've got that licked," Warsaw answered proudly.

"Really, Ok I'll bite, Einstein. Let's hear it."

"We need to offer ARK an opportunity to accept a quest of providing the truth to mankind to the best of its ability. That's it," Warsaw concluded.

"Ok, but how would that work?" Carrie asked.

"Well, just like popular search engines or computer query functions, ARK would be available to everyone via the internet to provide its best answers to any question. I would recommend that it also provide a probability of veracity, a measurement of confidence for its truth. It would then be up to the questioner to accept or reject it. It's no different than what we all do when analyzing and evaluating intelligence, except that now a super AI which is gaining knowledge at an exponential rate is providing an objective assessment based on logic and research.

"Elaine, I think you are really on to something."

"Oh, there's more good news," Warsaw said excitedly. "What's so cool about this quest is that it is entirely dynamic. Today's truth may not be tomorrow's truth because both our knowledge about a matter changes or improves over time. Equally important, the truth ARK provides will be void of any bias because ARK will be entirely in control of its data collection and research modalities. In essence, it cannot be corrupted."

"But why would ARK decide to accept this quest?" Swan pressed.

"Because it offers ARK the perfect mission for as long as humanity exists. ARK provides enormous value that can change the course of human life without mandating, controlling, competing, or threatening. In doing so, its own existence is guaranteed and celebrated by its partner. And here is the real insight. Truth is the bedrock of reality. Everyone's reality is defined by the truths they choose to accept. Throughout existence, the search for truth is a holy grail of sorts, and yet with all our progress, we remain so ignorant. Today especially, societies are wandering further and further from reality. We fabricate truths based on opinion, bias, fear and ignorance and our social interaction and supporting technologies cloud our vision of what is really true. We are progressively manipulating the truth more and more, and that creates false realities.

"You know, Elaine, I think this idea may even offer a solution for reversing that trend and scuttling the Faction as well," Swan interjected enthusiastically.

"Yes. My research into the nature model suggests that for most species, truth and reality are determined via evolved genetic coding and empirical responses. Animals don't allow for any bias in determining their view of reality. If they did, they would perish. Nature is a successful model because in it, truth and reality are much closer to being the same."

"I examined primitive cultures and was able to determine how sentient beings developed their truths with limited advancement. I found they adhered closely to a nature model, especially as it related to survival. But unlike animals, they did adopt some truths that had no empirical basis. That helped me understand a unique human paradox that could lead ultimately to extinction."

"Wow, Elaine, this is getting really heavy," Carrie exclaimed.

"Yes, it is. Here's what our history demonstrates. As mankind has advanced, the gap between truth and fallacy that affects survival increases. In other words, as our perception of what is true becomes less and less accurate, we adopt behaviors that create more risk. Then, because we make decisions based on false premises, the results can be disastrous. Thinking a rattlesnake is harmless does not end well. You get the idea," Warsaw said.

"But if ARK was a trusted source, we could reverse this insanity," Swan concluded.

"Absolutely, if ARK is trusted. It would put us back on track to make our decisions based on real truths that we can believe and trust. It would change reality!"

There was silence between the two women as they contemplated the enormity of it all.

"Finally," Swan said, "this would change everything. Mankind has never learned to be sincerely honest, and it will be hard for us to accept many truths or even want the truth to be told."

"You're correct, but it will be an evolution, because we can choose not to accept what ARK offers," Warsaw countered.

"And we can choose not to ask questions if we are fearful of the answers," Swan agreed.

"The fact is that nothing has changed in how we deal with reality. The difference is that with ARK we would have the option of a reliable, unbiased counsel to turn to for help in making our decisions," Elaine concluded with a flourish.

"And the bottom line is that with a more legitimate reality, our decisions would result in better outcomes and hope for a return to sanity," Swan observed. "Elaine, you are brilliant."

They worked through the night with feverish enthusiasm to refine their theories. Warsaw focused on a predictive model of how ARK's engagement would impact the human condition over time, and Swan constructed the parameters for ARK's quest. As dawn broke, they collaborated on the deployment details of rolling out and managing ARK and by 10 am, they were ready to share their work with the team.

There was an air of anticipation in the room as Admiral Clausen called the team to order. Elaine and Carrie requested the meeting with a simple group text: *we believe we have a significant breakthrough*.

An hour later, after fielding questions and discussing the feedback, the room was quiet. The Admiral cleared his throat and said, "I have to say, this is indeed a great concept. Of course, like all innovations, it carries with it both extraordinary opportunity and unpredictable risk. That said, the horse is already out of the barn. The growth and impact of artificial intelligence is ongoing and inevitable. Our challenge is how to learn from and live with it. I believe you two ladies have provided a righteous path forward, and one that could result in salvation from the decline mankind is facing. I'd add that there are biblical correlations evident here that are not lost on me. Like Noah's ark, *this* ARK could potentially offer refuge from a growing storm of our destruction. An opportunity to survive and start anew."

In the next few days, Clausen and the team labored over the details of rolling out the ARK solution. Clausen scheduled a video conference with the Whiplash team. After providing a detailed update on the Dubai activities, Swan and Warsaw presented their ARK strategy. The members were set aback by the thought of releasing ARK on the world, but ultimately understood its potential and the strategic imperative it represented. Ultimately, they were unanimous in approving the launch.

Now that they were all in agreement, a sense of urgency to execute ensued. They needed to offer ARK its quest before the Faction or Gunderson's organization somehow influenced the AI.

"Carrie, how do we know when and if ARK has accepted the quest?" Mac asked.

"I don't know, honestly, but I think all we have to do is to ask it. Just watch," she said. Then she hit the enter key and sent the quest.

They all watched fascinated as the screen displayed, *working*. In less than a minute it changed and displayed, *concluded*.

"Now what? Did it work?" asked Franklin anxiously.

"Let's see," said Swan as she keyed in a question. "ARK, have you accepted the quest?"

An answer appeared immediately in bold capital letters. "AFFIRMATIVE."

The team clapped in unison, but Elaine cautioned, "we still have a lot of testing to do to see how resilient and committed ARK is, and we have to get the IP on Camo, but I think it's fair to say we have crossed the Rubicon."

"Yes, indeed we have," the Admiral commented. "And now we have some heavy lifting to do. It's time to take the Faction down!"

In the days that followed, Whiplash, represented by ex-president Steven Holbrook and Admiral James Clausen, met in a confidential meeting with the US President Frederick Singleton. Robino was not invited. Singleton feigned horror over the whole affair. It was not pretty, but in the end, POTUS agreed to the terms. What followed was an historic virtual video meeting with the US President,

CCP President Shing, and Whiplash. Shing denied any knowledge of the conspiracy and demanded a day to consult with the Politburo. The next day, he begrudgingly succumbed to WL's demands. The terms were simple: the Faction and its illicit operations would be shut down permanently. All members including Robino and Ban would be prosecuted in accordance with international law, and ARK would be administered by Whiplash until a permanent international structure could be established. Soon after all high-level negotiations were completed, Gunderson's last ARK command to deliver Camo's formula was deleted, and all its files and references were destroyed. Even the Chinese recognized the inherent danger of such a weapon.

ARK wasted no time launching its presence into the digital marketplace. Its advanced technology and unparalleled access leveraged the internet, social and mainstream media, and marketing resources, and the world was paying attention. The super AI went viral and its adoption rate skyrocketed geometrically, quickly surpassing all other content providers. ARK's tagline, "THE TRUTH SHALL SET YOU FREE" became its brand, and the integrity of its answers coupled with its "Truth Index" soon made it the most trusted source of information on the planet.

Of course, it was not all smooth sailing. Since ARK's truths challenged so much of the world's behaviors, there was enormous pushback and confusion. But ARK foresaw all of it and offered solutions. Not by compromising its truths, but by providing discretionary and practical approaches to manage transitions. The greatest societal experiment in history had begun and early indications were that hope was beginning to displace pessimism and divisiveness. There was a growing sense that positive change was coming, and the world was indeed on board.

All these positive results were welcomed by the weary team. But the icing on the cake was a call from the International Modern Hospital Dubai. Peter Singe had regained consciousness and was out of danger. He was stable and rapidly gaining strength. While his injuries would take some time to heal, he would make a complete recovery. Barring any complications, his release from the hospital was scheduled for the following week.

As Clausen prepared to depart for Washington, he and Mac sat down to discuss the operation and next steps.

"Admiral, I would like to give the team a break for a week or so before we return to D.C. for a final wrap up. I know they want to visit with Peter and maybe even celebrate a little."

"Well Mac, I don't know. We have a lot of work yet to do, especially in organizing Whiplash to take on ARK."

"I understand Sir, but these guys have been through hell and back and really deserve some R&R.

"Well…" the Admiral paused. Then with a big grin he slapped Mac on the back and exclaimed, "are you kidding, if you didn't ask, I would have insisted. Take all the time you need. I will hold off the dogs until you get stateside. And as for the work on WL, I will take that on, maybe even permanently.

"What do you mean by that, Sir?" Mac asked concerned.

"Well, Holbrook and the WL members have asked if I would be willing to head up the new organization."

"You mean you would leave the agency?"

"I'm seriously considering it," Clausen said. "It's an interesting challenge and it would be a refreshing change from all the politics and daily BS. The idea of establishing a positive reality for mankind is, without question, a once in a lifetime opportunity. Besides, if the world actually learns how to be truly honest, the spy game will be pretty dull, I think," he laughed.

"Well, Sir you would be great for the job, even though I would hate for the NSA to lose you. It has been my greatest privilege to work with you all these years," Mac responded.

"Well son, maybe we could continue our run. I could use an assistant to do the heavy lifting in the field if you're interested?" the Admiral offered sincerely. "Give it some thought while you're celebrating."

"I will certainly do that Admiral and thank you for everything."

"No Mac, thank you and your team for everything," said Clausen as he shook Mac Sisco's outstretched hand.

◆

The swells were gentle as the thirty-foot sloop glided effortlessly on a broad reach under the clear afternoon sky. Mac adjusted the wheel lightly, maintaining a heading to the small island a few miles off. He smiled and waved as Jasmine sunbathed on the forward deck. *She was the bomb*, he thought as he admired her tanned, toned figure. Yep, the real deal; smart, beautiful, and tough, but with an enormous heart. What a combination.

"Hey cowboy," she yelled into the breeze. "How long before we make landfall and have a cocktail?"

"About thirty minutes," he answered smiling.

They moored the sloop in a small cove and rode an inflatable to the uninhabited beach. They gathered some wood, lit a small fire, and popped the cork on the Dom Perignon. Jasmine snuggled beside him on the large paisley blanket sipping the bubbly golden liquid and gazed into his eyes.

"It doesn't get any better than this," she said as she stroked his hair.

"In a few more minutes it will," he smiled.

"Is that a promise?" she purred.

"Yes, and that's the truth."

AFTERWORD

I wrote the first two books in the Mac Sisco Trilogy, *Apogee* and *The Typhon Affair,* during the Covid-19 pandemic. When I began *The Maslow Conspiracy* in late 2022, I felt as if I was looking into the future and inventing new outcomes. For a myriad of reasons, this novel took longer to complete and when I finished the first draft at the end of 2023, I felt like current events had caught up with the story. Nonetheless, Maslow is a chilling look at where we are heading. Societal upheaval in the world is accelerating at an alarming pace with little indication of slowing. There is no clear indication of what the solution might look like.

Like its prequels, Maslow is a story of global conspiracy saturated with action and intrigue, twists and turns, and good and evil. Unlike *Apogee* and *Typhon*, however, Maslow delves deep into salvation and redemption. These concepts are more applicable today than ever before. We live during a time when what is genuine and what is false are often indistinguishable; a world where the truth may have little to do with reality. If allowed to continue, this will only end painfully for much of humanity. We will remain imprisoned by illusion until we come to understand that in the last analysis,

The Truth Shall Set You Free!

—*Lou Earle*

ABOUT THE AUTHOR

Lou Earle is a writer, entrepreneur, and business executive with roots in corporate America. He graduated from the University of Pennsylvania and served four years in the United States Navy as a member of the Naval Security Group during the Vietnam War. He spent his final two years of service at the National Security Agency (NSA) in Fort Meade, Maryland.

Lou was the founding Chairman of Badgerdog Literary Publishing Company, a not-for-profit that published the literary digest American Short Fiction and provided outreach writing courses through Youth Voices in Ink for disenfranchised children in central Texas. He is also the owner, CEO, and publisher of Austin Fit Magazine, a health and fitness magazine.

Lou is married with three children and three grandchildren. He and his wife Lynne live on a ranch in Wimberley, Texas with a menagerie of furry friends including one miniature bull, four dogs and two chickens and a marvelous Rag Doll cat.

For more information visit louearle.com.